Crossroads

Crossroads

Skyy

www.urbanbooks.net

Urban Books, LLC
78 East Industry Court
Deer Park, NY 11729

ISBN 13: 978-1-60162-327-0
ISBN 10: 1-60162-327-5

First Trade Paperback Printing January 2012
Printed in the United States of America

10 9 8 7 6 5 4 3 2 1

Distributed by Kensington Publishing Corp.
Submit Wholesale Orders to:
Kensington Publishing Corp.
C/O Penguin Group (USA) Inc.
Attention: Order Processing
405 Murray Hill Parkway
East Rutherford, NJ 07073-2316
Phone: 1-800-526-0275
Fax: 1-800-227-9604

Dedication

This book is dedicated to all the Nerds, Geeks, and Weirdos. Feel free to be who you are and offer no apologizes for who you are.

Acknowledgments

It's here! The new book has arrived. I am currently listening to "I'm Here" from *The Color Purple*. It has been a long process. I didn't know if I was going to make it through but I'm here.

Disclaimer: This book is a lot different from Choices and Consequences. The characters have grown up a lot, partly because I have grown up a lot. It's amazing what you can learn in a year or even a few months. I hope you like the new direction. So sit back, grab a glass of something and turn on some music. Music is all through this book, listen to the songs that the characters are listening to if you can; it will only make it better for you.

Thank you to my family for being there for me, especially my fabulous aunts who might not agree with my choices, but you love me anyway, and my cousins and extended cousins who have given me great role models to look up to.

Bimbim: My Miyako and one of the most genuine people I know. I hope you know how much I care about you and only want what's best for you always.

Cat and Tiffany, it's been a long road filled with people who didn't make the cut, but both of you are still here. Love having you on my team J.

Meshanna and Cache, my fabulous Cancer Connection, I know I can count on both of you to tell me what I don't want to hear.

Acknowledgments

Shawn, the man in my life, I look forward to seeing what is ahead in your life. Thanks for keeping me fed and with internet and teaching me what you know.

To all the people who are a part of my life, I love you all:

The sexiest studs and great friends, who I can't imagine my life without: Angel, Chereny, Ashlee, Kira, Precious, April and Romeo.

The sexy femmes that are also some of the best-friends a girl can have: Dana aka Oohzee, Cassie, Jolie, Rachel, Byrd, Bri.

My families, real, gay, and publishing, life would suck without you.

1

The hot New York sun didn't compare to the heat radiating from Lena's body. Her legs were trembling, her softest place moist from anticipation. Denise was right on the other side of the brown hotel door. Lena stared at the golden numbers on the door right above the peep hole, number 1839. She would remember that number for the rest of her life.

Lena proceeded to knock, but found herself hesitating; something wasn't right. She turned around, took a deep breath and then set her eyes back on the golden numbers. She couldn't do it yet. Lena walked back down the long hallway and stopped in front of the wall-length mirror standing at the end. She stared at her curvaceous body. Her long, black hair, naturally wavy and bouncy, was as flawless as her black mini dress that seemed to cling in all the right places. The black Jimmy Choo platform sling backs adorning her feet added the extra sexy touch that would make any man offer her the moon and the stars. All she wanted was for Denise to offer her love.

Lena's stroll back to 1839 was slow and steady. The butterflies in her stomach seemed to turn to birds fluttering. Her palms began to sweat. The only thing standing in between her and Denise's arms was that door. Lena could hear the TV playing inside the room; Denise was definitely there. Lena knew it was now or never. She knocked on the door.

"One second." Denise looked at the door, wondering who was interrupting her dose of Celeb-reality. She still couldn't believe she had joined the masses in watching *Basketball Wives* and *Real Housewives of Atlanta*. The small black alarm clock on the dresser flashed 9:39 P.M. It couldn't be housekeeping; it was too late.

Denise rose from the comfortable spot her body had created in the plush hotel bed. The cool breeze hit her; she looked down at her blue and white boxers and sports bra; it definitely wasn't appropriate to open a door in. She stepped into her old basketball sweat pants and put on a white wife-beater.

Denise peered through the peep hole, but could see nothing. She knew someone's finger was placed over it.

"Who is it?"

Lena's heart skipped a beat. "Management." Lena lowered her voice, hoping it wouldn't be easily recognizable. Her heart began to pound as she heard the dead bolt. She knew she was about to have a heart attack as the door slowly opened.

Denise's inner alert system sounded. Something wasn't sitting right with her. Why would management have their finger over the peep hole? Her television wasn't loud, and the room was paid for a week in advance. Denise paused as a sly smile covered her face.

"You think I'm dumb enough to fall for that, Cool." Denise joked as she swung the hotel door open. As the door opened, her expression instantly turned to pure shock.

Lena smiled.

Denise's eyes widened like a deer caught in headlights. Speechless, Denise turned her head then turned back; she knew she had to be dreaming.

"You left and I didn't get to say good-bye." Lena immediately found herself staring into the woman's big brown eyes.

Denise's muscular biceps protruded as she crossed her arms.

"Soooooo, you came all the way here just to say good-bye?" Denise affectionately responded. "Or is there something else you want to say?" Her eyes slanted, still fixated on Lena and the dress that was wasn't leaving much to her imagination.

Lena's body trembled. She didn't know if the pounding from her heart or the throbbing between her walls was harder. She could feel Denise peering into her soul, trying to understand what would make her leave the comfort of her beautiful loft in Memphis with her superstar husband to stand at her hotel room door. Denise continued her straight-faced stare. Lena felt the walls closing in on her. Things weren't going as planned. She figured she would be in Denise's arms at first sight.

"I realized that I didn't want to say good-bye. I can't say good-bye because, Denise, I love you. I know it took me a minute to realize it, but if you will have me, I'm yours." A single tear fell from Lena's right eye.

Denise blinked. She uncrossed her arms, dropping them to her side. Her straight face was emotionless. Denise lowered her head, a thousand thoughts running through it. *Was she for real? Would she leave again? What about the baby?*

Denise glanced back at Lena. She had never looked so fragile. Lena's beauty was breathtaking. Denise's eyes roamed her excellent physique. Women paid good money to get injections and surgery to have what Lena developed naturally. Denise couldn't speak; even with all of her questions there was only one thing she could think to do.

Denise, long arms extended, placed her hands on each side of Lena's frame. Neither could speak; only short breaths escaped them. Denise passionately placed her lips against Lena's softness, the stickiness of her lipstick binding them like glue. Slowly their lips parted, their tongues eager to meet each other like it was the first time. Lena's arms wrapped around Denise's tall frame, and she could feel the heat between her legs turning into a full-fledged fire.

They made their way into the hotel room without letting go of their fervent embrace.

The sound of drama from the TV show in progress faded from their minds. Denise removed Lena's black dress before there was a chance to blink. Lena eased her way onto the king-sized bed.

Denise admired Lena's body. There wasn't a flaw in sight. Lena's big, brown nipples were protruding through her black lace bra. Denise took a step forward. She ran her fingers up the sides of each of Lena's thighs until reaching her matching black lace thong. She slowly slid the small piece of soft, Italian lace down Lena's legs, revealing her sweetest place. Denise placed her index finger in Lena's soaking wet walls, and smirked.

"Are you sure it belongs to me?" Denise rubbed Lena's clit, causing goose bumps to cover Lena's legs and arms.

"Yes, baby, it's—"

"Ladies and gentlemen, we've begun our initial descent into the Charlotte area. We're currently twenty-six miles from the airport and should be touching down in ten minutes."

Lena jumped at the flight attendant's announcement. She looked around, noticing her view was not of Denise's hotel room, but of the back of a seat. Lena sighed as she pulled her iPod headphones off.

"Looks like you were having a good dream."

Lena looked over at her neighbor. The older white woman closed the thick Stephen King book she was reading. A warm smile appeared on her face. Lena smiled back, feeling comfort from the woman's smile.

"It was a great dream. I didn't snore, did I?" Lena whispered.

The woman laughed. "No, you didn't, you were a great neighbor. Much better than the last one I had." The woman placed her book in her blue travel tote. "Is this your final destination?"

Relieved, Lena smiled and laid her head back on the seat. "No, I have a layover before making it to where I'm headed."

"Well, I can tell you are anxious to get to your destination. Must be a good man waiting at the gate for you."

Lena wanted to laugh, but instead she smiled. She would let the woman think that a man was the reason for her happiness, but she knew the truth.

Her mind drifted back to her dream, causing her body to tingle. In a few hours it would become a reality.

2

Denise stood in front of the tall skyscraper. She finally knew what Dorothy felt like when she opened her door to find out she wasn't in Kansas anymore. Denise felt like the country mouse in the big city. Whenever she'd traveled before, it was with a group of teammates. This time she was alone and completely clueless. She was amazed she made it out of JFK, triple amazed that she reached her destination without getting lost.

Denise took a deep breath and walked through the large glass doors. She had never been in such an elegantly designed building. The marble floors were so clean, they gave off a shimmer. Denise walked over to the information desk behind which was seated an older gray-haired woman.

"How may I help you?"

"Umm, I'm looking for the Miller-Lewis Agency."

The woman gave Denise an awkward glare. "My goodness, where are you from? Texas? Mississippi? I haven't heard an accent that deep in my life. You gotta be Southern."

Denise smiled. She wasn't sure if it was a compliment or an insult. "I'm from Memphis, actually."

"Oh, Memphis. Ever been to Graceland?" The woman's bright aqua eyes popped open.

"No, I haven't. Well, I've passed by it a million times, just never took the tour."

"Oh." The woman's excitement level disappeared. "Oh well, I'm sure it's nice. You want the twenty-seventh floor."

"Thank you."

The woman smiled again. "You have to love that Southern hospitality. No one ever says thank you anymore. You are welcome."

Denise smiled and walked off. Denise dropped her duffle bag on the elevator floor. She watched as the lights ticked off the numbers of each floor. She suddenly felt nervous. Her heart began to race. Denise studied her reflection on the mirrored walls. Strands of her hair were flying from her ponytail. She removed the holder and smoothed her long hair before tightening it again.

The elevator door opened right into the agency. Denise stood frozen in her spot. She was expecting to walk through a door; that way she, could take a moment to exhale.

"Are you coming in?" the receptionist behind the glass desk in front of the opened elevator doors asked while giving Denise an awkward look.

"Yes, I am," Denise said as she got off just as the doors were closing. She walked up to the desk.

The blonde was attractive, and she knew it. If her clothes weren't expensive, then she really knew how to bargain-shop. Her hair was cut perfectly in a Victoria Beckham signature bob. The receptionist was busy applying her lipstick. She looked at herself in a small desk mirror then looked up at Denise.

"Well, who are you here to see?"

"Mariah Murphey. I'm Denise Chambers."

"Have a seat." The receptionist pressed a few numbers on her multi-line phone.

Denise walked over to the chic waiting area complete with two white suede oversized chairs and matching couch. There was a white shaggy throw rug underneath the glass coffee table. Sitting on top was one single purple orchid plant and the newest copies of *Sports Illustrated, ESPN, Vogue, Vanity Fair,* and *RollingStone*. Denise felt out of place sitting in the chair in her Freedom University sweat pants and T-shirt.

"Denise?"

Denise looked up to see Mariah walking toward her. Her red hair pulled back into a tight up-do. Denise wondered if Mariah ever took her hair down. Denise smiled; it was good to see a familiar face.

Mariah, always in an elegant pantsuit with the same up do, began scouting Denise when she was a freshman. Denise always thought she would go with a black sports agent if the time came; however, Mariah won her over with her bigger than-life personality and her focus on business. While other agents were trying to tempt her with big dreams, Mariah kept it real.

Denise stood up and shook Mariah's hand. She noticed the vacant expression on Mariah's usually cheery face. Something seemed a little off, but Denise couldn't place it.

"Let's go back to my office."

Denise followed Mariah down a long corridor. She glanced into other agents' offices, each showcasing some of their triumphs with pictures of their clients on the walls. Denise walked into the office. She looked around. Denise expected an open glass room like the ones she'd seen on TV. Instead Mariah's office was filled with various shades of brown with hints of red in a few places.

Mariah sat down at her desk. Denise sat in the chair in front of the desk. Denise didn't know what to make of Mariah's expression, which was very straight. She was used to a big smile.

"Denise, there really isn't an easy way to say what I have to say, so I'm just going to let it out."

"Um, sure. What's up?"

"We have a problem. I've been working my ass off to try to correct it but—" Mariah pulled out a few sheets of paper. She slid them over to Denise.

Denise's heart dropped at the print out of *Commercial Appeal*, *Memphis Flyer*, and *Freedom Daily* newspaper articles, each about her injury caused by her bi-polar ex-girlfriend Rhonda.

"Why didn't you let me know about this?"

"I don't know. It all happened so quickly. I was just so focused on getting better and getting here. Why? What's the problem?"

"The problem is that your doctors have stated that you will need physical therapy for a few months."

"Yeah, just for physical conditioning reasons, and it's during off season. What's going on, Mariah?

Mariah gave Denise a grave look. "Denise, the Liberty no longer wants to pick you up."

The words hit Denise like a ton of bricks. Her hands began to shake. "But, what . . . why can't I just play for them and show them that I'm OK?"

"Because it's deeper than that, with the past issues of lesbians harassing teammates, and worse, they don't want the woman who is coming into the team with lesbian drama on her record."

Denise could feel her dreams slipping from under her. "So that's it? Is there no other team?"

"I'm so sorry, Denise, but at this time, no. There have been some offers for you to try out next year after a lot of this has died down."

Tears began to flow from Denise's eyes. "This can't be happening. What am I supposed to do? Where am I supposed to go? I don't have anything. This really can't be happening to me." Denise's hands were shaking, her heart was beating fast. She could feel the walls closing in on her. She tried to take a deep breath but found it hard to breathe.

Mariah noticed Denise's expression. She rose out of her chair and rushed over to Denise.

"Denise, are you all right? Do you need a doctor?"

"No, I . . . need . . . a . . . career." Denise couldn't control the tears, which flowed like the Mississippi.

"Denise, I'm so sorry. I don't want you to think of this as an end. It's only one year, then you can play. I'm not giving up on you. I'm going to help you in any way I can. You aren't the first person this has happened to. You can play, just not this year."

"This can't really be happening. What am I supposed to do? Where am I supposed to go?"

Mariah's heart was breaking as she watched Denise fall apart in front of her. She had watched some of the most arrogant women and men come in and out of her office over the years. The one who really deserved to make it had lost everything.

"You are already booked in the hotel for a week. Go there and just relax. If you need more time, don't worry about it. I promised you I would take care of you, and I'm a woman of my word. Just relax, think about what you want to do. Consider staying in New York, or maybe moving somewhere else. Whatever you need, I'm here for you. I'm only a phone call away. I can have a driver downstairs to take you to the room." Mariah placed Denise's hand in hers. "Denise, I'm going to make something work for you. I give you my word."

Denise wanly glanced at Mariah, her eyes red, tear ducts full. She couldn't speak. She slowly nodded her head. Denise stood up and walked out of the office, passing by all the offices she had planned on seeing over and over. She glanced at the receptionist, who was too engrossed in a phone call about a pair of shoes to see her walking out of the office. The elevator doors closed, Denise watched the numbers going down, her happy and anxious feelings replaced with feelings of disparity, agony, and confusion. She was lost.

3

The Charlotte airport was massive. Unlike the Atlanta airport, and its train that speeds you to your next terminal, the Charlotte airport was made for walking. Lena looked down at her next gate, GATE D. She looked up at her current gate, GATE A. Just her luck. Lena started on her cross-airport trek, watching handicapped and overweight people enjoying the handicap carts that would take them swiftly to their next locations. Lena thought about playing the pregnancy card, but changed her mind; she could use the walk.

After an hour, a large slice of cheese pizza and two bottled waters, Lena's last plane began to board. She felt someone looking at her. Out of her peripheral she noticed a familiar face. She turned around to see a woman from her last flight.

Lena immediately realized what feeling she got from the woman. She had to be gay. The short red-bone's style reminded her of the first time she met Cooley. The woman's baggy jeans, oversized Nike shirt and blue and white Jordan's were the first giveaway. Lena studied her masculine walk. She had a blue and white fitted cap pulled down with her hair pulled back in a ponytail. Lena's mind was so fixated on Denise that she didn't pay attention to the woman on the first flight.

The stud smiled at Lena. Lena returned a smile.

"Now boarding our First Class, A Plus and Business Class passengers," the male gate agent said over the microphone.

Lena headed to the door, and the stud followed, ending up right behind her. Lena could feel the stud's eyes on her, and made sure not to turn around.

Lena sat down on the second row and let the window shade up. She smiled. In a few hours she would be in Denise's arms.

The attractive stud walked on the plane, and Lena's eyes met hers. The stud looked at her ticket then glanced at Lena.

"You were on my last flight, right?" The stud flashed a smile.

Lena noticed her white teeth. "Yeah, I think so." Lena felt herself getting nervous. Did the stud think that she was interested because of their small exchange at the gate? Lena turned her head toward the window as the stud put her book bag in the overhead compartment and sat down and buckled her seat belt. Lena closed her eyes, hoping the stud would think she was 'sleep.

"My name is Terrin." The stud reached her hand out.

Lena looked at Terrin; she noticed her almond-shaped eyes, hazel with a hint of emerald, slightly slanted on the edges, and very alluring.

"I'm Lena." Lena shook Terrin's hand, very soft but strong, just like Denise's hands.

"So is New York your final destination, Ms. Lena?"

"Yes, actually, it is." Lena smiled.

"Business or pleasure?"

"Pleasure, definitely pleasure."

"Ahh, must be nice. Business for me; however, I have a feeling this flight might be a bit pleasurable."

Terrin and Lena looked at each other at the same time, their eyes connected.

The flight attendant stood at their seats with a big smile on her face.

"Can I get the two of you anything to drink?" The flight attendant smiled, while the passengers in coach struggled to get past her and to their seats. Lena had never sat in coach before, and she never planned to.

"Bottled water please," Lena said.

Terrin asked for a Coke. She quickly focused her attention back on Lena.

"Pleasure, huh, let me guess, you are going to meet your woman?"

The corners of Lena's mouth quirked upward. "What makes you think it's a woman?"

The flight attendant handed them their drinks.

Terrin took a sip of her Coke. She smiled. "Are you saying it's not?" Terrin smirked.

"I'm not saying it is or isn't. I just wondered why you would assume it was a woman."

Terrin sat up in her seat and leaned in toward Lena. "Let's just say it's my lesbian intuition."

"Are you saying I look gay or something? Did your 'gay-dar' go off on me?" Lena motioned her fingers like quotation marks. She heard her bestfriends, Carmen and Misha talk about their gay-dar in numerous conversations.

"My gay-dar." Terrin laughed. "If that's what you want to call it. Or if could have been the fact that no straight woman would have been looking at me the way you were. Also, no straight woman would have smiled back when I winked at you. And . . . no woman who isn't gay moans a woman's name in her sleep."

Lena's jaw dropped. Her cheeks flushed red from embarrassment. "How did—"

Terrin gave a sly grin. "I was sitting in front of you. Don't worry, Lena. Your secret is safe with me." Terrin finished her small cup of Coke.

The flight attendants manned their posts as the plane began to coast. They began to go over all the safety rules and regulations. Lena pretended to listen while Terrin opened a copy of *Sports Illustrated*.

As soon as the flight attendants finished, Lena turned back to Terrin.

"So, let's say you didn't hear me. Would you have guessed I was gay off your other comments?"

"Not really. But I can't lie. I was surely hoping you were, when I changed my seat number to sit by you." Terrin looked ahead with a grin on her face. Lena blushed.

"Look at you, little sneaky. What were you expecting, to put me into the mile-high club?"

Terrin laughed. "No, I was just hoping to have a great conversation while on the flight. Then when we landed, I was going to ask for your number so I could take you out in New York."

"Oh, so you had it all figured out."

"I had the long trek from our last terminal to come up with it."

Lena blushed; Terrin was definitely charming. "Well, great conversation we can have. The rest, I'm not too sure about."

"Well"—Terrin looked down at her watch—"I have two hours to change your mind about that, just like I changed my seat."

Their eyes locked on each other again. Lena's face felt warm. She twisted a few strands of her hair around her finger. She was openly flirting with a woman and it wasn't Denise.

"So why are you going to New York?" Lena asked.

Terrin frowned. "Conference. Very boring stuff, a bunch of nerds sitting around talking. Nothing like you going to meet your little love. So is it gonna be all romantic and cliché? Her holding a sign with your name on it, you run into her arms at the gate?"

Lena laughed; the Cancer in her loved the hopeless romantic aspect of Terrin's words. "No, she actually doesn't know I'm coming. It's complicated," Lena said, thinking about the messy situation she created for herself.

They paused their conversation as the flight attendants performed their duties of alerting passengers of the various procedures and exit doors while the plane coasted to the runway. The plane finally took off. Lena watched as the lines on the runway passed by. The take-off was her favorite part of flying. She watched as the houses and land below began to look like hundreds of little boxes.

Terrin leaned closer to Lena. "Oh, you just gon' pop up on the chick. That's brave. What makes it complicated?"

"Trust me, you would need more than two hours."

"OK. OK. Well, give me the *Reader's Digest* version," Terrin said, looking at Lena.

Lena couldn't resist.

"Well, long story short, she was my college roommate that I cheated on my boyfriend/new husband with, but that doesn't really matter because he's cheated on me a million times. But I realized that I can't live without her, so I had to do what I had to do. You know what I'm saying?"

Terrin's eyes tightened, and her bottom lip fell slightly open. "Wow, I smell a Lifetime movie of the week. Guess he can't be too happy right now."

Lena's mind drifted to Brandon. She knew he was probably furious. He might even be on another plane coming to kill her and Denise. "I don't know what he's thinking. I care, but I just couldn't do it anymore. I . . . I love her.

Terrin gazed into Lena's brown eyes. "Do you think she feels the same way?"

"She does. Well, she did. I hope she still does." Lena looked out the window. The thought never occurred to her that Denise might not feel the same way about her anymore. She had hurt Denise so much, she could only hope it wasn't too late.

"In that case I wish you nothing but good luck. I hope she takes you in her arms and gives you the best kiss you ever had."

"Is that what you would do if you were in her shoes?" Lena gazed into Terrin's eyes.

"If it was me, I would forgive probably anything coming from a woman as beautiful as you."

Lena and Terrin exchanged smiles. Lena looked back out the window. Terrin was attractive, and witty, but she couldn't hold a candle to the love of her life. Denise was it, and she knew it. She was on her way to meet her destiny.

4

Cooley shifted her position in the uncomfortable airport chair. She noticed a white couple sleeping, their legs hanging off the ends of the row of three connected chairs, their duffle bags worn and dirty. Cooley figured they must travel a lot. She couldn't imagine falling asleep in an airport. She wouldn't be able to protect her bags if she was 'sleep, and the idea of someone stealing even the smallest of her belongings would get her a one-way ticket with airport security.

Cooley looked down at her watch. Two hours to spare and she had nothing to do. The airport was virtually shut down; she should have been in Atlanta by the time her flight was going to board. All because she forgot to print her boarding pass. Cooley made a mental note to never do that again.

She arrived an hour early, only to find all the kiosk stations at the AirTran station broken and only one ticketing agent, who seemed to be moving at a pace equivalent to a snail. The three people in front of her were becoming restless. The couple next in line walked up to the ticket counter. Cooley wanted to laugh. There in front of her stood a real-life Norbit and Rasputia.

The large woman was loud, making sure everyone knew how tired she was of waiting. She constantly shifted her weight from one overrun flip-flop to the other. Cooley felt sorry for the frail, little man with her. He looked so unhappy. Cooley wanted to tell the woman to shut the fuck up, and tell the man to run as fast as he could.

As soon as the man made a quiet gesture for the woman to calm down, she went off.

"Don't tell me to calm down. Hell, we gon' miss our plane, dealing with this bullshit. But I'd bet you would like that, wouldn't you?" She hissed at her husband.

All he could do was turn his head and sigh. Cooley knew that it couldn't be her. She would have to pull a "Chris Brown" on a woman like that . . . and she didn't believe in hitting women.

The couple's turn came. The agent's face dropped, knowing he had a headache headed his way. The agent typed their information in, printed their tickets and proceeded to check their five bags.

"OK, that will be one hundred and ninety dollars," the tall male agent stated.

"What! Why?" the Rasputia look-alike snapped.

The man in front of Cooley looked down at this watch and huffed. He shifted his weight from his right leg to his left. Cooley knew exactly how he felt.

"Ma'am, airline policy states that your first checked bag is fifteen dollars, a second one is twenty-five, and each additional bag is fifty dollars."

The woman rolled her eyes. Cooley wanted to scream but remained calm. She still had thirty minutes to get to her gate. She could make it. The reaction on the man's face in front stated that he didn't even have that long to make it to his destination.

"I didn't know anything about that. It didn't say that when I booked the damn flights. I don't think I should have to pay that much to check my bags. Hell, I bought the plane tickets. Y'all always trying to get over on us. That's why your companies are going under." She rolled her neck while her hand flew around.

"Ma'am, the policy has been in effect for a very long time. It is included in the information you are supposed to read before you accept your ticket, and"—the man handed her the reservation page she brought with her—"right here, right on the bottom of your page, it even says it." The agent didn't budge as the gayness in his voice responded in a nasty/nice tone. That only irritated her more.

"See, this man about to . . ." she whispered under her voice, but loud enough for everyone to hear. "Well, I need to talk to a supervisor because that is ridiculous. That's more than I paid for the ticket. And I don't like your bad-ass attitude"

"I told you not to pack all those damn bags to begin with," the woman's frustrated husband chimed in.

Cooley smirked; he had a little backbone after all.

Rasputia shot him a glare that would scare children.

The agent rolled his eyes. "One moment please," the agent said, walking over to another booth to call for a supervisor.

"What the fuck!" The man in front of Cooley finally snapped. "I'm missing my flight over this bullshit!"

Cooley couldn't help but smirk; she felt the exact same way.

The woman looked back at the man. She felt no remorse for causing a line of people to miss their flights over her mistake.

The husky man in front of her had on a leisure suit, but his stance showed that he didn't have any quarrels about going at it with her, if need be.

The woman's husband just shook his head. He hoped the man laid a good smack down on his wife.

The gate agent signaled for the woman to come over. He handed her the phone and walked back over to his line of angry travelers.

Cooley looked down at her watch. If she could get her ticket, get through security, and run to her gate in ten minutes, she could still make her flight. Cooley pulled her blue fitted cap off and wiped her forehead.

She glanced over at the woman, who was arguing with someone on the phone. Her livid face let Cooley know she was losing. Cooley smiled. She hoped they made her pay the full amount. Cooley glanced at her husband. His face was borderline angry and irritated, not by the airport, but by his nagging wife.

The agent was overworked and stressed. The man in front of Cooley was going off about having to take another flight. Cooley had to give it to the agent. He was keeping his cool under a lot of pressure. Cooley's boiling point was reaching its peak. Now she was down to six minutes.

"I know you are dealing with a lot, but can I make my flight?" Cooley's turn finally approached. She handed the agent her ID and confirmation number. The agent sighed. "I'm sorry, but that flight is already boarding, but I can get you on another flight. I do apologize." The man seemed to relax a little at seeing someone who was obviously "family" like him.

Cooley cringed. "How late will it be?"

The agent began to type rapidly. "Well, your final destination is Atlanta. We can get you on a flight at 10:03 A.M."

Cooley sighed. She knew she wasn't in a major rush to get to Atlanta, she was just ready to bid farewell to Memphis. "Whatever." Cooley looked down at the agent's ID tag. "Morris, I see you are dealing with a lot. It's cool." Cooley flashed Morris a smirk, her deep right dimple setting in.

The gate agent smiled; His eyes went from stressed to relief. Cooley knew it was amazing what a smile could do. A nice smile and deep dimples could melt the heart of almost anyone.

The agent printed Cooley's ticket and handed it to her. "I've also upgraded you to first-class for your troubles," Morris said as Cooley handed her large suitcase to him.

Cooley pulled her credit card.

Morris shook his head. "Don't worry about it."

Cooley smiled, showing her deep dimples. "Thank you, man. Hope your day goes better." Cooley winked as she headed toward security.

Now she was dreading that three hour wait. Cooley's eyes began to shut. She shook her head. Cooley picked up her Gucci book bag and put it on her back. She walked through the bare halls of the Memphis International Airport. The brown walls were unappealing. Something about the AirTran side made that whole side just look cheap.

Cooley made her way to the sad excuse for a food court. Everything was closed, but Backyard Burger was in the process of opening. It was eight in the morning, but the idea of a good Backyard burger didn't sound bad. Something to eat could help her mood.

Cooley walked over to the bookstore across from the food court. She glanced at the table of bestsellers. She picked up a copy of *Eclipse* from the Twilight series. Denise and Carmen were hooked on the series. Cooley thought the movies were all right, but she couldn't bear to be spotted reading a book made popular by teenage girls. Cooley spotted the small section of African American novels. She scanned through the various titles, most dealing with some type of hustler, pimp, or stripper. Cooley didn't know what was with the sudden increase in hood-related books. She picked up *Sleeping with Strangers* by Eric Jerome Dickey and read the inside of the book.

"That's a good book," a soft voice said.

Cooley turned around to see a cute and petite brown-skinned girl standing behind her. Her green shirt let her know that she was an employee. She looked young, but she had to be at least eighteen, since she was working and not in school. Cooley liked her short haircut. She usually liked girls with long hair, but since Rihanna started rocking hers short Cooley started feeling short, rocker looks on sexy black women.

"Is it? I'm real behind in his books. I think the last one I read was *Chasing Destiny*."

"Well, this is a series around a hit man. They are really good books, but I suggest reading them in order. That's the first one."

Cooley nodded her head. "Well, then I guess I will take your advice,

"Great." The girl smiled as she walked behind the counter.

Cooley picked up a box of Dentyne Icebreakers and a PowerAde. The girl began to ring her purchase up.

"So tell me, Chasity," Cooley said after reading her nametag. "How can a person go about getting to know you better?"

Chasity looked up, her face covered with surprise. "Um, excuse me?"

Cooley was confused. She knew the girl was flirting with her, or was she? "I was just wondering how a person can get to know you better. You seem to really know your fiction and I could use—"

"I don't think that's a good idea. I doubt my *boyfriend* would like that." Chasity quickly put the items in a bag and handed Cooley her credit card and bag.

Dumbfounded, Cooley took the items and walked out the store. Cooley wasn't used to rejection. The girl was cute, but she wasn't all that. Usually Cooley could have pulled her with little effort at all.

Cooley walked into the women's bathroom. She looked at herself in the mirror and gasped. It all came back to her. The large scar crossing her left cheek, mostly healed but still with a brown scab over it. *No wonder,* Cooley thought to herself. She pulled out her small tube of Neosporin and dabbed a little on the ugly mark.

Cooley grabbed a bite to eat and made her way back to her gate. More passengers had shown up, the dusty traveling couple still sprawled over the chairs. She took a seat and pulled out her iPod and headphones. She scrolled through the playlist section, trying to find the right playlist to fit her mood.

"This is our gate."

The familiar voice sent chills down Cooley's spine. She looked up to see Misha walking toward her gate, and next to her was Patrick, the man who not only stole Misha away, but impregnated her in the process.

Misha's and Cooley's eyes met. Patrick looked at Cooley, his smile turning into a glowering stare.

Misha looked as though she had seen a ghost. She looked at Patrick and whispered something to him.

His face didn't change; he nodded his head and stood in the same spot like a tall bodyguard as Misha walked over to Cooley.

"I thought you were already gone," Misha said as she got closer.

"Missed my flight. So we are on the same flight, I see."

Misha sighed "I guess so. Look, I just wanted to make sure everything was—"

"Misha, you don't have to say anything. Just go be wit' ya boy before his head explodes."

Misha looked back at Patrick, still standing in the same spot, staring at them. Cooley looked at Patrick.

She couldn't figure it out. He was wearing a pair of khaki board shorts and a yellow graphic tee from American Eagle and a pair of sandals. Nothing about him seemed special. Cooley knew her designer jeans and shirt were ten times better-looking than what he had on. Cooley dressed fly whenever she left the house. Just because she was going to be on a plane was no reason to not look good.

Patrick, on the other hand, looked like he had rolled right out of bed and headed to the airport. He didn't look like he belonged next to Misha, who was dressed in a cute pair of shorts and a white blouse that hung off of her shoulders.

"So are we cool?" Misha asked.

Cooley tried to not focus on how beautiful Misha was. Her smooth brown skin had a glow to it. Her long, thick, black hair bounced with any slight movement.

"We're cool." Cooley realized she was completely focused on Misha. She noticed Misha's eyes glance in the direction of her right cheek. Cooley's body tensed, and she turned her head.

"I see it's looking a lot better." Misha could feel Cooley's uneasiness. She suddenly wished she didn't say anything. "Well, um, I guess we will see each other around? Maybe we can have a bite in Atlanta sometime . . ."

Cooley shook her head and gave Misha a sardonic smile. "Riiiightttt, maybe. Well, you better go be with your boy before he comes over here." A piece of her wanted him to walk over. She wanted to get him back for the sucker punch he'd landed the day they met. She had never fought over a woman until that day at Misha's dorm room. She made a vow never to do it again.

Misha put her hand on her hip. Cooley's nonchalant attitude always irritated her. "Cooley, I really want us to be friends."

Cooley felt her anger rising. In front of her was the woman she loved. Standing just a few feet behind Misha was the man she played her like a fool for. "Misha, I can't do this right now. Maybe when I get over the fact that the woman I *loved*, the woman I was supposed to be with, is now with, and pregnant by some nigga. I'll be able to talk, but not now. So can you please just leave me be?"

Misha looked at Cooley, a pained look in her eyes. "I'm sorry, Carla. Take care of yourself." Misha turned around and walked back to Patrick.

They walked over and sat at the gate across from Cooley. Patrick put his arm around Misha. He glanced over at Cooley and smirked. Cooley wanted to jump up and beat his ass; instead, she picked her things up and moved to a chair facing the gate wall. The last thing she wanted to do was have Patrick flaunting his victory in her face.

The last hour passed by quickly. Cooley boarded the plane and got comfortable in her first-class seat. She placed her book bag beneath her feet. As soon as she looked up, she found herself face to face with Misha and Patrick again. They stood there in silence while waiting on the line of people placing their bags in the overhead compartments to move.

Misha looked down at Cooley. She mouthed the words "I'm sorry."

Straight-faced, Cooley put her headphones in her ears and opened her new book. The short flight to Atlanta was going to be the longest flight of her life.

5

Lena's plane landed and began to coast to the gate. She had slept the rest of the flight. She looked over to see Terrin still reading her *Ebony* magazine. Lena glanced down at the page and gasped.

"Can I see that?" Lena asked as she looked at the magazine.

Terrin handed her the magazine.

Lena couldn't stop staring at Denise's face. There she was, the woman she loved, standing in a picture with other top African American women basketball players. A small profile of Denise was on the next page along with profiles of each player. Her smile was radiant even on the page.

Lena took a deep breath.

"Know someone or something?" Terrin said, looking down at the magazine.

"Yes, I do." Lena couldn't stop smiling.

"Ohh. One of them must be your girl. Which one? Wait let me guess." Terrin looked at the page. She pointed at Denise. "Chambers, isn't it?"

"How could you tell?"

"Lucky guess, or maybe the fact that you were calling out to Dee in your sleep."

The plane stopped, and the door opened. People immediately began to get up and gather their items. Lena and Terrin stood up and headed out of the aircraft. The terminal was filled with passengers. Terrin and Lena walked toward baggage claim together.

"So, you are doing it big, huh? Got you a basketball player."

Lena thought about Brandon, her pro basketball player, who was probably tossing her things out on the streets as they spoke. "I guess I have a thing for basketball players." Lena instantly realized how she sounded when Terrin's face dropped a bit. "I didn't mean it like that. I don't purposely look for ball players or anything." Lena felt like she was having an outer body experience. "I really sound like a groupie right now. But it's really not like—"

Terrin laughed. "Let me stop you before you give yourself a heart attack. I knew what you meant the first time. No need to explain. A lot of women dig that tall, athletic look. Us shorter chicks get the short end of the stick, literally."

Terrin and Lena laughed. Lena felt back at ease.

Lena and Terrin finally reached the baggage claim area. Terrin turned around to Lena. "I know you are here for your girl, but I wouldn't be me if I still didn't try to get your number."

"Now you know that wouldn't be right."

"So your ball player won't let you have friends? Not a good sign in a relationship." Terrin shook her head.

Lena smiled. "It was really nice meeting you, Terrin."

Terrin shrugged her shoulders and smiled. "Well, in that case, it was nice meeting you, Lena. Maybe we will run into each other again one of these days, if Chambers doesn't work out."

Terrin took a couple of steps backward then turned around. Lena watched her walk to the baggage area where the luggage was starting to circle around.

Lena walked toward the front door. She noticed an ATM machine, thought about using her joint account but figured Brandon would be watching it. If she was in the same situation, she would have turned his access off by now. She remembered her emergency card, her American Express her father told her to never leave home without. She thought about her father. What would he think if he knew his princess left her Prince Charming to be with Cinderella? Lena shook her head, hoping to shake her uneasy feelings as well.

Lena withdrew three hundred dollars and put it in her bag. She walked out the front door and headed to the taxi area. The assistant quickly got her a cab.

The Middle Eastern driver looked at her via his rearview mirror. "Where to?"

Lena realized she had no idea where she was going.

"Um, can you take me to Saks Fifth Avenue?"

The driver nodded his head and pulled out.

Lena pulled her cell phone out and turned it on. As soon as the Sprint logo disappeared, her voice mail and text message alerts began to blaze. 10 New Voice Mails, 17 New Text Messages. Lena opened her text message inbox.

Hubby Cell 10:03 A.M.: You doing some low down shit Lena.

Hubby Cell 10:06 A.M.: Fuck you Lena go be with that dyke.

Lena continued to go through the messages. As the time wore on, the angry messages turned to desperation and hurt.

Hubby Cell 2:11 P.M.: Lena please, just come home.

Hubby Cell 2:45 P.M.: Please Lena, I need you, I love you. Let's work this out.

Lena felt tears forming in her eyes. She cleared the screen and dialed Carmen's number.

Carmen picked up on the first ring.

"Oh my God, Lena! I cannot wait for you to see my loft. It's not as swanky as your million-dollar pad, but damnit, I'm gonna dress it up and—"

"Carmen, wait a minute," Lena said, cutting off her ecstatic friend. "I wanted to know . . . umm . . . do you have any contact info on Denise? Like her hotel?"

Carmen looked around her storage unit to see if there was anything important she was forgetting. "Umm, I don't know the number, but I think it's an Embassy Suites."

"Do you know where?"

"No, I don't. Just call her cell. I'm sure she'll answer for you."

"Have you talked to her since she arrived in New York?"

"Actually, no. I called, but it went to voice mail. I'm guessing she was in her meeting. She had to meet her agent as soon as she got there. Hey, where are you? I want you to meet me at my new crib. It's on Harbor Town, so we are real close"

Lena forgot she didn't tell anyone she was going to New York. "I can't right now, but I'll call you as soon as I'm free." Lena hung up. She looked out the window at the fabulous city.

Lena picked her phone up and scrolled to Denise's name. A picture of Denise popped up. She smiled. The time was near.

The driver was waiting in front of the office, just as Mariah had promised. He smiled and opened the door for Denise. Denise climbed into the luxury town car and closed the door. She looked at the beautiful building that held her nonexistent future. Suddenly it didn't look as shiny and beautiful. She saw bird droppings on the walls and trash on the ground. New York suddenly looked grimy and unappealing.

Denise heard her phone vibrating from inside her duffle bag. She rummaged through the side pocket until finding the phone. Lena's face flashed on the screen. Denise sighed. She took a deep breath and answered the phone.

"Yeah?"

Lena's eyes widened, her heart racing. "Hey, Denise, hi."

"What's up?"

"I was just, um, I was calling to check on you."

Denise rolled her eyes up, hoping the cool air conditioning would stop any tears from falling. "I'm fine."

Lena smiled. "That's good to hear. Um, Carmen said she tried to call you to get your hotel and room number, but you didn't answer. I was, um, about to go into her house."

Tears ran down Denise's face. Her voice trembled. She struggled to get it under control. "Uhhh . . . I'm at the Embassy Suites, downtown. I don't know the room number. Just tell her to ask for my room." The feeling of failure set into Denise's soul. Lena was married to a pro ball player and she was now nothing.

"Great. Well, I'm sure you are doing super important things, so I'll talk to you later. Miss you." Lena couldn't stop smiling, completely oblivious to Denise's somber tone.

"Bye." Denise hung the phone up. She couldn't tell Lena the truth. She didn't want to tell anyone she was a failure. She looked up at the driver. "Hey, are there any stores around here? Like a liquor store?"

"Sure. I'll take you to one. Celebrating, huh?"

"Yeah," Denise uttered.

It was ironic. She'd spent years turning down drink after drink because she wanted to be perfect when she started her career. She was cautious her whole life. The idea of not pleasing her grandmother, or ending up like the other people in her family had struck fear in her for years. Now that she didn't have a career anymore, she could drink like a fish and it wouldn't matter.

Lena smiled as the taxi pulled up to Saks. She paid the driver and stepped out of the car. She didn't have anything to wear, and she wanted to look perfect for her special night. The large store was filled with designer clothes, accessories, and perfumes to help her create a look that would make Denise want to eat her alive. She made a mental note; she needed a sexy dress to surprise Denise with, some smoking lingerie to entice her, and something comfortable to chill in when they had their first breakfast as girlfriends.

Lena opened the doors to the store that would help make her dream come true. First stop, the dress; last stop, Embassy Suites.

6

The flight couldn't land quickly enough. Cooley shifted in her seat, as the plane coasted to the gate. Her palms were sweating. She noticed the flight attendant talking but couldn't make out what she was saying. Everything sounded like the teacher on Charlie Brown. Cooley looked around. She made sure everything was packed, so she could just fly off her seat.

The attendant gave the go-ahead to leave. Cooley jumped up and off before the other passengers in first-class could even stand up. Cooley didn't look back. She scurried to the subway inside of the Atlanta airport.

Luck seemed to be on her side, as the doors opened as soon as she made it down the stairs. Before she knew it, she was walking up the escalator to the baggage claim.

Cooley sighed. Her good luck had run out. She'd made it to baggage claim before the bags had been taken off the plane. Cooley stared at the escalator; at any moment Misha would be appearing, probably hand in hand with Patrick. The thought made Cooley's stomach turn.

Cooley stared at the baggage claim belt, hoping that she would develop ESP and cause the bags to begin to fall. The loud buzzer made her heart race. Slowly bags began to fall to the now rotating belt. Cooley stared at the opening like she was waiting on a million dollars to come out. Her heart began to beat hard.

She turned around to see Misha and Patrick walking toward the baggage area. Cooley jerked back to the baggage belt. Her hands began to tense up; she was experiencing a new feeling. A woman was making her nervous.

What the fuck is wrong with you? Cooley thought to herself. She caught a glimpse of her reflection in the metal baggage claim. She didn't recognize herself. She felt herself becoming the one thing she vowed never to be. She was becoming weak over a girl. She had become just like the punks she talked about. She had allowed herself to enter the constant stream of women who let other women affect them all in the name of love. Her father would be turning over in his grave if he saw what she had become.

When I get out of this airport, I swear no woman is ever going to get me like this again. Fuck love. That shit is for the birds, Cooley thought to herself.

Cooley shook her head. She took another deep breath. *Get a grip. You are Carla Cooley Wade.* She saw her Gucci bag headed her way. Cooley grabbed the bag off of the belt.

"Excuse me, but can I get your autograph?"

The low, sexy voice sent chills down Cooley's spine. She smirked. She knew the voice instantly.

"No autographs. But if you give me your number . . ." Cooley turned around and smiled. Sahara stood in front of her with a Kool-Aid smile on her face.

Sahara pulled her shades off, tossing her silky hair in the process. "What are you doing here?"

"Well, I was told that the new A&R rep was arriving at the airport, so I decided to hop in my new ride and come pick you up myself. I hope you don't mind." Sahara extended her hands.

Cooley wrapped her arms around Sahara's small waist. "Not at all." Cooley nodded her head. She glanced down at Sahara's petite, thick frame. The pair of Seven jeans she was wearing fit her thick thighs like they were painted on. She looked thicker than Cooley remembered, and her designer rags a big upgrade from the stripper heels and cheap clothes that adorned her last time they were together. The brown stiletto boots just added to her sex appeal.

"Like what you see?" Sahara took a step back, modeling her outfit for Cooley.

"You could say that. I don't know what you have been doing, but keep it up, 'cause you look damn good."

Sahara looked passed Cooley. "Umm, seems like I'm not your only fan here." Sahara nodded her head.

Cooley turned around to see Misha staring in her direction, while the oblivious Patrick watched for their bags.

Cooley smiled; the tables were turned in her favor. "Nah, it's nothing like that. So, are we gonna stand here all day, or are you gonna take me to check out your ride?"

"After you." Sahara smiled.

Cooley turned back toward Misha. "Give me one moment, OK?" Cooley walked off before Sahara could respond. Her hands were no longer sweating; the nervous feeling was replaced with her usual cocky confidence.

Misha quickly perked up when she noticed Cooley walking in her direction.

"Hey, um, I'm out of here, but I wanted to come back and say good-bye, and I wish you two all the luck in the world." Cooley looked at Misha. Patrick quickly turned around. His straight face amused Cooley.

"Thanks, Carla. Keep in touch, OK." Misha gave Cooley a friendly hug.

Cooley manned up, giving Misha a strong hug, a hug filled with love. She wanted Misha to feel her one more time.

"Sure. I will. And, hey, I'm sorry about everything, man. You have a really wonderful woman, and congratulations on the bundle of joy." Cooley extended her hand toward Patrick.

Patrick hesitated but finally shook Cooley's hand. "Thanks."

"Well, I got to run. Take care of yourself, Misha."

"You too."

Cooley turned around and walked back to Sahara. She wrapped her arm around Sahara as they walked out of the airport. Deep down, Cooley knew it was the last time she would ever see Misha.

"Oh shit, so you riding like this?" Cooley grinned at the cherry red BMW.

"You know I had to ride well."

"OK, do I want to know what you are doing right now?" Cooley placed her bag in the empty trunk. She could tell the car was brand-new by the unused trunk and drive-out tags.

"You will find out in due time. Trust me." Sahara pushed her keyless entry to unlock the doors. They got in the car and drove off.

Cooley placed her shades on as they drove down the busy Atlanta expressway. "So, um, I wanted to apologize for—"

"Cooley, save it. There's no need for it, trust me." Sahara looked at Cooley.

"Nah, it wasn't cool for me just to leave you at the crib like that. It was a big mistake on my part, and I really do apologize for it." Cooley put her hand on Sahara's thigh.

She had turned Sahara down during Christmas break because of her love for Misha.

"Well, thank you for the apology. I do appreciate it. I can't lie. I was a little upset by you leaving me."

"Really?"

"OK, truth is, I was real upset. Cooley, you know there's been something growing between us for a while now. Hell, by the way you used to look at me I would have never in a million years thought you had anyone waiting back in Memphis."

"I know. Trust me, it wasn't that I wasn't feeling you. Misha and I just sorta happened and it grew. I never meant to hurt you." Cooley ran her hand through Sahara's long wavy hair. She glanced at the radio, which was talking about Jam Zone.

"So, tonight is the big Jam Zone listening party for the new artist they have signed to the new R&B division," the male DJ stated.

"Yeah, I'm real excited to check out the new acts. I heard they got some that are gonna be killin' the game," the female co-host added.

"Big-ups to Jam Zone. They're doing big things in the city," the male responded. "Speaking of Jam Zone, one of their artists isn't doing so well right now. According to MediaTakeOut, rapper Supa Sonic has been dropped from the label."

"What!" Cooley yelled.

Sahara stared at the bumper in front of her.

"According to the Web site, Big Ron and the other Jam Zone artist and execs have grown tired of Supa Sonic's antics. Supposedly, she crashed a private party at Big Ron's house. Some say she pulled a girl out of the party by her hair," the male DJ added as Cooley listened.

"We hear that she was seeing the female and was up-set that the girl went to the party without her; however, no reports were filed," the female co-host added.

Cooley turned the radio down.

"Do you know anything about this?" Cooley turned to Sahara, whose bleak expression said it all.

"It's true. Sonic has lost it for real. It's the drugs. They tried to get her help, but she didn't want it. Big Ron didn't have a choice. She was acting crazy every-where she went, especially at clubs."

"Damn, why didn't I know about this? Every time I call her, I get her voice mail."

"She hasn't been answering her phone since it hap-pened. Big Ron told her she had to get out of the house."

"That wasn't her house?" Cooley put her hand on her head. She couldn't believe what she was hearing.

Sahara shook her head. "No, it belongs to the com-pany. That's why you are able to still stay there. No one has seen her since the incident happened."

"Man, I wish someone would have called me. I would have tried something. I feel so bad. I wouldn't be here today if it wasn't for Sonic."

"Cooley, there was nothing anyone could do. She didn't want help. I think she actually moved from blow to—"

"Don't tell me that." Cooley pulled her iPhone out and texted Sonic's phone. "I'm sending her a text. I hope she will respond. Damn! I can't believe this."

"Well, hopefully she will text you back, but don't count on it. One thing I learned about Sonic is that when she doesn't want to be found she won't be."

Sahara looked over at Cooley. Cooley's eyes were tight. Sahara stared at the large scar on Cooley's cheek. "Cool, I don't know if you want to talk about it, but"— She ran her finger across Cooley's jaw.

"Don't." Cooley jerked her face away. "I . . . I don't really want to talk about it."

"OK, OK, I just—"

"Just nothing. I don't want to talk about it." Cooley took a deep breath, realizing she was snapping on Sahara for no reason."

Sahara glanced at Cooley. "Cool, you are supposed to be a whole lot happier right now. You are about to start an amazing career. I know we should go out tonight and celebrate, party like rock stars."

"I'm so not in a party mood." Cooley rested her head on the window. Sahara made her remember her scar. She didn't want to be seen looking the way she did.

"Oh my God, I'm gonna need you to snap out of this funk. You are about to see a really big artist. You should be excited, not moping over something that isn't that serious."

"How can you say it's not that serious? Look at me. I look—"

"You still look just as sexy as you did the first time I saw you." Sahara smiled. "I kinda like it actually. Gives you a little hardness. Sexy." Sahara winked.

Cooley couldn't help but smirk. She had to give it to Sahara. She knew what to say to make her feel better, even if she was lying.

"Wait . . . how do you know so much about my job anyway? I thought all you were doing were a few videos."

Sahara smiled. "Well, I got another job now in the company."

Cooley's eyes widened. "Really, and that is?"

"You ask too many questions. You will find out real soon, trust me."

"OK sneaky ass. I can't wait to find out."

Cooley looked out the window at all the big houses. She looked over at Sahara's beautiful face. Cooley wondered if this time it would be right. She put her hand on top of Sahara's hand. "Did I tell you that I'm really glad you picked me up?"

"No, but I'm glad to hear it." Sahara licked her lips.

Cooley felt her nature rising.

"Man, I am not in Memphis anymore." Cooley looked out the window. She knew her life was changing. She looked over at Sahara. For the first time in a while she felt like her old self.

7

Lena walked into the beautiful hotel. A group of businessmen's attention quickly turned to her, her tall black, Manolo Blahnik stilettos clicking against the floor.

Lena decided to keep it chic and sexy. She wanted to give Denise a true wow factor.

The businessmen followed Lena with their eyes. Her short, black jersey halter dress caused the men to stand at attention. She pulled her beautiful long black hair down, letting her natural curls flow.

Lena noticed the front desk agent salivating at the sight of her. She smiled. It was perfect; she should be able to get whatever she wanted out of the young, white male.

"Well . . . welcome to the Embassy Suites. My name is Phillip. How can I be of assistance to you?"

Lena placed both of her arms on the counter, causing just enough of a gap in her dress so that Phillip could get a better view of her cleavage. "Hi, Phillip, my friend Denise Chambers asked me to meet her at her room, and I can't, for the life of me, remember her room number."

Phillip pulled himself away from looking at her smooth skin. "Uh, yes, um, let me look that up for you."

"Oh, thank you so very much. You are a life-saver, she would kill me if she knew I forgot it." Lena flashed her pearly whites. Phillip was putty in her hands. In seconds she had Denise's room number. It was show time.

***

Denise knew liquor was not her friend. Instead of feeling better the vodka made her feel worse. The taste was horrible. The orange juice didn't help the burning of the cheap vodka going down her throat. Denise didn't care; she suffered, waiting on the effects to kick in. Soon she found herself sitting on the edge of the plush bed crying like a little baby. All the years of blood and sweat she'd given to her craft were coming out in her tears.

Mema's face circled in her mind. She thought about how much she missed her grandmother and how disappointed she would have been about her last years in college. Denise's unhealthy relationship with Lena was the cause of it all. She knew karma was kicking her in her ass for messing with Lena, and Rhonda. She had broken her own rules, no women until after college. Everything that had happened Denise brought on herself.

Denise thought about her mother Tammy. She felt more like her mother than ever in life. Her mother had a drug habit that made her incapable of making responsible decisions. Tammy's drug was crack; Denise's drug was Lena Jamerson-Redding.

In the midst of her self-pity party she heard a faint knock at the door. Denise ignored it. There was another knock, this time a little louder. Denise stood up and stumbled, her head spinning.

Using her hand on the wall as a guide, she walked toward the door. She looked out the peep hole, but all she saw was black. Either she was hearing things, or someone was playing at her door.

There was another knock on the door. Denise flung the door open and froze. Lena stood face to face with Denise.

Lena looked into Denise's eyes. Her voice soft, and with affection, she said, "Hi, Denise."

"Lena?" Denise inquired doubtfully, the vodka more powerful than she imagined. Now she was seeing things.

"Yeah, it's me." Lena reached out to Denise and touched her arm.

Goose bumps covered Denise's arm.

"Can I come in?"

Dazed and confused, Denise opened the door. Lena walked in the room. Denise couldn't help but notice the sexy black dress and heels that Lena was rocking. She felt her body heating up just as the vodka had done earlier. She bit her tongue. A surge of pain came from her throbbing tongue. It wasn't a dream or the effects of the liquor. Lena was in her room.

"Lena, what are you doing here?"

Lena looked around the room. She turned back toward Denise. She had a whole speech prepared that left her mind at first sight of Denise.

Lena's voice trembled. "Well, you left Memphis, and it started with me not being able to say good-bye." Lena sat on the edge of the bed.

"So you came to New York to say good-bye to me?" Denise slurred. She walked past Lena and sat down in her plush leather chair.

Lena was a little confused. She expected to be in Denise's arms by now, not explaining herself. "Well, no, I . . . Denise, I was sitting at home staring at the wall. I kept thinking about you. Everything I did, everything I watched brought me right back to you. I realized something that I . . . I honestly knew a long time ago, but I was too afraid to admit it. I'm ready, Denise. I want to give us a real chance."

Denise's face was completely unreadable. Butterflies began to flutter in Lena's stomach. At this point in her fantasies, Denise grabs her and kisses her. But Denise sat in the chair, almost lifeless, her eyes fixed on Lena.

Denise stared at Lena. A piece of her wanted to take her in her arms and hold her, but something bigger was holding her back.

"What did Brandon say?"

The response caught Lena off guard. That was not the response she was expecting. She looked at Denise. Denise had not moved or blinked.

"Well, I actually just left. When I got to the airport, you were gone, so I just got on a plane."

"So he doesn't know you are here?"

"Not exactly, but—"

"Figures," Denise muttered. She stood up, the face that was straight a minute before now covered with agitation. "You know what, Lena, you need to go."

"Huh?" Lena's hands began to tremble. This definitely wasn't in her fantasy. "What do you mean?"

Denise snapped. "You know what? Everything is making sense to me now. Lena, you don't give a damn about me or Brandon. All you care about is yourself." Denise glowered.

Lena's tremble turned to a rapid shaking in her hands. She wanted to think Denise was joking, but her facial expression said otherwise. "What are you saying? Dee, what is this?" Tears began to form in Lena's eyes.

"For two years you played me and Brandon. My dumb ass was so in love with you, I was willing to take you anyway I could get you. Hell, the only reason I dated Rhonda was to attempt to get over you! And what do you do, you run right back to him. You let me fuck you, then you go back to ya boy."

"Denise, it's not like that, and you know it."

"So now you want to be with me? For how long do I have you? A day? A week? Do I get to be your weekend lover then when you realize that I'm not the one again you go running back to ya millionaire ball player."

The bass in Denise's voice frightened Lena. "Denise!" Lena stood up. "Why are you being so mean to me?" She glanced into the bathroom; she noticed the empty bottle of vodka.

Denise looked away from Lena. She wasn't as appealing as she was earlier.

Lena walked into the bathroom and grabbed the bottle. "What the fuck is this? So you're drinking now? Denise, what the hell is going on?"

Denise grabbed the bottle from Lena's hands. "Nothing you need to worry about. Look, I'm sorry you came out here, but you might as well go back to ya man 'cause this here, it isn't happening, not now or ever again."

Denise and Lena stared each other down, but not backing down from their position. Lena's whole body was quivering, Denise was perfectly still like a stone statue.

Lena stared deep into Denise's eyes, looking for a glimmer of hope; all she saw was anger and resentment.

Lena didn't know what to do. She stood in her expensive dress, completely lost. She had only one more option, to completely beg.

"Denise, I know that I haven't been the best. I know I might have been selfish. But I also know that I'm here right now in your room asking you to just take me and love me like you said you would. Whatever I did, I'm sorry for it. I'm trying to make things right. I'm trying to show you that I'm all in this time. Don't do this. Please." Lena's lips quivered.

Denise knew she was serious. She could tell Lena meant every word pouring from her mouth, the mouth she loved to kiss more than any in the past. Lena's beautiful face was covered in fear and pain. Her face was a little fatter than normal. It dawned on Denise.

"You're pregnant, Lena. You're having his child. You will never be completely mine. There's no getting around that."

"I can, Denise." Lena grabbed Denise's hand. "I know, but we can make a really great life here."

"Life? What life? I don't have a life here . . . or with you!" The word spewed like venom from her mouth.

Lena's face cracked into a million pieces. "So you really do want me to leave?" Lena responded, still unable to accept the truth.

Denise's shattered dreams were now joined by her shattered heart. Denise walked closer to Lena. Lena's perfume aroused every part of her body. Denise grazed her hands down Lena's arms.

They both got goose bumps, each longing for the other.

Denise studied Lena's eyes, now glistening from tears. Denise wiped the falling water from Lena's face.

"I can't do this anymore."

Lena's body tensed up. She felt like she had been hit by a train.

Denise walked over to the door. She turned and looked at Lena, who hadn't even turned around. Denise wanted to cry, she wanted to hold Lena and make love to her for days, but she couldn't. She had put herself last for too long, she had her own problems to deal with, and Lena's drama would only hurt her already horrible situation.

Lena turned around. Her lip started to quiver at the sight of Denise standing at the door. Denise opened the door. Lena could feel herself breaking down.

Denise looked away, staring at the wall. She couldn't see Lena's face. If she saw her face, she would change her mind.

Lena lingered for another moment. She knew it was over. She broke down. The small tears were now waterfalls flowing down her face like Niagara Falls. She ran out the room, crying harder than she had ever cried in her life.

8

Cooley couldn't get comfortable. The thought of her enjoying the place that Sonic called her own was unsettling to her. She didn't sleep in the master bedroom; she opted for the guest room she slept in each time she visited Sonic. Her bad sleep caught up with her, causing her to oversleep. Sahara's loud knock on her door woke her up when her alarm clock failed to.

Cooley smiled as she sat across from Sahara at Cheesecake Factory. She wouldn't go out to a club like Sahara wanted, but she couldn't resist the chance to eat Cheesecake Factory. The large menu didn't matter to Cooley; she was addicted to their Buffalo Blast. The chicken bites had just enough kick to them for her. Almost as good as her favorite wing spot back in Memphis. She made a mental note to find the best wings in Atlanta. She couldn't live without hot wings.

Sahara's hot body added even more spice to Cooley's taste buds. She was amazed by Sahara's transformation. Curiosity was getting the better of her. She wanted to know what Sahara was doing at Jam Zone, and did she have to fuck for her position, like many women in the company?

The idea of Sahara working in the strip club she found her in the year before didn't sit well with Cooley, and the idea of some exec having his way with her really made Cooley's blood boil. Sahara was sexy beyond words. She could have any woman or man that she wanted.

Cooley noticed the twinkle in Sahara's eyes every time they looked at each other. She wondered why Sahara hadn't brought up the scar across her face again since the other day in the car. Cooley never caught her staring at it; Sahara looked at her like she always had. She had to notice it. After all Cooley could see it in a mirror a mile away.

Dinner went over with success. Cooley pressed for the secret job of Sahara's, but she wouldn't budge. She also never mentioned Cooley's scar, how she got it, or the woman who came in between them. Cooley's eyes wandered to Sahara's plump breasts. She was by far more attractive than Misha, yet she couldn't see it when she was still devoted to Misha. Love was a son of a bitch.

Cooley woke up bright and early for her first day at work. She didn't feel like the anxious intern, but this was more pressure. Overnight she had gone from student to executive, and she didn't want to make any mistakes.

Cooley had her first day outfit laid out and ironed to perfection. She started her normal routine of showering and primping to create her perfect look. Cooley didn't get the same joy out of getting ready like she used to. No matter how perfect her look was, she knew it wasn't.

She stared at her imperfection. She rubbed her ointment on her scar. The prickly feeling disgusted her.

She took the tip of her finger, pressing her finger nail against the scab. A twinge of pain shot through her, but she continued until a piece of the scab lifted. Cooley sighed, she slowly pulled a piece of the crusty scab off of her face. Most of it didn't hurt, it peeled off easily. She stared at the light-colored spot scar on her face. It wasn't as bad as before, but still was unsightly and didn't belong on her face.

Cooley sighed. She was able to deal with it better than before, but she knew plastic surgery was in her near future.

Cooley hated the weather in the South. The humid air was filled with moisture. She could smell the rain that was supposed to fall by afternoon. Cooley stared at the Jam Zone logo and took a deep breath. Her new life had officially started. She exhaled and opened the door.

"Good Morning, Ms. Wade," the cute, young receptionist greeted her.

"Hey, Tina. You can call me Cooley or Cool or whatever you like." Cooley smiled. A lot had changed. Last time she was in the office she was treated like any other intern. Now she was called by her last name. Suddenly Cooley didn't sound as good as it used to. She wondered, was it time for a new nickname, or even worse, time to start using her government name? "Tina, do you think I should go by another name?"

"Well, Big Ron calls you Cool, so why don't you just go by that?"

"Hmm, good point."

Tina smiled. "Thank you, Ms. W—I mean Cool. Are you excited to be here?"

"Can you see it on my face?" Cooley looked at Tina.

Tina blushed. "No, you are fine. You look very . . . cool. Would you like to know where you are supposed to be?"

"Oh shit, yes, I do." Cooley felt her body tense up from her nervousness. "Man, I'm trippin'."

"It's fine." Tina pressed a combination of numbers on her phone. She stood up and walked around her glass desk. Tina pulled her gray blazer down and adjusted her twisted skirt. "Follow me."

Cooley greeted other associates and artists as they walked down the long corridor. She felt herself calming down. She glanced at the large platinum plaque on the wall. Supa Sonic's first album cover dominated the majority of the plaque. Cooley's happiness was bittersweet. She made a mental note to try to get in touch with Sonic.

"So here we are. Welcome to your new office, Cooley." Tina opened the door.

Cooley's face lit up with pride as she walked into the nice size office. It was bare, no gold or platinum plaques on the walls like the other A&R reps. The chocolate carpet was only joined by a large dark chestnut desk, a chair for her, and two extra chairs for company. Her bookshelf was empty, and there was no stereo or awards.

"Man, this is . . . this is . . ."

"Bare," Tina joked.

"No, amazing." Cooley looked at Tina, who was unimpressed by the office. "It might not be anything in here, but it has the most important thing of all." Cooley walked over to her desk. She picked up the small nameplate. She looked at the CARLA "COOLEY" WADE written on the plate. "This is really all I need for now."

Tina smiled. "Well, enjoy your nameplate and empty office. I need to get back to the front. Welcome, Cooley. Oh, and you have a meeting in an hour with Ron."

Cooley sat down in her plush black chair. "Thanks, T." Tina closed the door as she walked away. Cooley couldn't resist the urge. She put her hands on the desk and pushed herself, causing the chair to spin around real fast. "Hell yeah!" Cooley laughed.

A knock at the door ended her childish antics. Cooley grabbed the desk so her chair wouldn't move. She sat up straight. "Ummm . . . come in."

A petite, young woman walked into the office. Her locks, oversized jeans, Jordan's and black button-down gave away her sexual orientation immediately.

"Greetings, Ms. Wade. I'm Teyanna, but most people call me Tee."

"How are you, Tee?"

"I'm, well, I'll be better when you decide to make me your assistant." Tee held her head high, her thin locks hitting her on her shoulders.

Cooley leaned forward and put her arms on her desk. "Wow, that's straight to the point."

Tee walked forward. She put a manila folder on the desk. "If you take a moment to view my resume, you will see that I have extensive experience in the field. As of recently I was the assistant for Supa Sonic and Danger Dane."

"Sonic? You were with Sonic?" Cooley's eyes widened.

"Yes, I was with her for the last few months until . . . well ,until recent events. I am a hard worker and I promise—"

"Hey, do you know where Sonic is?"

Tee's lower lip quivered. "Umm, well . . ."

"Come on, Tee, I'm just trying to locate her. She's my friend, and I'm worried about her. Hey have a seat ok." Cooley motioned toward the chair.

Tee hesitated but sat down. She pulled the chair closer to Cooley's desk and leaned in. "I'm not supposed to say anything, because . . . well . . . she's sorta banned from around here."

"OK, just let me know. I promise I won't tell a soul."

"Right now she's in New York. She's kicking it at an old girlfriend's house until the spot isn't so hot."

"Really? Wait, why does she feel the need to hide? I mean, all I heard was that she was fired."

Tee's lip curled. "Yeah, right! Ms. Wade—"

"Call me Cool."

"Oh, OK. Well, Cool, it's a whole lot more than that. I know 'cause I was practically staying there for the last two months. Sonic went off the deep end for real. She got into heavier drugs. I was on O.D. watch."

"Damn, are you serious?" Cooley's mouth dropped. She thought about the piles of cocaine and weed that was always present wherever she and Sonic would go. "So what was it? Pills? What?"

"Worse. Crack."

"Hell naw! I don't believe that. Tell me you are bullshittin'." Cooley's mouth dropped further.

Tee shook her head. "I wish I could say it, but I can't. Man, I saw the pipes myself. I tried to get her to get some help, but I'm just the assistant. She wouldn't listen to me."

"No, no, no! I can't believe you are telling me this shit." Cooley leaned back in her chair.

"I'm sorry." Tee sank down in her chair.

"Damn!" Cooley ran her fingers through her curly hair. She sat back up. "Fuck that, I need to get in touch with her. I gotta help her out. You got a way to get in touch with her?"

"Yeah, I'll get it to you." Tee stood up. "So, um, I know you might not want to talk about it, but I was wondering about the position."

Cooley laughed at Tee's awkward look. "Sure, I'll give you a try out. I think you might just be a good fit for me."

Tee smiled, showing almost all of her teeth. "Great!" She pulled out an iPhone. "In that case, Cool, you have to be in Big Ron's office in one hour and then you have your first artist planning meeting directly after."

"Oh, so you just knew I was going to hire you, huh?"

Tee smiled. "Let's just say I wanted to be prepared. Now, is there anything I can get you?"

"Yeah, well, I need some stuff for this empty-ass office. Can you work on getting me things that go in an office? You know, kinda take the cue from the other people."

"Done. You will have something by the end of your meetings today." Tee turned around and walked toward the door. She turned back toward Cooley. "Oh, by the way, thank you for the opportunity. I won't let you down."

"Dig that."

Cooley sat back in her chair. She wanted to enjoy the moment, but she couldn't get Sonic off her mind.

She thought about her new life. Denise popped into her mind. "Oh shit," Cooley said to herself. She hadn't checked in with her bestfriend and she was way overdue.

Cooley picked up her phone. It went straight to Denise's voice mail.

"Wuz up, bruh. I'm sitting here in my phat-ass office in ATL and I realized I hadn't talked to you yet. Bet you off becoming a supastar. Well, get at me. I might hit New York soon. One."

Cooley hung the phone up. She looked down at her watch. Her meeting with Big Ron was quickly approaching. She sighed. It was time to work.

9

The bright sun felt like it was burning through Denise's brain. She quickly closed her eyes. She sat up in the bed. The ache hit her like a sledgehammer to the head. She closed her eyes as tight as she could, but it wasn't keeping the bright light out.

She stumbled to the bathroom, felt her way to the sink without turning the light on, opened her eyes and splashed water on her face. *What the fuck was I thinking?* Denise said, staring in the darkness.

Denise turned the hot water on. She slowly pulled her clothes off, letting them fall to the floor. She cautiously stepped into the dark shower. The hot water hit her body with full force. She let the water run down her back.

Denise pulled the ponytail holder off of her hair. She let her thick hair absorb the water. She made a mental note never to drink again.

Thirty minutes later, Denise decided to venture back into her bright hotel room. The sunlight hurt, but not as bad as it did originally.

Denise fell back to her bed. She stared at the white stucco ceiling. Thoughts rushed through her mind. What should her next move be? Everyone in her life was off doing amazing things and she was back at square one.

Denise sat up. She looked around, until she eyed her duffle bag. She walked over and picked the bag up. She threw it on her bed and plopped back down. She searched through the pockets, trying to remember where she put her cell phone. Her hands roamed through the bag until coming across the thin iPhone Cooley insisted she get. The screen was black. She turned the phone on, only to be hit with the low battery logo. She grabbed the charger before the phone cut back off. Her fingers hit the screen, dialing her voice mail.

"Hey, boo, just calling to see if you made it to New York. Give me a call. Nic and I are looking for a place. God! How did I let her talk me into staying in Memphis? Anywho call me."

Carmen's voice made her smile. At least if she was going to end up back in Memphis she had somewhere she could crash.

"Bruh! Why the fuck is Misha on my damn plane? This is some bullshit. Call me."

Denise pressed delete at Cooley's drama.

"Denise, I just wanted to call and check on you."

Denise recognized Mariah's sweet, but strong voice.

"I'm actually working on something for you right now. It's not basketball, but honestly it might be better. I'll call you in the morning with more."

Denise was puzzled. She couldn't believe there was anything being better than basketball.

"Denise, this is Lena."

Lena's voice hit her harder than an SUV.

"I'm, well . . . I have a surprise for you. I will talk to you soon."

Suddenly the previous nights events flooded to her memory. Lena wasn't a dream, she was there last night. *Oh my God, what have I done?* Denise thought to herself, remembering the things she said. She could see Lena's face as though she was still there, standing in front of her. She saw the tears rolling down Lena's face.

Denise disconnected from her voice mail. Her body felt numb. Not the drunk numb she experienced the night before, but an emotional numbness. Lena came for her, and she'd sent her away.

Denise sank down in her bed. She didn't see how things could get any worse.

The hotel phone blared, causing her head to pound. "Hello?"

Mariah's stilettos click-clacked on the marble floor of her office building. "Denise, I have been calling you all day. What is going on with your phone?"

"I didn't have it on. I needed some time to—"

"I'm sorry to cut you off, but I'm on my way into a meeting. I need you to be up and dressed and in the hotel bar at noon. Can you do that for me? "

"Ummm . . . sure. Why? What's going on?"

"I'll explain when I get there. I think something amazing is headed your way. Just be in that bar. I have to run." Mariah hung the phone up and walked into the meeting room.

Denise stared at her phone. She scrolled down to Cooley's number and pressed SEND.

"You would call when I only have about five minutes to talk to yo ass," Cooley said as she picked her curly fro.

"Fuck! I got something really, really important to tell you."

Cooley looked up at herself in the mirror. "What's up?"

"I can tell you later. It might take long—"

"Just spill it."

Denise's voice trembled. "I'm not playing basketball." The words coming out of her mouth sounded surreal. She fought back tears.

Cooley's mouth dropped. "What do you mean? Dee, what the hell?"

"My injury from . . . Rhonda and the bad press . . . the team changed their minds." Denise struggled to get the words out. Saying them still seemed surreal.

"That's some bullshit! How can they do that? Bruh, are you OK? What do you need me to do?" Cooley sat down in one of the chairs in front of her desk.

"I don't know anything right now. Mariah called me this morning, said she got something she think might work for me. I'm meeting her at one."

"I'm so sorry, bruh. Have you told C?"

"No, I don't know how to tell her. I know she is gonna worry. I don't know what I am going to do. I have no career, no place to stay, nothing."

"Dee, please, you always got somewhere to stay. If this gig with Mariah doesn't work out, get yo ass on a plane and come to ATL and chill out here. You know I got you."

Tears streamed down Denise's face. "You know that's not my style. I can't be living off you."

"Man, if you don't shut that shit up! You are my family and I would love to have you here with me. Fuck basketball! Everything is in my industry. I can get you a job and we can be the two rich bros."

Denise laughed. "I love you man."

"Love you too, no homo."

They both laughed. Denise felt a bit of ease. Cooley headed out of her office. "So, guess who picked me up from the airport?"

"Who?"

"Sahara." I swear she showed up just in time. Misha and that damn Patrick were stalking me. But I had the last laugh in the end. Misha's face dropped when she saw Sahara's fine ass.

"Cool."

"Yeah?"

Denise looked down. "Lena showed up here."

Cooley paused in her tracks. "What do you mean, Lena showed up?"

"She showed up. She told me she wanted to be with me and everything."

"And you hit me with the bad news first. That's great. Where is she now?"

"Cool, that isn't good news. I was drunk and I said some fucked up things. I told her to go back to her man."

"You were drunk!" Cooley yelled.

Everyone looked around at her with puzzled expressions.

"You don't drink, Dee."

"I know. Blue Top too."

"Ah, hell naw."

"I feel horrible. I don't know what to do. Do I call her and tell her I want her . . ."

"Dee, look, I really hate to cut this short, but I gotta go meet with boss man. But I want to say this. Let it be. Dee you need to really focus on you right now. I love you, but the last thing you need is the drama of a pregnant, married woman."

"But I feel I should apologize."

"Give it some time. Just not yet. Focus on you. I gotta run bruh, but I'll call you as soon as I get out of here. I might even make a trip to NYC. I got to take care of some business there."

"OK, let me know. I got the hotel room for the week."

Denise hung up with Cooley. She put her phone on the desk. She noticed the time on the clock. Mariah would be there in two hours. She needed to completely sober up. Denise inhaled; she knew something had to happen for the good soon.

***

Lena stared at the door to her loft. She didn't want to stay in New York another minute. She grabbed her things from her room and headed straight to the airport. She booked a thousand-dollar non-stop flight home. She was back in Memphis before the sun completely came up.

She could hear Sade coming from the inside. She knew Brandon was home. He always listened to Sade when he had a lot on his mind.

She unlocked the door and pulled it open. The place was ransacked. A gallon of SKYY vodka lay over on its side, empty. Dishes were everywhere, chairs were turned over. Brandon had wrecked the place.

Brandon walked from around the corner. Their eyes met. Sade's voice filled the air as they stared at each other. Brandon's straight face dropped.

"You're back."

Lena lowered her head. "Yes. I see you did some redecorating."

Brandon walked closer. "Well, when a man's wife runs off to New York to be with some bitch, naturally, he might be a little angry."

Lena dropped her purse and keys on the kitchen counter. "Brandon, we need to—"

"No! Fuck talking, Lena! What the fuck are you doing back here?"

"This is my home."

"*Was* your home."

Lena walked closer to Brandon. "Are you fucking kidding me?"

"Does it look like I'm fucking kidding?!" Brandon knocked the one remaining kitchen table chair over.

"Brandon, nothing happened. I just wanted to—"

"Wanted to what?"

"I just needed to say good-bye. We didn't do anything. I didn't even spend the night in New York. We
talked, and I went straight back to the airport." Lena
walked past Brandon, he followed.

"And you couldn't do that in Memphis? You couldn't
pick the damn phone up or send her a fucking e-mail?"

"No! I . . . I don't want to talk about it." She looked up,
and Brandon was replaced with Denise. She blinked,
causing Brandon to reappear. Lena's body began to
tremble. Her stomach knotted up.

"You don't have a choice. We are gonna talk about
this now! What the fuck, Lena? How am I supposed to
respond to this shit?"

"I don't know. Probably the same way I responded
to finding out about your other bitches, and your son!"
Lena's side cramped. She tried to massage the cramp
out of her right side.

Brandon's lips tightened, his broad shoulders sunk
in. "Really, Lena, you want to go there then cool. Yes,
Lena, I fucked off. But that's all I did. I fucked those
bitches. They didn't mean shit to me! You, Lena, you
fucking loved that girl."

"I never . . ."

"I heard you!" Brandon's body now trembled along
with Lena's. Tears streamed down his masculine face.
"I heard you in her hospital room. You told her that you
were in love with her."

With one swoop, his hands crashed into the expensive brown vase on the small table, causing it to crash
to the floor.

The knots in Lena's stomach now filled her whole
body. She stood frozen.

Brandon couldn't take his eyes off the shattered vase,
broken in a million pieces, just like their marriage.

"How the fuck am I supposed to feel about that?
Those bitches never meant more than a quick nut to
me. I never gave my heart to any of them, only you!"
Brandon cried. His body filled more with hurt than
anger.

Lena and Brandon stared at each other face to face.
Both faces filled with raw emotions. There were no
words. Lena's body ached. Her body was hot. She could
feel steam rising from her, sweat trickling down her
body. She couldn't be angry, she knew he was right.
She loved Denise. If Denise had her, she wouldn't be
standing there right now.

Brandon's frustrated expression quickly changed.
He took two steps back. A look of pure terror took over
his face.

"Lena!"

The trickling of sweat wasn't sweat at all. Lena
gasped as she noticed the drops of blood falling from
her.

10

Denise looked at herself again in the full-length mirror on the hotel room wall. She pulled her hair back into a ponytail. Her jeans were creased, loose-fitting but still very professional. She opted for one of Cooley's polo shirts that somehow ended up in her luggage.

Her eyes weren't as red or puffy as they were a few hours earlier. She had popped two Tylenol, which helped tremendously. Denise sighed. It was five till show time.

She walked out of her room. She looked at the numbers on each door. Denise wondered where Lena was. She wondered if she was in one of the rooms in the hotel. She made a mental note to check with the front desk before leaving.

Denise spotted Mariah's red hair immediately. She noticed a small, white man dressed in a pair of jeans and a blazer chatting with Mariah. From the two pink cocktails sitting in front of them and his crossed legs, Denise could tell he was family.

Mariah noticed Denise out of her peripheral. She said something to the gentleman and stood up. Mariah walked over to Denise. A big smile radiated from her face.

Denise noticed Mariah's thick legs.

"Dee, you made it. Great! Come over. There's someone I want you to meet."

They walked over to the gentleman, now sipping his cocktail.

"Marco, this is who I was telling you about," Mariah said, holding on to Denise's arm.

Marco turned and looked Denise up and down. His eyes widened, and his right lip slanted up. "Well, well, well . . . Mariah, you never do me wrong. She's fabulous." Marco put his right hand over his face.

"Hello, I'm Denise." Denise extended her hand.

Marco placed his fingers in her hand. "My pleasure. Please have a seat."

Mariah and Denise sat down at the table.

"So, Denise, tell me, have you done any modeling?"

"Modeling?" Denise said, shocked by the question.

"No, she hasn't," Mariah stepped in. "Which is perfect, 'cause she's your undiscovered superstar."

"I like it. She is stunning. We can try it, test her and see what comes from it. Can you have her at the studio tomorrow morning, by seven?"

"She will be there."

Marco stood up from the table.

Denise felt dumbfounded. She listened as they mapped out details, discussing her as though she wasn't sitting next to them. Mariah and Marco gave each other a Hollywood hug and fake kiss on each cheek.

Marco looked at Denise one more time. "Fabulous. Simply fabulous." He walked away as his cell phone began to ring.

Mariah waited until Marco was out of the front door. She turned around toward Denise and squealed. "This is amazing! I told you I would take care of you!"

"Mariah, what's going on? I'm not a model."

"I know, but you can be. You have the look and you are on your way to landing a serious contract." Mariah grabbed her bag.

Denise was hesitant. "Mariah, I don't know about this. I'm not a model. I can't walk in heels. I don't wear dresses."

"Denise, come with me." Mariah began to walk out of the bar. She turned around and looked at Denise, still confused and still sitting in her chair. "Well, are you coming?"

Denise got up and followed.

Denise and Mariah walked down the busy Times Square. Denise admired the view. It was beautiful, but dirtier than she'd always imagined. Stands filled with I Love NY merchandise, hot dog stands and more lined the streets. Tourists covered in New York paraphernalia took pictures of famous buildings.

Denise noticed the large picture of Diddy. She smiled, thinking about Cooley, who loved anything Diddy.

"Well, we're here." Mariah stood in the middle of the street.

"Where is here exactly?" Denise said, surveying her surroundings.

Mariah threw her hands up. "Here, the heart of the city. Look around, do you see all these billboards. Fashion, music, movies, TV . . . all meet right here." Mariah smiled. "Look over there." Mariah pointed at a long billboard ad for Jocku Couture.

"Yeah. What about it?"

"Denise that could be you in a matter of weeks. I was talking to Marco and he was stressing about his campaign. He wasn't happy with the look and wanted something else. I knew you would be perfect." Mariah squealed.

Denise's eyes widened. She looked at the ad featuring a man and a woman dressed in the Jocku line. "Jocku, that guy was from Jocku?"

Mariah nodded her head. "You just met Marco Jerroud. The owner and designer of the Jocku brand."

"Damn, why didn't you tell me? I would have done—"

"Hold it. That is why I didn't tell you. I wanted you to be relaxed and come as you are. Trust me, I knew he was going to love you. Your face and body, simply stunning."

Denise smiled. "Get the fuck out of here. What's so stunning?"

"Denise, have you never really looked at your face?" Mariah ran her finger across Denise's jaw. "You have high cheekbones, flawless skin complexion, height, you're thin, built right. You are perfect for modeling."

"Mariah, I don't know about this." Denise took a step back. The whole idea was overwhelming her. Mariah grabbed Denise's hands. She looked her in her eyes. "Denise, I told you, that I have faith in you and I am not giving up on you. It might not be basketball, but like I told you it could possibly be so much more. The contract with Marco is worth a whole lot more than your basketball contract. I know you are what they are looking for."

"I don't know the first thing about modeling."

Mariah smiled. Her red hair blew in the wind. "All I want you to do is go in there and be yourself. Let me handle the rest."

Denise opened the door to her room. Things ran through her mind. She pulled her button-down off and threw it on the chair. She sat on the bed. Questions filled her head. Mema entered her head. She could picture her grandmother smiling at her.

"Mema, this is unreal. If I should wake up and go to this shoot tomorrow please give me a sign." Denise closed her eyes and opened them back. Nothing happened. She sighed.

She picked up her remote and turned the wide flat-screen on. Tyra Banks' face appeared. Denise looked around at her room. She watched as Tyra handed model hopefuls their photos from their shoots for that week. Denise couldn't help but laugh. She had her sign.

Cooley sat in Big Ron's personal lobby. She was nervous. She had never been nervous around him before, even as an intern. She knew that was one of the reasons he liked her, she was down-to-earth and about business. Cooley pushed the nerves to the back of her head and realized she had nothing to be nervous about.

A Ronnie Marko video came on. She noticed a familiar body lying in a chair. She smirked as she watched Sahara sitting on the beach with her shades on. She knew she was responsible for Sahara getting into videos. She remembered the first time she saw Sahara's name on MediaTakeOut. The internet blog site gave her a good review, stating that her body was banging harder than the song's video she was featured on.

Sahara had been on her mind since she dropped Cooley at her home. She thought about their original meeting, the threesome that changed Cooley's mind about women. She never felt that way about a woman before then . . . until Misha.

Cooley's mind went back to the last time she saw Sahara. They made an amazing couple. Everyone said so. She gave it up for Misha. She changed so much of herself for Misha. She wondered if it was time to really concentrate on Sahara the way she probably should have.

Cooley decided to try to make a date with her, just to see what would happen.

Cooley's head turned when she heard a familiar beat coming from Big Ron's office. It was the track she had created. Her body tensed up, confusion on her face.

"Cool, he will see you now." Maranda, Big Ron's personal assistant and known mistress, smiled.

"Thank you." Cooley stood up. The nerves she pushed back were trying to gorilla their way back to the front.

Cooley opened the big brown door. Big Ron's office was very impressive. Instead of gold and platinum plaques, his walls were filled with art work and collectible items.

Cooley's eyes focused straight on the large *Scarface* poster. Under it was a glass display box. Inside held one of the original cigars used in the movie. Cooley realized it had to be the female part of her that just didn't allow her to get excited over *Scarface,* like almost every man did. She couldn't count how many houses she'd been to where men created special Scarface rooms or small shrines. Even if they couldn't afford it all, they at least had the *Scarface* poster.

Big Ron looked up at Cooley, his gold grill flashing like a Cheshire Cat. "Aww, lookie here . . . our own Scarface."

"Ahh, man." Cooley smiled as Ron's baritone laughter echoed through the room. Cooley tried to hide her feelings. Her scar was her ultimate soft spot.

"I couldn't believe it when I heard it. Did you get the flowers?"

"Yeah, thank you so much. I was real surprised when I got them." Cooley eased down in the chair across from his desk.

"Well, we are glad you are OK. Stop fuckin' wit' those crazy bitches and get you one good girl. A God-fearing church woman. That's what I did."

Cooley nodded. She wanted to laugh, knowing that his good church woman had no idea he was banging his assistant every day. "So this track . . ."

Ron smiled. "Thought you would remember it." Ron pressed stop on the remote. "It's hot shit, Cool; you did real good with it."

"Thank you, sir."

"Chill with the *sir* shit. I think of you as one of my sons . . . daughters. Hell, as Cool." Ron laughed.

Cooley just shook her head.

"I can say that Sonic did one thing right, and that was bringing you to Jam Zone. I can't wait to see what you do with your first artist."

"I was going to ask about that. I was interested in going to visit my friend in New York and check out some artist while I was up there."

"No need. We got your first artist already."

Cooley's right eyebrow rose like the Rock. "Really?"

Ron smiled. "Yeah, and that is the track for her first single. Want to hear the song?"

"Of course." Cooley sat back in the chair.

Ron pressed play. The track began to play. Cooley noticed it had been slowed down a bit. A beautiful, soulful voice started to sing. Cooley listened to the words of the song.

Your face, your voice, your style so fine
Make me, shake me, take me I'm yours.

The woman's voice reminded Cooley of the Songstress from Floetry but with more mainstream sound. The song was sensual, very erotic. There was a familiarity to the voice that turned her on. She loved it.

"Man, that's hot. I can't believe I made that track. Wow."

Ron nodded along with the beat. "Thought you would like it." Ron pressed the stop button. "She is already blowing the minds of people, and we haven't officially released anything. We got her on a Drake mix tape, and it was on from there. She can sing, dance, and she's sexy. We got the next Beyoncé on our hands, and I know it."

"Wow! I'm excited, Ron, I really am. I can't wait to meet her."

Ron snickered. He pressed the intercom button. "Maranda, send her in."

Cooley looked at Ron then looked at the door. She heard the door knob turning.

"We wanted it to be a surprise. So . . . surprise!"

Cooley's mouth hit the floor. Sahara walked in with a big grin on her face. A tall man walked in after her. Cooley recognized his face.

"Cooley, you know Sahara." Ron responded. "And this is James; he is the head of your department. He will also be overseeing everything, teaching you the ropes."

Cooley bit her lip as she passed Sahara.

Sahara grinned, excited by her surprise.

Cooley walked up to James and extended her hand.

James looked Cooley up and down. His black three-piece suit made him look out of place with the hip-hop crowd that filled the hallways of the building.

He stared Cooley down. A sly smile appeared. "So, the famous Cooley. The intern turned executive. Our very own P. Diddy."

"I wouldn't say all that." Cooley pulled her hand, but James held firm.

"Neither would I, but I guess time will tell."

"James, play nice," Ron interjected. "Cooley is an amazing asset. Put her to good use."

"I'm sure I will." James finally let go of Cooley's hand. "I have to get back to work. I will see you soon. Sahara, Ron."

James' devilish smile appeared again, causing sirens to go off in Cooley's head.

He walked out the door, closing it behind him.

"What's his deal?" Cooley asked.

"Let's just say that he's not your biggest fan. He wanted to develop Sahara, but I knew with your dynamic, you would be the right person for the job. Not to mention, he thinks I'm losing my mind for hiring you in your position straight out of school. Hopefully you won't prove him right." Ron's cheery disposition was back in business mode.

Cooley felt pressure she hadn't felt before.

"Oh, Cooley is gonna be great. I know it." Sahara smiled.

"Well." Ron leaned back in his expensive leather chair. "Go out and make some greatness."

"Thank you, Ron. I won't let you down, I promise."

"Wait a moment, Cooley. Sahara can you excuse us for a moment?" Ron's cheery demeanor seemed to change to a more serious nature.

Sahara, excused herself, throwing Cooley one more smile before closing the door. Cooley suddenly felt nervous again.

"Yes, Sir." Cooley felt like she was standing in front of her father, waiting to be scolded.

"Now, Cool, you know I have a lot of faith in you. But I won't deny that it took me a while to decide to put you on Sahara's project. You know I am aware of you two and the past you shared. I want to make sure you know not to let personal affect your business."

"You don't have anything to worry about. I'm here to work."

"That's what I needed to hear." Ron's smile reappeared. "Now get out of here and go work."

Cooley walked out of the office. She glanced at Sahara, who was deep into a conversation with another artist. Cooley wanted to scream. If anything could make her fail, it was Sahara.

11

Lena stared at the white walls in her room. A cold draft came under her hospital gown, but she didn't move. She couldn't stop staring out the window. The beauty of the bright blue sky and thick clouds didn't matter anymore. All she could see was grey skies.

The nurse walked into the room. Lena didn't budge.

"How are you doing, Mrs. Redding?"

Lena didn't respond.

The nurse sighed as she wrote down Lena's vitals.

Brandon paced the floor outside of Lena's room. Nurses walked by, all concerned about the star athlete. Lena's nurse walked out the room. Brandon paused, his eyes widened, hoping for good news.

"I'm sorry, Mr. Redding. There's not any change as of now."

"But she is . . . physically?"

"Physically, she will be fine. Emotionally, that's another question." The nurse put her hand on Brandon's shoulder. "I know it's hard, but I'm sure she needs you right now."

Brandon's feet felt like they were covered in cement. He stared at the hospital door, afraid to walk in. Guilt filled his heart. He knew he had to face it, but didn't know if he was ready.

Thirty minutes passed before Brandon built up enough nerve to walk into the room. He put his large hand on the silver door knob. Brandon took a deep breath and walked into the room. He looked at Lena's back. She hadn't moved since they allowed her to turn over.

He walked back out of the room and closed the door. Brandon put his fists against the wall and rested his head on them. He fought to gain control. He couldn't let Lena see him cry. He knew he had to be strong for her right now.

Brandon turned around and looked at the hospital door. He couldn't make his feet move. He grabbed his cell phone. There was only one thing he could think to do.

Lena heard a soft knock on the hospital room door. She didn't answer. She just continued to stare out the window. She heard the door open, and faint steps hit the floor.

"Lena." Carmen walked around the bed. She looked at Lena, whose face was sullen. "Lena, baby, I'm here. Brandon called me."

Carmen walked over to the bed. She put her hand on Lena's thigh. Lena's leg felt like an icicle. "Your leg is freezing, honey." Carmen pulled Lena's sheet up over her legs. "I'm just going to cover you up." Carmen pulled a chair close. She put her hand into Lena's. "I don't expect you to say anything. I'm just going to sit here until you want to say something, OK."

Lena's body felt a little warmth take over. She blinked her eyes. They immediately began to swell with tears. "Carmen."

"Yes, hon?"

"My baby is gone."

Lena began to cry. Her silent tears turned to a hysterical cry. She felt as though her world was crashing around her.

Carmen stood up and wrapped her arms around Lena. Lena's tears soaked into her purple shirt. Lena cried and cried. Carmen was silent. She rubbed Lena's hair and occasionally stated, "Let it out."

Brandon stood outside the door, crying along with his wife.

Brandon walked down to the chapel. He entered the small, candle-lit room. Brandon slowly walked to the front. He lit one of the small candles at the front. He knew he wasn't Catholic but was willing to try anything at that point. He placed his hand on the large Bible sitting on the podium. Emotions filled his body. He fell to his knees and sobbed. Nothing mattered anymore. He didn't care about Denise, basketball, his fortune, or anything else. The only thing on his mind was his beautiful wife. He knew it was over. There was no way to repair the damage. His anger and their arguing took away their unborn child.

Carmen and Lena looked at each other. Carmen rubbed the back of Lena's hand. Lena finally stopped sobbing; now they sat in silence.

"Carmen," Lena sighed.

Carmen smiled.

"I'm glad Brandon called you."

"Oh, girl, of course. Don't even think about it."

"I'm just glad it wasn't my mother. She is going to irritate the hell out of me, I know it. I never even told her I was pregnant."

"Really." Carmen blinked. "I guess it's a good thing your parents didn't know."

Lena forced a smile. "I have never felt so empty."

"That's understandable."

"No, C, I feel even worse because my emptiness isn't just because of losing my child, I went to New York."

Carmen's eyes widened, her mouth dropped. "When?"

"Yesterday." A single tear rolled from Lena's face. "I asked Denise to take me."

Carmen covered her mouth. "Oh my God."

"She was drunk, C, really drunk. She yelled, she kicked me out and told me to come back to Brandon. She doesn't love me anymore, Carmen. She doesn't love me, and now I don't have a baby either." The tears began to flow again.

Carmen didn't know if she was more furious or concerned. "Denise was drunk? That's crazy. Girl, I'm sure it's something more. That's not like her at all."

"I saw it in her face. Her eyes were void of emotion. She doesn't love me anymore, I ruined it."

Carmen slightly squeezed Lena's hand. "Lena, baby, right now I want you to take your mind off Dee and even off Brandon. I want you to focus on you and what you need to do for you. All the rest will fall into place, I promise you."

Lena knew Carmen was right. "What's on TV?" Lena pressed the channel buttons attached to her bed. Lena gasped. She stopped on the channel that broadcasted the chapel. She saw Brandon sitting in the pew with his head down in his lap. An older white priest rubbed Brandon's back while chanting what looked to be a prayer. "Brandon."

Carmen felt her heart breaking for Lena and for Brandon. She didn't realize what type of effect losing his child was taking on him.

"Lena, do me a favor, OK."

Lena looked at Carmen.

"I know that you have unresolved issues with Brandon, and with Denise. But please take a minute and put all the past aside and realize that he is going through it too."

"I know, and I will. Carmen, I'm really glad you stayed in Memphis. I don't know what I would do if you and Misha were gone."

Carmen smiled. For the first time she was really happy to still be in Memphis. She realized she did have a purpose after all.

Carmen waited till Lena was asleep before walking out the room. As soon as she made it to the closest waiting room, she pulled her phone out to call Denise. She was livid. She hadn't talked to Denise since she made it to New York, Denise hadn't called or anything. Now to find out she was drinking and being mean just did it for Carmen.

Denise's loud ringer woke her up. The *America's Next Top Model* marathon was now on, the only season she ever watched, featuring Eva Pigford. She knew it was Carmen, from the ringtone.

Denise sat up in the bed and braced herself for a lecture. "Hello."

Carmen paced the floor. "You have a hell of a lot of explaining to do and don't even try to lie to me."

"Hello, Carmen. How are you?"

"No, how the fuck are you? So you drinking now? What in the hell?"

"Carmen, you—"

"And being mean to Lena. Hell, being mean at all. Denise, what is going on?"

"Well, if you shut up long enough I could tell you," Denise snapped. She sighed and ran her hand over the top of her head.

Carmen paused. She'd never heard Denise talk to her like that. "Carmen I lost my contract. I'm not playing ball."

Carmen flopped into the closest chair. "Denise, why didn't you call me and tell me? That explains so much."

"I didn't know what to say. It just happened so fast. I was upset, I got drunk. As far as Lena, I really feel horrible about that. I really do."

"It's OK. I'm sure she will understand. Denise, I really wish you would have called me. I haven't heard from you or Carla. I'm stuck here, and no one is letting me know what's going on."

"I'm sorry." Denise stood up. "How is Lena?"

Carmen paused. "Umm, Denise, are you sitting down?"

Denise froze. "Carmen, what is going on?"

"Lena lost her baby."

Denise's heart dropped. "No! No! Tell me you are playing." Denise fell back down on her bed. "No, I'm coming home."

"Wait, Dee." Carmen looked up. "Don't do that. Please, don't even tell her you know."

"Carmen, I have to apologize. Shit, this is all my fault."

"It's not your fault. Don't blame yourself. But right now Lena needs to take time to find Lena."

Denise knew Carmen was right. "Tell her I am sorry, OK. I really am."

"Denise, what are you going to do?"

"Well, I really don't know yet. But I'll have more info tomorrow. Carmen, I'm really, really sorry about Lena."

"I know you are. But, Denise, I know you are going through a lot, but please remember there are better ways than liquor. You don't fucking drink. I can only imagine how you were."

"Trust me, it won't be happening again. But, C, I gotta get up hella early. I'll call you tomorrow with more news."

"OK, babe." Carmen hung the phone up. She thought about Nic. She had never thought the day would come that she'd be doing better than her friends.

She stood up and headed back to Lena's room. Carmen turned the corner and ran into Brandon.

"Carmen! Is she . . . Lena . . ." Brandon frantically spoke. His eyes were bloodshot.

Carmen wrapped her arms around Brandon. Brandon hugged her back. "Brandon, go in and talk to your wife. All the past bullshit doesn't matter anymore. Focus on you and her. Tell Lena I'll be back to check on her later, OK."

"Thanks, C."

Carmen smiled. It was the first time Brandon had ever called her C. She always felt a little out of place around him, knowing that her bestfriend was in love with his woman. In that moment, they were friends.

12

"Why didn't you tell me?" Cooley stared at Sahara. She didn't know if she was more upset or happy.

Sahara smiled. "I wanted it to be a surprise, and so did Ron. Why do you seem upset?"

Sahara closed Cooley's office door. Cooley fought to remain calm while in the meeting. Ron talked about all the great things they were going to do together. Cooley couldn't focus beyond the surprise. Everything was different now.

"I'm not upset, I just wish I would have known."

Sahara walked closer to Cooley. "Baby, this is amazing. We are going to be working." She put her hands on each side of Cooley's face.

Cooley instantly jerked her face away from Sahara. "Sahara, please."

Sahara pressed her lips together. "Why are you acting like this? We thought you would be happy. Damn, do you hate me that much?"

"Sahara, I don't hate you at all." Cooley sighed. "You just don't understand." Cooley looked at Sahara, whose face was like a hurt child. "Look, I'm real excited to be working with you. But this just puts a damper on some other things."

"Things like what?"

Cooley couldn't believe that two hours earlier she was ready to have a date and consider making Sahara her girlfriend. She knew now that couldn't happen.

Cooley made one promise to herself; she would not date an employee or colleague.

"Man, I don't know why karma is fuckin' wit' me like this, but damn!" Cooley sat down on the edge of the desk.

Sahara walked close. She stood in between Cooley's legs. "Cooley, I can't think of anyone I would want to be in my career and in my life other than you. Don't you see? This is destiny. We keep trying to change what obviously is meant to happen." Sahara pressed her hands against Cooley's face, her palm on Cooley's scar.

Cooley looked at Sahara, who was unaffected by the wound.

"Sahara, I can't mix business and pleasure. I won't. We can't do this."

Sahara took a few steps back. Cooley tried to not focus on the short shorts exposing Sahara's milk chocolate legs.

"So, I'll go and get a new rep. I'm willing to do that if it means a chance for us."

Cooley grabbed Sahara by her wrist. "Don't do that. We can make you a hit, and you know it. Girl, fuck relationships. This is business, and you never let your personal feeling get in the way of business. Now, we gon' make you a star. Besides, I'm not in a position to be looking at any type of relationship. I can't go down that road anytime soon."

Sahara pulled Cooley close. She pressed her lips against Cooley's lips.

Cooley wrapped her right arm around Sahara, pulled her body as close as she could. She parted her lips allowing Sahara's tongue to enter hers.

Cooley ran her fingers through Sahara's thick wavy hair. She wanted to take her on her desk. She thought about it, considering there wasn't anything on it but her nameplate. Cooley felt her nature calling for Sahara's body.

She pulled away. "Girl, please don't make this any harder than it has to be."

Sahara smiled. "I'm not. I just figured I deserved one last kiss. Now, let's get to work." Sahara sat down in the chair and crossed her legs.

Cooley huffed and shook her head. "All right then." She walked around the desk and sat down. "Let's do this."

Brandon and Lena sat in silence. There was so much to say, but neither knew the right way to say it. Lena looked at Brandon's vacant expression. She could tell he was just as numb as she was. It had been a while since she realized how beautiful a man he was. He did love her and she knew it. She knew she loved him too, just didn't know if she was in love with him anymore, or ever.

Lena thought about their relationship. She always knew Brandon was sleeping with other women. She wondered why she was so adept to turning a blind eye to his indiscretions. Maybe it was because she knew deep down, that she was the one he truly loved. She was the one he married.

"Brandon."

Brandon's face lit up as he looked at his beautiful wife. "Yes, baby."

"I wanna go home."

Brandon stood up. "I'll go and check on that right away." Brandon walked out of the room without hesitation. There were no questions. He just wanted to do whatever she wanted.

Lena's mind drifted back to Denise. She thought about the things Denise said to her. She knew Denise was right. She had been very selfish. She played on Denise's emotions without really thinking about how her actions could be affecting Denise. She was no longer upset by Denise. She realized that on some level she deserved exactly what Denise did.

"OK, they said they were actually preparing to release you now. I tried to bribe them into speeding it up, but they weren't going." Brandon attempted to crack a smile.

Lena knew he was trying. "Thank you." Lena watched as Brandon made sure nothing was left behind. She studied his broad muscular shoulders. She overheard a few nurses gabbing about how sexy he was. She was married to one of the hottest basketball players in the nation, yet she couldn't stop thinking about another woman. They had years invested, and she didn't know if she wanted to throw all of it away.

The hot Memphis weather was uncomfortable as soon as they hit it. Lena sat in the wheelchair while waiting on Brandon to get the car. She watched as Brandon attempted to keep a smile on for a group of men who were excited to see one of their favorite Memphis Grizzlies up close and personal. Brandon politely told them he couldn't stop. They looked over to see Lena and quickly let him continue.

They drove in silence, both unsure of the right words to say to the other. Lena stared out the tinted windows on Brandon's Escalade truck. The *Jamie Fox Show* played from the XM radio. Even his funny anecdotes couldn't make the couple laugh.

"I'm going to pull in here and get your prescription filled real quick if that's OK." Brandon pulled into the local Walgreens. Lena forced a tight-lipped smile.

"Do you need anything else?"

"No, I'm fine." Lena continued to stare out the window.

Brandon lingered for a moment before hopping out of the truck.

Brandon walked into the store. Normally he would notice the looks people gave him as he passed by, but today he was completely oblivious to the cashiers' and customers' whispers. He walked down the card isle, glancing at the "I'm Sorry" section. None of them said what he wanted to say. He knew there wasn't a card to say, "I'm sorry I made you lose our baby."

Brandon picked up a small teddy bear. He wondered if it would cheer Lena up or if the sight of a teddy bear would just bring more painful memories.

The thought of their baby came back into his mind. He always wanted a baby by Lena. A tear fell from his eye while standing on the isle. He held up a card and acted like he was reading it in hopes of gaining his composure before someone saw him.

Once he was ready, he placed the card back down and headed to the snack isle. Brandon picked up all of Lena's favorites. He filled the hand basket with mint Milano cookies, Cool Ranch Doritos, Sweet Tarts and other junk food. Brandon knew he would buy the whole store if it would make Lena smile.

Brandon found himself putting on a happy face again at the pharmacy desk. The pharmacist filled his prescription immediately just because of who he was. He signed autographs for the workers and took a picture with the staff. The last thing he wanted to do was smile, but he knew the public didn't want to think of him having any issues of his own, and if it meant getting the prescription quicker, he was willing to do it.

Lena watched as Brandon signed autographs for a group of young boys as he walked out of the store. She could see the pain in his eyes while he attempted to put on a happy face for the youth. She knew Brandon was a good man, and that he loved her. But she didn't know if their love was strong enough to make it through all the things they had been through in such a short period of time.

"Sorry it took so long, but the pharmacist filled it right away. And I got you some snacks and stuff."

Lena looked at her husband as he rambled on about the things he had gotten for her. She could tell he was trying hard to make her feel better. He was completely selfless, only concentrating on her. She knew he was being strong for her. She loved him for that.

"Brandon, we need to talk."

Brandon's face filled with fear. "I know."

"Brandon, I'm so sorry about everything."

Brandon held her hand. "Don't. You don't have to apologize. If I was being the man I should have been, you never would have gone."

"I wasn't doing too good of a job either."

"You were amazing."

"No, we both screwed this up. I just want to find a way to correct things. Brandon, I know I love you, and because of that I think we need to separate for a while."

The words sliced through Brandon's heart. He took a deep breath. "You are probably right."

"I don't want a divorce. I just . . . I just think that I've been my mother and father's daughter. I've been your girlfriend and wife. I've never just been Lena."

Brandon's lips quivered as his lips slanted upward. "I understand, Lena. Maybe a little time apart is what we need to bring us back together."

"Exactly. I can move back on campus."

"No, you keep the loft. I always wanted to purchase a real house anyway. I'll look into that as soon as we get home." Brandon kissed Lena on her forehead. "I love you and I only want to do whatever you want me to do."

"I love you too."

13

Denise couldn't get Lena off her mind. She sat out on the balcony of her hotel room. The amazing view of skyscrapers was breathtaking; she wished Lena was there to share it with her. Denise wanted to call her. She wanted to jump on a plane, grab Lena and hold on and never let go, but something was still holding her back.

Denise couldn't make sense of her feelings. She was about to embark on a new experience. The test shoot went well, and now her real photo shoot was coming up, yet nerves hadn't set in. All she could think about was Lena.

She longed for the simple days. The days before they shared their first kiss. Denise thought about all the things she would change. She would have never flirted with Lena. She would have fought back her feelings for Lena with all her might, never giving into temptation. Denise sighed. She didn't know if that was the truth or not.

Another part of her wanted to take everything back. She wanted to go back to the first day they met. She wanted to do it Cooley style, and sweep Lena off her feet. She wanted to go back to the night before Lena's wedding. She wanted to really put it on her, sex her so well, she would have never gone through with the wedding in the first place.

Denise thought about Lena's situation. She lost her baby. Denise's body filled with fear. What if she was the cause of the miscarriage? What if Lena was so upset over the way she treated her that she lost her baby? Denise's body was filled with remorse. She wished she had another bottle of Blue Top to numb her feelings again.

"Stop it, Neecie. You know better." Denise jumped. Mema's voice filled her head so vividly; it was like she was in the room.

"Why aren't you here? I need you and you are gone." Denise cried out loud. She was alone in a big city. She had no one, no grandmother, no friends, no Lena. Denise felt empty. Void of all love she used to have. She had never longed for Memphis before in her life.

"Stop it, Neecie. You're stronger than that." Mema's voice echoed.

Am I? Denise thought to herself. She had been strong her whole life, and now she was tired. She didn't want to be strong anymore. She wanted to crawl up and be weak. Let someone else be the rock, for a change.

Denise thought she heard a knock at her door. She looked inside at the large hotel door, but all she heard was silence. The knock came again, louder than before. Denise headed inside. She looked through the peep hole to see a red bush of curly hair.

"I have been calling you like crazy, woman." Mariah walked into the room without looking up from her BlackBerry. "Why aren't you answering the phone?"

"I guess it was on silent. I didn't hear it." Denise walked into the bathroom to check her face. The whites of her eyes were slightly pinkish. She dabbed cold water on her face and walked back into her room.

Mariah had made herself comfortable, sitting at the desk in the corner.

"I was trying to check on you. See if you are ready for tomorrow."

"I guess so." Denise sat on the edge of her bed.

Mariah's skin looked extra white under the florescent lights in the room. She crossed her long legs. "Well, I just wanted to wish you luck. This could be big for you Denise. It could open a whole lot of doors." Mariah noticed Denise's gloomy expression. "What is wrong honey?"

"Just a little homesick." Denise forced a smile.

"Well, that's understandable." Mariah stood up. "No, actually it's not. Denise, you are in New York, about to shoot for a hot clothing line. How can you be homesick?"

"I just miss a few people, that's all. I'll be OK."

"I hope you will. Because the last thing you want to do is mess this up. Opportunities like this don't come around too often. Grab on and make the best of it." Mariah's lips curved upward, bringing a tight-lipped smile on her face.

"Mariah, have you ever been in love?"

Mariah paused. She sat back down in the chair. "Once, yes."

"Mind telling me what happened"

Mariah's face grew pale. "Well, I come from a very wealthy family where women are supposed to have children, join social groups and committees, not be aggressive sports agents."

"So he wanted you to be a housewife?"

"He wanted me to fall in line with all the other people from our expensive boarding school. That just wasn't me."

"Do you regret leaving him?"

"Sometimes." Mariah's smile was gone. "But I needed to do what was best for Mariah, not what my family or he wanted." Mariah stood up. She walked over and sat next to Denise. "Who is she?"

"She is . . . no one."

"You sure about that?"

"No, but I will be soon."

"I understand." Mariah turned her body toward Denise. She saw the pain in Denise's eyes. "Denise, you have been so worried about others for so long that I think it's time for you to do what is best for you right now. It's your moment. Don't let it pass by. Enjoy it. You deserve to." Mariah stood back up.

Denise nodded her head. she knew Mariah was right.

"I hate to run, but I have a business dinner. Call me if you need anything."

"I will."

Denise walked Mariah to the door. She closed it, still thinking about WHAT Mariah said. Mariah had only said the same thing Carmen and Cooley had preached over and over. Maybe it was time for her to focus on herself.

Denise slumped down on her bed. She looked out at the blue sky. She loved Lena, but she knew it was time to focus on Denise.

"This time, Denise, you will stick to the plan. No time for love until after I succeed in what I want. Whatever that might be."

Denise closed her eyes while her heart began to rebuild the wall Lena had broken. This time she welded it shut.

14

Lena slowly walked into her beautiful home. Brandon had instructed the staff on what they needed to do. Everything looked so normal, the mess she walked into earlier was gone. The maid had the house looking as perfect as it usually did. Things seemed back to normal, but Lena knew things would never be back to normal again.

Lena walked past Brandon, the chef and the maid. They all watched her as she curled up with one of the plush pillows on the large leather sofa. The coldness of the leather cooled her down.

Lena closed her eyes. She could hear the faint chatter of Brandon talking, but could no longer make out what he was saying. The maid, Melinda, covered her with a throw. Lena quickly drifted off into a deep sleep.

Lena heard someone calling her name. She thought she was dreaming. The voice grew louder. She felt pressure on her leg. Lena opened her eyes. Brandon's face came into focus. He was standing right in front of her.

"What time is it?" She rubbed her eyes and began to sit up.

"It's seven in the morning. You slept the whole night." Brandon put his hand on her shoulder. "No, you don't have to sit up. I just—"

Lena noticed a large duffle bag on his arm. "You're leaving?"

Brandon lowered his head. "I have some promotional engagements and a charity basketball game in Cali this weekend." Brandon sat on the edge of the coffee table. "And I talked to Torrence; she's working on the house hunt now. Hopefully by the time I get back I'll have us a new house that I can stay in while we do . . . you know . . ."

Lena sat up on the couch. Something in her wanted to tell him to say, but a bigger part of her wanted him to walk out the door, at least for a little while. "OK." She gazed at Brandon.

"The maid and chef are on call. They will be here whenever you need them. Call me if you need me, OK?" Brandon planted a sweet kiss on Lena's lips. "Are you sure you want me to go?"

"Brandon, I'm OK. Just go do your job."

Brandon forced a small smile. He walked to the front door.

Lena watched as her husband walked out the door. "Brandon!"

Brandon turned around, and their eyes fixated on each other.

"We will be OK in the end."

Brandon smiled. "I know." He walked out, closing the large iron door behind him.

The loft never seemed so empty.

Lena stood up. The cold hardwood floor sent chills through her body. She walked over to her state-of-the-art stereo system. She placed her red classic iPod on the docking system and pressed play. Jazmine Sullivan's hit "Lions, Tigers and Bears" instantly began to echo through the speakers through the house.

Lena sighed, the lyrics to the song resonating in her soul. She knew the reason that she lost Denise was because of fear. She feared loving a woman. She feared giving up everything she had grown accustomed to.

Lena walked into her kitchen. She opened the French doors on the large expensive refrigerator. The cold air added to her cold feet. She reached for the milk and paused. Lena shook her head; she didn't have to watch what she drank anymore. She pulled out her chilled bottle of Ciroc and the Tropicana orange juice. Lena mixed a quick cocktail. She let the elixir trickle down her throat. She could feel it hit her empty stomach.

Her fingertips glided across the smooth wall as she sauntered down the hallway toward her room. Everything was in the right place, everything just as she left it, but nothing seemed to be right. The tracks changed on her iPod, and Stevie Wonder began to belt out "I'd Never Dreamed You Leave in Summer." The words spoke to Lena. Everything she knew had disappeared within the course of a week. It was only her.

Reality hit and Lena couldn't move. Her hand trembled, and the cocktail fell, breaking the glass and spilling all over her polished floors.

But Lena didn't feel anything. She stared into the pitch-black abyss of the nursery.

She crept into the room and turned on the night light. The glow of the small light illuminated the beautiful Tiffany blue walls with white trim, two cribs: one for Brandon Jr. and one for the baby that would never get a chance to sleep in it.

Lena sat in the rocking chair she had purchased to nurse her baby. She slowly rocked back and forth as Stevie sang and played the piano. The numbness was coming back, starting at her toes, tingling up her body until making it to her eye ducts.

Lena couldn't take it anymore. She ran out of the room. She ignored the liquid and small pieces of glass entering her feet as she ran through the hallway. She ran into her room and shut the door.

Lena fell to the cold hardwood floor as she cried a river of tears. She put her hands on the floor. Lena curled her body into a tight ball. She rocked herself back and forth as she screamed; she wailed as Stevie wailed. The question entered her mind as he asked it. Why didn't Denise stay? Why didn't her unborn baby stay? Why did Brandon leave her in this state?

Lena cried until her eyes couldn't produce enough tears to flow. She cried as her tears dried up and her eye lids grew heavy. She slowly closed her eyes, falling into a deep slumber, knowing she would probably be crying in her dreams.

15

Denise pulled up in front of a big warehouse. She looked at the address to make sure it was right. She was relieved when she noticed a small Marco Jerroud Designs nameplate on the door. Denise stepped out of the car and paid the cab driver. She put her messenger bag over her shoulder and headed into the building.

Denise was amazed at the interior of the building. She couldn't believe it was the same place that looked like an abandoned warehouse from the outside. At 6:45 in the morning the office was buzzing. Men and women hurried around with stacks of drawings, racks of clothes and more.

"Can I help you?" the receptionist sitting at the small desk in the front asked.

Denise walked up to the glass desk. The receptionist looked like she belonged on a magazine cover and not sitting behind a desk answering phones. Her thin body made Denise look fat. Her blond hair was pulled up in an up-do.

"Yes, my name is Denise—"

"Chambers. They are expecting you." She pressed buttons on the phone. "Denise Chambers is here."

Denise looked around at the various high-fashion photos on the walls. Everyone wore the clothes. She couldn't believe she had the opportunity to do what Beyonce, Brittany Spears, Tyson Beckford and so many before her had done.

"Denise!" Mariah said as she came from the back. Her pantsuit screamed expensive to Denise. Mariah wore it well. Her black shoes added height to her curvy frame. She was thin, but not model-thin like the woman behind the desk. "Come on, they are ready for you."

"I'm nervous as hell, Mariah," Denise said as they walked swiftly.

"Don't be, you will be fine."

They walked into a bright white room. The natural light from the windows illuminated the room, making it seem lighter than normal. There were three makeup stations set up on one side, two models sitting down while teams of people primped them.

Denise noticed the photography area. It was a simple white area surrounded with lighting umbrellas. Mariah motioned for Denise to take a seat in the empty makeup chair.

As soon as she sat down a tall, skinny black man wearing white skinny jeans and a white button-down shirt with the middle button buttoned only walked up. He pulled her ponytail holder off and started rustling his hands through her hair without saying anything to her.

Denise looked at Mariah with a horrified expression. Mariah smiled and shook her head.

An hour later the chair turned around. Denise gasped; she didn't recognize herself. Her hair was in a million wild curls. Dark eyeliner covered her smoky eyes.

Mariah walked up to her. "Well, damn." Mariah giggled.

"I don't know if I am mortified or intrigued," Denise said, staring at her glam look. She picked her phone up and snapped a picture. She sent it to Carmen and Cooley.

"Come on, time for wardrobe."

Cooley sat at the end of a long rectangle table. The team assigned to Sahara's image went over tons and tons of pictures with Cooley. Cooley heard her phone go off. She picked it up while taking a swig from her water bottle. Denise's new image appeared. Cooley spewed her water all over the table. "Damn, I'm sorry. Umm . . ."

Before she could finish, Tee was cleaning up her mess. She nodded her head. She loved the assistant. "Excuse me for a moment." Cooley hurried out of the office. She pressed send on her phone.

"Yeah," Denise said as two women put various clothing items up to her body.

"What the fuck! Don't do that shit to me no more. I was in a meeting and almost choked to death. What the hell are you up to?"

"I really don't know yet. I'll have to tell you later. I gotta go. About to put some boots on."

"What!" Cooley yelled.

Denise hung up and laughed. She knew her friend was a second away from a heart attack. Her phone instantly began to ring. It was Carmen. She sent it to voice mail and opted to send her a text message.

Can't talk. Modeling. Call you later.

"OK, OK, let's do this!" Marco said as he walked into the room with his team behind him.

The wardrobe women helped Denise into a pair of tight-fitting jeans and a fitted shirt that had the look of a basketball jersey. She struggled to walk in the tall shoes they handed her.

Mariah noticed her and ran over to hold her hand.

Denise stood in front of the white wall.

A scruffy-looking man walked up. He snapped his finger, and an assistant handed him a camera. "And let's go!"

Denise was confused. She stood there as the photographer snapped picture after picture. "What am I supposed to be doing?"

"Model!" the photographer said.

"What the hell does that mean?" Denise questioned, completely out of her element.

"Hold it!" Marco said. He walked up to Denise and looked her in her eyes. "This isn't working." Marco turned around. "This isn't working! This is not the look she should have at all."

Marco walked over to the rack of male clothing. He pulled a pair of black jeans from the rack. "Put these on. And take those shoes off."

Mariah handed her the jeans. Denise looked confused. Mariah's eyes looked down. Denise looked around. Everyone was wondering why she wasn't' changing. Denise unbuttoned her jeans, embarrassed to be changing in front of a room of people. She put the loose-fitting jeans on, instantly feeling more comfortable.

"And these." Marco handed her a pair of male boots.

Denise was really relieved. She sat down as a helper pulled her shoes off and put the boots on.

Marco gave a slight smile. "Now, Denise, I want you to give me Denise. Take pictures like you would if you were at home."

"Yes, Sir."

Denise stood back up in front of the camera. The photographer began to snap pictures. She looked into the camera, intensity in her eyes. Marco and Mariah watched a computer off to the side, occasionally nodding and talking to the other associates. Denise let go of all her thoughts. She didn't realize just how comfortable she felt in front of the camera.

Five hours later Denise felt like she had done three days of work. Her looks changed. They mixed male and female clothes together to create Denise's style. She even took some pictures in boxers and a lace push-up bra.

The makeup remover felt good against her skin. She felt the removal of layers of foundations, making her face feel light again.

She looked down at her phone. There were twelve missed calls from Cooley and Carmen.

"Denise, come here," Mariah called over to her.

Denise walked over to the computer.

"We just wanted to show you a few of your shots," one of the associates said as she pressed the mouse.

Marco and Mariah watched Denise's facial expression as images of her flashed on the screen.

"Damn, are you serious? That is really me." Denise felt an overwhelming sense of pride taking over her body. "Wow!"

"Didn't know you could look like that, did you?" Mariah said as the images flashed of Denise in a short skirt with no shirt on, holding her chest.

"Man, my friends are gonna trip. This whole thing is a trip."

"Well, do you want to *trip* more often?" Marco looked at Denise with a stern face. "Because we would like you to become the new face of Jocku."

"Are you serious?" Denise put her fist up to her mouth.

"Very much so. My original look for this season wasn't sitting right with me. I needed something new, and you are it. It's fabulous. I'm rushing these images and replacing the original campaign, that is if you accept the job. So is that a yes?" Marco responded, trying to keep his stern expression.

Denise was speechless; it all seemed surreal. Marco noticed her expression. "Maybe this will make you say yes quicker."

Marco scribbled on a piece of paper and handed it to Denise.

Denise turned the piece of paper over to see more zeros than she had ever seen before.

Denise's body froze. Her eyes bucked, and her mouth dropped.

Mariah hugged Denise. "I told you things were going to work out. Say yes, woman."

"Uhhh, yeah," Denise said, trying to figure out if she was dreaming or not.

"Great. Welcome aboard." Marco stood up and shook Denise's hand. He walked away with his group following him.

Denise looked at Mariah. "Is this for real?"

"It is. Are you ready to be a model?"

"I guess so."

"So, big model, what do you want to do first?" Mariah asked as they walked out of the warehouse. She pressed the button on her BMW.

Denise hesitated. It was identical to Lena's car. She quickly shook it off and got in the car.

"We have to celebrate."

"I don't know. There's so much I need to do. I gotta find a place to stay. When do I sign the actual contract?"

"The contract signing is tomorrow morning. I have to say, this is exciting. This is big for both of us. Now I have a model to add to my portfolio, not to mention a nice commission for myself. Now we have to get you a place to stay. I'm sure Marco will let you stay in one of his places until you get on your feet," Mariah rambled.

"Man, this is unreal. I can't believe this."

"Denise, take a deep breath. You can relax right now. Like I said, what do you want to do to celebrate?"

"I really would like to just go to sleep." Denise put her head back on the head rest.

"Go to sleep? You are seriously no fun. How about a club or something?"

"Nah, I'm not really a club person."

Mariah looked at Denise. "You are really one of a kind, Denise Chambers."

Denise looked at Mariah and smiled. She noticed a billboard. "Well, there is one thing I would like to do." She pointed at the billboard for the Broadway play *Wicked*.

"You want to go to a musical?" Mariah frowned.

"Yeah, I've always wanted to go to one. I mean, I used to go to the shows when they would come to town but never actually on Broadway. Why are you frowning?"

"I just never expected you to be into that type of stuff."

Denise laughed. "Well, my grandma was real big on old movies and musicals. I was watching them before anything else. I fell in love with classic movies. I love them. Call it my guilty pleasure. She also used to take me to plays. She always talked about coming to New York to see a musical like *Cats*. Man, she was elated when she heard *The Color Purple* was a musical. But she died before—"

Mariah put her hand on Denise's thigh. "In that case let's do it up. Tomorrow night. I'll make all the plans. After you sign the contract, we will have a night out on Broadway."

Denise smiled. "Mariah, thank you so much, for everything. I didn't know what I was gonna do. I didn't know I could do anything besides basketball. Thanks for helping me when you didn't have to."

"It's no problem. Besides, after tomorrow you won't be my client anymore."

Denise's head whipped back around. "What do you mean?"

"I mean that believe it or not, I'm a sports agent. You have to sign with a modeling agency that can take care of you and get you where you really need to be. That's not me."

"Damn, that sucks." Denise looked at Mariah. "Are you sure there's nothing that can be done?"

"I'm afraid not, but it's all good. I did what I set out to do. Now we can focus on a friendship instead of a working relationship."

"Of course." Denise looked out the window. Things were finally looking back up for her.

16

Cooley sat at the end of the long conference table. Her week wasn't as exciting as she expected. Instead it was an endless circle of meetings. So much was already in place before she got there. Sahara was becoming a bona fide star on the mix tape scene. Her collaborations with major artists were all over the airwaves. They had taken the same approach as Drake and Nicki Minaj, Sahara was big, and her album wasn't dropping anytime soon.

This meeting was different from the others. She felt Sahara's eyes on her. Sahara wasn't present for the other meetings, due to various engagements at nightclubs that had her out of town a lot. Cooley scribbled on a notepad with her pen, trying not to look down the table. She wasn't quite sure how she was able to not stare when Sahara walked in, let alone not sneak in any peeks during the long, boring planning meeting.

Sahara couldn't take her eyes off Cooley. She tilted her head, slanting her oval eyes. She just didn't get it. Sahara couldn't tell if Cooley was trying to act uninterested, or if she really was. Sahara was determined to win the ultimate prize, Cooley's heart. She planned her outfit to the tee, hoping to accentuate her finest assets, which included her round apple bottom, thick thighs, and perky breasts.

Today she took a page out of Alicia Key's handbook. She picked a pair of grey pants that fit her so right, they could have been painted on. She added a pink and grey halter shirt that not only made her breasts look like juicy ripe grapefruits ready to be picked right off the tree, but showed off her flat stomach that hours in the gym with her trainer afforded her. She knew what was on the mind of every man in the conference room. They all wanted to undress her right there, but with Cooley, she wasn't sure. The one person she wanted to take her body on a midnight ride wasn't showing the interest she wanted.

"So let's discuss video. The good thing is that the two songs out now are both blazing. We just need to pick which we are going to use as the front-runner." Marco stood up. The dark Italian man strutted to the stereo system.

Cooley wanted to laugh. The men on the team were very envious of her. No one could understand why Big Ron put so much faith in a gay-ass girl fresh out of college.

"At first I thought we should come out with a bang, make the people dance. But we all saw what she could do in the collabo with The Dream. So I think the front runner should be 'One Night.'"

Marco pressed play on the stereo. A hot bass line echoed through the room, causing everyone to start nodding their heads to the beat. Cooley wanted to run out the room. The words of the song made her want to laugh and yell at the same time.

So Cool, but so hot, you make me feel right
You're the champ no need for a fight
He was no more the moment you entered my sight
My destiny fulfilled, all in one night.

Cooley's lips pressed hard against each other. She lowered her head, trying not to laugh. She could feel Sahara's eyes burning a hole in the side of her head. She couldn't resist.

Cooley turned her head and looked directly at Sahara. Sahara nodded while she grinned. No words exchanged, but so much was said. Cooley knew the song was about her.

James noticed the exchange between the two. Suddenly everything was making sense to him. He had been trying to get Sahara for months but with no luck.

The words of the chorus played again. His mouth dropped as everything became completely clear. The rumors about Sahara and Cooley were true. She was gay and Cooley had her. James' piercing eyes shot back at Sahara, who was completely oblivious to his glare. That let him know Cooley still had her.

"So let's hear ideas." Marco stopped the song. "I was thinking that, since she's talking about leaving her man to be with this other dude, I think that we should do a hot video playing off of the actual words of the song."

"Umm, can I say something?" Sahara raised her hand.

Everyone nodded.

She stood up. "I agree with Marco. I was a big fan of the old Dru Hill videos; you know, the 'Sleeping in My Bed, Never Make a Promise' and '5 Steps.' Those videos told such great stories. I want my video to do the same, in the 'Sleeping in My Bed' feel."

"OK." Marco looked at Sahara. "In what ways?"

Sahara smiled as she began to walk toward the end of the table. "I was thinking we could show a woman whose man isn't paying her the right attention, like she's sitting up bored while he focuses on video games and his friends. They go to a club and she runs into this other person. That's when she no longer seems interested in him. Instead of watching him play games, we see her off in a corner texting and smiling. So in the end he walks in on her with someone else in the bed."

Everyone was hanging on to her every word.

"But to add a twist, we see her in bed with a woman."

Cooley's head jerked up. The men were silent, but their looks screamed NO.

Sahara stood in her place, irritated.

Marco stood up. "Sahara, sweetie, that will never work. We are not putting you out like that."

"Why not? I'm a lesbian. My songs are about my experiences with women. Why can't I be real?"

Sahara's words angered James to his core. "Because we want to sell records." James snapped.

Cooley couldn't take her eyes off of Sahara.

"Why the hell can't I sell records if I am gay? Katy Perry hit it big singing about kissing a girl."

"That's a white pop singer," Marco added. "Not a black soul artist."

"OK, so what about Wanda Sparks? Since she came out, she's bigger than ever."

"Again, a completely different genre altogether; it's not gonna happen."

"Well, explain Nicki. She's the hottest female rapper in the game. Hell, did you even listen to her verse on Usher's 'Little Freak'?" Sahara waited on a response. She made sure she was prepared before she came into the room.

"Nicki Minaj is also different. You aren't a rapper, you are a R&B diva in the making we are going to bring out as super mainstream," Marco added.

"This is some bullshit." Sahara folded her arms.

"You can think what you want, but it's not happening." James' deep voice rumbled. "You might as well give up the gay shit 'cause nothing about your image is going to say gay. Not your videos or anything else."

"Cooley!" Sahara looked at Cooley, her eyes filled with despair.

Everyone turned their attentions to Cooley.

Cooley looked up, all eyes on her. "Well, I think that being out right now is not the best idea."

"Cool!" Sahara stomped her foot against the ground.

"Chill out." Cooley looked at Sahara, and she immediately followed instructions, sitting down in her chair and rolling her eyes.

The idea that when he talked she argued, but when some gay bitch said stop, she shut up infuriated James even more.

"Can you be out? No. Our focus is on making these people fall in love with you. We are going to make Sahara a house hold name. As far as the video, I think the idea isn't bad, but it needs some tweaking."

Cooley stood up. She could see Marco's and James' dislike for her written all in their expressions.

"I think that instead of you being the woman in question that it should be someone else. I think you and your song should come in as the soundtrack. Maybe having your song playing on a radio in the house, or when they are at the club, you are on stage singing."

The other associates looked at each other; the idea was growing on them, including Marco.

James sat with his same straight face.

"I think we should get a great director and let them work out the details then meet again so we can go over it. Oh, but 'One Night' is for sure gonna be the single." Cooley picked up her phone and organizer. "Now I think we have discussed everything we need for today. Let's do this again tomorrow same time, have some dates mapped out for everything. Have a good day, fellas."

The meeting room quickly cleared. Sahara grabbed Cooley's arm before she could make it into the hallway. "Close the door."

Cooley looked at Sahara. She knew she meant business. Cooley closed the door.

"What's up?"

Sahara sat on the edge of the desk. "So is this how it's gonna be. You don't answer my phone calls. When we are in meetings you won't look at me."

"Sahara."

"Fuck that, Cooley. No matter what, we have always kept it real, and right now you being phony as hell."

Sahara's attitude intrigued Cooley. She felt turned on by her aggression. "Damn, girl you got a little too much bass in your voice right now." Cooley laughed as Sahara rolled her eyes. "Chill out, I'm just trying to do my job."

"Well, you aren't doing a good job of it." Sahara stood up.

"What the fuck?"

"Please, Cooley, look at today. You were like a fucking mute in that meeting. I'm supposed to be your artist. Why are these other men trying to run shit?" Sahara paused.

Cooley lowered her head. She knew Sahara was right. Sahara noticed the look in Cooley's eyes. She smiled. "Oh, I see. You try so hard to ignore your feelings so that you aren't letting it show in your work."

Cooley shook her head in defeat. "Damn, I'm trippin'. Well, it's your fault!"

Sahara's eyes bucked. "What the hell? How is it my fault?"

"You walk in here wearing that shit. Trying to fuck wit' me. You trying to throw me off my game."

Sahara grinned. "Oh, but you supposed to be the champ, remember. I shouldn't be able to throw you off anything." She walked closer to Cooley.

"Yeah, well, I was the champ. I've been retired for a minute. I'm a little rusty." Cooley's eyes locked on Sahara's.

"I don't believe that. I just think you're a little down right now. I know you have been through a lot, Cooley. I can see it in your eyes. That passion, that fire that made me fall for you to begin with is dying out. But I can see there's a dim light still flickering. Let go, Cooley. Bring that fire back. That's what I fell for, and that's what Ron saw in you."

"And I suppose getting with you is supposed to bring it back?" Cooley moved away from Sahara. "Nah, shawty, it's more than that. I think that psycho bitch fucked up my mojo when she fucked up my face." Cooley turned away from Sahara. Sahara walked up behind Cooley. She put her hands on Cooley's broad shoulders. Sahara began to massage Cooley's shoulders.

"I know the scar is an issue for you. But, baby, I didn't fall for your face. I fell for your personality. I fell for that confidence, that attitude that you had. When I see you, I don't see that scar, I just see Cooley. You need to stop seeing the scar and remember who the fuck you are."

Cooley turned around to Sahara. A warmth came over her body. Sahara wasn't sexy in that moment, she was beautiful. Cooley wrapped her arm around Sahara. She put her right palm on the back of Sahara's head, pulling it to hers.

Sahara wrapped her arms around Cooley's neck. They kissed.

Cooley didn't want to let go. She felt the fire growing. Their tongues danced the familiar dance of love.

Cooley pulled away. "I want to do this. Don't think that I don't. But I just—"

Sahara put her index finger on Cooley's lips. "Shhh. I'm not trying to put pressure on you, Cooley. I'm just trying to make what should have happened a long time ago happen. Cooley, there's a reason we keep ending up together. We are connected, and you know it. We can't keep fighting fate."

Cooley smiled. She opened her lips, allowing her tongue to lick Sahara's finger. "Sahara, I don't want you to think I'm not interested, 'cause that's not it. But, baby girl, I'm in a different place right now. You see how this shit is already affecting my work. I gotta be focused, and too many times in the past I let women fuck that up."

Sahara frowned. "I'm not trying to mess anything up, Cooley, I'm trying to enhance."

"Well, right now the best way you can enhance is to just give me the time I need to figure my shit out. If it's meant to be, it will be." Cooley held Sahara's face. Sahara nodded her head like an innocent little girl. Cooley kissed her forehead.

Sahara slowly pulled herself away from Cooley and turned to walk away.

Cooley shook her head as Sahara's ass bounced. "Ummm-mmmmm."

Sahara laughed. "You so silly. It's yours. You just have to claim it." She winked and walked out the door.

Cooley looked up at the ceiling. *Damn, that girl gon' make me wife her.*

17

"Sooooo, what did you think?"

Mariah and Denise walked out of the crowded theatre.

Denise's face lit up. She turned around and looked up at the Marquee lit up with lights.

"Man, I have an all new respect for my hometown. I never in a million years thought a musical would be named after Memphis."

Mariah's red hair glowed under the bright lights. She held on to Denise's arm. "I don't know why you come down so hard on Memphis anyway. I loved visiting there. I can't wait to go back so I can go to Graceland."

Denise's mouth curled. "I guess."

"What? Tell me about it. How is the house inside? I bet it's magical."

"I wouldn't know. I've never been." Denise smiled as they walked down the street.

"Are you kidding me?" Mariah's hazel eyes lit up. "How could you grow up in Memphis and never visit the home of Elvis. He's the king!"

Denise frowned. "No, he's y'all's king. Now let's talk about going to the Neverland Ranch and then we are in business."

They both laughed.

Denise and Mariah continued to walk. Denise noticed all the marquees. "Man, this is amazing. I don't see how you live in New York and you haven't seen every play on this strip."

"I've seen most of them actually." Mariah smiled "I love *Wicked, The Lion King* and *The Color Purple.*"

"Man, I'm so mad *The Color Purple* isn't playing anymore. I really wanted to see that."

"I'm just waiting on them to bring back *Dreamgirls.*" Mariah smiled.

Denise found herself staring at Mariah. "M, you have a really amazing smile," Denise said as they walked into her hotel lobby.

Mariah blushed. "Why, thank you. How about we get a drink at the bar?"

"Sounds good."

The two sat down at a small round table in the bar.

The bartender walked over to them. She looked at Denise then looked at Mariah. The older black woman looked confused by Denise's appearance. "What can I get for you two?"

"I'll take a Manhattan. Denise?" Mariah looked at Denise.

"Umm, a Coke please."

Mariah started to laugh. "On this big day you're only gonna have a Coke?"

Denise shook her head. "I've had my share of drinking this week. I don't drink."

"Well, drinking cheap vodka is always a bad idea. You know what"—Mariah opened her purse—"cancel my drink order and can we have a bottle of Dom?"

The waitress nodded and smiled as she took Mariah's card and walked away.

"You are having a drink with me, and something good." Denise couldn't help but smile at Mariah's excited face.

Mariah noticed Denise's look. "What's wrong?"

"Oh, nothing. I'm just . . . The other day I thought my life was over, and now it seems like my life is beginning all over again."

"I told you, Dee, to stick with me. I wasn't going to see you suffer at all."

Denise's smile turned more serious. "Mariah, why me? I mean, you have a lot of clients, and I'm sure the same thing that happened to me has happened to others before me. Do you do this all the time, or did you do it just for me?"

"Oh, I definitely don't do it all the time. Let's just say, I see something really special in you, Denise. You are so sincere. I couldn't let you go back to Memphis. I didn't want you to leave New York broken."

"Well, I really, really do appreciate everything you have done," Denise said as the bartender popped the bottle of champagne and poured some in each flute.

Denise picked up a glass. "And to show you just how much I appreciate you"—Denise held her flute out.

Mariah took her flute and gently tapped it against Denise's.

Denise put the glass to her mouth and swallowed the expensive bubbly. "Not bad."

"I told you. Stick with me, Denise; you will experience things you never imagined."

One hour and one bottle down, Denise and Mariah walked to her hotel door with a new, half-empty bottle of champagne in hand. They abandoned the champagne flutes and opted for the ghetto-fabulous option of drinking straight from the bottle. Denise knew she was drunk, but it was a different feeling. They were like high-school kids smoking their first joint. Everything was funny.

"Man, I feel great. How about you?" Mariah flung her shoes off and plopped down on Denise's bed.

Denise unbuttoned her button-down and let it hit the floor. She pulled her shoes off.

Mariah stared at Denise's bi-ceps; her black wife-beater clung to her flat stomach. Denise lay down on the bed next to Mariah.

"I haven't felt this good in a long time." Denise turned toward Mariah. Their eyes met. Both were silent.

Suddenly they both erupted in laughter at the same time, and a bit of Mariah's spit landed on Denise's lip.

"Dang, girl."

"Oh, shut up. I'll get it." Mariah leaned in and wiped her liquid from Denise's face.

Suddenly things weren't funny anymore. Denise and Mariah gazed into each other's eyes.

"What's happening here?"

"I don't know."

Denise and Mariah continued to gaze. Denise didn't know if it was the champagne causing her heart to race.

Mariah's hand made its way on Denise's lap.

"Mariah."

"Denise."

There were no more words. Denise grabbed Mariah's head. Her fingers instantly entangled her wild red mane. Their lips locked, and Mariah climbed on top of Denise.

With ease Denise unzipped Mariah's dress and threw the Versace creation to the side.

Mariah ran her fingers through Denise's hair while Denise's lips kissed their way over Mariah's smooth white skin. Mariah's wetness soaked through her black and white lace thong. She grinded her pelvis against Denise's.

Denise unbuttoned Mariah's matching lace bra and threw it carelessly. Denise paused. Mariah's small pink nipples were a change from the brown of the black women of Denise's past. Lena entered her head.

"What's wrong?" Mariah said noticing the pause.

Denise dropped her head on Mariah's chest. "Shit!" She looked up at Mariah's confused face. "I'm sorry, Mariah. I can't do this."

"Denise, what's wrong? Did I do something?"

Denise couldn't help but let out a frustrated grunt. "No, you are great. I'm just . . . damn, I'm just a fucking fool." Denise wrapped her arms around Mariah's butt and picked her up, placing her back on the bed.

Mariah was speechless.

"I got some serious personal shit right now, and I'm just not ready to take this step."

"Well, it's OK . . . I guess." Dumbfounded and horny, Mariah looked around for her bra. "I guess I should leave."

Denise clutched Mariah's arm. "Wait. Mariah, I don't want you to go."

"Well, I'm confused, Denise. What do you want from me?"

Denise looked at Mariah in her eyes. "Let me hold you." Denise climbed into the bed.

Mariah smiled. She crawled in the bed next to Denise. They embraced.

Denise kissed Mariah on the nape of her neck sending, shivers down Mariah's body. Mariah turned toward Denise. They kissed the night away, falling asleep in each other's arms.

18

"Mrs. Redding!" Rosario ran into the bedroom. She shook Lena. "Mrs. Redding, Mrs. Redding!" The older Hispanic woman continued to shake until Lena's head moved.

"Whhhaaa," Lena murmured, shaking her head.

"Mrs. Redding, why are you on the floor. Is everything all right? Do I need to call the doctor?"

Lena looked at Rosario's frightened face. "What time is it?"

"It's noon, Mrs. Redding. Maybe I should call the doctor or Mr. Redding."

"No, I'm fine. Just help me up." Lena held her arms up while the housekeeper helped her to her feet. Lena glanced over, catching her reflection in the mirror. Her eyes were blood-shot, and her hair was tussled all over her head. "I guess I just fell asleep."

"You broke a glass. I cleaned it up in the hallway. Are you sure you are all right?"

"Define all right?"

"I . . . I don't understand." The short Hispanic woman looked confused.

Lena noticed how neat her hair was, pulled back in a perfect bun. "Rosario thanks for cleaning up the mess. I'll be OK. Take the day off, with pay."

Rosario, didn't budge. "I don't know if that is a good idea Mrs. Redding."

"Oh, I am fine. I just had a rough night. I'll be OK. I promise. If I have any problems, I'll call Brandon."

"Are you sure?" Rosario asked, hoping for a yes so she could enjoy some free time.

"I'm sure. I think I'll go shopping or something."

"But what about baby?"

"What!" Lena's head jerked. "Oh shit, Brandon Junior." Lena hit her forehead with her palm.

"Yes, ma'am. Babysitter supposed to bring him home any minute."

Lena sighed. "OK, can you call and find out if they can keep him another day or two? Doesn't matter the cost."

Rosario nodded her head and walked out the room.

Lena walked over to her mirror. She pulled her brush out and began to stroke her hair. She didn't like her image. Her face looked worn, like she'd aged in one night.

"She said that is fine. They will bill regular," Rosario stated, standing in the door.

"Thank you, Rosario. You can leave now." Lena continued to brush her hair as the housekeeper disappeared.

Lena walked across her bathroom and ran a tub filled with hot water. She pressed a button, causing jets of bubbles to come from the tub. Lena undressed and slowly stepped into the large Jacuzzi tub and laid back, allowing the steam rising from the bath to create a mist.

The phone began to ring. She looked over to see Carmen's number lighting up on the LED screen. Lena pressed the intercom button on the wall.

"Hi, C."

"Heeeyyyy, honey. How are you?" Carmen's attempt at a concerned voice humored Lena.

"I don't really know. I feel . . . I really don't know what I feel."

Carmen took a sip of her water. "That's to be expected. I wanted to see if you wanted to come see my new place. Maybe we could grab a bite to eat or something."

"Actually I would. I can't stand being in this house much longer. I'm taking a bath now. I'll call when I get out, so I can get directions."

"Great." Carmen hung the phone up.

Lena dipped her head under the water. The sound of the bubbles was soothing to her. She held her breath and wondered how long she could hold it. As her chest started to grow heavy, Lena came up from under the water. She released the breath she was holding. It felt like she released all of her pain at the same time. She looked over at her reflection in the mirror. She looked better already. She was ready to start her steps toward recovery.

Lena pulled into the apartment complex. She smiled when she saw Carmen standing on the balcony smiling back at her. She stepped out of the car, the hot sun soothing her.

"Hey, Le-Le." Carmen waved frantically.

"Hey, Carmen!" Lena smiled as she headed up the stairs.

"Hey, Lena, baby." Nic stood in the door watching Lena come up, Nic's long wavy hair hung down her almost to the middle of her back.

"Oh my God, how long are you letting your hair get?" Lena said as Nic wrapped her arms around her. Nic's tall frame seemed massive next to Lena's short body.

"Girl, I'm about to cut it. It was a dare between C and me. She wanted to see how long it could grow. It's hot, and it's getting on my nerves. I'ma go bald like Cooley."

"No, the hell, you aren't." Carmen hit Nic as Lena walked into the house. "But I am kinda tired of all your hair being in the bed. Hey, girl." Carmen hugged Lena.

Lena looked around the living room. "Wow! This is nice. Good job, C."

"Thanks, girl. I mean, it's not your house, but it will do for now."

They walked into the bare apartment. They sat on a small sofa covered with a red couch cover and big black and red pillows.

"Well, this is comfortable. Where did you get it?" Lena's body sank into the plush couch.

Carmen smirked. "Girl, from Craigslist. I saw it on the curb notice. It was from Collierville, so I knew it couldn't be that bad. Girl, y'all rich people are crazy. She had put so much stuff out. There wasn't anything wrong with the couch but the awful color and a tear in the back fabric. I hit Marshalls and bought this cover, and it was all she wrote."

Lena smiled at her friend's happiness. "Carmen, you are so silly."

"I'm serious. My mama taught me one thing, one person's trash is another person's treasure."

"I know that's right." Nic walked by and kissed Carmen on her forehead.

Carmen blushed. Lena loved seeing Nic and Carmen together.

"So, Carmen, what do you want to do today?"

"Well, maybe we can go look at furniture. See if you see anything."

Carmen looked at Lena. "Are you sure? 'Cause I'm down for whatever you want to do."

Lena smiled. "I think it's a great idea. I need to get you a house-warming present."

"Well, let's do it." Carmen smiled. She was OK with second-hand things, but she couldn't help but enjoy the idea of getting one really nice item from Lena.

Nic walked out of the kitchen. "OK, can you not spend my whole paycheck please?"

"I won't." Carmen and Nic kissed.

Lena smiled. She wondered what Denise was doing at that moment. Lena's cheery disposition was fading quickly.

Carmen noticed Lena's dreary face. "Well, girl, let's get out of here and have some real fun."

"Carmen, you know I really admire your relationship with Nicole. It must be nice." Lena stared out the window of her BMW while Carmen drove.

"Girl, I can't lie. It's wonderful. But you know what? I went through a whole lot before I found her. So, trust me, you are going through some tough times now, but things are going to get better."

"I hope so. I don't see how they could get worse."

"Well, you know what they say, what doesn't kill us makes us stronger."

Lena smiled. She turned back to look out the window. Mary Mary's rendition of "Yesterday" began to play on through her speakers. "I'm starting to think my iPod has a mind, because it sure does know what to play at the right time."

Carmen laughed. "Or maybe God is trying to tell you something."

The two looked at each other.

Lena put her hand on top of Carmen's. "Maybe you are right. Well, God, I'm listening. Whatever you want to tell me I'm listening." She closed her eyes and listened to the words. Lena took a deep breath. It was time to forget about yesterday and focus on today.

19

Denise jumped at the loud knock at her door. She looked down to see Mariah sleeping soundly. Damn. She got out of bed. She didn't have a hangover, but the drinking made her forget about her bedmate. Denise looked at the clock. They had slept the day away. She knew she had to stop drinking.

Denise walked to the door and looked through the peep-hole but couldn't see anything. She knew someone was holding their finger it.

"Who is it?"

"Housekeeping," a high-pitched voice said.

There was a vague familiarity to the voice. Denise put the doorknocker over the door and cracked it open. "Oh, shit!" She smiled as she saw Cooley standing with a rolling luggage bag.

"So you gon' let me in, fool?"

Denise looked back at the bed. "Hold on one second."

"What the—"

Denise closed the door and ran over to the bed. She slightly shook Mariah.

Mariah turned over and smiled. "Hey, you."

"Mariah, I hate to rush you, but my bestfriend is at the door, and you don't have on any clothes."

Mariah's eyes widened. She sat up in the bed. "Oh, OK, I'll go the bathroom." She got out the bed, her red hair wild and all over her head. She grabbed her dress and ran to the bathroom.

Denise walked back to the door. She opened it to see Cooley standing with her arms crossed.

"It's about damn time." Cooley pushed the door all the way open and walked in. She paused in the doorway. Cooley sniffed. She looked at the bed then looked at Denise and smiled. "Who is she?"

"What? I don't know what you're talking about." Denise walked into the room.

"You lieeeee! I can smell a woman in the air. You don't wear Bond Number 9. You probably don't know what Bond Number 9 is."

Denise sat on the edge of the bed. "How do you know—never mind." Denise knew Cooley knew her fragrances. Cooley sat her bag against the wall. Denise noticed the curious look on Cooley's face. "What, man?"

Cooley grinned, her dimples deep. "She's still here, isn't she?"

"Oh my God! You really are in the wrong business. You need to be a private detective."

The bathroom door slowly opened. Mariah walked out with an embarrassed smile. Her hair was wet, curls stringing down her back.

Cooley did a double take. She looked back at Denise then turned back to Mariah. Cooley extended her hand.

"So she made you hide in the bathroom? That's sad, Dee."

"No, I actually needed to get dressed. Hi, I'm Mariah. And I'm guessing you are Cooley." Mariah extended her hand.

Cooley smirked; she had never heard her name so proper before.

"Good job on guessing my perfume."

"Well, I always know a good scent, and it's a pleasure to meet you, Miss Mariah. I'm sure we will see more of each other."

"I'm sure we will." Mariah smiled. "Well, Denise, I need to get out of here. You will be all right getting to the studio, right?"

Instantly Mariah was back in business mode. Cooley was impressed.

"Yes, ba—Mariah, I can manage. Thank you again."

Mariah blushed. "Anytime. Call if you need me."

"I'll call you later."

Mariah grabbed her purse and left.

Cooley poked her head out the door to make sure the coast was clear.

Denise rumbled through her duffle bag. She braced herself for Cooley.

Cooley closed the door and turned around, leaning against the door.

"Really, Dee."

"What?" Denise cackled.

"You know what? I'm not even gonna say what you think I'm going to say. She seems cool, good taste in clothes. Thick-ass legs for a white girl. I even like the red hair. At least she's not a blonde."

"Mariah is just a friend. Nothing happened."

"Riiighhhhttt." Cooley walked farther into the room. "Whatever you say. Carmen gon' kick yo ass when she finds out you fucking Vanilla now. And you got an old Vanilla drop too."

"I'm not fucking anything. She was my sports agent. She helped me land the modeling gig, which I gotta get ready to get to. Wait, what the hell are you doing here anyway?"

Cooley stretched out over the bed. "Well, I got some business to look into here. On top of that, I got this girly-ass picture of my friend and figured she had lost her damn mind, so, I had to come and check on you."

Denise snickered. "It's not like that. Dude, you won't believe. I'm the new face of Jocku."

Cooley sat up on the bed. Her eyes widened. "You are bullshittin' me."

"I'm serious. Mariah got it for me."

"Dee, you aren't a model. Hell, have you ever worn heels?"

"Yeah, once, but it's not like that. You'll see for yourself. Come go with me to the studio. They took some pics of me for my first ad, and I'm going to see it today." Denise gleamed with pride.

"Damn right. I can't believe this, my dog, I mean, my girl is a model. I might have to put you in one of my videos." Cooley stood up.

Denise pushed her back on the bed.

"Man, this is just for work." Denise walked over to the mirror. She brushed her thick black hair.

Cooley's mouth twisted. "Yeah . . ." Cooley watched her friend primp in the mirror, something Denise never enjoyed doing. "I think I'm having an outer body experience right now."

Denise looked at Cooley's reflection in the mirror. "Why do you say that?"

"Because I'm sitting on the bed, waiting on yo ass to get out the mirror and I could care less about looking in one at all."

Denise turned around. "Dude, are you still trippin' about that?" Denise pointed to Cooley's right cheek.

Cooley lowered her head. "I just don't feel like I'm me anymore sometimes."

"Carla, your face was never what made you. It was your swagger and your confidence. You have to realize that your face might have attracted women in the beginning, but it was your words and attitude that made them fall crazy for you."

"Thank you, Dr. Phil, for those inspirational words. But I've heard them before." Cooley threw a pillow at Denise as they both laughed.

Denise hailed a cab.

Cooley laughed, calling Denise a New Yorker. Cooley took the sights in while listening to Denise gush about her photo shoot and Mariah.

Her mind drifted to Sahara. Sahara's smile warmed Cooley's body. Misha entered Cooley's mind, the warm feeling replaced with an icy cold.

"Dee, what did you really think of my relationship with Mish? Do you think she ever loved me?"

Denise turned her head toward Cooley. Her forehead wrinkled slightly from the question. "I think that you both loved each other, but not as much as you or she thought you did."

Cooley's right eyebrow rose. "Elaborate."

Denise shifted her body toward Cooley. "Well, don't laugh, OK."

"Oh God, what the hell are you about to say?"

"OK, check this out. I was reading the Twilight Series."

"Damn here you go." Cooley giggled at the thought of Denise being apart of the vampire phenomenon that had taken over the planet. She decided to hide her secret of liking the series for a little longer.

"Shut up. You liked the movies too, and I know it. I'm surprised you haven't picked up the book." Denise smiled.

Cooley threw her middle finger at Denise. She hated when Denise was right.

"But, seriously, in the book the girl Bella is all in love with the vampire, but she also loves the werewolf."

"Remind me why I am listening to you right now."
Cooley turned her head.

Denise hit her on her shoulder.

"Man, for real, this shit was deep. Jacob, man, loved
the hell out of Bella, and even though Bella loved Jacob,
her heart already belonged to someone else, Edward."

Cooley turned back to Denise. "Soooo, you are saying . . ."

"That we are the Jacobs of the world. Misha and
Lena, they are Bella. They love us, we are good for
them, but their hearts already belong to other people."

Cooley and Denise looked at each other. Cooley
shook her head. "I can't believe that shit actually made
sense."

They both erupted into laughter. The cab driver even
smirked at their silly conversation.

"I guess that makes us the wolf pack."

"Team Jacob."

Cooley paused. She nudged Denise. "Hell, naw, you
did not just say that. I think you are going femme for
real."

The taxi pulled up to the large building. Denise
checked her look as Cooley paid for the cab.

Cooley shook her head. "I don't know who you are
anymore." She crossed her arms, like an emotional
woman.

"Shut the hell up." Denise grabbed Cooley's arm as
they walked to the building.

The scene was a lot less busy than the other day. It
was fairly quiet. A faint sound of Lady Gaga played over
the speakers.

Cooley grinned at the skinny supermodel wannabe
sitting behind the desk. She smiled back. Cooley made
a mental note to check on her when they left.

"Hello, Ms. Chambers." The receptionist stood up. Her Chanel skirt was hugging her nonexistent thighs. She walked from behind the desk. "Follow me." The receptionist glanced at Cooley again.

Denise and Cooley walked behind her, noticing her attempt to switch. Cooley looked at Denise, both thinking the same thing.

"Damn shame," Cooley whispered.

"No ass at all," Denise mouthed.

They both giggled.

The receptionist opened a large black door. Denise and Cooley walked in. Marco looked up from the computer in front of him. His associates and brand directors sat in anticipation.

"Ahh, Denise." Marco pressed his hands together.

"Hello. This is my associate, Carla Wade."

"Greetings, Ms. Wade. Please." Marco motioned for Denise and Cooley to sit down. "I'm going to let Armund take over."

Armund's chair swiveled around; he stood up, his long frame towering over everyone. "Well, as you all know, the first ad campaign just wasn't working for us. Then Denise came along. Everything has come together so well that we are rushing out this out immediately. This will be in every major magazine in the nation."

Armund pushed a button on a small remote in his hand. Denise's image caught her and Cooley completely off guard.Both were speechless, completely ignoring the claps around them.

Denise struggled to catch her breath, and Cooley was flabbergasted. Denise's image covered the large white wall, her hair wild and curly, her black halter shirt revealing her rock-hard abs, with the Jocku logo on it. From the top up, she was feminine, a sight she was unfamiliar with. Below, a pair of baggy jeans similar to the ones she wore on a daily basis.

"Wow," Denise muttered.

"This will not be the only one. This is just the first of a few campaigns we are running. The billboard should be placed by the end of next week." Armund sat back in his chair.

Marco noticed Denise's and Cooley's vacant expressions. "You do not like?"

Denise's head quickly turned to Marco. "Oh no, it's amazing. I just . . ." Denise looked at Cooley, whose mouth was still slightly dropped. "I have just never seen myself like that before."

Marco smiled. "Such humility."

"Let's see how long it lasts," Armund stated.

Cooley and Denise sat in the taxi in silence.

Denise quickly realized how unimportant the model was after taking the picture. She wouldn't be involved in picking pictures or anything. She was the face. She showed up and did whatever they told her to do, a role she was not used to playing.

"Did I do the right thing?" Denise uttered, interrupting the awkward silence.

Cooley looked up from her iPhone. "What do you mean?"

"This whole thing, it's not me. I'm not that woman who was on that wall. What the fuck was I thinking?"

"Dee, I'll admit I was very . . . *very* shocked by the look. But, fuck it, if you gotta dress like a damn girl to make yo money, than you do it. I can't lie, you looked good, dude. I was impressed, really. No joking. I think you might just have stumbled into a serious career here."

Denise could tell from Cooley's serious expression that she was sincere. "I'm a model?" Denise questioned.

"Looks that way."

Denise tried to fight it, but slowly a smile appeared on her face. It wasn't basketball, but she liked it just the same.

20

Lena's pillow was stuck to the side of her face. She pulled the pillow off. It was still damp. She had cried herself to sleep again. The idea of moving on was harder than she expected.

Lena consumed her days with shopping and redecorating. She dragged Carmen out with her to buy useless items. Carmen didn't mind, as the things Lena replaced came to her half-furnished apartment.

Brandon didn't mind the excessive spending. He handed her a new Black card. If spending helped her get over her depression he was OK with it. Anything to help her heal and him feel better for the mess he felt guilty for causing.

Lena forced herself out of bed. She knew it was going to be a down day for her. It was one in the afternoon and she was just waking up. The cold floor alerted her senses. She made a mental note to buy a nice rug for her floor.

Lena walked into her kitchen. She had dismissed her maid; she had grown tired of her worrying for Lena in Spanish every morning.

The silence in her loft was irritating. She turned her plasma on loud. The sound of Wendy Williams ranting about the hot gossip of the day helped, but not a lot.

Lena knew it was time. She had been dreading the phone call, but her mother's constant voice mails were a nagging reminder. She knew if she didn't contact her mother soon she would show up. Lena sipped her espresso. The strong coffee woke the rest of her body up quickly.

She stared at her phone. She pressed the button for her mother's cell.

"Lena, you better have one great excuse for not calling me." Karen Jamerson held a black Dior dress up to her in the full-body mirror in the upscale boutique.

"Mom, are you busy right now?"

"If you call shopping for the UNCF fundraising gala tonight busy, then yes, but you know I'm never too busy for my beautiful daughter."

A huge knot filled Lena's throat. The words stung. She sighed. "Mother, I have something to tell you."

"Yes, do you have this in a six? Make it an eight?" Karen handed the dress to the eager store clerk. "Yes, dear?"

"Mother . . . I . . ." Tears filled Lena's eyes. "I'm so sorry, Mom."

Karen's body trembled. "Lena, what is going on?" she sat on the plush chair next to the rack of designer threads.

"Mom there's something I should have told you a while ago but . . ."

"Lena please just tell me before I have a heart attack." Karen held her hand over her mouth.

Lena took a deep breath. "Well, um, I . . . See . . ."

"Lena!"

"Mom I'm not going back to school this semester." Lena closed her eyes and sighed.

Karen let a sigh of relief. "Is that it? Lena don't ever have me scared like that again. I'm over here thinking something horrible happened." Karen stood back up as the assistant brought over a new outfit. Karen gave the navy dress a thumbs up.

"No mom it's nothing worse than that. I just know you and dad were expecting me to finish this year, but . . ."

"Oh Lena, please that is totally understandable. You are a newlywed. You have a house to prepare, hopefully including a nursery soon."

The words pierced Lena. She wanted to cry but held it in. "We are taking our time on that." Lena couldn't tell the her mother the truth. Telling her mother would bring too many questions she wasn't prepared to answer.

"Well, don't take too long, I do want my granddaughter to see me in my glory years." Karen admired her beauty in the three way mirror.

Her mother's conversation was too much to bear. Lena couldn't hold the tears in. She didn't get the chance to find out if she was having a girl or a boy. "Well, I just wanted to let you know so you wouldn't be expecting a graduation this year."

"I will let your father know. My darling I bet you are swamped over there. Do you need me to come to town?"

"No!" Lena caught herself. "No, mother things are fine."

Karen paused. "If things are fine Lena, why do you sound like they aren't? What is really going on?"

Lena wanted to come clean. She wanted to tell her mother everything that was going on in her life but she couldn't. "I'm just really tired."

"Well, how about we go away for a week. Hamptons or some where exotic."

"As nice as that sounds I need to get this house to-gether. Maybe later."

"OK well I really need to figure out what I am wearing to this benefit. Oh but Lena, if you ever go so long without calling me I will be there so fast you will think I used a rocket instead of a plane."

Lena hung up from her mother with a sense of relief. She didn't have to worry about her mother showing up and prying in her life for a little while longer. She knew she should have told her that Brandon wasn't living there, but she knew that would warrant a visit for sure.

Lena finished her espresso and got up from the table. She had shopping to do, and had already lost half of her day.

21

Cooley got in the taxi and handed a small piece of paper to the Indian cab driver. "Can you take me to this address?"

Cooley turned down the invitation from Mariah and Denise to go to Avenue Q with them. She let them talk her into going to see *The Lion King* the night before. Cooley had to admit, *The Lion King* was a lot better than she expected, but the thought of watching puppets sing crazy songs just wasn't appealing to her.

Cooley received the call she had been waiting on. Tee called with the address and phone number for Sonic. After a long conversation, she knew it was time for her to step in.

Cooley looked out the window. She would have to enjoy Harlem another day. They pulled up to the tall apartment building. Cooley looked up at the numbers on the wall. She was there. She paid the cab driver and got out of the car.

Cooley pressed the buzzer for apartment 506. Instantly a buzzing noise echoed, and she heard the lock unlatch. Cooley walked into the building. The hallway of the building had an old smell to it. The paint on the walls was chipping, with tiles on the floor scuffed and broken in places. The rank smell of sweat and mildew hit her as she got into the small elevator. She tried to hold her breath until making it to the fifth floor.

Cooley walked down the long hallway. The few working lights flickered on and off. Cooley examined the sounds coming from the passing apartments. Someone was watching BET in apartment 501. She could hear Keyshia Cole's mother's voice clearly.

Cooley stopped at her destination. She tried to listen. There was music coming from the apartment, but she couldn't make out the lyrics. There was a lingering smell of weed coming from under the door. She knocked twice.

Cooley heard the various locks unlocking. The door opened. A petite woman opened the door. Cooley knew the face, she just couldn't place it. The woman smiled, throwing her long Beyoncé curls behind when she moved her head.

"Hey, Cooley." The woman reached out.

Cooley hugged the girl, trying to remember where she knew her from.

"Hey . . . ummm . . ."

The woman pulled back and looked at Cooley. Cooley could see the disappointment.

"Bee-Bee. We met at Sonic's house in ATL when you came last summer."

Cooley looked at the girl for a moment. There was a familiarity to her. Her booty shorts and T-shirt were form-fitting. Cooley noticed the cursive B.B. tattooed on her leg. Cooley smiled. It hit her.

"Oh, shit. Girl, yeah, I remember you." Cooley hugged her again. Her model name was Bee-Bee, but around the office she was known as Brain Busta. The woman could put Super Head out of business.

"How are you doing?"

"I'm OK, trying to make it. Got some gigs lined up, doing a Nelly video soon. I might be going on this new reality show on VH1." Bee-Bee smiled and turned her face, hoping Cooley couldn't tell she was lying. "So, you coming to get this bitch up out of my spare room or what?"

Cooley walked into the tiny apartment. The smell of weed and incense made Cooley feel nauseous. She never understood why people thought that was a good combination.

"Where is she?"

Bee-Bee frowned. "In the bedroom, watching videos, I think. I'm glad you came 'cause I was about to put her ass out."

Cooley ignored Bee-Bee. She wanted to curse her out. Sonic was the reason she had anything at all. Sonic gave Bee-Bee her first gig in the videos. She took it and ran with it, becoming one of the million whores of Jam Zone.

"Let me go talk to her," Cooley said, walking toward the room. She could see the TV lights flickering from the room to the wall.

Bee-Bee grabbed Cooley's arm. She slanted her eyes and licked her lips. "Before you do, let me take my moment to say you looking real good. I'd love the chance to see you in better circumstances. How long you gon' be in New York?"

Cooley couldn't help but shake her head. She let out a laugh. She couldn't believe what women would do to try to get on top. "Thanks, but I'm leaving in the morning."

"Well, I'll be in ATL soon. We should hook up." Bee-Bee pushed her thick frame up against Cooley.

"Yeah, well, have fun while you're there. Now, if you don't mind." Cooley walked past Bee-Bee, leaving her dumbfounded in her spot.

Cooley walked into the messy bedroom.

Sonic looked up from her spot in the bed. Her hair unbraided and wild on her head; she had on an over-sized white tee and her boxers, Her usual plump cheeks were sunk in, she had lost a lot of weight, she looked ill. Sonic's eyes popped when she saw Cooley's face appear in the doorway. She didn't know if it was Cooley for real or if it was the drugs.

"What the fuck? Cool, is that you?" Sonic sat up on the bed, trying to adjust her eyes.

"Yeah, it's me," Cooley said, walking farther into the bedroom.

"Oh, shit." Sonic sniffed and rubbed her nose. She leaned over and opened the drawer next to the bed.

Cooley's eyes darted down. She noticed the glass tray filled with white powder and a razor blade. Cooley's eyes almost popped out when she noticed a small pipe in the drawer as well.

"What you doin' here? Hell naw, man." Cooley grabbed the plate from Sonic.

"What you doin'?" Sonic looked up at Cooley. She knew she didn't have the strength to jump up at that moment.

"Sonic, what the fuck is wrong with you? Look at this shit! Look at where you are!"

"Don't fuckin' come in here and judge me, Cooley! You think you all that now 'cause you working at Jam Zone. You wouldn't be shit without me!"

Cooley tried to ignore Sonic's rants. She noticed a duffle bag in the corner. She picked it up, realizing Sonic's few possessions were in it. "Get the fuck up. We are going."

"I ain't going nowhere!" Sonic said as she lay back in the bed.

"You right. You did help me, and now I'm helping you. Sonic, you're better than this, and you fucking know it. These damn drugs and shit, I'm checking you into rehab."

"I don't need no damn rehab. I need a hit record, so I can get back on my feet. You gon' get me a hit record, Cool? Or you too busy working with that bitch!" Sonic threw her hand in the direction of the TV.

Sahara's face flashed across the screen. It was her MTV spotlight. Sahara's face normally would have calmed Cooley down. But she felt rage at Sonic's words.

"What the fuck are you talking about?" Cooley could feel the anger rising.

Sonic lit her blunt. Instantly the room filled with the thick cloudy haze. "I don't know why you brought that stuck-up-ass bitch to the crib anyway. I knew she wasn't shit. Now they all catering to her ass like she fuckin' Beyoncé or some shit, ho trippin' about letting a nigga smash."

Cooley felt a large knot in her throat. "Did . . . did you?"

Sonic looked over at Cooley. "Nah, she too damn stuck-up. Always saying she belonged to someone else. I know you hit it though. Man, girls drop the panties for your ass." Sonic's laugh turned to a whooping cough. She grabbed a hot beer and took a swig from it.

"It's not even like that." Cooley looked at the TV again. She couldn't believe Sahara wasn't seeing anyone else. She looked back at Sonic. "Man, look, are you gon' let me help you or not?"

"What, you got a hit for me or what? I know if I get a hit, they will let me come back to the company."

"Sonic, I want to help you, but you have to help yourself first. You need to go to rehab."

"I said—"

"Sonic, if you want your career back, you'll do this. Do it for me."

The only sound from the room was the television. Sonic stared at Cooley.

Cooley wasn't breaking. She stared right back at Sonic with a stern look on her face.

"You promise to get me a hit if I do the rehab thing?"

"I promise."

"A'ight. But can you make it a nice one. These wack-ass centers just make me wanna leave."

Cooley sighed. "I'll do the best I can. I'm going to pick you up tomorrow morning after I get everything together."

Sonic stared at Cooley. "You know I always liked you, Cool. Even when we first met, I normally don't let others come around me like that. It was something about you. I knew you were true." Sonic lit a cigarette and took a puff. A'ight, man, I'll do it for you."

Cooley smiled. "Any time."

Sonic looked at Cooley, who was tapping away on her phone. "Aye, Cool. Thanks, man."

Cooley let the crisp New York air hit her. She felt a sense of pride. She was able to get Sonic to do something no one else was able to do. She hailed a cab and headed back into the city.

And we are bringing it to you first. The hottest new singer out of ATL's Jam Zone: Sahara. This girl is is hot, and this song is blazing. Lemme know what ya think. Hit the line.

Cooley listened to the radio coming from the cab. Sahara's sultry voice sounded amazing against her beat. Sahara entered her head. Cooley felt the warm sensation taking over her body. She thought about Sonic.

Sahara wasn't some whore that fucked her way to the top. She was really all about Cooley.

Cooley smiled. She thought about Denise and her Twilight reference. Maybe she wasn't the werewolf after all. Maybe she was the vampire, trying to stay away from someone who was made for her. Cooley knew she didn't want to resist anymore.

22

Cooley didn't realize how much rehab would cost. The idea of rehab for the stars was out of the question. She knew Sonic would have to settle for rehab for the D list.

"Talk to me," Cooley said, answering her phone.

"Hey, Cool. Everything is set. I have your ticket for tomorrow like you asked. And everything is set for Sonic as well. I thought it would be best to let her just show up. I didn't want them charging you, in case she didn't show." Tee walked down the busy hall at Jam Zone and sat at her small cubicle in the intern room.

"Thanks, but you didn't have to do that. I'm sure she will be there." Cooley looked at her face in the mirror. The last piece of her ugly scab had fallen off, leaving a longer white mark, no more hideous skin.

"Well . . . I just wanted to be on the safe side." Tee knew what she was implying. Cooley knew her assistant had lost all faith in Sonic, just as most had.

"Thanks. How are things going with the house hunt?" Cooley rubbed Neosporin on the area. She was glad the ugly, bubbled up scab was completely gone. Now she was determined to get her face as close to normal as possible.

"I have three appointments set for you when you get back. Are you sure you want to get an apartment? I mean, the mansion."

"It's always best to have your own. Remember that, young blood. Let me go. I'll call if anything changes."

Cooley hung up from Tee. She brushed her curly hair. She was starting to feel more like herself. Cooley heard Sahara's single play on the small bathroom radio. Her heart raced. She couldn't wait to get back to Atlanta for more than one reason.

Cooley's text alert rang out. She picked her phone up. It didn't have a number. She opened it.

SORRY, but I can't.

Cooley reread the text. She called Sonic's phone number. The operator chimed in with the usual disconnect message. Worry quickly set in. She called Bee-Bee's number.

"Hello!" Bee-Bee yelled in the phone.

"Hey, Bee. It's Cooley. Is Sonic—"

"Fuck Sonic! That son of a bitch is gone, and she took my shit with her!" Bee-Bee threw her glass of cognac against the wall.

Cooley's heart pounded. "What are you talking about?"

"I'm saying that bitch left in the middle of the night and took my damn jewelry with her. I swear I bet not find her, fuck the police—I got something else for that ass."

"Damn, Bee-Bee. I'm sorry. I don't know what to say."

"See, this is what happens when you try to help someone. Be glad you didn't take that cone-head-ass bitch back with you! I gotta go."

Cooley hung the phone up. She sat on the toilet seat. Her mind raced. *Where could Sonic have gone that quick?* Cooley thought to herself. She needed to find her; she needed to save her friend.

***

"Hey, bruh, wanna grab a bite?" Denise stood in the door.

Cooley looked at Denise, her eyes filled with worry.

"What's up, C?"

"Sonic . . . she just, she left." Cooley fought back emotion.

Denise walked into the bathroom. "Bruh, I want to say something to you without you getting upset," Denise murmured.

Cooley's glazed eyes looked at Denise.

"Your expression right now, the feelings you are feeling. Bruh I've been there. I know how you are feeling right now. But there's something you need to realize. Something it took me a long-ass time to realize. You can't save someone who doesn't wanna be saved. Sonic gotta want the help, or else you gon' be out of a lot of cash for nothing."

Cooley sighed. She knew Denise was right. She was there with Denise all the times her mother skipped out on rehab. She was there the final time when Denise almost choked her mother to death. She knew in her heart Sonic was lost, and wasn't going to be found until she wanted to be.

"You said something about food?" Cooley stood up.

"Yeah, let's go grab a bite. It might make you feel better."

Cooley and Denise walked out of the room. Cooley inhaled, trying to push Sonic and her drama to the back of her mind, but she couldn't shake the feeling that something wasn't right.

"You know I'm going to miss living right on Broadway."

Denise and Cooley walked out the front door of the hotel.

"It's right here at all the action."

"Speaking of, where are you gon' go? Yo ass hasn't looked for a spot at all."

"Well, I'm going to crash at Mariah's for a spell until all the checks clear and I book another job."

Cooley smiled. "Umm, crashing at Mariah's, huh?"

"Shut up. It's not like that."

"Riiigghhh—damn!" Cooley stopped in her tracks.

Denise looked at her friend, noticing her eyes were fixated on something else. Denise looked up, and her jaw dropped. The large Jocku billboard with her photograph hit them dead-on.

"Damn, that's my friend!" Cooley pulled her phone out and began to snap pictures of the billboard.

Two young black girls walked up to Denise and Cooley. They looked at the billboard and back at Denise. "Is that really you?"

"Yes, that's me," Denise proudly responded.

"Wow, can we take a picture with you?" the shorter of the two asked.

People around started to look at Denise. The tourists pulled their cameras out, hoping to get a picture with a model.

Cooley took the camera from the two girls. They stood on either side of Denise. Denise smiled, the two girls gleamed.

"Thank you."

"No problem."

The two girls walked off. "I can't believe we just met a supermodel."

Cooley and Denise laughed at the girl's statement.

An Asian couple walked up to them. The elderly woman held her camera out to Cooley, unable to speak English.

Cooley frowned at Denise. She reluctantly took the camera and snapped a picture.

"OK, let's roll before I become your picture girl."

"Aww!" Denise put her arm around Cooley's neck. "It's OK. I'll make sure you always have a job as my assistant."

"Fuck you!"

They joked as they walked up the street. Denise looked back, her billboard farther in the distance. She thought about her grandmother. *I hope you are proud of me, Mema.*

Lena stared at the nursery door. The whole house was undergoing a transformation, but Lena couldn't bear to open the one door that she knew she needed to. She took a deep breath and pushed the door open. The furniture and toys all gone from the house; she couldn't bear it. Brandon had hired a nanny to keep Brandon Jr. at his place while he was on the road. The only thing to remind Lena of the painful past was the walls. The pastel colors on the wall were the constant reminder that the room was for a child, a child that would never be. Lena knew it was her last major project.

Lena couldn't take her eyes off the walls. She stood next to buckets of white, blue, and gray paint. Her gray Grizzly sweat pants rolled up to her knees, her bare feet cold against the clear tarp on the floor. She had to change the color of the room.

Lena picked up the small canister of blue paint and walked to the wall. She dipped the thin paint brush in the navy paint. With one stroke, blue hit the face of a white rabbit on the mural in the room.

Lena's body began to tremble. Emotions rushed up to her hands. She screamed as she threw the canister of paint against the wall. Blue splattered all over the wall and the floor. With Lena's rapid heartbeat, heavy breathing, she knew she couldn't do it. *Fuck it. I'll hire someone.*

Lena loved what money could do. Within two hours a company sent a painter to her house to do the easy paint job. He promised a completely new room by the end of the day. She promised an off-the-books bonus if he was right.

The loud smell of paint was making her head hurt. Lena changed out of her sweats into a pair of 7*7*7 Nostalgic Luxury Roxanne jeans with a fitted black T-shirt. Lena pulled her hair down out of its ratty ponytail and brushed it until her waves bounced and fell just the way she wanted them. She opened her armoire to find the right jewels to complete her look.

She opened the top drawer and nearly lost her breath. Right on top of all her beautiful Tiffany silver was the small charm bracelet that Denise bought her. She held the bracelet up and put it on her wrist. She could feel Denise near her. She didn't want to lose the feeling. She closed her armoire and walked out of the room.

Lena took a seat in a small artsy café on South Main. South Main was one of the things she loved about her loft. She was surrounded by art galleries and trendy clothing shops that carried only a few of each product. She could rollerblade or walk up and down the street or head down to the river to think. Carmen was right. If she had to be in Memphis, this was the way to do it.

Lena stared into her martini glass. The orange slice floated in the glass. She stared until the orange was nothing more than a blur to her. She heard the bell on the door open. There was another customer besides her. She didn't look up to see who would be enjoying her new little safe haven; she just stared into the glass.

"Well, isn't this a surprise?"

Lena glanced up from her drink. She thought she was dreaming. Terrin stood with a big smile on her face. Her dimples deeply inset like the rapper turned preacher turned back rapper, Ma$e.

Lena smiled. "Wow, this is." Lena felt herself blushing. She didn't know why. Terrin's look was completely different. She traded the Jordan's and baggy jeans for a professional black pinstriped woman's suit that was perfectly tailored to her body.

"I was walking past the window and something told me to look up, and to my surprise I saw you." Terrin glanced down at the extra chair at Lena's table.

Lena motioned for her to sit down.

Terrin sat in the chair, placing her briefcase on the floor. "What are you doing back in Memphis?"

Denise entered Lena's mind. She shook her head, hoping to shake out Denise's beautiful face as well. "Things didn't work out after all."

Terrin's eyes widened. "I'm sorry to hear that." Terrin looked at Lena. She cracked a smile. "Do you want to talk about it?"

"There's really nothing to talk about. I made some mistakes and now I'm paying for them." Lena forced a smile. "But I'm dealing with it. And I would rather not focus on it."

Terrin's eyes locked into Lena's. "Well, I am sorry that things didn't work out. I hate that you are not happy. But on the flip side, something great is happening right now."

Lena put her elbows on the table. She placed her chin in her hand. "Is that right?"

Terrin mimicked Lena. "Yes, it is."

"Do tell."

"Well, with the unfortunate dismissal of the basketball player, I now have the option of giving you this." Terrin reached in her pocket and pulled out her wallet. She handed Lena one of her business cards.

TERRIN MCFAYE—D.D.S.

"Oh, so can you give me some laughing gas? I could use it right about now" Lena smirked.

"I could, but that's not the route I usually like to take. Maybe I can make you laugh without the use of drugs." Terrin smiled.

Lena nodded her head in approval.

"So, Miss Lena, what do you have planned for the rest of the day?"

"Nothing. They are painting at my loft, so I just wanted to get out for a while. I think I might go shopping or something."

"Well, what do you know? I was just about to go shopping too. Want to check out Indigo Moon?"

"The new store down the way? Sure. Why not? Let me just pay."

"I got it." Terrin walked over to the counter and paid for Lena's cocktail.

Lena took her last big gulp; she needed the extra boost of alcohol to get her out the door.

The two walked down the sidewalk commenting on various artworks and items they saw in the windows of a few galleries and stores. Lena made a mental note to check out a dress in one small boutique. She was impressed by Terrin.

"So what type of store is this supposed to be?" Lena asked as they approached the neon blue sign.

"My friend owns it, actually. It's really a mix of fashions you really can't find in Memphis. I'm sure they carry those jeans you have on right now." Terrin looked Lena up and down. "Seven, right?"

"Yes. So you know your labels, I see."

"Yeah, I'm a label whore."

Terrin and Lena laughed.

"They have the new Jocku line. It's supposed to be this mix of—"

"Couture sporty. I heard about it. Overpriced sweat suits and jeans."

"Well, let's check it out."

The two walked into the urban store. Lena's text message went off as soon as she walked into the store. She looked down at the text.

CALL ME, I HAVE NEWS.

Carmen's call would have to wait. She was enjoying her company.

ME TOO, GIVE ME A FEW.

Lena pressed send and looked up. Alicia Keys and Jay-Z's "New York State of Mind" was blaring over the system.

"There's the Jocku line." Terrin pointed over toward the far wall.

Lena smiled as she looked in the direction of the store. Her body froze. Her hands began to shake. Lena's heart dropped out of her chest at the sight of Denise's face on the large wall display. It hit her with maximum impact.

Lena closed her eyes. Surely she was dreaming. That couldn't be Denise. She opened her eyes and felt her knees buckle.

"Lena, are you all right?" Terrin put her hand on Lena's back. Terrin's words sounded like the teacher on the *Peanuts* cartoons. Lena felt the room spinning. She darted out of the store.

Lena struggled to catch her breath. She looked down at the pavement.

Terrin ran out of the store after her. She put her arm around Lena. "Lena, are you all right? Do I need to take you to a doctor?"

"I just need to sit down," Lena said, trying to get control of her shaking hands.

Terrin guided her to the bench at the trolley stop. "Talk to me? Are you OK? Are you OK? What can I do?" Terrin panicked. She'd never seen anything like that.

"I . . . I will be OK. I think I need to just go home." Lena couldn't tell Terrin the real problem. That the love of her life was covering the back wall of the store. She didn't know what to think. Her mind raced. Why was Denise on the wall? Why was she dressed the way she was? Why did she have to look so damn good?

"Let me drive you home? Where do you live?"

"You don't have to do that. I actually live down here."

"Really? Where about?"

Lena pointed at the tall building down the street.

Terrin looked at Lena and laughed. "Tell me you are joking."

"No. Why do you say that?"

"You live in the Lofts. I live in the same building. OK, it's official. You are stalking me." Terrin smiled.

Lena couldn't help but smile back. "Hey, I've been living there for over a year, so maybe you are stalking me. What floor are you on?"

"I'm in a studio on the second floor. What about you?"

Lena hesitated. "I'm on twelve."

Terrin's eyes widened. "Wow, big baller! I'm gonna be moving on up eventually. Let me help you to your place."

"Actually"—Lena held on to Terrin's hand. "I think I just needed some fresh air and a little time to myself. Can I get a rain check?"

Disappointed, Terrin stood up. "Of course, you can. And I'm going to keep you to that. Remember, I know where you live." Terrin winked.

Lena smiled. Terrin was great at making her smile. Terrin turned and walked away. Lena watched her. Terrin could grow on her.

Terrin turned and looked back at Lena. "I knew you were watching me walk!" she yelled from down the street. "Here's something to really watch."

Terrin walked, switching her thick ass.

Lena cracked up.

Terrin turned back and waved. "Rain check, Ms. Lena!"

"Rain check!"

Lena waited until the coast was clear. She picked her phone up and pressed send on Carmen's name. Carmen answered the phone quickly.

"Why did it take you so long to call me back?!"

"Carmen, please come to Indigo on Main. I need you just to get in your car and come."

"Wait, Lena, there's something—"

"Tell me when you get here, just come."

Carmen parked and quickly got out of her car. Lena wanted to laugh. Carmen took her statement literally. She walked up in a pair of flip-flops, some Freedom University sweat pants, and an old oversized Freedom shirt. Her hair was pulled back in a ponytail that flopped from side to side as she walked. Lena stood up off of the trolley bench.

Carmen stretched her arms. Concern was etched in her face.

"What the hell, Lena?"

"Go in that store."

"This better be important." Carmen walked to the store doors. "Are you coming?"

Lena shook her head; she couldn't bear to walk through the doors.

Carmen sighed and walked in the store. A minute later she walked out with her hand over her mouth. "I'm sorry, Lena, I didn't want you to find out like that."

"You knew!" Lena scolded. "You knew this shit and didn't tell me?"

"Lena, that's why I was calling you. I saw the picture in *Jet*. I talked to Denise earlier. She said it's gonna be in most of the major magazines. I was trying to warn you before you opened a *Vogue* or something."

"How? Why?" The spinning was coming back. Lena sat back on the bench.

Carmen sat next to her. "Well, when the basketball thing didn't work out, her agent hooked her up with the modeling gig. They are using her as the face for this campaign."

"The face? That means I'm going to see her everywhere! This is too much."

Carmen put her arm around Lena. "Lena, you have to face it and get it over with. You have to work on moving on."

"I'm trying, I really am. It's just. Denise—"

"Is in New York and you are in Memphis. You will never be able to get your friendship back if you don't release her. Go. Meet some new people. Hey, how about we go tonight. I heard Onyx has some amazing music at night."

The trembling was gone. She knew Carmen was right. She needed to get out. "OK, let's do it."

Carmen smiled. "Great. Meet you there at nine."

"It's a date."

23

Denise sat next to Mariah on the small metal seat. Mariah looked at Denise and smiled. Denise tried hard not to show her excitement for her first ride on a subway. Mariah interlocked her fingers with Denise's. Denise looked at Mariah, her lips curved upwards with a smile.

Denise could feel the attraction between them. Mariah's pale skin against her brown skin almost made her hand look darker than it really was. She had never been attracted to a white woman before. Denise didn't know if it was just a preference or the thought of what her grandmother would do to her if she brought a white woman home. Denise knew where her grandmother stood with the situation. Her grandmother loved black love. She would always rave that there was nothing better.

Denise thought about the few white girls who crossed her path. She was never really around any, except the occasional ghetto white girl or the Beckys, white girls who were groupies. Mariah was different. She was professional and mature. She could sing a Taylor Swift song as quick as a Keyshia Cole song. And she didn't have a white girl's body. Denise knew her hips and ass were real; she had it back in the day, before injections gave even the flattest woman an ass like J-Lo.

"Denise, what's on your mind?" Mariah noticed Denise's vacant expression.

"Nothing much, just thinking about some stuff."

"Want to share?"

"Nah, it's nothing really." Denise glanced over at Mariah. Her brooding expression puzzled Denise. "It's nothing. I'm serious."

Mariah lowered her head. "No, it's not that. Denise, can I ask you a question?"

Denise nodded.

"How are you able to do it?"

"Do what?"

"Ignore what is happening between us." Mariah let go of Denise's hand. "A week ago, you were about to make love to me and then you stopped. Now when we are around each other, it's as though nothing ever happened."

Denise sighed. She didn't know what to say. Thoughts ran through her mind. She couldn't tell her the truth. "I'm sorry; it's not like that at all. I just have a lot going on right now."

Mariah's arched eyebrows lowered. She looked at Denise, lips locked tightly together. "Denise, let me tell you something about me. I am a grown woman. I don't play games, I don't sugar-coat the truth. For this friendship to work, I expect the same from you. So tell me the truth. What is really stopping you from doing what I can tell you want to do?'"

Mariah's forwardness sparked a flame in Denise. She shifted her body to Mariah. "All right then, you want the truth, I'll give it to you." Denise put her palm on Mariah's knee. "I like you, I like you a lot. But I still have feelings for someone else."

"And it has nothing to do with my color?"

Denise's jaw dropped . "Why would you say that?"

"Because I'm not dumb, Denise. I notice how you switch up when there's a group of black people around us. You don't act the same. You seem tense."

Denise didn't know what to say. She knew Mariah was right. It shocked her that she was so obvious.

"It's not that I have a problem with the fact that you're white, it's just that I've never considered dating a white woman before. It's different for me."

Mariah nodded her head up and down. "OK, well, that's a start. As far as this other woman, is it something you want back?"

Denise thought about Lena. The yearning for Lena wasn't as strong as it used to be. "Nah, it's not like that. I invested a lot of time in that for nothing. I won't do it again."

"Is it that you don't want to or you don't need to?"

"Both, but mostly I don't want to. Do I still think about her? Yes. That's why I stopped the other night. Mariah, I like you, but I don't want to bring you or any other girl into my life when I know I haven't gotten rid of all my feelings for someone else. That is how bad shit happens."

Rhonda entered Denise's mind.

"That's how I lost my career. I only messed with Rhonda because of Lena. Trying to get over Lena, I brought someone into my life, and it almost killed me and my bestfriend."

Mariah held Denise's hands. Denise could see the warmth in her eyes.

"Denise, I don't want you blaming yourself for that. The woman was crazy, certifiably. I swear, Denise, you are so hard on yourself. Even when I met you when you were starting school, I could see it then. You are so intense, so focused. I wonder if you ever let loose and just have fun."

Denise and Mariah's eyes locked into each other. Denise wanted to see into Mariah's soul. She wanted to see if this woman was as real as she was coming off.

"I always had to be strong. I had to be there for my grandmother, for my friends."

"And in the process who was there for you?" Mariah inched closer to Denise. "Denise, don't look at me as a potential girlfriend. Just look at me as a woman you are enjoying your time with. I'm not one of these little girls running around here. I just want us to enjoy being together, free to do what we please."

The heat between them became an inferno as the other commuters disappeared. Mariah leaned closer. Denise pulled Mariah's face to hers. Their lips met, tongues aflame searing hot wet kisses between them.

Denise stroked and pulled Mariah's fiery red hair. She didn't want to let go.

The color no longer mattered. They strolled through New York's streets, fingers locked, occasionally grasping at each other, hands often roaming freely, discovering secrets in open view of the city's indifferent pedestrians. Denise felt free, free to do whatever she wanted to do, not holding back in fear.

Mariah unlocked the door to her Soho loft. They didn't make it to the bedroom. Denise scooped Mariah into her strong arms. Mariah locked her legs around Denise. Their tongues craved each other. Denise pushed Mariah's body against the wall. The streetlights cast an ornate backdrop of shadows. Mariah's feet slowly touched the floor. Denise unbuttoned Mariah's skinny jeans, pulling them down while Mariah pulled her blue-and-white blouse over her head.

On her knees, Denise pulled off Mariah's black lace panties. She hadn't seen a pussy so bare and smooth. The small landing strip of reddish brown hair was smooth and lay neatly.

Denise spread Mariah's legs. Her index finger grazed Mariah's clit before entering her hot pussy. Denise looked up at Mariah who was looking up at the ceiling. Her naked body was appealing, but something was holding Denise back. As beautiful as her body was, it couldn't hold a candle to the soft, thick curves of Lena's body. Lena had the body of a goddess and Denise couldn't help but compare and contrast the two. Mariah was new and different, and while beautiful, the differences stood out, so that Denise couldn't possibly ignore them.

Denise stood up.

Realizing nothing was happening, Mariah looked at Denise bewildered. The worried expression said enough. "Denise, come on."

"Mariah, I—"

Mariah walked away from Denise. Denise wanted to shoot herself. She watched Mariah's naked frame walk up a few steps. She pulled a sliding shade door.

Denise followed. "Mariah, I'm—"

Mariah pulled Denise into the room. Denise fell against the king-size bed.

"Fuck that, Denise. Don't talk." Mariah got on top of her. She unbuttoned Denise's belt and pulled it off with one tug. "Denise, you are not about to have me all hot and bothered and keep stopping." She unbuttoned Denise's jeans. "So I've decided that since you can't seem to get things poppin', I'll just take over. Maybe you aren't as hard as I thought."

Denise's head turned fast. "What did you just say?"

"I'm saying, maybe I just need"—Mariah yanked on Denise's pants.

"Man, fuck that!" Denise pulled Mariah to the bed and rolled over on top of her. Denise sat up on Mariah. She pressed her hands against Mariah's wrists, making sure she couldn't move.

Mariah fought back a smile.

"Don't ever question how hard I am. Obviously, you let my little photo shoot get it twisted in your head."

Mariah's pussy was soaking wet; she grinded her pelvis against Denise. "Then why don't you stop acting like a pussy and show me then."

Denise laughed. She was turned on by Mariah's attempt to be hard. She knew what Mariah was doing, and it was working. No woman had talked to her like that before.

Denise leaned in and planted her lips against Mariah's lips. Her fingers made their way down to Mariah's throbbing heat.

Denise eased her hand under Mariah's backside, pulling her body closer. "You want it?"

Mariah didn't respond. Her eyes locked in on the intensity in Denise's brown eyes.

"Tell me you want it." Denise stared back; this was a battle she was not going to lose. "Say it!" Denise's voice was low but strong.

"I want it," Mariah whispered.

"Louder." Denise pulled Mariah closer.

"Please, give it to me!"

Denise didn't know the feeling. She felt so primal. The sweet, caring side was gone; the hunter was alive and was ready to claim her prey. She stroked Mariah's breasts, rubbing her finger against her hard pink nipples. Her tongue sucked on Mariah's right nipple, sucking it, licking it, then more sucking.

Blood rushed to Mariah's face, causing her to turn nearly the same color as her hair. She moaned for more, and Denise obliged.

Denise's tongue entered Mariah's heat, her tongue dancing around Mariah's swollen clit. She sucked on the knot as her tongue vibrated around it.

The sucking and vibrations made Mariah yell. The neighbors were going to know Denise's name by the end of the night.

Denise pressed two fingers into Mariah's swollen hole while she sucked and caressed her breasts. She pressed in another and opened her wider as she slowly stroked the moaning woman. She began to thrust the fingers harder, faster and deeper into the cavernous dripping pussy, and Mariah began to tremble.

Denise went harder, turning her long fingers to stroke the top inside wall of her burning pussy. When she found the spot, Mariah's body jerked. Denise hit it over and over, causing Mariah's body to twitch and jerk like she was having convulsions.

"Denise . . ."

Professional went out the window. Mariah shouted obscenities with each thrust. The trembling grew faster, Mariah's legs bucked, tensing to a straight position. Her back arched, her mouth dropped. Words wanted to escape, but she couldn't speak. The approaching orgasm took over all her senses, leaving her helpless and at the mercy of Denise's strokes.

Denise felt her fire blazing, throbbing; she was ready to explode right with Mariah. She hit Mariah's spot again, this time pushing in the last finger and twisting her hand as she did. Denise rubbed the spot with every stroke. She pressed her body farther up against Mariah as Mariah tilted her pelvis forward.

Spread wide open, Mariah's hands clawed at the sheets as she struggled to move her now filled pussy closer to Denise.

"Fuck me. Please fuck it," she begged for the release that was building. It was coming, they were cumming.

Mariah, mouth wide open, tried to scream, but she couldn't. Denise gave her tongue to Mariah, which she gratefully took. She sucked it hard as Denise hit Mariah's G-spot while rubbing her pulsating clit.

Mariah reached for Denise's hand as Denise pressed harder into the woman. Her legs tensed to the point of cramps, and her hands pulled at Denise's flesh. She couldn't hold out any longer.

Mariah's orgasm erupted, and a flood covered Denise hand. The wetness triggered Denise's release. She shuddered and impaled Mariah as her muscles tensed. Mariah rode the fingers with wild abandon, screaming Denise's name as the tortuous orgasm spasmed throughout her body.

Both breathing heavily, Denise didn't want to leave Mariah's warmth. She slowly stroked and felt the tension of Mariah's pussy subside. She rubbed her clit.

Mariah licked her lips and reached for another lingering kiss as Denise slowly massaged the woman's pussy again. Mariah moaned and slowly rode the fingers stuffed inside of her.

Denise watched as the woman below her opened in wanton submission, taking the four fingers deep inside of her. She thrust herself down one last time before the final orgasm took hold of her. The strained expression on her face released the scream before her body lost its rigidity. She was spent.

Denise felt the hunter starting to retreat. She slowly pulled her fingers from inside and grazed the swollen clit as she did. Mariah's body involuntarily convulsed. Denise smiled as she collapsed on the bed next to Mariah, who wrapped her arms around her. Her rising chest was all else she could move. The hunter was gone, and Denise sealed the evening with a kiss to Mariah's forehead. Both women were spent.

***

The small restaurant was crowded with dressed-to-impress black women and men. The colorful art from the connecting art gallery adorned the walls with small price tags in each corner. The aroma of waffles and chicken made Lena's stomach rumble, making her realize how hungry she was.

Lena sat at a small table for two. She ordered a pomegranate mojito while waiting on Carmen. She watched the groups of couples and friends chatting over their meals, men and women having a good time together. She rarely had that feeling when she went out with Brandon and the other basketball player couples. She didn't know why she couldn't enjoy that part of her life which was slipping away from her.

"Sorry I'm late." Carmen sat down in the empty chair. "I couldn't find anything to wear."

With her fingers, Lena gestured like a person talking. Carmen playfully hit her friend. They both laughed.

The waitress brought over Lena's drink. Carmen took a sip before Lena could, and then decided to order the same thing.

The band began to play. Lena and Carmen moved in their seats to the soulful cover of Jill Scott's "A Long Walk." Others in the crowd also enjoyed the band.

"This is nice, huh?" Carmen leaned in, raising her voice so Lena could hear over the music.

"It is. I'm glad we came." Lena smiled.

Something was telling Lena to turn around. She glanced at the door. "Oh shit, we're being hunted." Lena laughed as two males watched them from the door.

Carmen looked at the two guys. "God, I hope they don't come over here." She rolled her eyes.

"Too bad." Lena said as the two men walked toward them.

"Excuse me, but my friend and I couldn't help but notice you two lovely women sitting here," the shorter of the two said.

The men looked completely different. One was short with a small beer gut poking out from his linen. The taller of the two caught Lena's eye. His mocha skin was smooth, facial hair lined perfectly. As he smiled, he resembled Morris Chestnut.

"You couldn't, huh?" Carmen tried to hide her disgust for the short man staring at her like she was a piece of meat.

"What can I say? I saw something amazing and I had to come over. My name is Chester." He held his hand out.

Carmen reluctantly shook his hand back.

"And"—the taller man extended his hand to Lena—"I'm Kenneth."

"Hello, Kenneth."

"And you are?" Chester licked his semi-chapped lips.

"Carmen." Carmen frowned.

Chester ignored her facial expression. "So, Miss Carmen, why would your man leave you alone on a Friday night?"

"He's at work." Carmen quickly responded.

Chester's face fell like a sad boy who just learned there's no Santa Claus.

"Oh well, it was nice meeting you." Chester's eyes began to scan the crowd for a new challenge.

"Is your man working too?" Kenneth flashed his smile again.

Lena blushed. "Actually I—"

"Lena. Lena Redding."

Lena looked up to see Nicole Crescent standing with two other basketball wives. Nicole was the leader of the Memphis Grizzlies basketball wives. Married to the highest-paid athlete had its perks. Nicole's huge diamond ring sparkled in the light.

"Hello, Nicole." Lena stood up to greet the ladies. "How are you ladies tonight?" Lena flashed her smile. They had been courting her for their group since her marriage. Nicole would like nothing more than to have the only woman who could truly compete with her in the looks department as her "frienemy."

"We're great. About to meet the fellas at the rooftop." Nicole's eyes darted over toward Kenneth. "Are you meeting Brandon there?" She smiled, knowing she was interrupting.

Lena knew Nicole could be ruthless. She would run to Brandon in a heartbeat. It was unacceptable for wives to flirt with other men. Nicole didn't like the fact that Lena wasn't under her wing like the other wives.

"Actually no, my friend Carmen and I were just grabbing a bite before heading home."

"Right. OK, well it was nice seeing you, girl. We should do lunch soon."

"Let's. Just give me a call." Lena smiled.

"I'll have my assistant set that up. See you later, Lena." Nicole and the other women walked off, giving one more glance at Lena as they walked to the door.

"Brandon Redding, huh?" Kenneth chimed in.

"Yes, he's my husband." Lena sat back in her chair.

Kenneth nodded his head. "Lucky man. Well, it was nice to meet you ladies."

Kenneth and Chester walked off. Carmen couldn't help but laugh. "Sorry, girl." Carmen snickered. "He was a cutie."

"I'm dammed if I do and dammed if I don't." Lena sat back in her chair.

"Maybe you're gonna have to look outside of the city." Carmen looked at Lena. "Or at girls." She grinned.

Lena threw a piece of ice at Carmen. Terrin entered her mind. "Actually I did meet a woman."

Carmen's eyes bulged. "Really now. Do tell."

The band's cover of Maxwell's "Bad Habits" echoed through the room.

"There's not much to tell. I met her on the plane to go see"—the thought of Denise caused Lena's stomach to knot up. "You know."

Carmen nodded her head, knowing it was hard for Lena to think about Denise.

"Then I ran into her today. Actually, she was with me when I had my little episode."

"Wow, girl." Carmen sipped her drink. "That sounds a little like fate to me. To meet someone in the air then see them again."

"Yeah, and she lives in my building."

"Oh, hell yes, sounds like fate to me," Carmen replied. "You should call her. See what she's about."

"I might just do that. "Lena thought about Terrin. Maybe she would try it out.

Lena let the sweet taste of her Moscato d'Asti wine trickle down her throat. The three drinks at the restaurant didn't put her on the level she wanted to be on, so she hoped the wine would take her to that higher level, but she knew she should have gone for something stronger, like vodka.

Lena opened her small laptop and turned it on. The Apple logo flashed across the screen. The first step was done. She turned on the computer. Lena knew the only way to face her issues was to hit them head-on.

Lena opened up the browser. A beautiful Bing.com photo popped up of Australia. *Sydney*, Lena thought to herself. That was far enough from Denise. She could fly to Sydney and never worry about seeing Denise again. *Yeah, right. with my luck I'll get off the plane and see a big picture of her as soon as I hit the baggage claim.*

Lena let her fingers touch the letter keys. She took a deep breath and typed in JOCKU. As soon as she clicked on the official Web site she was hit. Denise in various outfits spread across the Web site.

Butterflies filled her stomach. She continued to breathe through her mouth, letting the butterflies exit one by one. Amazement set in. She never saw Denise looking the way she looked. Denise was still dressed in male clothes, but with hints of feminine attire.

Lena noticed a black halter top; she made a mental note to purchase it. This was a different side of Denise; she liked it even more than the tomboy she fell in love with.

Questions filled Lena's head. *What was Denise doing right now? Had she met a model to fall in love with? Was the new look purely for the modeling, or was she dressing more feminine now? Was she ever coming back to Memphis?*

Lena picked her phone up. She wanted answers, and there was one person who could give them to her.

The phone seemed to dial more slowly than normal. All the questions she had were escaping her brain. Lena silently prayed for Denise's voice mail to pick up.

"You are gonna love this," Mariah said as she straddled Denise's lap. She stuck her finger in the chocolate sauce. "Taste it."

Denise laughed as Mariah's index finger entered her mouth. "That is some serious chocolate," Denise said as the rich taste took over her taste buds.

"Wait till you try it on those."

Mariah reached for a strawberry. She dipped the ripe fruit in the dark chocolate. She held the chocolate-dipped strawberry up. "Come and get it," she joked as some of the chocolate fell from the strawberry to her chest and rolled down her right breast.

"I think I will." Denise leaned in, licking the line of chocolate down until she reached Mariah's nipple.

The touch of her tongue excited Mariah's body, and her nipple instantly perked up.

Sarah Bareilles "Gravity" echoed from Denise's phone. Her body froze. She looked up confused. Only one person had that ringtone, Lena.

Mariah looked puzzled. "Do you need to get that?"

"Ummm . . ." Denise looked at Mariah. She felt like a child about to get in trouble for something. Mariah's lips tightened.

"It's her, isn't it?"

"Yes."

Mariah stood up. She smiled. "Well, go answer it."

"I . . . Are . . ."

"Denise, you do not owe me an explanation for anything. You aren't my girlfriend, remember. Go answer the phone. It might be important."

Denise realized the phone stopped ringing. She let out a sigh of relief and smiled. "See, it's not ringing anymore. No need."

"Denise." Mariah ran her hands through her hair and touched Denise's face. Softly she said, "Go call the girl back."

The new-found hunter in her wanted to ignore Lena and take Mariah in that spot, but the Jacob in her got her to stand up and go the room. She pressed send on her phone.

***

Lena listened to Denise's voice on her voice mail. She smiled; she missed Denise's deep, smooth voice. She knew the beep was coming. She took another sip of wine.

"Denise, hey, this is umm . . . Lena, but I'm sure you know that. Well, I jus . . ."

Lena's phone beeped. She looked at the screen. Denise's face appeared on the screen in front of her. She froze, the green answer button flashing in front of her.

Lena took a deep breath and pressed the button. "Hello."

Lena's voice sent chills down Denise's back. "Uh, hi, Lena, it's Dee." Lena's body trembled. Denise felt butterflies starting to flutter. "You called me?"

Lena stood up and began to pace the floor. "Yes, I, um, I did." Beyoncé's version of "Kissing You" by Desiree began to play from her stereo system, making the talk ten times harder. "I just, it's been a while, and I wanted to call and—"

"Lena, can I say something first?" Denise sat on the edge of the bed. She could hear the hurt in Lena's voice as she tried to get her words together.

"Sure," Lena stopped pacing.

"Lena, when you came here I was in a really bad place. I had just found out I wasn't going to be playing ball and I was drunk. I said some things I really regret and I am really, really so sorry for them."

Lena smiled as tears began to form in her eyes. "Denise . . ."

"I'm so sorry, Lena. I can't believe I was so mean to you. Carmen told me about what happened. I'm so sorry. I wanted to call you, but I didn't know what to say."

"Denise, I think it's fair to say we've both done some things that we regret. I just want us to move past them."

Denise smiled. "Me too. I miss you as a friend."

Friend? The word hit Lena head-on. "So is that it Dee? You only want to be my friend?" A tear fell from Lena's eye.

Denise's heart skipped a beat. The line was silent.

"Denise . . ."

"Lena." Denise felt the knot forming in her throat. She looked up; Mariah's nude body sat on the couch, flipping through the channels.

Lena's body entered her head. There was no comparison, Lena's body surpassed Mariah's in every way. But the drama that went along with Lena took away from all her beauty.

"I'm sorta seeing someone."

Lena felt her knees going weak. Denise's words hit her harder than any punch ever could. She held on to the side of the desk. Tears streamed down her face. Her voice trembled. "Oh."

Denise felt her eyes beginning to water, her heart breaking right along with Lena's.

"Lena, I'm so sorry, I never wanted to—"

"I have to go. Good-bye, Denise." Lena hung the phone up without waiting for a response. She couldn't bear it anymore.

She threw her phone against the wall. She didn't want any reminder of Denise. She knew if she kept the phone, she would pass her number or her face in the phone. She'd given up everything for Denise, and now she was alone and heartbroken.

Lena cried the Mississippi. She wiped the tears until her face was numb and raw. She couldn't take it anymore. Denise's happy face haunted her. The thoughts of Denise holding another woman infuriated Lena.

She ran to her kitchen. She grabbed the first bottle she could get her hands on. The strong 1800 Platinum tequila burned worse than vodka ever did. She loved the feeling; numb was better than hurting.

Lena heard a knock on her door. She ignored it. There was no one she wanted to see right then.

The knock continued.

She looked at the door. The door was evil, and whoever was on the other side had to be destroyed. Lena stormed over to the iron door, pulling it open with all of her rage.

"What!"

Lena's reaction caused Terrin to jump. She stood there dumbfounded.

Lena paused. Terrin's look was back to how she remembered her from the airplane. Her baggy khaki, board shorts and pink and grey polo shirt hung down with a pair of brown flip-flops.

"Oh, I'm sorry," Lena said, wiping her face.

"I'm really sorry. I didn't mean to interrupt anything. I just I was worried about you from earlier so I wanted to do something"—Terrin reached down and picked up a large box—"to brighten your day."

Lena looked at Terrin, whose face was covered with concern. Lena stood up straight. "I'm sorry, you just . . . I'm sorry, come on in," Lena said, pushing the door farther open.

Terrin walked into the house.

"Lena, sweetie, what's wrong?" Terrin said as Lena poured herself a glass of tequila.

"Nothing," Lena lied. "Would you like something to drink?"

Terrin sat the box on the table. She walked over to Lena. "No, and I don't think you need anything either." She took the glass from Lena as she was tilting it to her mouth. "Come here and open my gift."

Terrin's smile warmed the coldness in Lena's heart.

Terrin took Lena by her hand and guided her to the table. They sat down at the table. Lena looked at the box with Edible Arrangements written on it. Lena looked up at Terrin.

"You really didn't have to do this."

Terrin smiled. "Open it before you make that statement."

"I can't."

"Fine. I'll do it for you." Terrin pulled the box near her. "See, after I left you, something hit me. I recognized the person on the wall, so I googled it and realized who it was."

"Terrin, I'm sorry—"

Terrin interrupted Lena. "Then, I also realized that this woman on the wall had such an impact that you couldn't be in the store. She hurt you in ways that I can't even imagine. Your face, it looked like you were in a dark place. I wanted to do something to bring some light into your life."

Terrin pulled the display out. Beautiful suns carved in pineapple along with pineapple daisies and strawberries sat in a green woven basket. The ice on Lena's heart was melting rapidly.

"This is so beautiful. Thank you, Terrin, but . . . I don't deserve it." A tear fell from Lena's eye. "Denise did hurt me, but honestly I hurt myself." Lena looked up at Terrin, whose eyes were fixated on her. "I strung her along for two years. I knew she loved me, I knew I loved her, but I couldn't let go of my life and Brandon. She deserved to do and say what she did to me. Now, she's with someone else, and there's nothing I can do to change that."

Terrin stood up. She walked over to Lena. Lena put her head on Terrin's shoulder. Terrin wrapped her arms around Lena, "Lena, you were in a bad situation, and you dealt with it the best way you could. Coming out is a difficult thing, and if a person truly loves you, they will understand that."

"But . . ."

"No buts. Look, trust me, I understand your situation. I know it has to be hard to be getting over your first female love. I just want to let you know that you don't have to do it alone. In fact"—Terrin pulled Lena to her feet—"get your shoes."

"Terrin, I don't need to go anywhere. Look at me, I look a mess."

"You look beautiful." Terrin's eyes met Lena's.

Lena felt a twinge in her stomach. Terrin smiled. Lena couldn't help but notice her beautiful smile.

"Where are we going?"

"No questions. Just put your shoes on and let's go."

Lena and Terrin pulled up to a small hole-in-the-wall club. Inside was packed with a diverse mix of people. Lena quickly realized there were no men. A butch white woman stood on a small stage butchering her version of "Honkey Tonk Badonka Donk" by Trace Adkins.

"Karaoke? This is your great idea?" Lena said as they maneuvered through the crowd.

Terrin greeted many of the women.

"Yeah. What better than getting drunk and singing off-key?" The bartender handed Terrin a beer before she ordered, and a karaoke book.

"Hey, T, who's your friend?" the white woman asked from behind the bar.

Lena liked her black Harley Davidson vest.

"Rosco, this is Lena. Lena, this is Rosco, the owner."

"Nice to meet you, Lena. Boy, T, you sure know how to pick them," Rosco said, looking Lena up and down.

"Chill out, it's not like that. We're just here to do some karaoke."

"Yeah, OK. What can I get for you, darling?"

"Umm, what's that?" Lena pointed to a bucket of a red liquid.

Terrin started to laugh.

Rosco laughed. "Well, we call that Anything. Drink it and by the end of the night you will be down for anything."

"Can it cure a broken heart?"

"Oh yeah." Rosco smiled.

"Well, I'll take that."

Rosco grinned as she poured a cup of the cocktail.

Terrin shook her head.

"What?"

"I just want to see how much you get down." Terrin flipped through the pages of the song book.

"Please, I'm an Atlanta black socialite, I've been drinking since I was ten."

"OK, Miss Thang, let loose."

Lena stood up. "I think I will." She turned and walked over to the karaoke DJ.

"So, how new is she?" Rosco asked Terrin.

"Very. Only one girl in her past."

"I bet you are looking to change that. She's beautiful. She could be the one."

"I'm two steps ahead of you. That right there could be my future wife."

"In that case . . ." Rosco walked over to the karaoke DJ as Lena made it back to her seat. She whispered something to the big butch woman's ear.

"What was that all about?" Terrin asked as Lena took a drink from her cup.

The powerful concoction caused Lena to cough.

"Damn, that is powerful." Lena made a face. "I'm going to sing a song."

"Wow. Can you sing?"

"Maybe." Lena smiled. "Or maybe not."

"This is gonna be great." Terrin sat back with her elbows on the bar.

The butch karaoke DJ stood up. "OK, now we have coming to the stage a very special treat. Ladies, start your engines. We have a newbie and a KC's Bar virgin in the house."

The women in the bar swooned while looking around.

"Lena, come on up to the mic."

Lena's eyes popped. "Damn, that fast?"

"Let's say I have some connections." Terrin looked at Rosco, who winked.

Lena downed her drink and sauntered to the front. Women began to cat-call as soon as Lena hit the stage.

"Easy, ladies, let's not scare her before we get her," the DJ said.

Lena looked over and blushed. The music began to play.

Terrin couldn't stop smiling.

Lena looked at her while singing the words of Mariah Carey's "I Don't Want to Cry." Terrin couldn't take her eyes off Lena.

The crowd hung on to her every word, as Lena belted out the song. She felt the words like they were coming from her soul. She wanted to cry, but she didn't. Instead, she focused on Terrin, who was mesmerized.

The song ended, and the crowd went wild. Lena blushed as women attempted to talk to her while giving her compliments on her song. She walked over to Terrin, who was still clapping.

"Stop it."

"What? Girl, I was not expecting that. Damn, you got a voice on you," Terrin roared. "What are you doing next?"

"Nothing at all. That was all I needed to do. I just want to have fun now. Thanks, Terrin, for bringing me out. I needed this."

"Any time."

Terrin and Lena's eyes locked. Lena knew she was losing it. She was hurting over Denise, but couldn't help but feel an attraction to Terrin. She didn't know what to think. She had never been attracted to another woman before.

Lena sat back and watched an overweight woman attempt to be Effie White by singing "And I Am Telling You."

Carmen's voice entered Lena's head.

"The best way to get over one is to get under another."

24

Thoughts of Lena woke Denise up in the middle of the night. She pulled herself free from Mariah and walked into the living room and sat on Mariah's couch. She couldn't shake the images of Lena filling her mind. She pictured her crying, each tear burning a hole in Denise's heart. Her heart wanted her to call, but her brain told her no.

Denise looked around at Mariah's amazing apartment. *How did I get here?* Denise questioned herself. Her life was nothing like it was supposed to be. A part of Denise wanted to walk out the house, get on a plane, and go back to Memphis.

Then she thought about what she had waiting in Memphis. She had no career there. In New York she had three modeling gigs booked. In Memphis she had Lena. But then she remembered that Lena was still very married. In New York she had a beautiful, successful woman helping her to reach heights she never knew existed.

Denise lay back on the couch. She knew deep in her soul that she had made the right decision. *Mema, am I making the right choices? Give me a sign*, Denise thought as she looked up into the darkness. She drifted off to sleep while waiting on the sign.

***

The sound of Mariah talking on her cell phone woke Denise up. She realized she was still sleeping on the couch. She looked up to see Mariah fully dressed in a black business suit. Her wild, red hair was pulled back in a precise up-do.

The loud smell of coffee brewing woke Denise up further. She stood up and walked into the kitchen.

"Yes, well, we can get her twice that amount for sure." Mariah kissed Denise on her cheek. "Well, that is what we pay you for, make it happen, Jeff." Mariah held the coffee pot up.

Denise shook her head, declining the offer.

Mariah poured a cup of coffee and took a sip. "Well, I'll be in very soon. Have things right when I get there. Good-bye." Mariah hung the phone up and took a deep breath. "Hey, you."

"I'm sorry about last night."

Mariah looked at Denise. "What are you talking about? Last night was amazing."

Denise thought about the rounds and rounds of sex they had. She felt the need to make up for the awkward moment with Lena. "Well, you know, the phone call."

"Denise, really, it was not a big deal. Again, you are single."

"I know. I just felt it was a bit disrespectful for me to take the call."

Mariah shook her head. "Oh, Denise, sweetie, you have to give up some of that southern gentleman thing. This is New York. There was nothing disrespectful about it. It wasn't like you were talking to her while I was going down on you. Speaking of, when am I?"

"No time soon." Denise cut Mariah off. "I give, not receive."

"We'll see about that." Mariah winked. "So are you heading back to the hotel or staying here?"

"I'm going back to check out and get the last of my things. Then I was going to go look around for places."

"Why, Denise? I said it was fine for you to stay here."

"I just would feel better having my own place."

"I guess. It's kinda foolish though, don't. you think? You don't know where you are going to end up next. What if you are sent to Paris or something?"

"I doubt that will happen."

"Well, don't sign anything until I look it over." Mariah took a bite out of a bagel.

Denise couldn't believe how quickly Mariah could turn on her professional side.

"Well, I have to run. You want a ride?"

"No, I'll take the subway."

Mariah laughed. "Right. Take a cab."

"Fine."

Mariah pecked Denise on her lips and headed out the door.

Denise poured a glass of orange juice and sat down on the couch. She picked up her phone and called Carmen.

"I am so going to kill you," Carmen exclaimed.

"I'm sorry, C. Things have been crazy."

"You and Cooley are such sucky friends, you know that. You leave me here to rot away in Memphis while you are off modeling and hanging out with stars. This is some bullshit."

"Carmen, as soon as I'm settled, you can come visit me."

"Whatever."

Denise listened to Carmen rant about her boring life. She knew deep down Carmen didn't mean it. She loved being a housewife more than anything else.

"Carmen, have you talked to Lena today?"

Carmen flipped through *Black Hair*. "Not today. Why?"

"She called me yesterday."

Carmen paused. "What happened?"

"I hurt her again. I didn't mean to. I told her about Mariah."

"Ugh." Carmen rolled her eyes. She hadn't met Mariah, but she didn't like the idea of Denise dating a white woman. "Why did you tell her about the white girl?"

"Why she gotta be the white girl, Carmen?"

"Because I just know you could do better."

"Said the girl dating Rico Suave."

"At least she ain't white."

"Carmen, you sound real wrong right now, and you know it."

Carmen rolled her eyes again. "I know. Look, it's not just that she's white. I'm just in hater-bitch mode right now."

Denise chuckled. "Hater bitch?"

"Yes, I'm hating because you are in New York and I'm not." Carmen stood up. "I just miss my friends."

"Don't worry, we will see you soon. But can we get back on the main issue? What about Lena?"

"Denise, let it go. You told her, so she knows. Now maybe she can work on herself, and move on."

"I felt so bad. I heard her crying. Carmen, it was breaking my heart. Can you just check on her for me today and make sure she's all right?"

"Of course."

"Thanks. Let me go. I have to meet my agent."

"Oh, shut the fuck up! I hate you and your fabulous life." Carmen sighed.

"I love you too. Bye."

***

Denise looked around the hotel room one last time to make sure she didn't forget anything.

Cooley walked into the room holding a bottle of orange juice.

"Well, look who decides to remember it's her best-friends last day."

Cooley hit Denise on her arm. "You better have fucked her if you left me in this room alone."

Denise sat on the bed. She grinned. "Cooley, I think I channeled you last night."

"What? Get out."

"Man, I fucked the hell out of that woman."

Cooley laughed. "Hell yeah, that's my dog! Was she good?"

"Amazing. Wild as hell."

"I knew she was wild. I could tell by that red hair. I bet she's a lady in the streets and a super freak in the sheets."

"You right on that."

The two friends gave each other daps.

"Things were great until Lena called."

"Uh-oh, what now?"

"I told her I was dating."

"No shit?" Cooley sat in the desk chair. "What did she say?"

"She was crying, but she was trying not to let me know. I felt like shit afterwards."

Cooley looked at Denise. "Man, you did the right thing. Lena might have been the shit in college, but honestly besides looks, she ain't got shit on Mariah. You gotta think about the big picture. Fucking with Mariah will have you rich. Fucking with Lena will have you broke, living in Memphis, and dodging her crazy-ass husband."

Denise nodded in agreement. "You're right. Mariah is amazing, and I wouldn't have shit without her. Oh, and her attitude is the shit. She is cool with not being my girl."

"That's 'cause she is a grown-ass, independent woman. Those types don't have time for full-time girlfriends. They know the deal. It's about being happy." Cooley stood up. "And being happy right about now is all that matters."

Denise stood up. "I wish you could stay longer."

"Me too, but duty calls. Look out for Sahara's album to drop; it's gonna be hot."

Cooley and Denise hugged.

"Let me get out of here before I miss my damn plane. Love ya, bruh and remember . . . do what is going to make you happy and make you money."

"Get money, huh?"

"Damn right."

Cooley walked out of the room, leaving Denise with a whole new outlook on life.

Lena's eyes slowly began to focus. She looked at the beautiful painting of a woman's body on the wall. *That's nice*, she thought to herself as she turned back over. Lena jumped up. *I don't have that painting.* Lena looked around the room. *Oh my God, where am I?*

Lena crawled out of the queen-sized bed. The cold hardwood alerted her senses even more. She could hear a TV from outside the bedroom. She hesitated, afraid of what she would see when she walked out. *I'm still dressed. That's a good thing.*

Lena tiptoed out the bedroom. Wendy Williams' voice grew as she walked closer. She smelled something cooking. It smelled amazing. She peeked around the corner. Lena let out a sigh of relief when she saw Terrin standing in the kitchen flipping pancakes.

Terrin caught Lena in her peripheral. She turned her head and smiled.

"Hey, drunky! Pancakes?"

"Oh my goodness, what did I drink last night?" Lena sat down at the small iron table. It was covered in splashes of paint.

"Two large cups of *anything*." Terrin walked over with a plate of four pancakes. She placed it in front of Lena. "I must say it was an amazing sight."

Mortified, Lena looked at Terrin. "Did I make an ass of myself? Don't tell me. Considering the fact that I woke up and didn't know where I was, I'm pretty sure I did."

Terrin sat at the table. "Actually, you just sang a few more songs. You get really flirty when you're drunk."

"What!"

"Let's just say you wanted to act out the song, 'I kissed a girl.'"

Lena covered her mouth. "No! I didn't."

Terrin shook her head. "Yeah, you did. But it was cool. You are a good kisser. I can tell you that."

"I kissed you?"

"No, you kissed my homegirl Rena. But she said you were a great kisser."

"OK, shoot me now."

"Aww, now." Terrin smiled.

Lena felt the butterflies waking up in her stomach.

"You needed to have fun, and you did. I didn't expect you to let loose like that. It was very sexy."

"Sexy? A drunken girl singing and kissing on folks is sexy?"

Terrin let out a chuckle. "It was, actually. You were free to do what you wanted. Something I have a feeling you don't do."

Lena blushed. "Well, when you have to watch your appearance in fear of ending up on Mediatakeout.com it's kinda hard to let go."

"I bet." Terrin stood up and walked into the kitchen. "So, tell me something Lena, and if I'm getting too personal, feel free to tell me." Terrin came back in holding a pitcher of apple juice.

Lena nodded her head giving the go-ahead.

"What is the deal with you and Brandon? I haven't read on MediaTakeOut that you are getting a divorce." Terrin giggled.

Lena swallowed the piece of pancake in her mouth. "Well, he moved out, but we are supposed to be taking this time to figure out what we really want."

"Do you know what you really want?" Terrin stared into Lena's eyes.

Lena felt the heat rising in her seat.

"I'm not one hundred percent sure of anything yet."

"But you are sure that you like women." Terrin didn't lose eye contact. She stared at Lena, trying to see into her brain.

Lena didn't know what to say. Her deer-in-the-headlights expression said it all.

"You don't have to answer if you don't want to."

Lena looked down at the pancakes in front of her. "It's a simple question. I can't believe it's so hard to answer."

"It's cool, Lena. It's a confusing time for you. I remember when I first realized I was into women."

Lena looked back up at Terrin. "It's just that I've never wanted women before. Then Denise came along. I was never attracted before her. Until recently I thought that I was only attracted to her, but lately, I'm finding myself looking at other women."

Lena locked eyes with Terrin. Terrin blushed. Lena's long hair fell on her face. Terrin reached over, pushing the fallen hair behind Lena's ear. She put her palm on Lena's cheek. Lena felt the warmth in her hand. She grazed her cheek against Terrin's hand.

"Lena, I know we haven't known each other long, but I knew on the plane that there was something drawing me to you. I'm a believer in fate, and I think there's a reason we were on that plane together. I saw you in the café, and hell, we live in the same building. Someone is trying to tell us something. I can't lie. I don't want to ignore it."

Lena sighed. "I just . . . Terrin, I don't want to get involved with you, knowing I have my situation with Denise."

"I understand. I don't expect you to jump into my arms. I would just like the chance to really get to know Lena Redding for who she is. Maybe help you in finding who you really want to be."

Lena's heart was racing. She studied Terrin's oval face and smooth caramel skin. Her big brown eyes were drawing Lena in. Her leg trembled as butterflies ran throughout her body.

"I just don't want to hurt another woman."

"Lena, if hurting me in the long run helps to heal you, then go right ahead. I'm a big girl, I can take it."

The warmth turned to a full fire. Lena shifted in her seat. She couldn't think straight with Terrin staring at her. She wanted Terrin's hand on her. She wanted to feel the warmth of Terrin's body next to hers.

"I think I need to go home."

"Are you sure?" Terrin questioned, trying to hide her disappointment.

Lena stood up. "I have a lot to think about. But if it's all right with you, I would like to see you again, maybe tonight."

Terrin's lips curved upward. She stood up and wrapped her arms around Lena.

Lena felt a familiar safety in Terrin's arms, the same safety she felt when Denise held her.

"That sounds great." Terrin reluctantly let Lena go.

Lena felt like she was floating all the way to her home. She unlocked the door and pulled it open. She walked in with her eyes closed and sighed.

"Where have you been?"

"Shit!" Lena jumped at the deep voice. She opened her eyes to see Brandon standing with an awkward expression on his face. "You scared the living daylights out of me."

"Lena, where have you been all night?"

"Umm, I was at Car—"

"Before you form your mouth to lie, Carmen has called here three times looking for yo ass." Brandon's voice rumbled.

Lena's eyes widened. She looked at his tall physique. He looked amazing in his jeans and blue polo shirt.

"See, I wasn't even about to say Carmen's. You know my sorority sister, Carla. We had a girls' night out last night."

"Girls' night out, huh?" Brandon huffed. "Right, Lena." Brandon walked to the bedroom.

Lena followed.

"Did it include the nigga you was with at Onyx?"

Lena rolled her eyes. She wanted to kill Nicole. "See, I knew that bitch was gonna take that shit the wrong way. I wasn't with that guy, his friend was trying to get at Carmen. Wait, why are you questioning me anyway? I haven't talked to you in forever."

"I'm not really questioning you. I just thought we were past all the lies. And it's tacky as hell for you to be all up on some nigga in public like that. Then you stay out all night!"

"I wasn't on anyone. I didn't even know the guy, and I told you where I was. I'm not lying to you."

Brandon stopped and looked at Lena.

Lena sighed. "OK, so I was lying, damn. Truth is, I went out with a friend I met in this building, and I got drunk and fell asleep on her couch. But it wasn't a guy, and I really wasn't on anyone at Onyx."

Brandon stared at Lena. "A friend in the building, huh? Gay or straight."

"Brandon, what the hell . . ."

"Gay or straight, Lena?" Brandon opened his dresser drawer.

Lena tried to read his straight face.

"She's gay."

Brandon started laughing. "Wow, OK. Well, I just stopped by to get some things. I won't be long."

"Brandon, don't act like that!"

Brandon continued to pull clothes out with a smirk on his face. "I'm not acting like anything."

"Ugh, whatever." Lena sat on the edge of their bed. She didn't like his nonchalant attitude. She preferred when he got angry.

"So, what's up, Lena? Are you gay now or something?" Brandon turned to Lena.

"You are seriously pissing me off right now."

"What's the deal with Denise? I saw her modeling shit. Guess she got up to NY and trying to blow up. What? No time for seducing my wife anymore?"

Brandon's words cut Lena like a rusty knife. She rolled her eyes. "I don't know. I haven't talked to her in forever."

Brandon pressed his lips together and nodded his head. "Well, wife, I guess I have everything I need."

Lena watched as Brandon pushed his expensive clothes into one of their pieces of luggage. Although angry, Lena was strangely attracted to him. She walked up behind him and put her arms around him.

Brandon turned around to her.

"What are you doing?"

Lena smirked. "I don't know."

Brandon frowned. He pushed Lena away. "Well, do that when you know what you are doing." Brandon kissed Lena on her forehead and walked out the room, leaving Lena's face on the floor.

Lena's fire was burning hot. Between Terrin and Brandon, she had to do something. She didn't have anything to pleasure herself, no toys to help her get the orgasm her body was pleading for. Lena pulled her pants off and shirt over her head. She stretched her body across her expensive comforter, spreading her legs apart. Her fingers rubbed her swollen button, making her pussy wetter than before.

"Lena, you know something . . ."

Brandon walked into the room. Lena jumped. Brandon's eyes bucked. Lena looked at Brandon, Brandon stared back. He walked over to the bed, pulling his shirt off.

Lena sat up and unbuttoned Brandon's pants. His jeans fell to the ground.

Brandon's manhood stood at attention. Lena's hands stroked his hard shaft. Brandon slowly got on top. Their mouths met. Brandon kissed his passion into Lena's mouth. Lena scratched her fingers down Brandon's broad backside.

Brandon pulled Lena's leg up, slowly entering her fire. He moaned as Lena's cave curved around his dick.

Lena closed her eyes. Brandon's tongue danced on her nipple while he stroked in and out, in and out. Her fire burned for him. Lena moaned for more; she had forgotten how he felt inside her. Her queen missed his king.

Brandon stroked as though he was on a mission. He wanted to fuck all lesbian thoughts out of Lena's head. He wanted to remind her why she married him, why they were together for so long.

"God, I love you, Lena," Brandon murmured in between sucking on her erect nipples.

"I love you too." Lena's passion spoke for her. The pleasure was creeping up her leg, making its way through her thighs. Every stroke of Brandon's massiveness brought Lena pleasure and pain, pure ecstasy.

Lena's body jerked. She dug her nails into Brandon's back, and the pain brought Brandon's orgasm. Lena and Brandon exploded together, both dying a thousand deaths that they hadn't experienced together in a long time.

Brandon and Lena struggled to catch their breath. Lena rolled over, placing her head on Brandon's hard chest. Brandon ran his hand through Lena's hair. Words escaped them; they just lay together.

Lena woke up a few hours later. Brandon was sound asleep, snoring next to her. She smiled, her womanhood still sore from the workout he put on her.

Lena sat up in the bed, her leg ending in her wetness from their orgasm. Her smile began to fall. Happiness escaped her; she felt empty.

Lena stood up staring at Brandon's face. He looked the same, his chest going up and down. She looked at the tattoo of her name written on his chest, a tattoo he only got because she caught him in a compromising position.

Lena walked into the bathroom, her pussy still sore from their romp. She looked at herself in the mirror. Her body felt good, but her soul felt empty. Lena turned the shower on and got in. The warm water from the three shower heads hit her body in all the right spots. She washed the scent of sex from her estranged husband off of her body.

Lena walked back into the bedroom. Brandon was no longer in the bed. She could hear the shower running from the guest bathroom. Lena looked in her closet. She looked at all her designer clothes. She thought about Nicole and the other basketball wives. She was like them in so many ways, but also completely different.

She knew that with Brandon her life could never be like her first year in college. She missed the days of just seeming normal like Carmen and Denise. She knew being with Brandon meant embracing the high-society life she grew up in and detested.

"Hey." Brandon walked back into the room in just a pair of basketball sweats and no shirt. He sat on the side of the bed. "I guess we need to talk."

Lena looked at Brandon. She realized they had opened a can of worms they couldn't just close. She knew life would be easier if she just stayed with him. She would never have to tell her parents she was getting divorced. But she knew her love for Denise had opened another can that also couldn't be closed. She was attracted to women.

"Brandon, I don't really know what to say at this point."

"Lena, it's obvious we still have something. Why can't we just try to—?"

"Brandon we never had an issue in the bedroom. It's the other shit."

"So what do we do, Lena?

"Brandon, can you sit here and tell me that you will never cheat on me again? That you won't run across that one groupie you just can't resist?"

Brandon's forehead wrinkled. "Can you sit here and tell me you are never going to want to fuck another woman?"

Silence filled the room. Lena lowered her head.

Brandon's anger began to flare. "That's some bullshit, Lena. You are not fucking gay!"

"I don't know what I am. God, this is frustrating!" Lena threw her hands up. "I don't know anything right now. I don't know who I am anymore. I know nothing!"

Lena's body was trembling. She had come face to face with reality, and was confused.

Brandon could see the agony in Lena's face. He stood up, walking over and placing his arms around her.

"Lena, calm down." Brandon didn't know what to think of Lena's tantrum. He didn't recognize his wife anymore. Brandon's head dropped. He rubbed his hand through his hair. "Lena, I don't know what to do anymore. I don't know how to help you, how to be there for you with this. I don't know if I can sit back and wait on my wife to realize if she wants to be with me or not."

Lena looked at Brandon, his brow wrinkled, lips locked. She was breaking him. "I'm not asking you to wait."

Brandon looked at Lena. She had never given him permission to move on before; it hurt him to know she could give him that option so easily. "When you figure out what the hell you want, you know where to find me. Just hope someone else hasn't found me first."

Lena wanted to yell at him for his statement, but she couldn't talk. She watched as Brandon gathered his things. She wanted to tell him to stay, but something was holding her back.

Brandon looked at Lena, hoping she would say anything, but she didn't. He shook his head. The muscles in his arms bulged as he held his anger in; he gave up and walked out the room.

Lena looked at the large print of their wedding photo hanging on the wall. They looked so happy, so in love, but it was all a sham. She wondered how they pulled it off, how they were able to fool everyone, including each other. Behind the smiles were secrets. Brandon's baby's mother had interrupted their wedding celebration, only to be detained with a story about a crazed fan. Lena, holding her own secret, let Denise make love to her for the first time only hours before they said, "I do."

Brandon finished getting dressed in the guest bathroom. He peered at his reflection in the mirror; he had done so much dirt to Lena over the years. All the groupies that he shared his bed with had caught up to him. Karma was taking care of him; he was losing his beautiful wife.

Brandon opened the door to see Lena standing in the doorway of their bedroom. Their eyes met. Two beautiful people who had a beautiful wedding, and a beautiful life now falling apart in front of them.

"I don't want to lose you in my life." Lena wrapped her arms around his strong torso. Brandon put his arms around Lena, holding her as though it was the last time.

"You will never lose me in your life. I love you and always will."

"What do we do now?"

"You can keep the loft, your car, and we can work the rest out."

Lena buried her head in Brandon's chest. She felt safe in his arms, but not the type of safety she desired. "OK."

Brandon fought his tears back. He pulled away from Lena. He placed a single kiss on her lips; they both knew it would be the last.

25

Cooley's beautiful desk was covered with papers, CDs, and photos of Sahara. The singles were bona fide hits. She knew it had to be backed up with the best CD possible. She pressed the track button on her remote, skipping to the next possible song for the CD.

Sahara's voice enticed Cooley. She fidgeted in her seat. Cooley tried to remember the last time she had sex. She knew it was too long. She needed some and she needed some bad. Sahara's pictures didn't help the situation. Her smooth caramel skin, round ass and plump breasts were calling to Cooley, and she wanted to answer. A slow knock on the door brought Cooley out of her sexual trance.

"Come in!" Cooley shifted in her chair.

The door opened slowly. Tee walked in slowly.

"What's up, Tee?" Cooley noticed the pained expression on Tee's face. Her eyes red and puffy, her lips pressed tight together. "What's wrong?"

"Cool," Tee's voice trembled, "I'm so sorry."

Cooley stood up. She walked from behind her desk. "What is going on?"

Cooley's phone began to blare. She picked the phone up and checked her messages.

R.I.P Keisha "Supa Sonic" Jackson. Jam Zone has lost a family member today. Sonic you will always be loved and missed.

Cooley held her phone tight. The text blurred. She couldn't move. "What happened?"

Tee struggled to respond. "She . . . she OD'd" Tears began to fall from Tee's face.

Cooley fought the tears back. "I need a moment. Close the door behind you," Cooley said, never looking up from her screen.

Tee immediately obeyed.

It felt like a bus crashed into Cooley. Her legs felt weak. She sat on the edge of her desk. Cooley closed her eyes, trying to block the images of Sonic running through her head. She could see her so vividly; the last time they saw each other, Sonic's frail state. *This is all my fault.*

Tears streamed down Cooley's face. Cooley knew the news must have hit everyone. Her phone started to blare back to back. She couldn't pick it up; she couldn't face anyone. Guilt took over her body, as the images of Sonic played like a movie in her brain.

Cooley didn't hear the door open. Sahara walked in, her makeup flawed with streaks from her overflowing tears. Sahara walked over to Cooley. She put her palm on Cooley's shoulder.

Cooley didn't look up. Sahara's hand was like a magnet, bringing the emotions all the way to the surface. Cooley leaned into Sahara. Sahara wrapped her arms around Cooley.

"It's my fault, it's all my fault," Cooley cried.

"No, baby, it's not." Sahara held Cooley in her arms, rocking her gently.

"I shouldn't have pushed her. I pushed her. Oh God. Why! Why!" Cooley's voice cracked. She wrapped her arms around Sahara. Sahara was only the second woman to see her cry. She held on to her, not wanting to let go.

"Carla, it's not your fault. She wouldn't want you blaming yourself. You did what you could. You were a friend to her, she knows that. Don't do this to yourself. Come on, baby, don't do this, Carla."

Cooley looked up at Sahara. "What did you call me?"

Sahara's big brown eyes widened. "I'm sorry, I didn't."

Cooley put her index finger up to Sahara's soft plump lips. "My name, I never liked when people called me by my real name." Cooley gazed into Sahara's beautiful eyes. She ran her fingers through Sahara's wavy hair.

Sahara looked at Cooley with a confused glare.

"I liked that."

Cooley slowly pulled Sahara's face to hers. Their lips gently met. Sahara parted her lips, allowing Cooley's tongue to enter into a passionate dance. Sahara held on to Cooley's T-shirt, wrinkling the fabric with the imprint of her fingers.

Cooley's hand rubbed through Sahara's long hair, letting her fingers roam freely down her scalp. Cooley slowly pulled her face from Sahara's.

"I need you," Cooley whispered.

Sahara nodded her head.

"Anything, baby. Need me, let me be there for you. Cooley, just let me love you," Sahara pleaded, her eyes filled with water.

Cooley wiped the first tear to fall down Sahara's face. "Call me Carla."

26

Denise sat in the hallway. She looked at the row of gorgeous women sitting around her, all holding their portfolios tight. Go-see appointments never seemed so long and boring on *America's Next Top Model*. Denise looked at the women around her. She could see the drive and determination in their eyes, drive that she didn't have.

Denise sighed. Her eyes shifted, catching glimpse of a beautiful chocolate model. The model smiled, Denise smiled back. She had never seen teeth that white or that perfect before in all her life. The model's hair was pulled back in a bun. Denise noticed her striking facial features. Her cheekbones were high and defined, resembling Naomi Campbell in her early days.

"Denise Chambers," a short woman standing in the doorway called.

Denise took a deep breath and stood up. She walked toward the door.

Someone tugged on her pants. "Good luck in there."

The chocolate beauty's African accent intrigued Denise. Denise snuck another look at the girl before walking to the back.

Denise wanted to die. She stood in a black floor-length evening gown that was worth more than everything she owned. She tried to focus on not tripping in the stiletto heels they put her in.

Denise tried to stand tall. Her new agent told her the designer was a big deal and personally asked to see her. Deep down she hoped it would be as easy as the Jocku booking, but from the looks of the dresses, she knew she would be a hard sell.

Two double doors opened. Melanie Guston walked in the room. Mariah had schooled Denise on the hot designer. From Mariah's praise she expected a stunning beauty; instead, the woman looked more like Denise than any other person she'd met in the industry. Melanie's hair was braided in three big corn rows to the back. Her blue-and-white Jordan's matched her blue-and-white Jordan jogging suit.

Denise tried not to stare as two women fitted the dress around her. She couldn't believe the same woman in the jogging suits created the dress she had on.

Melanie's eyes shifted to Denise's face. Melanie's eyes widened. She put her hand up to her mouth.

Denise suddenly felt nervous as the woman stared at her with a surprised look on her face.

"Is everything OK?" Denise questioned. She got the funny feeling something was wrong.

Melanie's eyes were glossy. She blinked. Denise didn't know what had happened. It seemed Melanie's body was the room, but her mind was obviously somewhere else.

Melanie turned away. She walked to her desk and sat down.

"So you are Denise." Melanie's voice was light and airy.

"Yes, ma'am."

"And your last name is Chambers?" Melanie asked, looking down at a folder.

"Yes."

Melanie glanced back at Denise. Her face was flushed. Denise didn't know how to respond.

"You have very stunning features, Denise. Good for print, but what about runway?"

"I've never done runway." Denise cringed at the thought of walking down a catwalk. "I honestly just started modeling. I was really a ball player." Denise noticed Melanie staring at her again. "I'm sorry, but did you want me to turn another way or something?"

Melanie snapped back to reality. "I'm sorry, you just . . . you just are the spitting image of someone I know."

"Oh." Denise responded. She hoped her face didn't show the confusion she felt.

Melanie closed the folder. She stood up and walked over to Denise. She began to circle the platform, evaluating every inch of Denise.

"And do you want to do runway?"

"Honestly?"

Melanie's right brow rose. "Yes."

"No." Denise looked directly in Melanie's eyes.

Melanie stared back, her lips curved upward. She let out a chuckle. "Well, at least you are honest. You can go change now."

The two women helped Denise down off the pedestal. Denise flipped the shoes off before heading to change.

Melanie watched as Denise walked away. She motioned to the two women. They exited the room, closing the door behind them.

Denise came out of the dressing room feeling comfortable again.

Melanie was sitting in her chair. She looked up at Denise and motioned for her to come and sit in a black chair next to her desk.

Denise sat down. Her eyes met Melanie's.

"Your eyes . . ." Melanie's soft voice was almost a whisper. "Stunning. You get them from your mother."

"I don't know if I got them from her or not. I never really paid attention."

"You weren't close with your mother?" Melanie hung on to every word coming from Denise's mouth.

"No, we weren't close at all."

Melanie's eyes were glossy again. "A shame."

Denise felt her body tensing up. Nerves were getting the better of her.

"Well, my mother wasn't really around. I was raised by my grandmother."

"Oh, OK." Melanie sighed.

Denise felt a hint of sorrow in Melanie's voice. "Well . . ."—Melanie stood up—"You are no model, Ms. Chambers."

Denise looked up around her. She looked at the door. "I wouldn't say that. I'm just—"

"No, I would." Melanie lit a Slim cigarette. "You stumbled into this, but you do not want it. You don't like the life of a model. I can tell."

Denise shifted in her seat. Her Jocku jeans were slightly baggy with her tight-fitting black tee.

"So I guess that's your way of saying you're not interested?"

Denise felt incredibly comfortable next to the designer.

"As a model, no." Melanie walked away. "But there could be something more. You remind me a lot of myself, Denise, a butch woman in a career not normally suited for her." Melanie picked up a brown envelope. "But somehow we are making it work." Melanie walked back to Denise and handed her the envelope. "Be there."

Denise looked at Melanie with a curious look. "Wait, you are using me?"

"Heavens, no, you are not a model." Melanie laughed.

Denise didn't know if she was more embarrassed or angry.

"Then what is this?"

"An invitation. Just be there. Now, good-bye, Denise Chambers." Melanie clapped her hands. Immediately the two fitters walked back into the room.

Confused, Denise walked out the room, envelope in hand.

Lena knocked on the brown door. Terrin didn't have the sliding door she had, since her loft place didn't take up a whole floor. Lena's hands tingled like she had been sitting on them for hours. She shook them, hoping the sensation would ease.

"I'm coming," Terrin yelled.

Lena froze. She almost hoped Terrin wasn't home.

Terrin opened the door, causing Lena's eyes to widen at Terrin's muscular arms in her wife-beater. Her stomach had a slight pot belly like a person who overate. Lena found her attractive.

Terrin smiled. "Well, this is a pleasant surprise."

Lena blushed. "Well, I wanted to say thanks for everything from the other night. I was wondering if you, um, wanted to grab a bite to eat or something." Lena lowered her eyes, trying to hide her embarrassment.

Terrin's face lit up. She quickly scanned Lena's frame. She couldn't believe how sexy Lena was. Lena's hair hung down on her shoulders. "Are you asking me on a date?"

Lena smirked. "I'm asking if you want to grab a bite to eat."

"Sure, I'd love to go on a date with you." Terrin winked. "Let me put on some real clothes." Terrin opened the door.

Lena walked in. "I think you look OK," Lena said as Terrin walked off. She knew the look well. Basketball shorts and a wife-beater was her favorite outfit on Denise.

Terrin's shorter frame didn't compare to Denise's, but it didn't matter to Lena. There was something else pulling Lena to her.

"Please don't come out looking all fresh. I didn't get dressed up." Lena sat on the small brown sofa. She noticed the small DVD collection; they had similar tastes in movies.

"Girl, whatever," Terrin yelled from the back. "I just gotta keep up with you."

"I didn't dress up."

"Yeah, even with your jeans and white tee, you look like you stepped out of a fashion magazine." Terrin walked out, her basketball shorts replaced with a pair of Ed Hardy jeans with an Ed Hardy graphic tee covered with a diamond skull.

"Wow, you dress fast." Lena stood up.

"I was actually getting ready to change and go to the club."

"Oh, I'm sorry, I didn't—"

"Lena, it's cool. It's just the club. Same ole dykes I see all the time. Your offer is much more appealing."

Terrin's smile sent chills down Lena's spine.

Lena walked closer to Terrin. "So, why don't we just go where you were going."

Terrin paused. "You want to go to the gay club?"

"Sure, why not? I've been to a gay club before." Lena thought about her first gay club experience with Denise on New Year's a year back, the first time they almost kissed.

"Well, if you want to, let's do it."

"Do I need to change?" Lena said, looking down at her fitted seven jeans and white Bebe shirt, what she considered her plain-Jane clothes.

Terrin shook her head. "You look great."

***

The small club was packed with wall-to-wall lesbians. Lena held on to Terrin's hand as they walked through the dimly lit nightspot. Club lights flickered and flashed on the small dance floor. The pool table was inhabited with a group of butch women watching two others playing an intense game. The customers were predominately black women, unlike the karaoke bar Terrin took her to before. Lil Wayne's latest hit blared through the speakers as women bumped and grinded on the dance floor.

Lena was surprised by the look. It wasn't like any club in Atlanta. People were dressed down, not that many tight skirts and club outfits she was used to seeing.

"Are you all right?" Terrin looked at Lena with a concerned glare.

"Why do you say that?"

"'Cause you are cutting off my circulation." Terrin laughed.

Lena realized how tightly she was holding on to Terrin's arm. She quickly let go.

"I'm sorry. I don't know what is wrong with me."

Terrin took Lena's hands in hers, and their eyes met. "Don't be nervous, I'd never let anything happen to you."

Terrin's words soothed Lena. She felt her nerves calming down. Lena smiled as Terrin guided her through the club. They walked up to a table with three other women. The women looked at each other with confusion in their eyes.

Terrin shook her head as they made it to the table.

"What's up, y'all? This is Lena. Lena, these are my friends Precious, Angel and Cat."

Lena shook hands with each woman. She could tell they were sizing her up. Angel and Precious were both femmes, and Cat was the only stud.

"It's nice to meet you, Deena," Angel said in a nasty/ nice tone. She didn't know what to think of Lena.

"Nice to meet you too, but it's *Lena*." Lena sized Angel up first. She knew her type well . . . cute and was probably used to being the cutest in the group. The emergence of Lena would not work well for her ego.

Lena noticed a silver bracelet on Angel's arm. "That is a nice bracelet. I love that." Lena smiled.

Angel's face lit up. She loved compliments, especially from women who could take her in the beauty department. It meant they found something good about her.

"Thanks, girl I"—Angel's smiled dropped when she noticed the Tiffany silver hanging around Lena's arm and neck. "I got it from this little store in New York, paid a grip for it. But it was worth it." Angel pulled her hand back some.

"Well, girl, that is nice." Lena flashed her smile. She knew the silver probably came from a silver store out of the mall at the most.

"We weren't expecting Terrin to show up with anyone. This is a real surprise." The chubby Precious took a sip of her Apple Smirnoff.

"Chill, P," Terrin said, pulling a chair out for Lena.

"What? I think it's great. She is a cutie," Precious said to Terrin like Lena wasn't sitting there.

"I'm going to the bar. Y'all need anything?" Cat got out of her chair. She was the tallest of them. Her hair was cut in a short boy cut. Her clothes hung off her thin frame.

Lena hated when women wore clothes too many sizes too big. Even with the huge shirt, she could tell Cat had big breasts. Her sports bra did nothing, causing her breasts to hang down. Lena knew she was in need of a serious makeover.

"I'll come with you." Terrin put her arm on Lena's back. "Do you want anything?"

"Anything fruity would be nice," Lena said, knowing the club didn't have a full bar.

The club's crowd grew as the night went on. The DJ's mix of hip-hop, top forty and a few tracks of rock kept the crowd on the floor.

Terrin hung to Lena's side, pushing her chair close enough to rest her arm on the back of Lena's chair. Lena laughed at Terrin and her friends. She got along with them well. Even Angel warmed up to her.

Lena could feel the buzz of her fourth drink. She bounced her head with Beyoncé's "Get Me Bodied."

Terrin licked her lips and rubbed them together like she was L.L. Cool J.

"Let's dance." Terrin stood up.

"Oh, umm, I'm—"

"Not taking no for an answer." Terrin held her hand out.

Lena couldn't help but blush. She placed her hand in Terrin's, and they walked to the crowded dance floor.

Bodies pushed against each other as they moved to the beat. Lena popped her round butt right against Terrin's pelvis. Terrin nodded in approval. Lena let the music take over her body, swaying and grinding to the beat.

A tall, thick woman walked up in front of Lena and began to dance. Lena soon found herself in the middle of a six-person sandwich on the floor. She felt the woman's breasts rubbing against hers as Terrin's body grinded against her backside. Lena's pussy began to throb as she glanced down at the woman's cleavage.

"You sexy as hell, mama." The woman licked her red plump lips.

Lena smiled.

The woman pulled Lena closer, their pelvises grinding against each other.

Terrin watched as Lena rubbed her hands up the woman's thick thighs. Other woman watched the sexy show Lena and the women were putting on.

The woman gently grabbed Lena's hair, causing Lena's head to fall back into Terrin's chest. The woman kissed Lena on her neck.

Lena grinded her butt against Terrin in a sexy, circular motion, and Terrin pulled Lena closer to her. The woman followed suit, coming closer to the two. Marvin Gaye's "Let's Get It On" began to play. Women coupled up, grinding as though they were in the privacy of their own homes.

Lena and Terrin stared at each other as they gyrated to the beat. Lena felt her panties getting moist as she stared into Terrin's big brown eyes. Without hesitation, Lena pressed her lips against Terrin's. In that moment, nothing else mattered. There was no floor full of people.

Terrin's tongue massaged Lena's; it seemed like they were the only two in the room. Terrin's hands roamed up and down Lena's back, her index finger grazing the nape of Lena's neck, sending shivers down Lena's body.

Their focus broke as a woman bumped into them. Lena looked at Terrin, whose eyes fixated on Lena as though she wanted to take her right there.

"I'm sorry." Lena lowered her head.

Terrin's index finger pushed Lena's chin back up. "Don't apologize. Never apologize for doing that. Feel free to do it anytime you want."

Terrin's intensity was a pleasant change from her usual silly nature. Lena felt her internal fire burning.

"Terrin, how long did you want to stay here?"

"Ready when you are."

"In that's case, let's go."

27

"Shit!" Mariah jumped as she turned the lights on in her apartment. Denise sat on the couch staring in her direction. "You scared the shit out of me."

"I'm sorry."

"Why are you sitting in the dark?" Mariah dropped her briefcase on the floor and stepped out of her Louboutin heels. They were the only shoes she wouldn't kick off.

"I was just thinking." Denise stared into space.

Mariah sat on the couch next to her.

"Thinking about what?"

"My life."

Mariah's eyes slightly slanted. She pushed her red hair back behind her ears. "What about it?"

Denise glanced over at Mariah. She turned to her and placed her hands on Mariah's leg. "Mariah, I really appreciate all that you have done for me . . ."

"But?" Mariah slowly pushed Denise's hands away, her face covered with concern.

"Don't be like that." Denise put her hands over Mariah's. "It's not what you think."

"I think you are trying to let me down gently. Is that not right?"

Denise smirked. "No, it's not. I don't want to leave you alone. I just . . . Mariah this whole modeling thing really isn't for me."

Denise stood up.

Mariah watched as Denise paced the floor. Mariah sighed. She sat back on the couch.

"Is that it?"

Denise paused. "Yeah. I sat in that go-see and I looked at the faces of the women who actually love and want it. I knew then it wasn't for me."

"Denise, I was just trying to find you a job."

"Yeah, and I appreciate all that you have done. A normal woman would be in heaven. But it's just not me."

Mariah rested her elbow on the back of the couch and put her head in her hand. "So, what do you want to do, Denise?"

Denise plopped back down on the couch. "I have no idea."

"Well." Mariah sat back up. "You have your contract with Jocku that you need to complete. But, besides that, you have enough money to take the time to figure out what you want. You can stay here as long as you want."

"Thanks, but that's another thing. It's not my style to live off someone else."

"Denise . . ."

"But I also know that money I have won't go very far in this city," Denise said, looking into Mariah's eyes. "So I think that we should come up with some kind of rent thing."

Mariah laughed. "Denise, my apartment is paid for. I own this place. I don't rent."

"Oh. I guess that makes sense." Denise lowered her head. "OK, well, how about I pay some other bill. Maybe the cable or put in on utilities."

"Denise." Mariah held both of Denise's hands. "Not only do I have a wonderful job, but I'm a trust fund baby. I'm set, everything in this apartment is set. Hell, if I wanted to go buy a house in the Hamptons I could pay cash."

"OK." Denise looked puzzled. She'd never heard Mariah mention her fortune before.

"So any money you put toward anything would be only to make you feel more comfortable. So if that's what you want to do, drop a hundred on the cable bill. But it's not for me, it's for you. But any money you give me, I'll just put aside and give back to you later."

Denise lowered her head. She thought about Lena. Mariah's money made Lena's fortune look like chump change. Denise looked into Mariah's eyes. She felt a twinge of guilt.

"I'm not gonna win at this, am I?"

Mariah shook her head. They both laughed. Mariah turned around, laying into Denise's arms. Denise ran her hand through Mariah's hair. She kissed Mariah on her forehead.

"So, do you have any ideas about what you want to do?"

"Not yet, but I'll figure it out soon." Denise glanced at the envelope on the table. She picked it up. "I got this."

Mariah took the envelope from Denise and opened it. Mariah's eyes widened as she pulled a beautiful black invitation out of the plain envelope. Even Denise admired the beautiful invitation.

"Oh my God!" Mariah gasped as she read the invite. "Denise, wow! I knew it."

"What?" Denise sat up in anticipation.

Mariah flipped the invite around. "Do you know what this is?"

Denise shook her head.

"This is an invite to one of Melanie's exclusive dinner parties. I knew it."

"You knew what?" Denise leaned back

"Well, I got a call from Melanie's camp asking me about you."

"Why?" Denise felt on edge.

"I don't really know, but they wanted to know about where you were from and your basketball career."

"And you just gave up my info?"

"I figured she was booking you for a job." Mariah could feel Denise's anger. "But then I realized that Melanie could have just called your agent. So, I knew it had to be something more. I think you might be tapped."

"*Tapped?* What the hell is that?"

Mariah smiled. She placed her hand on Denise's thigh. "Denise, it's a good thing. Melanie has made a lot of stars. The last person she took under her wing is now a supermodel. You have to go to the party."

"What? You want to go?" Denise looked at Mariah.

Mariah's smile dropped. "I didn't get invited."

"What? But you would be with me."

Mariah stood up. "You don't understand, Denise. When I say exclusive, I mean exclusive. Only the person whose name is on the invitation comes to this. And those names don't usually include my kind. But you need to go."

Denise stared at Mariah, who picked up her shoes and headed to the bedroom. Denise stood up and followed.

"So you are saying that I can't take you because you're white?"

"A white, bisexual agent. Not what Melanie is known for."

"That's some bullshit, Mariah, and you know it." Denise sat on the edge of the bed while Mariah pulled off her work clothes.

"Don't look at it like that. It's just that Melanie is all about empowering black gays and lesbians in the industry. It really is a big honor to even attend."

"Well, I don't see it like that. I'm not going to go."

Mariah's head jerked around toward Denise. Her serious face was on. "Denise, look, if Melanie has taken an interest in you, you would be a fool not to go. Melanie can open a lot of doors for you, but she can also close a lot of them as well."

"So, if I don't go she'll blackball me? She doesn't seem too great."

"I'm not saying that, but I am saying that she is a very powerful person who knows very powerful people. Maybe even people who can get you back into the league sooner rather than later."

Denise's heart skipped a beat. The thought of playing basketball excited her. "You really think that could happen?"

"I can't say for sure, but if there is a person who might be able to help, it would be her." Mariah looked at Denise. She knew Denise's mind was racing. "What do you have to lose?"

28

Lena nervously looked around Terrin's apartment, staring at items as though it was her first time seeing them. Her hands were trembling. She shook them, trying to shake off her nerves. It was like it was her first time.

Terrin looked around her room. She lit every candle, giving the room a soft incandescence. The jasmine-scented candles permeated the room with an intoxicating fragrance. Terrin gave the room one more look over. She wanted things to be perfect.

Lena sat on the couch. She took a deep breath. She knew she had to get a grip. She laughed to herself; she didn't know why she was so nervous. It wasn't her first time at bat. Her mind drifted to Denise and the first time they made love. She was nervous, but more anxious than anything. This was different. Lena's heart was racing, and her palms were beginning to sweat.

Terrin peeked around the corner. She watched as Lena rocked back and forth on the couch. She smiled; Lena looked so innocent, and so beautiful to her.

"We don't have to do this." Terrin walked into the room, startling Lena.

"Oh, I'm good. I just—"

"You are just a nervous wreck." Terrin giggled. "Lena, we don't have to do anything if you aren't ready. I don't want to make you feel uncomfortable."

Lena's body began to relax. She sighed. "I'm sorry. I feel like a baby."

"Nah, it's not like that. You've only been with one woman. It's only natural to be a little nervous."

Lena walked over to Terrin. Terrin wrapped her arms around Lena's shoulders. Terrin's lips slowly planted a kiss on the top of her forehead. The last of Lena's nervousness dissipated.

"Can we just go to bed, and if the mood comes, then we explore from there?" Lena's big brown eyes brought heat to Terrin's body.

"That sounds great to me." Terrin smiled, hoping Lena couldn't see the longing in her eyes.

Lena's mouth dropped as she walked into the room. She looked at Terrin, who just smirked as she walked over to a set of candles and began blowing them out.

"I feel really bad now."

"Don't." Terrin blew the last of the candles out. "They are a fire hazard anyway."

"Do you have a shirt I can put on?" Lena pulled her shoes off. The cold hardwood chilled her body, causing her nipples to perk up.

Terrin tried to not notice them. She threw a white tee at Lena. Lena walked into the bathroom.

Get a grip, Terrin said to herself as she pulled her clothes off. She pulled her pajama bottoms up and got into the bed.

She listened as water ran in her bathroom. She wanted to enter. She wanted to see how Lena's body looked naked. Terrin never wanted to see a girl naked so badly before. Terrin's mind raced. She couldn't figure out what it was, but Lena had a hold on her unlike any girl before her.

Terrin's phone began to blare. She silenced the ringtone and ran out the room.

"You have some fucked up timing, you know that?" Terrin whispered as she headed to the kitchen.

"Shit." Cat inhaled from her rolled up cigar. She exhaled slowly, allowing the thick weed smoke to cloud her car. "My bad, dude. I just wanted to check on yo ass. You fuckin'?" Cat smiled causing her already tight eyes to slant even more.

"Would I have answered the phone if I was?" Terrin took a sip out of her bottle of water.

"You already hit?"

"Naah."

"Why not?"

"I don't think she's ready. She seems really nervous, and I'm not trying to rush her."

"Whhhuuutttt! Oh snap, you really feeling cutie, huh?" Cat grinned.

Terrin's face lit up. "I can't lie. It's something about her. I think she could be the one."

"T."

Terrin turned at the sound of Lena's sexy voice calling her name.

"I gotta go," Terrin whispered. She hung the phone up before Cat could say good-bye. Terrin took another gulp of the cold water before heading to the back.

Lena turned to the door when Terrin walked in. Terrin did a double take. Lena stood at the side of the bed, her perfectly manicured feet on the cold floor and Terrin's shirt hanging just low enough to cover the places Terrin wanted to see more than anywhere else.

"I don't think my shirt has ever looked that damn good." Terrin walked farther into the room. She fought to maintain her composure.

"You are so silly." Lena blushed.

Terrin pulled the covers back on the bed. The last thing she wanted to do was sleep.

Lena could see the lust in Terrin's eyes. She wanted to take the step, but something was holding her back. Her mind drifted to Denise.

"Well, I guess we should get in bed now. I can turn on a movie if. . . ."

"Terrin . . ." Terrin's eyes focused on Lena's. Lena's big brown eyes gazed into Terrin's. The sullen look worried Terrin. "I'm really sorry about everything, the fact that I'm so . . ."

"Lena, don't." Terrin quickly walked around to the other side of her bed. Lena's perfume lingered on her body. "You don't need to apologize for anything." Terrin placed her hands on both sides of Lena's face.

Lena looked at Terrin like a scared puppy dog.

"I know this is a big step for you, and I know you aren't over your feelings for . . . her . . ." The thought of Denise didn't sit well with Terrin. "I am just happy that you are here with me and that you are allowing me to be here for you."

Lena's eyes began to water. "I don't know what is wrong with me. Denise has a new girlfriend. I shouldn't care this much. I shouldn't let her affect me like this."

"Hey, you are completely justified in the way you feel. Honestly, Lena, she's the fool. 'Cause I find it hard to believe that there is another woman in this world that could compare to you."

Terrin wiped the tears that flowed down Lena's face. Lena felt a sense of relief. She felt safe with Terrin, like nothing bad would happen as long as she was in her arms.

Yet her mind still drifted to Denise. Images of Denise sexing another woman flooded her mind. She could see the woman's body, her chocolate skin against Denise's flesh. She could hear her moaning the way Denise had made hermoan.

Lena shook her head. She looked at Terrin, whose eyes hadn't left her.

"Terrin."

"Lena."

Their eyes completely focused on each other, their hearts beating rapidly and in sync.

"Take me."

There were no more words. Terrin's hand pulled Lena's face in close to hers. Their mouths met, immediately embraced in a sensual kiss. Lena's tongue invaded Terrin's mouth. Terrin greeted it with a slow suck, their tongues dancing.

Lena moved backward. Terrin wrapped her arm around her and pulled her into her arms with ease. Slowly, Terrin slowly lowered Lena onto her bed. The sexual beast inside of Terrin was roaring to get out.

Lena closed her eyes as her head hit the soft pillow. She didn't want to think about anything. The only thing she wanted to feel was pleasure. She felt her leg being lifted. She could feel the cool, wet tip of Terrin's tongue making its way up her thigh. Lena bit her lip in anticipation as Terrin's fingers gripped her thong, slowly pulling it off.

"Mmmm-hmmmm." Terrin murmured as her eyes finally set on Lena's completely naked body. It was better than she expected. There wasn't a blemish in sight, no unsightly marks or hairs.

Terrin ran her index finger down the very small landing strip on Lena's womanhood. Her pussy was so smooth, Terrin knew it had to be a wax job because no razor could do it. She smirked. Lena made her mouth water. She had to have her.

Lena was pleasantly impressed as Terrin expertly worked her tongue inside of her. Her body writhed with the teasing pleasure. Where Denise took her time,

Terrin dove head first into her. Lena found herself loving the aggression. Denise was always so afraid of hurting Lena that she was overly cautious. Terrin went in confident that she would please her, and it showed.

Terrin pulled on the clit with her lips as her broad tongue licked the full length of Lena's pussy, lips, and clit, extending it as she pulled and sucked with her mouth.

Lena moaned.

Terrin captured the head of the clit and teased its most sensitive spot. Lena felt her body jerk and Terrin took her cue.

Lena's body shook as the woman skillfully teased the tiny spot with barely the tip of her tongue. Lena wanted to escape as she felt the jolts shock her convulsing muscles.

Terrin held her tightly and pulled her closer; her mouth and tongue anchored on the tiny knot and danced around it.

Lena twisted to escape, her body bouncing along the mattress. Her moans caught in her throat. There was no escape. Terrin held her firmly in her mouth's grasp.

Lena's body continued to tremble. Shades of red danced in her head as the intensity of her orgasm grew closer. The lovemaking shook her to her core. No one had ever loved her this way. It was as though Terrin had been given a map of all of her pleasure spots and memorized each one. She deftly moved between the hard, swollen button of a clit and the cavernous, quickly flooding pussy.

Each stroke took Lena closer to her ultimate destination and farther away from her former loves. Brandon had long ago disappeared. Denise's face lingering in the recesses of her mind was quickly fading with each masterful stroke of Terrin's probing tongue.

Terrin wrapped her arms around Lena's ass. She devoured Lena, sucking the hot wetness that poured from within her. She let the taste linger momentarily on her lips. She wanted to savor every sweet drop.

Terrin slowed down long enough to spread the lips in front of her. The skin glistened in the soft moonlight filtering in through the high windows. She wanted to slow down, take in every moment, but she couldn't get enough.

Terrin was convinced. Lena's sweetness was her crack. She wanted to live inside of Lena, bury her entire head within the folds of those lips, feel the round soft curves of her walls close in on her, and drown her with her pleasure. Whether it was the saltiness of her sweaty skin, or the sweetness of the nectar pouring from her flower, Terrin had to have it.

She pressed her face into the heat of Lena's pussy and thrust her tongue deep inside.

Lena bit her lip. The explosion was present. Her legs bucked.

Terrin held on, wanting to capture it all.

Lena moaned, grabbing Terrin's shoulders. Her back arched as she exploded. All of her hurt, anger and passion flooded out with her orgasm, like a broken dam.

Terrin moaned as Lena's sweetness hit her tongue and filled her mouth. It was better than any piece of candy. Lena panted. Her chest rose and fell. Terrin looked up at Lena. Even covered in sweat she was the most beautiful girl she had ever seen.

Terrin rolled over to her side of the bed and wrapped her arm around Lena. They spooned and hugged close. Terrin wanted to say something, but her instincts told her to remain quiet. She held Lena, sealing the night with a kiss on the back of Lena's neck.

Lena knew she had to do something. She squeezed Terrin's hand and pulled her as close as she could, her ass pressed against Terrin's boxers.

Terrin knew what the gesture meant. She knew she had made Lena happy. That's all she wanted to do.

They fell asleep, both silent, both satisfied.

29

The large church was filled with the celebrity community. Almost everyone was dressed in black. Cooley tried to hold back tears under her dark shades. She stood in the line, heart beating harder with each step closer to the casket.

Big Ron sprung for Sonic's funeral. Cooley thought about her friend. She had died in a roach-infested hotel room. The rapper who once ruled the female rap game lay dead from an overdose, broke and alone. Guilt took over Cooley's body. She felt her knees buckle.

Sahara placed her hand on Cooley's shoulder. Cooley looked at Sahara's beautiful face. Her hair was pulled back in a bun. Sahara's black Armani suit made her appear regal to Cooley. She loved the toned-down look more than Sahara's normal sexy attire.

"I don't know if I can do this," Cooley's voice cracked.

"It's OK, sweetie. Just take your time," Sahara said as they drew closer to the casket.

The scent of the hundreds of flowers entered their noises. Large flower sprays covered in roses, gladiolas, and other flowers covered the front. It was beautiful; Cooley hoped Sonic was happy with the funeral and turn-out.

Cooley took a deep breath. One foot at a time, they walked up to the bronze casket. Cooley pulled her shades off. Her bloodshot eyes welcomed the cool breeze. She looked at Sonic.

Cooley's mind drifted to the first time they met. She looked more like she did that first night at the Jam Zone party than she did the last time she saw her alive.

"Bruh, I'm sorry," Cooley whispered. "I, I hope you can forgive me." Tears flowed down her face. "I"— Cooley turned her head; she walked away from the casket, unable to take anymore.

Cooley and Sahara took a seat on the second row. Cooley lowered her head.

James sat next to Sahara. "Wade's having a hard time, I see," he whispered to Sahara.

"Yes, they were very close." Sahara rubbed Cooley on her back.

"Sad story, but I guess that's what happens when you live like that."

Sahara wanted to slap James. She looked at his smug face. She was glad Cooley didn't hear him, or the funeral would have been turned out.

Cooley and Sahara listened as friends and industry associates talked about the good times they had with Sonic. Cooley laughed at some of the funny stories.

The preacher called for anyone else who wanted to say a few words. Cooley stood up and walked to the front.

"Umm." Her voice trembled. "I first met Sonic at a party during a Christmas trip my friends and I took while I was still in college. I walked up to her and said something crazy. She laughed, and invited me to sit down." Cooley smiled, thinking about their first meeting. "Sonic welcomed me with open arms. I . . . owe her a lot."

The crowd nodded as Cooley spoke. Cooley noticed Sahara's face. She was smiling, her makeup ruined from tears. Cooley looked down at the now closed casket.

"Words can't explain how I feel right now. I'll miss you, my friend." Cooley walked away from the podium.

Cooley privately said her final good-byes as she stood at the gravesite. The thousands of people who gathered at the church had trickled down to a few, since paparazzi wasn't allowed in the cemetery. Cooley quickly realized how fake the industry she loved was.

"I don't want to be like this," Cooley muttered.

"What, hon?" Sahara watched as the casket lowered to the ground.

"I don't want to be like this. I don't want to party my life away. I don't want to die with no real friends."

"Carla, you won't. You aren't like Sonic. You aren't on drugs."

"I know, but . . . Sonic never really let anyone in. She wouldn't even let me in when I went to help her. I am just like her. I don't let people in."

Sahara turned to Cooley. "Carla, you control your destiny. Make it what you want it to be."

Cooley knew Sahara was right. She held on to Sahara's hand tight. She threw a single white rose into the grave. Cooley knew she had changed, but she knew she had a long way to go. She said good-bye to Sonic, and to the last traces of the old Cooley.

30

Lena woke up to the strong smell of coffee. She looked at the clock and blinked. She couldn't believe how early it was. She crawled out of Terrin's bed. The cold floor alerted her senses along with the aroma of hazelnut.

"Damn, I didn't mean to wake you." Terrin stood up from her table. Terrin was completely dressed in black suit pants and a white button-down shirt.

Lena noticed Terrin's black leather pumps, a major difference from the Jordan's she wore most of the time.

"Is it Monday already?" Lena crept into the living room wearing one of Terrin's oversized T-shirts and a pair of boxer shorts.

"Yeah, back to reality for me." Terrin kissed Lena on her lips. "I gotta go to work, but you can stay here if you want."

"No. I need to get home before my maid puts out a missing person's report on me. I haven't had my phone in two days."

Lena turned around to walk back to the bedroom. Terrin followed.

Lena pulled the shirt over her head. She picked up her pink laced bra. Terrin stood in the door way admiring the view of Lena's backside.

Lena turned around, catching Terrin's peep show. She smiled.

"I swear, you are making me want to call in." Terrin shook her head.

"No, go to work. I'm not going to be the reason you miss work."

"I think spending the day in bed with you is a pretty damn good reason to miss work."

Lena threw Terrin's shirt at her, causing Terrin to laugh.

Terrin headed back to the kitchen.

Lena shook her head. She had spent two days in bed letting Terrin take her mind off of her problems. In the last two sex-filled days she didn't think about Brandon, and her thoughts about Denise weren't as frequent. Terrin was very attentive to her needs, which made Lena feel comfortable.

And she seemed to love to taste Lena. Lena had never had anyone want to lick her as much as Terrin wanted to. She was impressed.

Lena walked into the living room. Terrin added her black blazer to complete her look. She had traded her stud look for a professional look that Lena found very sexy. She could see Terrin's curves in the suit, something she only saw through Terrin's boxer briefs and wife-beaters when they were in bed.

"I will call you when I get in, OK?" Terrin wrapped her arms around Lena.

Lena nodded her head. "Let's get some sushi tonight."

"Sounds good."

Lena and Terrin parted ways.

Lena headed up the elevator to her lavish loft. She unlocked her door and walked in the dimly lit room. Lena placed her purse on the kitchen table and walked into the kitchen. She thought about Terrin and smiled to herself.

"It's about time."

"Ahhh!" The voice startled Lena, causing her to drop her bottled water. She turned around to see her mother, Karen, sitting in the dark living room. "Oh my God, Mother, you scared the sh—mess out of me."

"Well, maybe if you would answer your phone, you would have known I was here."

"How did you get in?" Lena walked out of the kitchen toward her den. She turned the light on.

Her mother sat in a pair of Donna Karan grey pants and a white blouse. Stunning at forty-nine due in part to great genes and in part to an excellent surgeon who helped make her look like she was still in her thirties, Karen sat with her Apple laptop book open.

"Oh, darling, you know I have my ways." Karen sat still with a calm look on her face.

"So, what are you doing here?"

"Well, funny you should ask. The other day I was surfing the Web and I came across this blog site called MediaTakeOut." Karen picked up her laptop. "Funny, the first thing that pops up is this." Karen turned the laptop toward Lena.

Lena's whole body froze as she looked at the heading.

Pro Baller Already Creeping on his New Wife. Hope she isn't reading this.

Lena picked the computer up from her mother. She clicked on the large link.

Seems Grizzlies superstar Brandon Redding was having a good time in Miami with an unidentified Hispanic honey. Bad thing is, Brandon is a newlywed. Pictures were snapped of Brandon in some serous positions, including kissing the Latin mamacita. I hope his wife isn't reading this, 'cause it's a wrap if she is.

Lena scrolled down to the pictures. She tried to keep a straight face as she looked at pictures of Brandon hugged up and kissing a sexy Latina woman. Furious, Lena closed the laptop.

"Mother, it's not what you think."

"Well, that's obvious. I could tell that, the second I walked into this ghost town of a house. I noticed all of Brandon's things are gone."

"You went through my house?!" Lena stood up and walked away. She didn't know if she was more upset with her mother for snooping or at Brandon for being so careless to get caught on camera.

"Don't you take that tone with me, young lady! What did you expect me to do? You obviously have been hiding a lot from me. Do you know what kind of embarrassment this has caused? Your father is furious. He was ready to take a hit out on Brandon."

"Oh my God!" Lena covered her mouth.

"I was able to calm him down. I told him I was coming to get to the bottom of things. Lena Jamerson-Redding, what is going on?"

"Mother, Brandon and I are separated."

Karen stood up, her lips pressed firmly together. "I knew it. I knew you and that girl—"

"Me!"

"Yes, Lena. You want to sit here and tell me it has nothing to do with that girl!"

Lena's face dropped.

"And before you form your mouth to lie." Karen picked up a piece of paper and opened it.

Lena stared at the American Express bill in her mother's hand.

"Plane ticket, New York Hotel."

"It's not what you think."

"Oh, really. What did you do go to New York for? A shopping trip?"

"Mother, please!"

"What else could it be, Lena?"

"Brandon has a baby! He had a baby by another woman! He has been cheating on me our whole relationship!"

Karen's straight face fell. "Why are you just now telling me this?"

"Because I wasn't trying to get you or Daddy involved. This is my life and my relationship. We had to figure things out on our own."

Karen walked up to Lena and put her hands on her shoulders. "Lena, you never have to go through anything without us. That is why we are there. We love you."

"I know, Mother. But this is my life and my relationship. I have to figure things out on my own."

"I understand, honey." Karen hugged her daughter. "But I must ask you, and I want you to be honest with me. Does she have anything to do with this at all?"

Lena paused. She could see the concern, and fear in her mother's face.

"No, Mother. Denise and I are only friends."

Lena let her mother out of the house. She couldn't bear to break her mother's heart. She looked around at the big space.

Instantly Brandon entered her mind. Anger set in. She grabbed her cell phone off the kitchen counter. Lena dialed Brandon's number, but got the voice mail.

"I am furious with you. Call me!" Lena slammed the phone closed. She walked back in the living room and sat on the couch. Lena turned the TV on. She screamed when Denise's face appeared in a Jocku ad.

When it rains it pours.

Lena turned the TV off and headed to her room. She had to get a grip on her life, and quickly.

***

Cooley and Sahara couldn't keep their hands off of each other. Sahara sat on top of Cooley's desk with Cooley's hand buried deep inside of her. Cooley kissed passion into Sahara's mouth. Each time they had sex, it was like the first time. Cooley was impressed. Sahara's sexual skills were unmatched. She even had Misha beat.

"Shit! Oh shittt! Cooley," Sahara moaned, as she grinded on Cooley's hand. Cooley's fingers hit her spots in perfect motion. Sahara's short dress sat up on her round ass as it bounced up and down.

Cooley glanced at the clock. "Girl, they gon' be here any minute."

"Wait, no," Sahara panted. "Not yet, almost there." Sahara grinded her pussy harder.

Cooley placed her thumb on Sahara's clit. She applied pressure, rubbing it in a fast, side-to-side motion. Sahara's body started to tremble.

Cooley bit her lip. She smirked as Sahara's body twerked. Their eyes met as Sahara exploded on Cooley's hand. Cooley pulled her fingers out. She sucked her index finger.

"Finger-licking good." Cooley laughed as she sucked Sahara's sweet flavor off her sticky fingers.

Sahara playfully hit Cooley as she jumped down from the desk. Their lips met again.

Cooley pulled Sahara close. She inhaled the *Berry Kiss* by Victoria's Secret that covered every inch of Sahara's body. Cooley loved the way Sahara used every product in the line from the bath gel to the final step of the body mist.

"Damn, you smell good enough to eat." Cooley ran her nose on the side of Sahara's neck.

"You can do that tonight. Send me to Miami in style."
Sahara playfully bit her lip as she pulled away from
Cooley. She walked over to the floor-length mirror and
began to fix her short halter dress and hair. She reap-
plied her lipstick. Cooley checked her look in a small
mirror in her desk.

Someone knocked at the door. Sahara opened the
door. Tee entered holding a stack of CDs.

"Hey, y'all, sorry I'm late. Cooley, I went through all
the CDs and these are the ones that I like the most."
Tee placed one stack of CDs on the desk. "And these
weren't that bad either," she said placing the last CDs
next to the other stack.

"Cool."

"What's all this?" Sahara said, walking over to the
desk. She picked up a CD.

"Well." Cooley flipped through the disks. "I do have
to find other artists. Can't keep my job off you alone."
Cooley winked at Sahara, whose pouty expression
showed she wasn't happy. "Don't be like that."

"Like what?" Sahara smirked.

"Whatever." Cooley raised her index finger and motioned for Sahara. Sahara smiled, leaning in toward
Cooley. She planted a kiss on Cooley.

A deep voice clearing its throat made them both
jump. They looked up at the three mortified execs
standing in the doorway. Marco crossed his arms.
James stood with a stern straight face.

Tommy, Sahara's publicist, stormed into the office.

"Out!" Tommy pointed at the door.

Tee looked at Cooley. Cooley nodded for Tee to leave.
Tee hurried out of the office.

Tommy slammed the door behind Tee. "Are you out
of your fucking mind?"

"I knew this was a bad idea." Marco paced the floor.

"What the hell are you all talking about?" Sahara stood with her head held high.

"When did this start?"

"So the rumors are true? You two are an item?" Tommy sat in one of the chairs in front of Cooley's desk.

Cooley tried to keep a straight face, not show her nervousness.

"Look, Sahara and I had something a long time ago that just arisen again."

"I bet." James huffed.

Cooley threw him a dark glare. "This is not to go public, you hear me."

"How is that any of your business?!" Sahara contested.

"It is our business because you are our artist, and a lot has been invested in you! If Big Ron—" James interjected.

"Big Ron knows about us," Cooley added. "He's known for a year."

"I don't give a fuck who knows. This is my department and I'm putting my foot down. Cooley, you are off of Sahara's project!"

"What!" Cooley hit her desk.

"Be glad I'm not firing you!" James yelled.

Cooley wanted to kick his ass but knew he was right.

"What! I don't want her off of my project!" Sahara's arms flew up in rage. "This is some bullshit!"

"It's not about what you want at this point. You are not about to ruin what we have worked our asses off on. And let me tell you right now, if this goes public, if a single person so much as even sees you giving googly eyes at each other, you are fired!"

James stormed out of the room. Marco and Tommy were shocked. Cooley was speechless.

Marco shook his head while closing the door. "Why, Cool? Why would you give him ammo like that?"

"What are you talking about?" Tommy looked at the others, confused.

"James doesn't like the fact that I walked in and got my job. He feels I should have started at the bottom like him."

"And the fact that he was sweet on you doesn't make it any better." Marco looked at Sahara. Sahara looked up.

"Look, all of this is irrelevant," Tommy added. "However, I do have to protect your image. This cannot go public now, for more than one reason."

Sahara stood in her place with her arms crossed. She was livid.

Cooley watched as Tommy and Marco walked out of the office. Cooley closed the door behind them.

"You OK?"

"No!" Sahara threw her hands up. "This is some bullshit. I'm not hiding my relationship."

"Yes, you are." Cooley stood in front of Sahara, her face straight. "We have to think of both of our careers now."

"So, you want to hide me?"

"No, I just don't want to lose my job or you lose everything you have worked hard for. James is an ass. You think he won't shelf your project? We got to think like adults here and not love-sick teenagers. We have both worked too hard. If we have to not be seen together in public, then that's just something we have to deal with."

Cooley wrapped her arms around the upset Sahara.

Sahara placed her head on Cooley's chest. "If this is what you want, then fine, but it's still some bullshit."

"Agreed, but we will make it through it." Cooley kissed Sahara on her forehead. She could only hope she was right.

31

Denise stood outside of the Park Avenue apartment building. She looked up at the tall building. She looked down on the invitation and sighed. She thought about Mariah. She didn't want to go in. Butterflies filled her stomach. A cool breeze caused her wrap to blow in the wind.

"Well, so we meet again."

Denise turned her head and smiled. "I see. Miss. . . ."

The chocolate beauty walked up to her. She smiled. Her bright white teeth were perfectly aligned. The beauty was even more beautiful. Her black mini dress showed off her long, toned legs. She stood so statuesque, Denise couldn't help her attraction.

"Farih . . . Farih Okoro. I see we are headed to the same place." Farih held up her black invitation.

"I see." Denise paused. "Wait, I thought these parties were for gay and lesbian people."

"Really?" Farih gave Denise a surprised look then smiled. "Well, now I'm sure I'm in the right place. Shall we?"

Denise stood stunned as Farih walked up the steps. Intrigued, Denise quickly followed.

"So, Okoro . . . that's—"

"Nigerian. My father is Nigerian," Farih replied as they rode the elevator up to the penthouse.

"Does it mean anything in particular?"

Farih smiled. "It actually means light-complexioned. When I was born I was very fair-skinned, so my father named me Farih. I'm still the lightest in my family."

"Wow, that's interesting."

"Yes, it doesn't really fit nowadays." Farih giggled. "I'm far from that. But hey, black is beautiful, right?" Farih glanced at Denise.

"It sure is." Denise agreed. Their eyes met.

The elevator door opened. They both walked down to the end of the hall. A large man in a black suit stood in front of the door. They handed their invitations to the man, who opened the door.

Denise tried to not show her amazement at the lavish penthouse. She could almost see her reflection in the shiny Italian marble floors. Beautiful spreads of fresh-cut orchids, calla lilies, and other beautiful flowers sat on most tables. Guests stood around talking.

Denise tried not to get star-struck by some of the well-known, and very closeted GLBT community that was in the room.

"Welcome, Denise." Melanie appeared in the door-way wearing a pair of slacks and a blue blazer. Two attractive models stood on either side of her.

Denise walked up to them and shook Melanie's hand.

"Thank you for having me. I must say I was surprised to open the envelope."

"Why is that?"

"Well, I . . . I guess I didn't get why."

"Denise, walk with me." Melanie walked away, leaving the two girls in their places.

Denise followed.

Melanie led Denise outside onto her balcony. The view of the city was breathtaking at their height. Melanie closed the sliding glass door behind them.

"So, you are wondering why you were invited here."
Melanie smiled.

"Yeah, I mean, I'm not that important. I have one
modeling gig, and even you said I'm not very good at
doing it."

Melanie let out a chuckle. "I said you are no model."
Melanie sat down in one of the two Monaco swivel
lounge chairs that faced the matching loveseat. She
motioned for Denise to sit. "Tell me, Denise, what is it
that you want to accomplish here in New York?"

Denise sat in the plush black chair. "Well, honestly,
after my basketball dream was shattered, I didn't know
what I was going to do. My agent and friend Mariah got
me the job with Jocku." Denise noticed Melanie staring
at her.

"And once Jocku is no more, what do you plan to
do?" Melanie's strong voice commanded attention and
made Denise nervous.

"Honestly, I really don't know."

Melanie stared at Denise. The tips of her lips curved
upward. "Denise, I must admit when I saw you in the
Jocku ad, I was impressed. Not with your modeling,
but with you in general. You have something about
you, something very special. I don't even think you
realize it."

"I can't say that I do. I was always known as the
ballplayer. Not really as anything besides that." Denise lowered her head. She couldn't help feel a little
ashamed.

"That is one of the things that make you unique. You
didn't come here hoping to be a star, even though you
have amazing star potential." Melanie smiled. "Tell me
a little more about your family, Denise. Your mother,
grandmother."

Denise's guard was up. She wondered why Melanie was so interested in her family life. Melanie's eyes were warm, Denise felt she was sincere, but something wasn't sitting right with her.

"Well, there's not much to tell. I already told you that my grandmother raised me. I don't know my father. As for my mom, she was on drugs."

Melanie's lip quivered as Denise spoke. "It's such a shame."

"What?"

"That you didn't know your mother." Melanie sat up. "Or your father."

"I guess, I just take it as it being life. I doubt there was much I missed out on."

"How can you say that?" Melanie snapped. "You could be just like them and not know it."

"I doubt it. My mom was a crackhead. That will never be me." Denise was irritated.

Melanie crossed her arms. "I can see the subject is sensitive for you."

"I'm just not used to anyone being so interested in my family life like this."

"I'm sorry if you feel I was prying. I just like to know what makes a person the way they are. Your features are so defined, I'm sure you got them from your mother. You should thank her for that. She made a beautiful child."

Denise noticed the change in Melanie's eyes. She looked as though she was going to cry.

"I can tell you that I do get my looks from my mother. We looked just alike. Her hair was longer than mine, but besides that, everything else seemed to be from her."

Melanie smiled. "I'm sure you did." Melanie couldn't take her eyes off of Denise. "Denise, what did your agent friend tell you about me?"

Denise thought about Mariah's words. "She just said that you are a good person to be in contact with."

"She is right. The fashion world is only one aspect of what I'm involved in. I believe in uplifting the black gay and lesbian community, especially the lesbian community. Helping us to finally have a voice in the entertainment industry."

Denise nodded. "That sounds great."

"When I see potential in someone, I like to take them under my wing, help them to be the best they can be." Melanie's eyes met Denise's. "I would like to take you under my wing, if you are interested."

"Why? Why would you want to do that, and what would you get out of it?" Denise stood up with her guard up.

Her stance caused Melanie to laugh.

"This is not the movies, Denise, everyone isn't out for blood. I told you, I see something special in you. And when you blow up I expect you to mention my name in your award acceptance speeches. Now, let's get back to the party. There is someone I want you to meet."

The two walked back into the living room. Denise noticed the decadent spread of foods. Waiters walked around serving cocktails to the guests. Denise noticed Farih talking to a group of people. Her beautiful smile lit up the corner.

"Ahh . . . I see you walked in with Farih," Melanie whispered. "That is a good pick, you two would be dynamite together."

Denise looked at Melanie and smiled. She liked the idea herself. Mariah entered Denise's head, ruining her dream of Farih.

"George."

Melanie and Denise walked up to a group of gay men. Denise couldn't believe her eyes as Melanie kissed the cheek of movie director George Kyles.

"This is Denise Chambers."

The men looked at Denise and greeted her with handshakes and nods.

George looked at her from head to toe. He reached his hand out and shook hers.

"You are the Jocku girl," George responded in a deep Southern accent.

"Yes, I am. It's a pleasure to meet you. *Devious Minds* was an amazing movie."

George cracked half of a smile. "You were right, Melanie. She does have the look."

Denise looked at Melanie, who nodded her head. She wanted to say something but stayed silent. Denise suddenly felt like she was on display. The men studied her like she was a piece of art.

"Tell me something, Denise. Can you act?"

"Act?" Denise repeated.

"Yes." George didn't take his eyes off of her face.

"I don't really know. I've never done it before." Denise felt like she was standing naked in front of a room full of people.

"Well, how would you like the chance to try?"

Denise's eyes widened. "Are you serious? Sure, I would like the chance to try."

George snapped his fingers. A young gay man walked up holding a bag. He handed a card to George. Denise could tell the young assistant was well trained.

"Be here. Let's see what you can do."

Denise looked at the card. The front was black with George Kyles Productions embossed in gold. She turned it over to see a location, date and time written on the back.

"I will be there."

Farih walked up with two glasses of champagne. "I thought you might want a glass."

"Oh, Farih, do you get more stunning each time I see you, darling?" George's flamboyant gay male side appeared as he kissed Farih on both of her cheeks.

"I only do it just for you." Farih schmoozed with the males, who were hanging on her every word.

George looked at Denise and Farih. "Are you two . . .?"

Farih looked at Denise and blushed. She turned back to the group. "Oh no, we just met."

"Thank goodness. That would be too much beauty in one relationship," one of the other gay males stated, causing everyone to laugh.

"Well, people, sit back and enjoy. Drink and eat, so we don't have anything to clean up afterwards," Melanie declared.

"Melanie, please, like you lift a finger in this place." George flicked his wrist.

"Well, my workers don't want a lot to do." Melanie snapped her fingers in a Z-formation. "Now get drunk, bitches."

The crowd laughed.

Denise no longer felt like the center of attention. She looked at Farih and smiled. She took a sip of the bubbly, determined to make the one glass last the whole night.

Denise and Farih walked out of the building. They'd spent the majority of the night at each other's side. Denise loved the way Farih commanded attention with her beauty and grace. She could hold a conversation with anyone. One minute she was talking foreign policies, the next, laughing about the crazy reality shows that covered TV.

Denise also noticed how sexy Farih was. Farih swayed her body to a song playing. Her body moved with little effort. She was naturally sexy, stunningly beautiful like Lena, but she had a regal appeal to her.

"So do you want me to hail you a cab?" Denise looked at Farih.

"That's sweet of you, however, I live right down the way."

"Oh, well, excuse me then."

They both laughed.

"At least let me walk you to your place."

"That would be fine."

Farih's smile caused butterflies to flutter inside of Denise. They walked down the expensive street.

Farih turned to Denise. "So tell me something, Denise. Did you really not recognize me when we met at the go-see?"

"I'm sorry, but no, I didn't. I don't read many fashion magazines. Let me guess. You are in some big campaigns, aren't you?"

Farih laughed. "You could say that."

"Like what?"

"Ummm, let me see . . . *Victoria's Secret*, *Cover Girl* and *Sports Illustrated*."

Denise froze in her spot. Her face dropped. "Are you serious?"

Farih chuckled as she nodded her head.

"Excuse me while I wipe the egg off of my face. You must think I'm an idiot."

"No." Farih placed her hand on Denise's shoulder. "I actually find it refreshing. You didn't flirt with me because of who I am."

"So you think I'm flirting with you?" Denise retorted.

"Aren't you?" Farih paused, and her smile faded. "You weren't. Now I have egg on my face." She turned to walk away.

Denise grabbed her hand and smirked.

"I was. Just glad to see you noticed." Denise winked her right eye.

"Well, this is my place." Farih blushed. "You wouldn't want to come up, would you, maybe for some espresso?" Farih's brown eyes were calling to Denise.

"Can I take a rain check? It's late, and I fear if I go up, I might not want to come out."

"There's nothing wrong with that." Farih didn't take her eyes off Denise's.

"I can't." Denise looked away from Farih's alluring eyes. She knew Mariah was at the house waiting on her. "But can I get a rain check?"

"Sure." Farih pulled Denise's phone out of its holster. She locked her phone number into the phone. "Call me. Good night Denise Chambers."

"Good night, Farih Okoro."

Denise watched as Farih walked into the building. She sighed.

What are you getting yourself into, Denise?

Denise quietly walked into the apartment. Her guilty conscience was eating away at her. She cared about Mariah, but she couldn't help the strong attraction she had for Farih.

Denise walked into the bedroom to find the bed empty and made up. She looked around, the place was empty. She looked at the clock on the wall. It was two in the morning, and Mariah wasn't at the apartment. Denise stood in the bedroom looking around. There were no signs of Mariah. Her work clothes weren't out. No shoes on the floor. Denise wondered if she came home at all.

Denise grabbed her cell phone and proceeded to text Mariah. As she prepared to press send, she heard laughing at the front door. Denise jumped, turning the bedroom light off. She peered through the door to the living room.

"Oh, that was crazy." Mariah stumbled into the house.

A tall white male held her up as they walked in the house. Denise moved back, making sure Mariah didn't see her.

Mariah flipped her shoes off. Her black pantsuit she wore to work was replaced by a form-fitting navy mini dress.

The male smiled, looking Mariah up and down with a lustful look. Denise knew what was on his mind.

Mariah smiled, turning toward the man. "Well, I had an amazing time."

"I did too," the male said. "So, how about a night-cap?"

Mariah smiled. She placed her hands on the male's broad chest. "Maybe next time." Mariah leaned in, pressing her lips against his.

Anger filled Denise's body. She wanted to storm through the doors, but something stopped her. She continued to watch the lingering kiss and embrace.

"Are you sure you don't want me to stay?" The male rubbed his body against Mariah. He kissed her on her neck.

Mariah seemed to enjoy it. She grabbed the male by his blonde hair, planting another kiss on him.

Denise felt her stomach turn.

"Not tonight hun, but trust me, I'll give you a rain check." Mariah smiled as she slowly pushed him toward the door.

Denise could see the small bulge forming in the man's pants. After a few more moments of contesting, the guy finally left. Denise felt her blood boiling.

Mariah locked the door.

Denise sat on the side of the bed, trying to keep her cool.

Mariah hummed a tune while walking to the bedroom. She turned the light on and jumped at the sight of Denise.

"Dee. Oh my God, you scared me," Mariah said, holding her chest from the fright.

Denise peered at Mariah with a dark expression.

Mariah could feel the anger coming from Denise. She turned toward the mirror and began to take her jewelry off. "How was the party?"

"You really gon' act like I just didn't see yo ass."

Mariah turned around. "What?"

"What the fuck was that at the door?" Denise stood up. Mariah's calm demeanor only angered Denise more.

"That was Ronald," Mariah answered as she turned back around to the mirror.

"OK, I see you trying to play real dumb right now, so I'm going to ask one more time. What the fuck—"

"First, Denise, before you finish that statement, you need to remember our arrangement. I am single, and so are you. We aren't exclusive, you don't have to answer to me, and I don't have to answer to you."

The words hit Denise like a ton of bricks.

Mariah walked past Denise like nothing was happening. She pulled her dress off.

Denise was speechless. She watched as Mariah pranced around the room like nothing was wrong. Mariah and the guy kissing entered Denise's mind again.

"So, you mean this whole time we been kicking it, you been kicking it with other people? And not just other people, you fucking with dudes?"

"Again we are both single. You can go out with other people too."

Denise paced the floor, shaking her head. "Nah, man! This isn't my style. I don't fuck random mutha-fuckas. I'm not trying to be sleeping with you, and you are fucking around with other people—ugh—and dudes. Hell naw, that's nasty as hell!"

Mariah's head jerked around. "So you are calling me nasty?"

"No. I'm saying you fucking with other people and not letting me know is not cool. Have you been out fucking some dude then coming back and letting me fuck you?" Denise's mind raced. Her ex, Crystal entered her mind. She'd caught Crystal having sex with a man in their dorm room freshman year.

"No, Denise. I wouldn't do that. I haven't been sleeping with anyone but you. But I won't make any promises that I won't be seeing other people, and possibly something might happen. If that's too much for you to handle, we can stop this now and go back to just being friends." Mariah stood on her side of the bed.

Denise looked at her with a disgusted expression. "Yeah, maybe I need to start looking for a new place."

Mariah sighed. "Oh, don't be dramatic, Denise. You don't have to leave. You can still live here, same deal and everything."

"I don't know if I will be cool with knowing you are fucking around with other people, seeing ole dude come up in here."

Mariah walked up to Denise. She reached out and grabbed Denise's hand. "Denise, I'm sorry, but I thought we both made it perfectly clear that we weren't in a relationship. You seemed to stress that more than I did."

Denise looked away from Mariah. She knew she was right, but didn't want to admit it. Denise took a deep breath. She looked at Mariah. All of a sudden she looked very different to her.

"Yeah, you're right. It's cool. Do your thing. I do think it's best we stop fooling around though."

"If that's what you want, then fine, but you really don't have to leave. If you don't want to sleep in here, you can sleep in the guest room. Nothing has changed."

"Yeah, I think I'll do that."

Mariah smiled. She hugged Denise.

Denise didn't hug back.

Mariah pulled away, her face covered in disappointment. She smiled, trying to hide her true feelings.

"So how was the party? Did you meet a lot of people?"

Denise nodded. "Yeah, I got an audition with George Kyles."

Mariah's eyes widened. "Wow, that's amazing. See, I told you it was a good idea to go."

"Yeah," Denise muttered, the shock of everything still affecting her.

Mariah noticed Denise's hesitation. "Denise, are you OK with this?"

"It's just I wasn't expecting to see that. I'll be cool. I'm tired. I'm going to bed."

Denise walked out the room and headed to the guest room. She almost forgot Mariah had another room in her house. She turned on the lights. The room was much different from the rest of the house. The walls were white with splashes of various shades of blue.

Denise closed the door. She sat on the side of the bed and stared into space. She felt played, even though technically she wasn't. The sound of her text alert going off brought her back to reality.

Farih: Wanted to make sure you made it home.

Denise re-read the message. Farih's smile entered her mind.

Yeah, I was just thinking about you.

Denise pulled off her shirt. Her text alert blared again.

Farih: What were you thinking?

Denise smiled.

That I should have stayed for that espresso.

Mariah knocked on the door. She slowly opened the door without waiting for Denise to answer. Denise looked at Mariah's sullen face. Mariah stood in the door.

"Are you sure you want to sleep in here?"

"Yeah, I'm good." Denise sat down on the floor and prepared to do her sit-ups.

"I didn't mean to hurt your feelings, Denise. I really thought we both had the same unders—"

"Mariah, we are cool. You didn't hurt my feelings. I was just caught off guard. We are good, trust me. I'm not ready for anything serious, and neither are you. It's cool, really. Don't worry about it."

Mariah's face stayed the same. She was confused, not really sure if she was happy or a little disappointed that Denise wasn't upset over the intimate part of their relationship ending. Mariah forced a smile. She turned and closed the door.

Denise began to do sit-ups. She thought about Mariah. The feelings she had developed were dissolving quickly. In mid sit-up her phone began to ring. She smiled when Farih's name came up. Denise sat up.

"Hey, you," Denise responded in her a deep, calm voice.

Farih sat up in her bed. She smiled. "See, you shouldn't have said no in the first place."

Denise laughed. "You're right. I won't make that mistake again."

Farih bit her lip. "What makes you think there will be another time?"

"Let's just say, I hope there will be."

Farih's face ached from her big grin. "I was wondering if you were busy tomorrow."

"What do you have in mind?"

"Well, I was going to go work out tomorrow. I was hoping you would be up for shooting some hoops."

"Hoops? What do you know about shooting hoops?"

"Don't underestimate the model." Farih smirked.

They both laughed.

"Sounds like fun. I haven't played ball in so long. I could use the practice."

"Well, great. Maybe we can make a wager, to make it interesting."

"Girl, I don't want to take your money." Denise sat on the side of the bed.

"I didn't say anything about money," Farih replied, causing both of them to blush. "Text me your address, and I'll pick you up at noon."

"Will do."

"Good night, Denise."

"Sweet dreams, Farih."

Denise hung the phone up. She suddenly wanted to thank Mariah for the make-out session with the guy. Denise headed to the shower with thoughts of Farih consuming her.

32

"How could you be so stupid?" Lena hit Brandon as he walked in the loft.

Brandon laughed.

"This shit isn't funny. My mother was here!"

Brandon walked into the kitchen and grabbed a bottle of water. "So, you are more concerned with your parents knowing than with the fact that I was kissing another woman."

Lena paused. She looked at Brandon, whose face showed a bit of irritation. "Well, we are, you know . . . so I pretty much expected you to be messing with someone else."

"Whatever, Lena." Brandon walked past her and sat in the chair. "So, is that all you wanted? 'Cause, damn, Lena, you act like your parents aren't gonna find out we are divorcing. I really expected your mom to show up when you lost . . ."

Lena shot Brandon an evil stare.

Brandon looked at Lena, his eyes widened. "Lena, you never told your parents we lost the baby?"

Lena turned away from Brandon.

Brandon stood up. "Wait a minute. Lena, you never told them you were pregnant!"

"I didn't get around to it."

"What the fuck type of shit is that, Lena?"

"Well, we were going through our shit, and everything was happening so fast. Besides, it's a good thing now because last thing I want is them all up in my business. Oh wait, you have fixed that for me."

"Lena, don't even try to put that on me. You the one who is hiding shit. We are getting a divorce. People are gonna find out."

"I know, but damn, Brandon, we could have handled it in a better way than ending up in the gossip blogs. Do you know how that makes me look?"

A knock at the door interrupted their discussion. Brandon walked to the door and pulled it open. His face dropped at the sight of Terrin.

"Can I help you?" Brandon stood in the door like a security guard. He looked down at Terrin's boyish appearance.

Terrin looked at Brandon's massive body. "I'm sorry. Is Lena here?"

Lena's whole body tensed up when she heard the voice. Her heart started beating fast. She rushed to the door and wedged herself in front of Brandon.

"Hey, what are you doing here?"

Terrin looked at Lena then at Brandon, his face covered with anger. "I was just coming by to say hey. I hadn't heard from you in a few days."

Brandon's tight-lipped expression dropped. He shook his head, letting out a chuckle while walking back into the house.

Lena closed the door behind her. "I'm sorry. I've had some family stuff going on." Lena lowered her voice.

"I see. Well, I guess, get at me when you want to." Terrin turned around.

Lena grabbed her arm. "Terrin, please don't be mad. It's not what you think. It's a long story, but trust me, it's not what it looks like."

"I hear ya. Well, you know where to find me, Lena."

"I will call you, I promise."

Terrin walked away without responding.

Lena took a deep breath then walked back into the house. She closed the door and looked at Brandon, sitting on the arm of the couch, staring at her.

"Don't start," Lena huffed, walking into the house.

"So, you want to talk about me and who I'm kissing. Hell, at least it's someone of a different sex." Brandon crossed his arms.

"Brandon . . ."

"So what? Are you gay now, Lena? You coming out the closet? Is that your new little boyfriend?"

"Brandon, please." Lena sighed.

"Tell me, Lena, how do you think it's gonna make me look when someone snaps a photo of you hugged up with some dyke?"

"That's not gonna happen."

"How do you know?"

Lena turned toward Brandon. "Because unlike you, I know how to do my shit in private."

Brandon's bottom lip dropped. "So, you really are messing with that girl?"

"I'm not messing with anyone. She's nice, we hang out."

"That's bullshit and you know it. What the fuck are you, some damn dyke now?"

Lena's mouth dropped.

"Answer my fucking question!"

"I'm not answering a damn thing." Lena rolled her eyes.

Brandon was fuming. He let out a loud growl. Pure rage consumed him. He flipped the dining room table over with one quick lift.

Lena jumped.

Brandon paced the floor.

"Brandon, please . . ."

"You know what? Fuck this shit. You wanna be a dyke, then go be a damn dyke. I'm done wit' yo ass."

"What the hell is that supposed to mean?"

Brandon rushed up to Lena. Lena ducked. Brandon looked at Lena's scared face. He backed off, shaking his head.

Lena's whole body quivered in fear.

"You know what? This shit is for the birds. You wanna go be gay, then do it. I'm not about to sit around and watch the shit."

"Brandon, you don't understand what I am going through," Lena cried. "I just gotta figure things out on my own."

"Do that then. But I'm not staying around to watch you ruin your life. I'm out of here." Brandon grabbed his keys and walked out the house. He slammed the door with so much force, it shook the room.

Lena stared at the door. She knew the only man she loved was never coming back.

33

Denise stood outside of the tall community center building. She watched people walk in and out of the doors. She thought about her days of playing ball at the local community center in Memphis, back when she played for fun, not for school or a scholarship.

"Hey, you." Farih smiled, walking up to Denise.

Even in a simple pair of jeans and a baby doll tee Farih looked like a supermodel.

"Ready to get your ass kicked?"

Denise laughed. "Right. Even though I'm rusty, I doubt you will kick my ass."

"I guess we will see then." Farih walked past Denise and headed up the stairs.

Denise followed. "So, I have one question," Denise said as they walked into the rundown facility. "Why are we playing here and not at some swanky place?"

Farih smiled. "I'll show you."

She opened a door. A group of young women were laughing in the small room. "Hey, ladies."

Denise watched as the young girls greeted Farih like she was a big sister.

"Everyone, this is my friend Denise."

"Hi, Denise," the seven girls chimed in unison. Denise waved back.

"Denise is a basketball player and model."

"I'm not a model," Denise chimed in.

"You played for Freedom in Memphis, didn't you?" One of the young women pointed at Denise.

"Yeah, I did." Denise was surprised. The girl reminded her of herself. Her long body was covered in oversized basketball shorts and shirt. The girl's hair was braided to the back.

The girl smiled. "I thought about going there when I graduate. Y'all got a good team, for a black school."

"We do indeed. You play?" Denise asked.

"Yeah, I do."

"Well, we are gonna have to play some then." Denise smiled.

The young girl nodded her head in approval.

Denise watched in amazement as Farih talked to the group like she was one of them. They talked about everything, from boyfriends to sex.

Farih gave honest answers. She didn't fill their head with nonsense like many would do. She didn't try to force the abstinence idea on them. She was honest, open, and the young women showed their respect in return.

Farih wasn't the supermodel in that room; she was just a woman who was sharing her knowledge and time with a group of young women who might not have anyone else to turn to.

Denise couldn't believe how down-to-earth Farih was; it was sexy as hell to her.

A bell rang, and the girls all stood up. They said their good-byes and headed out the door.

"So what did you think?" Farih picked up her bag.

"This is cool. It's great that you are doing this."

Denise and Farih walked out of the room.

"I can tell those girls really love you."

"And I love them too." Farih's face lit up. "When I was younger, I went to a place like this. I had a woman who I could talk to. I just wanted to do the same for others."

"Dig that." Denise was feeling Farih even more. "So, what's next?"

"Next, I kick your ass at ball."

They walked into a gym. A group of men were playing a pickup game. Farih pulled a basketball out of her bag.

The ball sent chills through Denise's body. She hadn't picked up a basketball in a while. She held the ball in her hands; it felt good.

Farih pulled her shirt over her head. The men playing the game found it hard to focus as Farih pulled off her jeans to reveal a pair of tight Nike Be Fast capris.

Farih's pants and sports bra also consumed Denise's thoughts; she knew how the men felt at that moment.

Some of the men began to wolf-whistle, and yelling in her direction. Farih smiled, ignoring the men's advances.

Denise felt very protective. She wanted to grab Farih and hold her so the men would know what the deal was.

"So, that's not bothering you?"

"Comes with the job." Farih leaned back. "I'm sure some of them are for you too." She winked at Denise.

"Hi, Farih." A gentleman in a Nike track suit walked up to them.

Farih stood up and hugged the gentleman. "Hey, Jessie. This is my friend."

"Denise Chambers. I know who you are. Played for Freedom. I thought you were going to be playing for Liberty this year."

Denise hoped her face didn't show her feelings. The subject was still sore for her. "I got injured, but hopefully I'll be back next year."

"Jessie is the coach of the young women's team here," Farih said as Denise shook his hand.

"Yeah, Denise, if you ever want to come around and drop some knowledge, I know the girls would love it."

"I will." Denise smiled. She loved the thought of helping young women.

The men's game ended. Farih and Denise headed onto the court. The men all paused as they watched Denise and Farih walk to the middle of the court. They all put their things down, ready to see the two women go at it.

"First to twenty?" Farih bounced the ball to Denise.

"Let's do this." Denise dribbled the ball. It was like riding a bike; she was back in her element, with the sexiest opponent ever.

The game grew intense. Denise's dream of a quick victory was quickly ruined. Farih was better than good; she was an amazing ball player. Her flirting ceased; she had her eye on the prize.

Farih's supermodel status was gone; she was now a ballplayer trying to beat Denise.

The men all stayed to watch the game. They yelled like they were watching an NBA game. Denise and Farih were both soaked in sweat. Denise knew she had to get back to working out; her energy wasn't what it should have been.

Finally, victory was hers as she shot a lucky three-pointer that caused her to win the game.

"Good game," Farih said. "Guess I didn't beat your ass, after all."

"Please, you came close. Too close. I wasn't expecting that."

"Man, that was the sexiest basketball game I've ever seen," one of the ballers yelled toward them.

"Yeah, maybe next time we'll join your game."

"Naa," the older man stated. "I'm not trying to get my ass kicked by women."

Everyone laughed.

Denise and Farih showered and changed then headed out of the community center. Farih signed a few autographs for a few kids who recognized who she was.

"You really have surprised me, Farih."

"Let me guess, you were expecting a stuck-up, prissy supermodel."

"Well . . . yeah." Denise laughed. "I definitely wasn't expecting what I got."

"Is that a good thing?" Farih looked at Denise.

"It's a great thing."

Denise and Farih's eyes met, and they both blushed. Denise was anxious, a feeling she hadn't had in years. She was anxious to see what was going to happen. She welcomed it.

Denise heard the familiar male voice outside of Mariah's apartment. It didn't bother her anymore. The only woman on her mind was Farih.

"Hey, Dee." Mariah smiled as Denise walked in the apartment. She was lying in Richard's arms while they watched a movie."

"Hey." Denise closed the door.

Mariah sat up. "Richard, this is Denise." Mariah's face was flushed.

Richard stood up. He was taller than Denise remembered. Denise shook his hand. She had to admit, he wasn't an ugly man. He reminded her of David Beckham.

"It's nice to meet you." Richard's voice was also deeper than normal.

"Nice to meet you too. Well, I'm tired. I'm gonna go lay it down."

"You've been playing basketball?" Mariah questioned when she noticed Denise's attire.

"Yeah, I went to a community center."

"That's great, Dee. I'm glad you are playing again. Keep those skills up."

Denise wanted to laugh at how quick Mariah was in agent mode. "Yeah, it felt good. I didn't realize how much I missed it."

Mariah smiled. Denise noticed Mariah's demeanor. She could tell Mariah was very happy. "Well, I'm gonna leave you two alone." Denise headed toward her room.

Denise knew her feelings had changed for Mariah. She sat her bag on the floor. Farih consumed Denise's thoughts. Denise knew she was dealing with feelings she'd never experienced before. The only other woman who had her open was Lena, but that was a forbidden love.

Lena's face entered Denise's mind. Lena was a forbidden love her heart didn't want to completely let go of.

Denise's thoughts were interrupted by her phone. She smiled when Farih's face appeared on her screen.

"Hey, you."

Farih relaxed back in her favorite black oversized chair. She put her feet up on the ottoman. "I just wanted to let you know I really had a great time today."

Denise felt a warm tingle in her cheeks. "I had a great time too. Thanks for taking me. I really enjoyed myself."

Farih grinned; she had never met a woman like Denise. "I was wondering if you would like to come to a photo shoot with me tomorrow."

"Photo shoot?"

"It's for Victoria Secret."

Denise paused. Butterflies fluttered in her stomach. "Victoria Secret? Are you serious?"

"I understand if you don't want to go," Farih playfully replied in her low, seductive voice.

"Naaa, I would hate to go watch you model in lingerie. That sounds like the worst idea ever."

Denise and Farih laughed.

"I'll pick you up at five."

"In the morning?" Denise frowned.

Farih let out a snicker. "The early bird catches the worm, Denise."

Denise was smitten. Farih's quick remarks kept her on her toes. "I think I can manage that." Denise lay back on her bed. "Hey, Farih, what's your zodiac sign?"

"Cancer. And you?"

Denise's body tensed. "That explains a lot. Hey, I need to get off if I'm going to wake up in the morning."

Farih sat up, taken back by Denise's change in attitude. "Oh OK, see you in the morning. Hey, wait. You didn't tell me your sign."

"Scorpio."

Farih smiled. "They say Cancer and Scorpio's the perfect match."

Visions of Lena filled Denise's head. "Yeah, I know. See you tomorrow?"

"It's a date."

Denise hung the phone up. The wall around her heart that Farih was breaking down was slowly starting to rebuild itself. Farih was too good to be true. She knew from her past that things that were too good to be true usually were.

34

Lena watched the polar bears swim from end to end of their new exhibit at the Memphis Zoo. The polar bear building was her favorite place to think. The underwater viewing room was dark, illuminated by the sun and the blue water in front of her from the wall-sized viewing glass. She took a sip of her Dasani water. She loved coming to the zoo midweek during the day. It wasn't crowded with people like on Tuesdays when the zoo was free. Lena was able to think in peace.

"Did you know you are staring at the world largest land predator?"

Lena turned around. A tall, brown-skinned man stood behind her. His slender body was fit, his clean-shaven face better looking than any other zoo worker she had seen before.

"Really? That's interesting." Lena watched the attractive guy walk down the stairs.

"Yes. I figured I'd tell you a little something since I see you here a lot." The man smiled. He extended his hand. "I'm Derek."

Lena read this name tag, Derek Harris, Zookeeper. "So you are the zookeeper. So you like, get to touch the animals?"

Derek let out a baritone laugh."It's a little more than that, but yes."

"I've never seen you around here before."

"I've seen you." Derek smiled.

Lena felt herself blushing. "So, what does a girl have to do to touch an animal?"

Derek's almond eyes slanted. "Go over to the farm area. There are plenty of animals you can touch."

They both laughed.

"I was thinking something a little more exotic than a cow." Lena drank some more of her water.

"I see the beautiful woman is trying to make me lose my job."

Lena laughed. "No, I'm not. I know it's impossible."

Derek sat next to Lena. He leaned in to her ear. "Nothing is impossible. Come with me."

Lena followed Derek through the employees only area of Primate Canyon, where the monkeys resided. They walked down a long corridor. The wild smell of monkey droppings hit Lena's nose. She wondered how they kept the smell from being so bad in the front of the zoo.

Derek opened a door that said DIRECTOR. "Sit in here I'll be right back."

Lena obeyed. She was impressed. The office window overlooked the gorilla exhibit. Derek's office was filled with rich browns, oranges and deep reds. A beautiful mural of a variety of animal faces covered half of the wall behind the brown leather sofa. Lena noticed a picture of Derek on his desk holding a baby white tiger. Lena got excited; she always loved white tigers.

The door opened. Derek walked in holding a tiny brown and white monkey in his arms. Lena's mouth dropped at the sight of the adorable creature.

"This is Katie. Our newest Atelidae." Lena looked at Derek confused.

"Spider monkey."

"Oh, she's so cute." Lena squealed. "Can I?" Lena held her hand out.

Derek nodded.

She petted the baby on her head. "Oh, she's adorable. I want one."

Derek's laughter rumbled. "See, this is why women don't need to see exotic animals."

Lena couldn't help but laugh.

Derek handed Lena a bottle. She put it to the monkey's mouth. It began to suck like a baby. Lena felt a mothering sense take over her body. She thought about her child. Lena pulled away.

"Thank you, Derek. That was amazing." She handed Derek the bottle.

"You aren't trying to leave me yet, are you? I risk my job and you are ready to bounce." Derek smiled.

Lena was impressed by his charm.

"I would like to stay, but I really need to be getting home."

"OK, let me put Katie back, and I'll walk you out." Derek turned around. "Don't pull a Cinderella on me, OK?"

Lena couldn't help but laugh.

Derek returned holding a bottle of anti-bacterial gel. Lena cleaned her hands, and they headed out of the office. Derek's slender frame was a change from Brandon's massive body, Lena liked it.

"So, Lena, what brings you to the zoo so often?"

Lena and Derek walked around the area, passing the various types of primates. Lena stopped in front of a sunbathing gorilla.

"I just come here to think. I love the zoo."

"Well, I must say, I have been watching you for a while."

Lena smirked. "Really? Stalk much?"

Derek laughed. "No, I just figured that someone as beautiful as you had to have someone waiting in the wings. I guess you can say I was waiting on the day a man comes in with you."

"Is that right." Lena looked at Derek's handsome face. "So what made you come up to me today?"

"I don't really know. Guess I got tired of letting you leave." Derek giggled.

They stopped at the gift shop. Lena pulled her keys out of her pocket. Derek stood fidgeting with his ID tag. Lena was amused that an obviously confident man was a little shy around her.

"Well, thank you again Derek. I really appreciate it."

"Hey, um, how about a private tour of the zoo? If you come late tonight, you can see things you'll never see during the day." Derek smiled.

"Is that legal?"

"Yes, we administrators have some clout," Derek boasted. "So how about it?"

Lena smiled. "OK, what time?"

"Ten." Derek reached into his pocket and pulled out a business card. "Just call me when you get outside."

"OK, I will. See you later, Derek."

"I'll be looking forward to it."

Lena was floating as she opened the door to her loft. She was excited about her special plans. She pulled off her flip-flops. The cool floor sent a chill through her body. She started thinking about what to wear; she had no idea what to wear to the zoo at night.

She heard a faint ringing coming from her purse. She ran to the table, trying to catch it in time. By the time she pulled her phone out, she had missed the call. She looked at her call log. It was from Terrin. Lena pressed send to call her back.

"I was just leaving you a message." Terrin tried to sound cool.

"I'm sorry. I didn't hear my phone ring. How was your day?"

"Long. Had this one child whose mouth was full of cavities. Poor kid had to have five teeth pulled."

Lena cringed. "Oh my God."

"Oh well, comes with the job." Terrin poured a glass of orange juice. "So I was wondering if you wanted to grab a bite to eat. I have been craving some of Onyx fish and chicken."

Lena froze. She knew that was the last place she needed to go. She suddenly felt guilty. Technically she was single and could do what she wanted, but she still felt a little guilty. "I, um, actually already have plans tonight."

Terrin's body tensed up. "Oh, a date?"

"Something like that."

Terrin covered the phone with her hand. She mouthed a few obscenities. She realized she didn't have Lena the way she thought she did. "Oh, OK, that's cool. Well, just get at me when you can."

"Are you sure you're OK with it?"

"Lena, I'm not your woman. I don't have to be OK with it."

Lena sat down at her kitchen table. "I know, but I don't want you to think badly of me."

"I don't, Lena. You are cool. I'll holla at you later." Terrin hung up the phone before Lena could respond. She didn't want Lena to hear the hurt in her voice.

Lena was in shock. She couldn't believe Terrin hung up in her face. She suddenly felt horrible. She didn't want to hurt anyone. She picked her phone up and called Carmen.

"Hey, girl." Carmen held the small cell phone with her shoulder while she seasoned the chicken she was about to cook.

"So I met a guy today at the zoo and he was real nice. He let me touch a monkey."

"What! Shit!" Carmen yelled as she almost dropped her phone. "Hold on Lena." Carmen placed the phone on the counter; she washed her hands and dried them on her shirt. She picked the phone back up. "OK, now you touched his monkey? What the fuck?"

"A real monkey, Carmen. He's the director over animals. Like the head zookeeper."

"Oh, that's interesting. Is he cute?" Carmen sat on her sofa.

"Yes, he really was. He invited me to come to a private tour of the zoo tonight."

"Oh, really? Now that sounds like fun."

"Yeah, but I told Terrin, and she sounded upset."

Carmen looked up. "So."

Lena headed to her bedroom. "What do you mean?"

"I'm sorry, Lena. When did you get into a relationship?"

"I'm not."

"Then you don't owe her anything."

"That's what she said but . . ."

Carmen stood up when she heard water hit her stove and sizzle. "Look, Lena, you are single, and you don't owe either one of them anything. If it's one thing I've learned from Cooley is that if you keep it real with the women, they really can't get mad at anyone but themselves."

Lena opened her closet door. "So you think I should tell Derek the truth too? That I'm a married but separated confused girl who's currently dating a woman as well?"

"Maybe not in those words, but yeah, oh fuck." Carmen ran into her kitchen. She pulled the boiling pot off of the stove. "I gotta go before I burn my house down. Have fun tonight."

"OK, girl." Lena hung up the phone. She knew Carmen was right. She took a deep breath and began to pick out the perfect outfit for her date.

35

Sahara pressed her lips against Cooley's. The tip of Cooley's tongue grazed Sahara's strawberry-flavored lips. Cooley's body was on fire. Sahara's legs straddled Cooley's lap, and she caressed Sahara's butt cheeks. Her thin lace cheekies were in the way of what she wanted.

Cooley took both of her hands and ripped the panties right off of her.

Sahara said, "Oh, you ass. Those cost sixteen dollars."

"I'll buy you another pair." Cooley pulled Sahara's face toward hers. "Fuck it. Just send me a bill." Cooley kissed Sahara's chest as she ripped the matching lace bra with her bare hands.

"Damn, nigga, you racking up a big bill here," Sahara teased while Cooley licked her way to her hard nipples.

"It's worth it," Cooley muttered as her tongue licked around Sahara's brown nipples. Cooley stood up out of her chair. Sahara's long legs held on to Cooley's waist. They kissed as Cooley slowly carried Sahara to the bedroom.

Sahara watched as Cooley pulled a familiar black leather bag out of her closet. She pulled a harness out and attached a thick black dildo to it. Sahara's pussy jumped in anticipation.

Cooley strapped up. She fastened the leather strap to her body. She looked at Sahara's naked body laying on her king-sized bed. Sahara's sexual appetite was unparalleled. Even Misha, who was the only woman who Cooley ever knew to keep up with her, couldn't hold a candle to Sahara. Cooley hated to admit it, but Sahara was even a little much for her at times. Sahara was her match. She knew it.

"Carla." Sahara watched Cooley pull her wife-beater over her head. Her black sports bra held in her lady lumps. Sahara loved to see Cooley's body. She had curves out of this world, but she kept them hidden under oversized clothes. "Carla, what am I to you?"

Cooley looked up. "What do you mean?"

"I'm not trying to freak you out or anything. I was just wondering if we are, you know, exclusive now. Am I your girlfriend?"

The word sent chills up Cooley's arm. "Uhhh . . ."

Sahara sat up. "I'm just trying to see where we are. I mean, I'm happy with whatever it is. I just kinda wanted to know."

"We are us. Why we gotta have a title on it?" Cooley sat on the edge of the bed.

"Cooley, don't freak out. I just was wondering. We don't have to have labels. Don't worry about it."

"Yeah, I've heard that before. Then a few weeks later you gon' be pissed if I don't call you my girlfriend." Cooley thought about Lynn, the woman she spent most of last year with while still craving Misha.

Sahara felt offended. She got out of the bed. "You know what, never mind."

"Where are you going?" Cooley watched as Sahara's naked body switched out the room. She sighed, following her.

"I expected you to know me a little better than this, Cooley. I'm not about to sit up here and let you compare me to those lame-ass bitches from your past." Sahara picked her panties off the floor. She tried to step into them, realizing Cooley had torn her underwear. "Asshole!"

Cooley walked closer and stopped. She looked down, realizing her silicone rubber manhood was hitting her leg. She looked back at Sahara.

They both burst out in laughter.

"Looks like we both are stuck with each other right now," Cooley joked.

Sahara tried to put her mad face back on. She pouted her lips out.

Cooley walked up to her, putting her arms around her. Sahara's ass rubbed against her manhood.

"Cooley, I accept you for who you are. Don't you know that? I'm not trying to put pressure on you. I just didn't want to refer to you as the wrong thing."

"I'm sorry, Sah. I'm just really just not into labels. Why mess with something that is going so great?"

Sahara nodded her head. She didn't care how she had Cooley, as long as she did. Sahara bit her bottom lip. She fell down to her knees.

Cooley's eyes widened.

Sahara began to stroke the eight-inch black dick.

"So, why are you studs so fascinated with a woman sucking your strap?" Sahara eyes shifted up.

Cooley licked her lips. She smiled. "I don't know, I just like it."

"So, you would like it if I sucked it right now?" Sahara flicked the tip of her tongue out. She grazed the tip of the dick.

Cooley shook her head, trying to remain calm. "How does this look to you?"

"Baby, you look damn good right now," Cooley responded.

Sahara closed her mouth, taking the rubber into her mouth.

Cooley put her hand on the back of Sahara's head.
She guided Sahara's head while she sucked back and
forth. Sahara was in total submission to her. Cooley felt
a rush come to her stomach.

Cooley watched Sahara's plump lips sucking her
fake manhood like she was Superhead in the flesh.
She reached down and grasped the fake scrotum at the
base of her dick. Holding it, she eased the cock farther
into Sahara's mouth. Sahara looked up at her as Cooley
nodded.

"That's right. You can take it all." Cooley watched
as Sahara's jaw dropped back and she opened wider
to receive the manhood. She felt the pressure against
her crotch as the tip pushed against the back of Sahara's throat. She slowly stroked the dick in and out
of Sahara's mouth as she watched the woman's lips
curl around it. She took it like a champ. Cooley never
wanted to sex Sahara so badly in her life.

Sahara pulled her head back and stood up. "Lay
down," she directed and pointed to the floor.

Cooley went with it, getting down on her cold hardwood floor.

Sahara positioned herself between Cooley's legs. She
took the strap back in her mouth. Her long hair fell
down in front of her face.

Cooley ran her hands through Sahara's hair. She
wanted to see it. Sahara took her hands and pulled
on Cooley's cotton boxer briefs. She felt the open slit,
placed in the front of men to use to pee. With both of
her hands, she ripped the cotton underwear with all of
her might.

Cooley jumped. "What you doing!"

"Now we're even."

Before Cooley could move, Sahara's tongue entered
her walls with force. Cooley's eyes bucked open. Her
mouth dropped.

Sahara sucked on her swollen knob, causing Cooley to feel like she had temporary paralysis. Only one other girl had gone down on her in her life. Now Sahara was making her into her little bitch.

Cooley tried to say stop, but the pleasure was so intense, she couldn't talk. Only moans left her mouth. No longer wanting to fight it, she laid her head back while Sahara worked her mouth on her pussy.

Cooley's body trembled. Sahara was dishing out what she had given to so many before her. It was the most pleasurable revenge in history.

Sahara never expected Cooley to taste so good. She held on to Cooley's thick legs. In that instant Cooley was all woman. The aggressor submitted. She wanted Cooley to feel her inside of her.

"Bae. Baeee." Cooley's eyes rolled around. "Shit." Her fingertips caressed Sahara's scalp. Cooley felt death approaching. Her toes stretched out, legs tensed up.

Sahara didn't stop. She continued to tongue-fuck her like her tongue was the strap. Cooley's body trembled as she came.

Sahara felt Cooley's warmth hit her tongue, and she sucked it up.

Unwilling to be outdone, Cooley wrapped her leg around Sahara. With one push, Sahara found herself on the ground and Cooley on top. The hunter was back.

Cooley pulled Sahara's legs up, placing them on her chest. She entered Sahara with her man. Sahara jumped as the tip entered her tight pussy.

They didn't take their eyes off of each other.

Cooley's stroke caused Sahara to stutter. "Shhh . . . shhh . . . ahhh."

Sahara's incoherent mutters excited Cooley. She pushed deep inside of Sahara's walls.

Sahara sat up. She pushed Cooley down to the floor. Sahara claimed on top, immediately riding Cooley like she was a championship jockey.

Cooley held on to Sahara's hips as her body gyrated against her pelvis. Sahara's plump breasts bounced up and down. Cooley loved Sahara's stamina.

She felt her body about to cum again, but Sahara wasn't ready yet.

Cooley tried to hold her orgasm, but it rushed out of her like a broken dam.

"You my *papi*." Sahara moaned.

Cooley nodded her head rapidly. "Ummm, *papi*."

Sahara lowered her body to Cooley. Their mouths met.

Cooley pulled Sahara's face close. Their tongues wrestled. Sahara's jaw dropped. She hit a note in a falsetto only heard when you reach the highest level of ecstasy.

Sahara's body fell on top of Cooley's. She rested her head on Cooley's chest. Cooley ran her fingers up and down Sahara's hair. Cooley didn't want to move. She wanted to stay in that position, with their sweaty bodies locked together.

"Let's do it," Cooley whispered.

"Damn! What the fuck are you, a rabbit?" Sahara panted.

"No, crazy-ass girl. Let's do it. Let's make this official."

Sahara raised her head. She looked into Cooley's eyes. "Cooley, don't just—"

Cooley covered Sahara's mouth with her hand. "I mean it."

Sahara couldn't hold it in. Her face lit up with a large smile. "OK then."

"Cool." Cooley put her hand on the back of Sahara's head, pushing it back to her chest.

They laid there, officially a couple.

36

Denise sat back watching Melanie critique a group of super-thin models. Denise was in awe. Melanie commanded attention. When she said move, the models moved instantly, all hoping to earn the job.

Melanie glanced back at her new protégé and smiled. "What are you staring at?"

Denise looked up. "I'm sorry, I just, that dress is beautiful." Denise looked at the model in a long blue-and-white chiffon print evening gown.

"Yes, I'm putting it on Zoë Saldana for her premiere. I'm glad you like it."

"Man, she's hot. She could definitely rock it."

Melanie looked the model over one more time. She clapped her hands. Her two assistants walked in and helped the model off of the platform. Melanie walked over to her desk and sat in her chair.

"So how are things going with you and Farih?"

Denise blushed. "It's cool. She's cool."

Melanie smiled. "From the look on your face, it's a little more than cool."

Denise dropped her head. She gazed back up at Melanie. "She is kind of amazing."

Melanie clapped her hands together. "That's great. I knew you two would hit it off. I bet y'all have some wild times."

"Oh, it's none of that yet. I actually haven't kissed her yet."

Melanie's smiled dropped. "Why not. Hell, if I had a young thing like that, I would live in her pussy."

Denise's jaw dropped at Melanie's comment. "I can't believe you just said that to me."

"What? It's the truth." Melanie shuffled through some pages of designs. "What is the holdup?"

Denise sat back in the chair. "I just like to take my time. I don't want to rush into something."

Melanie shook her head while looking at the drawings.

"What?"

"You haven't even kissed the girl. That's not taking it slow, that's slower than slow. So stop bullshitting with me. What's the real holdup? Or should I say who?" Melanie looked up at Denise. "Is it Mariah?"

"Oh, hell no." Denise snapped. "Mariah and I are beyond over. She's with her first love again. He's cool." Lena entered Denise's head. "I feel so stupid at times."

"So it's someone else?"

"A girl back home name Lena. She's married."

"Oh, not good."

"Yeah, but you see, she left her husband for me. Came to New York and everything. I was messed up over the basketball thing, drunk as hell. I yelled at her, told her to leave." Denise lowered her head. The thought of Lena's tear-filled face still stung.

"So why didn't you go back after her?"

"Because Lena was complicated. The whole thing was complicated from day one. She was an amazing, complicated woman. I can't deal with the drama, you know. And now I have this amazing woman staring me in my face who I really, really like, but when I try to take that next step, Lena enters my mind."

Melanie turned her chair around to Denise, her face covered with concern. "Denise, do you think that you think about this girl because you still want her, or because you feel guilty for hurting her?"

Denise stared at Melanie. Melanie had become like an older sister to her. She gave advice as well as Mema used to. "It's guilt. I love her, but I don't think I'm in love with her anymore. It kills me that I hurt her. That I brought pain to her life. I never wanted to do that."

Melanie put her hand on Denise's knee. "Denise, guilt is a hard thing to deal with. To this day I can't shake the guilt that I have about someone."

Denise noticed the sorrow in Melanie's eyes.

"I loved someone, and I wasn't there for them like I should have been. I blame myself for everything that happened to them. Unfortunately I can't apologize. I can't make it right anymore. You do what you have to do to find closure. So you can be right for yourself."

Denise hung on to every word. She could tell Melanie was sincere. She sighed. "I really do care about Farih; she is the most amazing woman I've ever met."

"Then you do right by yourself, so you can do right by her." Melanie stood up. "It sounds to me that this woman, Lena, put you in a situation that you both couldn't control. You did what you felt was best by letting her go. You can't blame yourself for her showing up a little too late. Tell me, Denise, how many times did she come to you and go back to her man?"

Denise thought about the years of the Lena limbo. She thought about how it felt when Lena would flip-flop from her to Brandon, all because she didn't know what she wanted.

"A few times."

"So why are you blaming yourself for finally putting an end to the cycle?"

Denise looked at Melanie. Her eyes widened. She realized Melanie was right. She stood up. She never meant to hurt Lena, but if the series of events hadn't had happened to bring that situation then it never would have happened to begin with. Denise felt like a ton had been lifted off of her. She smiled.

"Man. Denise Yvette Chambers, I think you have just had a breakthrough." Denise shook her head. "Thanks." Denise looked at Melanie. She was staring at Denise like she had seen a ghost. "What's wrong?"

"What is your middle name?" Melanie said, frozen in her place.

"Yvette," Denise replied, completely confused by Melanie's change in demeanor.

Melanie's eyes began to fill with tears. She turned so Denise would not see her. "Man, something got in my eye. OK, have fun with Farih. I'll see you later." Melanie swiftly walked off toward her bathroom, leaving Denise dumbfounded.

37

Lena gave herself one more look over. She opted for a pair of sexy skinny jeans and a baby blue halter top for her outing. She figured if she was to touch any more animals she would be OK with losing a pair of jeans and a shirt, not with one of her expensive dresses. Lena placed her flip-flops on and headed to the door.

Lena slid her heavy door open and jumped. Terrin was standing there with her hand in knocking position. They both jumped. Lena could tell something was up, by Terrin's stern look.

Terrin looked at Lena's sexy appearance. She took a few steps back and sighed. "Look, I know you are on your way out, I just wanted to come and say something real quick."

Lena closed the door behind her. She turned back and looked at Terrin. "What's up?"

Terrin took a deep breath. "Look, Lena, I know I'm not your woman, and I'm cool with that. However, I'm not cool with you sleeping around and coming back to me."

Lena was put off by Terrin's attitude. "Terrin."

"I'm not saying that you are sleeping with anyone. I just have to say what is best for me. I'm not about to be just a number on your list."

"Terrin, wait a minute here. I don't want you to think that it's like that, because it's not. But I just ended a marriage. I'm not trying to be settled back down this soon. I am going on a date, but I'm not trying to sleep around with various people. That's not my style." Lena felt her body heating up.

"It's whatever, Lena. Do what you want to do. But understand that even though I want to be here for you, I'm not going to sit around and let you play me for a fool. That's all I got to say. Have fun on your little date." Terrin walked off, leaving Lena speechless.

Lena knew Terrin cared about her, but she wasn't expecting that reaction. A piece of her wanted to follow Terrin and just give in, but something held her back. She shook her head and headed down the hallway. She had a date to get to.

Lena pulled into the abandoned zoo parking lot. There were two cars in the facility. She figured one of them had to be Derek's. She hopped out of her BMW and walked toward the front gate.

The parking lot was a little scary at night. The giant brick animal statues that lined the front entrance seemed bigger in the dark.

She noticed a tall figure standing by the gate. She smiled. Derek looked nice in a pair of dark denim jeans and a black button-down, a big change from his zoo-keeper get-up.

"Wow," Derek smiled. "You look amazing."

"Thank you." Lena hugged Derek. His cologne smelled amazing on him.

"I hope you're hungry." Derek held her hand as they walked into the zoo.

The beautiful pool that resembled the Reflecting Pool in front of the Lincoln Memorial was lit up with pink and blue lights. Lena was in awe. The beauty of the zoo was captured better at night than during the day. She thought it would have been beautiful for a party or reception.

They walked into the Cat Country Café. What once housed the lions and tigers now was transformed into a large cafeteria during the day that served Backyard Burgers and treats to customers. Lena was surprised to see a single table in the middle with two taper candles and a white tablecloth.

"Wow. You did all this for me?"

"Don't get too excited yet." Derek pulled the top off of her silver tray. A backyard burger and fries sat on the plate.

Lena laughed.

"I'm sorry I didn't have much time, had to work with what I could. But I made the burgers myself."

"I can't believe they let you do this." Lena sat in the chair that Derek pulled out for her.

"Let's just say, I have friends in high places." Derek sat in the chair across from her. "The head security guard is one of my bestfriends. We are the only two in the zoo tonight."

"Oh, so is this an all-the-time thing. Bring women to the zoo and wine and dine them with burgers and private tours?" Lena slanted her eyes.

Derek's deep laugh echoed through the building. "No, it's not like that. We wouldn't risk this for just anyone." Derek's eyes were fixated on Lena.

"So why me?"

"Let's just say, I saw something special in you."

Lena blushed. She thought about Terrin. She wondered what it was that made people say that they see something special in her. She wondered why Denise didn't see it anymore.

"So what's your story, Lena? Why are you able to be out with me? Why hasn't some man put a ring on it?" Derek mimicked Beyoncé's signature move.

Lena felt her stomach drop. She knew she had to be honest. "Actually someone did put a ring on it. I'm in the process of getting a divorce from my husband." Lena swallowed hard. "Brandon Redding."

Derek looked confused. Suddenly shock covered his face. "The basketball player?"

Lena nodded.

Derek sat back in his chair. "Wow, that's, that's a serious ex you have there."

"I'm sorry. I probably should have said something when we were around each other earlier."

Derek shook his head. "No, no, you're fine. I am actually flattered."

Lena gazed at him with curiosity.

"I mean, I'm flattered that you would even consider going out with me after you were married to a superstar athlete. I mean, you come from hanging out with celebrities. I hang out with animals all day."

Lena laughed. "I think it's pretty awesome that you get to hang out with animals all day." She placed a French fry in her mouth. "You know I've always dreamed of owning my own white tiger."

"Oh. See you are trying to kill yourself." Derek laughed.

Lena blushed.

"You know we have white tigers now."

Lena's eyes lit up. "Yes, I've seen them. So beautiful. I actually went to the Mirage in Vegas. They have all of Siegfried and Roy's white tigers. I was in heaven."

Derek was completely wrapped up in Lena. He put his napkin down, stood up and extended his hand. "Come on."

They walked through the dimly lit zoo. Derek opened a door in the Cat Country exhibit. The hall reminded Lena of the hall from earlier that day. The smell was just as bad. They walked up to a door. Derek unlocked it.

Lena's mouth dropped. Right next to the bars were the three newest tigers, including the two white tigers.

"How close can I get?" Lena started to walk close but was grabbed by Derek. He pulled her into his arms, instantly turning Lena on.

"This is as close as you get. Those are not pets, sweetie. They will kill you."

Derek and Lena's eyes met.

"Oh." Lena's stomach filled with butterflies. Derek slowly let go of Lena's waist. Lena knew that was one thing she loved about men. She felt protected in his arms.

They left the cat night-house and walked around the zoo. They talked about all types of subjects. Derek had been engaged, but the engagement was called off a few months before the wedding. Derek made Lena laugh. He had a goofy side that she liked.

They made their way to her favorite exhibit. The exhibition room was dark; the lights inside of the polar bear pools illuminated the viewing room. Derek sat down on the steps that Lena had sat on millions of times before.

Lena put her hand on the glass. "That water looks so beautiful."

"Yeah, thanks to lights and an amazing filter system." Derek snickered.

"So why the Memphis zoo? I mean, you've worked at some major places, why come here?" Lena questioned, leaning against the viewing glass.

"Why not? Honestly, Memphis has an amazing zoo. It's one of the only zoos to have the pandas. And with all the expansions, I expect Memphis to make it to some Forbes list very soon." Derek couldn't take his eyes off Lena's body. He tried to focus on her face, but her thighs and perky breasts were calling his name.

Lena smiled. "Derek, thank you, really. This has been an amazing night."

Derek walked over to Lena. "I'm glad you're having a good time."

Derek and Lena's eyes met. Derek put his hand on Lena's waist. Lena moved in closer. Derek leaned in, planting his lips against hers. Lena closed her eyes; she opened her mouth slightly, allowing his tongue to enter hers. Lena's eyes opened as Derek stuck his tongue down her throat. He held on to her, planting a wet, sloppy kiss on her.

Lena felt her French fries coming back up. She pulled away.

"What's wrong?" Derek questioned, his dick bulging in his pants.

Suddenly Derek didn't look so good. She noticed his bad skin. His ears were bigger than she remembered. And in his nose sat a big booger. Lena felt disgusted. She blinked. Suddenly he looked normal again, no bad skin, no big ears, but the booger remained.

"I'm so sorry, Derek. I can't do this," Lena said as she walked up the stairs.

Derek rushed after her, grabbing her by her arm. "What's wrong? Is it something I did?"

Yes, you tried to kill me with your tongue. "No, it's not you, it's me. I'm not ready for this. I thought I was, but I'm not. I'm so sorry."

Derek looked like a lost puppy. His mind raced, trying to think of something to make Lena want to stay.

Lena's mind was made up. The date was over.

Derek walked Lena to the front door. He pleaded for her to stay a little while longer, even throwing the offer to feed the pandas at her.

Lena gave him a hug and a kiss on his cheek, promised to call him, even though she knew she wouldn't. She walked out of the zoo, knowing she wouldn't be able to return for a while. She would have to find a new place to think.

Terrin opened her door to find Lena standing there. There were no words. She took Lena by the hand and led her into her house.

"Are you gon' D up or what?" Farih dribbled the ball with ease and a big smile on her face.

Denise wiped the sweat from her head. She didn't realize how out-of-shape a few months would make her.

"Just play," Denise snapped. She didn't like the idea of getting beat by a supermodel.

Farih smiled as she stood with the ball in front of Denise.

Denise looked her up and down. "You know you have an unfair advantage."

"Why do you say that?"

"Look at what you're wearing." Denise pointed at Farih's short pink velour shorts that hugged her chocolate thighs. Her little Victoria's Secret tank hugged her body, making her breasts sit up. "How the hell am I supposed to concentrate with you looking like that?"

"Excuses. Excuses. I thought you were supposed to be a good player."

Denise's mouth fell open. She nodded her head. "All right, you might look good, but that statement just cost your ass the game."

Farih began to dribble the ball. Denise bent her legs into her defensive stance. Farih attempted a cross-over but instantly found herself without the ball. Her mouth dropped as Denise stole the ball and scored on her. Denise smiled, dribbling the ball slowly.

"You want to repeat that thing about being a good player?"

Farih clapped her hands. "Finally, now that you can take your mind off my ass, we can play some real ball." Farih winked.

Denise smirked.

Denise and Farih showered, changed and headed out of the trendy gym. Farih's pink shorts were replaced with a pair of tight-fitting denim jeans and a black tee. Her ponytail hung, bouncing with every step. Denise opted to use her free clothes, wearing a pair of Jocku pants and a white T-shirt. They walked down the busy street to a small restaurant across the street.

"So did I impress you?" Farih smiled, taking a sip of her strawberry smoothie.

"You really did. Gave me a run for my money."

"No, I didn't."

They both laughed.

"But thanks for letting me get those few shots in early."

"Yeah, I was gonna let you win, but you was getting too cocky." Denise smiled.

Two young men walked up to the table and asked Farih to sign their *Sports Illustrated* swimsuit issue. Denise watched as Farih smiled and treated the boys like they were the most important people in the world. They walked off on cloud nine.

Farih looked at Denise's expression. "What?"

Denise shook her head. "Nothing at all." She took a sip of her mango smoothie.

"So tell me something I don't know, Denise."

"I don't know what you already know."

Farih sat up in her seat. "Well, I must admit, I did my research. I Googled you."

"Googled me?" Denise laughed. She hadn't felt that down-to-earth in a long time.

"Yes, I did. You were the superstar of your high school and college basketball teams. I was wondering why you opted for that small local school instead of a major school like Tennessee."

"I was recruited by Tennessee. Man, I would have loved to play there. But I didn't want to be that far away from my grandmother. She had gotten sick my senior year in high school. I didn't know if she was going to make it. She stayed with me until my junior year. Then she passed." Denise fought to hold back tears, thinking about her grandmother.

Farih put her hand on top of Denise's hand. "This is why I like you, Denise. You are so genuine. You don't run across people like you in this city, especially in this industry."

Farih's radiant smile caused Denise to blush.

"So, let me ask you something. You are like a super-model for real. Why were you at a go-see for Melanie? Aren't you past those days?"

Farih lowered her head. "Actually I wasn't really there for the go-see."

Denise's eyes widened.

"Melanie told me there was a new girl coming she wanted me to check out. She's been trying to hook me up for a while."

"Oh really?"

"Yes. Don't tell her I told you, but your whole go-see was a setup. She just wanted to see if you were going to be what she was hoping."

Denise's right eye rose. "Wait, so what?"

Farih laughed. "Denise, you were never going to be up for the job. So many people come into Melanie trying to get on, she said she had a feeling you were different. So she set the go-see to see if you were going to be like all the others, or if you were what she thought you were."

"This is a trip. I don't understand what the fuss is over me." Denise sank down in her chair. "I am just Denise."

"That's it right there. You aren't out here trying to take the world by storm. You are a genuine person. Your struggles, your attitude, you radiate this positive vibe that is infectious. I felt it the moment you looked at me."

"I think you were feeling more than my energy." Denise smiled.

"Is that right?"

"So you said you were sent there to check me out. I'm guessing you liked what you saw."

"More than you know." Farih locked eyes with Denise. They both blushed.

"You know, Farih, I can't lie. Besides the whole inspection at Melanie's house, I haven't felt this comfortable in New York. I've been feeling like something was missing. I thought I was just homesick, missing my friends. But now I feel so comfortable."

"You feel like you finally belong somewhere. Maybe you just needed to be around people more like yourself."

"Yeah, around a basketball playing supermodel."

They both giggled.

"Denise, I'm six foot tall, of course, I can play basketball."

"Denise."

Denise and Farih turned their heads. Denise gasped when she saw Mariah walking toward her. She sat up in the chair.

"Hey, Mariah."

Mariah looked at Farih and then back at Denise. "What are you doing in this area of town?"

"We went to 24-hour Fitness to play ball." Denise looked at Farih. "Oh, Mariah, this is—"

"Farih Okoro, right? I recognized you from the Victoria's Secret campaign." Mariah extended her hand.

Farih smiled, shaking Mariah's hand.

"It's a pleasure to meet you."

Mariah smirked. "Well, I'm on my way back to the office. I'll see you at home, Denise."

Denise nodded her head.

"Nice to meet you again, Farih." Mariah turned and walked out of the café.

"Roommate?" Farih questioned.

"Yeah, she's a friend I'm staying with until I find a place of my own."

"Ex-girlfriend?"

"No, not really."

"You've slept together. I can tell." Farih looked at Denise. "You don't have to tell me, I can tell."

"Yeah, we have, but it's not like that now, I promise."

"You don't owe me an explanation, Denise. I'm not your girl."

"But I want to let you know." Denise held Farih's hand. "I was going to move out, but I don't know what my future holds right now. I don't want to get into a lease then have to go back to Memphis or move to Atlanta if I don't find a job."

A young group of people walked into the café. They reminded Denise of the TV show *Friends*. "I just . . .

modeling isn't my thing. I might not be meant to be in New York."

"Don't say that. I think you have big things in store for you. You have to believe in yourself the way Melanie and I believe in you. If she didn't think you had potential, she wouldn't have put you up for the movie role with George."

"Yeah, but I've never acted a day in my life."

"I think you are going to do great." Farih smiled.

Denise's heart raced. "What are you trying to do to me?" Denise joked.

"The same thing you are trying to do to me."

Farih and Denise locked eyes. Denise hadn't felt that way since Lena, but this time the feeling was mutual.

A bright light flashed through the front window. Everyone in the café turned to see two papparazzi snapping pictures.

Farih turned her head. "Looks like we have fans." Farih smirked.

Denise looked at the cameramen. "They are snapping us?"

Farih nodded.

"Why?" Denise questioned, confused as to why people wanted to take her picture.

"Oh, it's because of you. I'm sorry. Do you want to go out the back or something?" Farih laughed. "Denise, you are soooo cute. You do realize that you are the face of Jocku. This isn't just about me. But no, I don't want to go out the back. They want a show, let's give them one." Farih stood up.

Denise followed suit.

The two walked out the door. The cameramen yelled called out their names.

"Farih, Denise, wanna smile for us?"

"Word on the street says you two are an item," the other cameraman yelled.

Denise instantly knew why celebs hated them.

Farih just smiled as they continued to walk. She whispered to Denise. "Are you ready to become famous?"

Denise looked at her.

Farih grabbed Denise's hand. She pulled her close and wrapped her arm around her.

"Are you sure about this?" Denise whispered. "Are you out?"

"I am now." Farih turned to the cameramen, who had continued to snap photos. "Did you ask if we are an item?"

"Yeah, are you two the new lesbian couple?" the bigger of the two photographers asked.

"You have to ask her." Farih looked at Denise and smiled.

The cameramen continued to snap and question.

Denise looked into Farih's eyes. She shook her head. "Fuck it." Denise pulled her close, planting a kiss on Farih's lips.

They pulled away, both laughing. The photographers followed them all the way to the car.

Both laughing hysterically, they drove off, leaving the cameramen behind them.

38

Lena sat in her loft listening to Alicia Keys' newest album. She took a sip of her Merlot. Lena picked up her fork. She placed a piece of her Godiva chocolate cake into her mouth, a present from Brandon. He knew how she loved Godiva chocolate cake. She looked over at the chair holding her birthday gifts: a little black box from her mother and father, a large box from Carmen and Nic, and even Brandon sent a small Tiffany box. That box made her smile. She knew that eventually they would be all right.

She hadn't bothered to open any of them. Brandon and Carmen had offered to take her out on the town, but she wasn't in the mood. She had a text box and voice mail filled with birthday greetings, but nothing from the one person she wanted to hear from.

Lena stared at her laptop until her eyes began to blur. She took a deep breath and pressed the sleep button. Her screen popped on, the last Web site she visited still present. Perez Hilton's blog site sent chills through her body.

Farih comes OUT.

Super Hawt supermodel Farih makes a public declaration of her sexuality with Jocku cover girl, Denise Chambers. After papz asked if they were an item, the couple decides it's better to kiss then tell by sharing a very public smooch for the cameras. The two laughed then left.

What a way to come out of the closet. Way to go, Farih. We can't wait to see more of this super sexy lezzie duo.

"Happy birthday to me," Lena said to herself as she stared at the photo of Denise kissing the gorgeous model. She scrolled down to other images of Denise and Farih laughing. Lena tried to remember when she had seen Denise smile the way she was in those pictures. She couldn't remember a time.

Alicia's song "Un-thinkable" began to play. Lena thought about Denise. Her heart ached. Lena didn't want to leave the house. The malls and magazines were covered with photos of Farih's and Denise's Jocku campaign. Since the outing Farih and Denise were the hot news. Denise had not only moved on, but was dating one of the top black models of the time. Lena knew she couldn't compete with that. She missed Denise more than ever.

Her mind drifted to Terrin and the last night they had spent together. After Derek had nearly choked her with his sloppy tonguing, she had realized there would be no more men in her life. She wanted the softness of a woman, the tenderness of a touch that ignited her in all of the right places. Terrin had been right there waiting.

Alicia's sultry voice sang the words to the song. Lena sighed. She wanted to be able to say she was ready to move on like Denise had. But was she ready? Lena thought about all she had put Brandon and Denise through. She thought about what she had put herself through. She deserved to be happy. She deserved to have someone special in her life.

Alicia hit the bridge, and Terrin entered her mind again. Her growing feelings for her neighbor wouldn't go away. Could she possibly love another woman the way she thought she had loved Denise.

Terrin's smile entered her mind. She thought about the times they had spent together. She blushed, thinking about the attention Terrin paid to her. Terrin made her smile and laugh, even when she felt like she would never laugh again. Why was she fighting something that had become so real to her? What was she waiting for? The smile. The easy way Terrin made her feel. Lena realized she missed Terrin. She only hoped she hadn't pushed her away.

Lena put on her fuzzy white slippers. She knew she didn't look her best, only dressed in a Victoria's Secret pink pajama set, but she didn't care. She walked out of the door without thinking twice.

Lena's heart began to beat fast when she heard Terrin's voice yell, "I'm coming."

Her knees began to shake as the sound of the dead bolt unlocked.

Terrin opened the door in a pair of baggy lounge pants and a black wife-beater. Terrin took a step back.

"Lena."

"Today is my birthday."

Terrin's wide-eyed expression crushed Lena. "I didn't know."

"I know. I just . . . it's my birthday, and I haven't been so depressed in my life." Tears filled Lena's eyes. She blinked, causing a teary river to flow down her face.

Terrin wiped Lena's face. "Lena, don't cry." She put her arms around Lena. "Everything will be OK."

"Will it?" Lena pulled away from Terrin. "I'm a mess. I couldn't even tell my mother I was pregnant, and that I lost my baby. How am I supposed to tell her that, that I might be gay?" Lena walked farther into the apartment.

Terrin followed.

"Lena, all of that is your personal business. You don't have to tell anyone if you don't want to."

Lena turned back toward Terrin. "I'm a coward. I'm afraid to be honest with the people that I love and I keep losing them because of it." Lena lowered her head. A single tear fell to the floor. "No wonder she didn't want me anymore."

Terrin rushed up to Lena. She held her by each of her arms. "Lena, listen to me. What you're going through, I can only imagine how hard it has to be for you. You were willing to give up your whole life for that girl and she let you go. Only a fool would do something like that."

Lena's eyes met Terrin's. "Why are you so wonderful to me? I don't deserve it."

"No, Lena, you don't know just how much you truly deserve."

"Terrin, I really think you are an amazing woman. You have been so great to me, and I've treated you like . . ."

"You've treated me like a woman who is going through one of the most difficult times in her life. You've treated me like a woman who is trying to find herself. I understand, Lena. I told you before that I'm here for you. Just let me be here for you," Terrin pleaded.

Lena put her hand on Terrin's arm. "I am not sure what is going to happen with me. I really can't tell you if I am gay, straight, bi or whatever. But sitting upstairs by myself, I realized that I didn't want to lose you too, but I just don't want to hurt you."

Terrin smiled. She held both of Lena's hands. "Lena, I told you in the beginning that I am here for you. I understand what you are going through. I've been there before. I want you to stop worrying about hurting me. If that happens, I will be OK. I'm a big girl." Terrin smiled and winked, causing Lena to laugh. Terrin rubbed her hands up and down Lena's arms.

"I don't deserve you."

"Ever think that we deserve each other?"

Lena stared into Terrin's big brown eyes. Her hands were trembling, and her heart was racing. Lena took a deep breath, her body warming up. "Are you sure you want me even with all my issues?"

Terrin's lips curved upwards. "Lena, you just don't get it. I've wanted you since I saw you at the airport. That shit hasn't gone away. In fact, it has only grown stronger. But I do want you to want me too. Can you say that you do?"

Lena nodded her head.

Terrin smirked while shaking her head. She pulled Lena in closer. Lena could feel Terrin's cool breath hit her ear. "Say it."

The heat was now a forest fire. Lena held on to the sides of Terrin's wife-beater. Her heart was pounding. "I want you too."

Terrin pulled her close. Lena closed her eyes as Terrin's lips met hers. She felt an electric energy fill her body. Terrin scooped Lena into her arms. She carried her all the way to the bedroom.

Terrin kissed her passion into Lena. Lena let Terrin's hands explore her whole body. Terrin slowly pulled Lena's pants off, pushing them to the side.

Lena looked into Terrin's eyes. She could see how much Terrin liked her; it was written all over her face. Lena closed her eyes as Terrin tongue-kissed her inner thigh. She felt a strong sucking there.

Terrin left a passion mark on Lena.

"Now, you belong to me."

Lena smiled. She loved the aggressiveness of Terrin;
it was a side she hadn't seen before. Lena's pussy pulsated and became moist.

Terrin ran her index finger across Lena's lower lips.
She entered her, stroking gently with her finger. When
she pulled out, Lena's wetness covered her. Terrin
closed her eyes and savored Lena's taste as she placed
her finger in her mouth. She had to have her.

Lena's body pulsed in anticipation as she felt the
warmth of Terrin's moist breath long before the vibrating tongue ever touched her. It's hard wetness pres-
sured against the clit was nearly too much for her to
bear.

Terrin sucked the little knob, loving every minute
of Lena's flesh. She could feel the subtlety of her soft,
thin flesh covering the mound, and she pushed it back,
exposing the taut, smooth skin on the head of Lena's
clit. The thin membrane exposed over the throbbing,
distended button offered no protection to the nerves
below. Each lick sent Lena into convulsions as Terrin
expertly satisfied her hunger for Lena's delicate flesh.

This woman knew exactly what to do with her tongue.
She was adroit in her lovemaking. Lena squirmed
and panted as Terrin licked circles around her clit
and slowly, deftly entered her with two fingers. Lena
moaned for more.

Terrin pulled on Lena's love button with the soft
flesh of her lips, sucked it and released it, sucked it and
released it, again and again.

Lena felt the wetness escape her body in small shud-
ders. It slipped across the entrance to her pussy and
along the crack of her ass. Terrin's tongue chased it
down.

Terrin eased out of her pants and climbed on top of
Lena. Pelvis to pelvis she grinded on top of her. Terrin
kissed Lena as they grinded their bodies in sync.

Lena felt a familiar intensity creeping into her stomach. She didn't know what to think. She hadn't known
grinding could feel so good.

Terrin let out a moan. Lena looked at Terrin, whose
eyes were closed. Lena realized that Terrin was feeling
the same thing she was feeling.

Lena began to thrust her hips harder against Terrin.
The thought of giving Terrin an orgasm excited her.
Lena bit her bottom lip. She decided to go for it. She
pushed Terrin over on her back.

Terrin's eyes opened. Lena continued to grind on top
of Terrin. Terrin's lips parted, and Lena licked Terrin's
lip before she could say anything. Their tongues met.
Lena and Terrin's eyes met.

"I wanna try it," Lena whispered.

Terrin's eyes widened. "I don't want you to do anything you aren't ready to do."

"I'm ready." Lena slowly crept down Terrin's body.
She pulled her boxer briefs off. Terrin's pussy was
neatly shaved.

Lena felt nervous, but it didn't take from her curiosity. She took two fingers and parted Terrin's lips. Lena
didn't know what to expect. Terrin's wetness covered
her womanhood. Lena closed her eyes and took a deep
breath. Slowly her tongue touched Terrin's softest
place.

"Just do what you like done to you," Terrin said, after noticing the hesitation from Lena.

Lena obliged. She began to lick her tongue around
and over Terrin's clit. Terrin let out a soft moan. Lena
suddenly felt a rush of aggression. She wrapped her
arms around Terrin's legs. She sucked on Terrin's pleasure knot, causing Terrin to moan even more.

Lena didn't know what the taste reminded her of,
but she liked it. She sucked and licked around the

walls, becoming familiar with Terrin's pussy. Terrin grinded her pussy into Lena's tongue. Terrin's moans only excited Lena more. She grinded her crotch against the sheets while devouring Terrin's pussy. She let out a moan. She could feel her orgasm coming closer.

Terrin grabbed Lena's hands. She wrapped her legs around Lena's body, pushing her back on her back. "I gotta taste you." Terrin pushed Lena's legs up over her head. She stuck her tongue in Lena's cave. She tongue-fucked Lena. Lena closed her eyes, moaning from the pleasure.

Lena felt a slight pressure toward the back. Terrin's thumb entered her asshole. Lena's body began to shake. Terrin's tongue-fucked her while her thumb moved in and out of the tight hole.

"I . . . I'mmm cumm . . ." Lena couldn't get the words out. Her body tensed up as her body exploded.

Terrin licked every drop off of her. She climbed back on top of Lena. Their eyes met. Terrin kissed Lena passionately.

Lena felt her pussy throbbing again.

Terrin moved on the side of Lena. She pushed Lena's ass against her pussy. Lena put her leg on Terrin's, while Terrin's fingers entered Lena again. She stroked in and out while Lena's round ass grinded against her. They both moaned for more.

She fingered Lena harder, while Lena twerked and jerked her ass against Terrin. Terrin's body began to tremble. She let out a loud moan.

Lena smiled as Terrin came.

"Shit." Terrin fell over on her back.

Lena turned over, laying her head against Terrin's chest.

"Girl, damn, you gon' make me put a ring on your finger," Terrin said, breathing heavily.

Lena smiled. She closed her eyes. There were no images of Denise floating around, only images of Terrin and her sweetness that lingered on her taste buds. In Terrin's arms, she let go of Denise.

Denise woke up in a cold sweat. The room was dark. The only light was coming from the street lights via the window. Denise looked at Farih sleeping peacefully. She climbed out of the bed, causing Farih to turn over, her naked body exposed, chocolate skin radiant in the city light glow.

"What's wrong?" Farih whispered.

Denise ran her fingers through Farih's hair. "Nothing. I just need some water. Go on back to sleep."

Farih was back in la-la land before she finished the sentence.

Denise tiptoed into Farih's living room. She sat down on Farih's leather couch. The coolness of the leather seeped through her thin cotton pajama pants and wifebeater.

Denise's mind raced. There was something she forgot but couldn't put her finger on it. She looked around Farih's beautiful apartment. Hints of her African heritage mixed with modern style created a trendy style. Denise looked at the wallsize black-and-white picture of Farih. Denise wanted to pinch herself, because things were too good to be true.

A sharp pain hit her on the right side. She couldn't shake the feeling that something wasn't right. She leaned back, resting her head on the back of the couch. Denise closed her eyes, hoping her memory would come back.

Lena's face entered her mind.

Denise's eyes popped open. She hit herself on her forehead. She picked up her cell phone to look at the date, June 29th. It was Lena's birthday. She scrolled through her phone to Lena's name. Lena's picture pulled up. Denise paused. It had been so long since their last talk. Maybe she didn't need to call.

The sharp pain attacked her side again. She took a deep breath and pressed send. Each ring seemed longer than the one before. Finally her voice mail picked up.

"The voice mail you are trying to reach is currently full."

Denise sighed. She pressed end, going back to the contact screen. She stared at Lena's face. Lena's smile made her smile. She pressed the screen, taking her to an empty text message.

Happy Birthday Lena ...

Denise stared at the message. She wanted to say more. She wanted to apologize for the way things happened again. She wanted to talk to her, make sure she was doing OK.

Too much time had passed. Denise knew it was too late for it. She pressed send and headed back to the bedroom.

39

Denise walked in the house and paused. Three large suitcases sat on the couch.

Mariah walked from her bedroom holding a Louis Vuitton bag. "Hey, stranger." Mariah smiled.

"Hey. What's going on?" Denise walked farther into the house.

"Well, Richard wants to spend a weekend at his house in the Hamptons."

"Damn. OK then." Denise sat down on the couch arm. "We just can't seem to catch each other, can we?"

"I know. Things have changed so much in the last few weeks." Mariah paused. She turned toward Denise. "There's something I have to tell you."

"What's up?"

Mariah held her hand out. A huge princess cut, pink diamond sat on her ring finger.

"Whoaaa! When did that happen?"

"Yesterday." Mariah's face was flushed pink. "I can't believe it myself. Rich asked me to marry him, and I accepted."

"Well, congratulations." Denise hugged Mariah. "I'm really happy for you."

"Thank you. I don't know what it is, but it was like we fell right back into place. To think we'd been apart for so long. It's like we just fell right back in love. We are doing something we should have done a long time ago."

"Well, you are glowing, so I know you're in love."

"I am. We are going to tell our parents this weekend, and I'm going to be moving in with him."

"That's wonderful, Mariah, I'm happy you are happy. So how long do I have to move?"

"Oh, Denise. Shut up you don't have to go anywhere. I actually was going to talk to you about keeping the apartment for me."

"Really?"

"Yes. I mean, I'm no fool. This place is paid for, and I'm not giving it up. So I was thinking, if you stay here and pay the utilities and stuff, then we can call it even. I trust you to keep it nice, and it's better than subletting to someone I don't know."

Denise wrapped her arms around Mariah. "Thank you so much! I will take great care of your place."

"I know you will." Mariah picked up her Birkin bag. "Oh ,how did your audition go?"

"I think I did pretty good. The movie is about a bas-ketball player whose mother is a crackhead. It's pretty deep stuff. But I can relate somewhat. I just haven't heard back yet. They said it would be a minute."

"Well, with all the press you have been getting lately, they would be a fool not to put you in it."

"Oh, you've seen it."

"Who hasn't seen the lesbian kiss seen around the world? I can't believe she let you do that."

"It was her idea." Denise smiled, thinking about Farih.

"Well, it was genius. How have the paps been?"

"A little crazy. We don't go many places anymore. They are always outside of her apartment. She's been staying in Melanie's guest room."

"Oh, I bet Melanie loves all of this." Mariah smirked.

"She's cool. Why do you say that?"

Mariah rummaged through one of her bags. "Let's just say Melanie is known for launching stars. You are in good hands. I heard about Puma too."

"Wow. Been keeping up, I see."

"It's my job."

Denise smiled. "Mariah, I really need to thank you. I wouldn't have anything if it wasn't for you. It really, really means the world to me."

"Denise, you're more than welcome. Just promise me that you are never going to change." Mariah held Denise's hands.

"I promise."

A knock at the door interrupted their moment.

"That's the car. I have to go."

"Let me help you with the bags."

"Ah." Mariah opened the door.

A tall black man in a black suit walked in.

"That's what he's for."

Mariah walked over to Denise. They hugged again. "See you when I get back."

"Bet."

Denise stood on the balcony and watched Mariah drive off. She looked out at the city. A deep sense of pride overwhelmed her. New York finally felt like home.

40

Cooley turned on her office TV. Sahara was making her first appearance on *106 and Park* to premiere her second video. Cooley watched the two co-hosts playful banter with each other. She picked her phone up. Sahara's plane had arrived two hours earlier, but she hadn't heard from her. Cooley sent her a text to see if she was still going to make it in time to watch the show together.

"Busy?"

Cooley turned her head. James stood in the doorway with a smile on his face. Cooley noticed his change in attire. His normal three-piece suit was replaced with a pair of khaki slacks and an Ed Hardy graphic button-down. Cooley pressed her lips together, forcing a tight smile.

James walked in without waiting on a response. "Good job on signing Blaque Reign." James sat in one of the chairs across from her desk.

"Thank you," Cooley replied. She knew he was up to something.

James looked up at the television screen. "Oh yeah, your girl is gonna be on there today isn't she? You know it was nothing personal with removing you from her project."

"I know. It was the right thing to do."

"And I must say, y'all are doing a great job keeping out of the gossip pages. Maybe you do value your job after all."

Cooley's eyes tightened. "What exactly is that supposed to mean?"

James looked at Cooley with his same smug smile.
"Nothing. You know, Wade, you have done some good
work around here. But I always think about something
that Big Ron told me once." James leaned forward.
"The bigger the balloon, the easier to pop. Do you know
what that means?"

Cooley bit the inside of her jaw. "Yes, I know what it
means. I don't really know what it has to do with me."

"That should be obvious."

Cooley sighed; she lowered her head and grinned.

James' smile faded, from Cooley's reaction. "Something funny?"

The *106 and Park* hosts called Sahara's name. Cooley
and James stopped to watch her come out on stage. Sahara walked out smiling and waving to the crowd. Her
black tights looked like they were painted on her thick
thighs. She sat on the couch next to Bobby Dee, a new,
hot R&B singer. He hugged Sahara. Cooley noticed him
checking her out.

"Do you two know each other?" The cute girl host
asked Sahara.

Sahara smiled. she looked at Bobby Dee. "No, this is
our first time meeting, but I love your new song."

"Yeah, I think we were in a club at the same time, but
we didn't actually meet. But it is definitely a pleasure."
Bobby Dee grinned at Sahara.

Sahara laughed it off, while the audience chimed in
with oohs and ahhs.

"Uh-oh, don't get nothing started on this stage," the
male host joked. "Sahara, are you single?"

Cooley wanted to laugh, as the question caused Sahara to blush. After the audience calmed down, Sahara
looked at the two hosts. "Yes, I am."

The audience went wild.

Bobby Dee perked up. "In that case." He playfully scooted closer to Sahara, placing his arm on the back of the couch around Sahara.

Everyone laughed.

Sahara playfully hit his arm. Cooley felt a twinge of jealously hit her side.

"Now that is what I call an attractive couple," James responded, his devious smile so big, he looked like the Cheshire cat. "Oh, and by the way." James reached into his pocket and dropped a business card on Cooley's desk. "I figured you would want this, you know, to take care of that." James pointed to the permanent scar on Cooley's jaw.

Cooley picked up the plastic surgeon's card. "Thanks, but no thanks."

"Don't be so difficult, Wade. We both know you could use it. It's the best practice in Atlanta. I know appearance is important to you. It is to all of us. I mean, you can't expect to sign hot stars without using hot people." James headed to the door, leaving Cooley speechless. "I'll let you get back to work, Wade." James walked out of the office.

Cooley looked back at the TV. Bobby Dee continued to sneak peeks at Sahara. They began to play the video. Cooley watched Sahara dance to her upbeat song. Her mind wandered. She wondered what Bobby Dee was saying to her while the video was on.

Cooley get a grip. You are not the jealous type.

Cooley shook her head. She knew she was tripping. She turned the TV off. There were better things she could do with her time.

***

"Hey, Cooley if you didn't need me for anything else, I was gonna head on out." Tee walked into Cooley's doorway.

Cooley looked up from her computer. She looked at the clock.

"Damn, it's six already." Cooley shuffled to pack her things up. She paused. "Hey, Tee, did Sahara call me?"

Tee shrugged her shoulders. "No, she didn't."

Cooley looked at Tee, puzzled. She knew Sahara should have been there a long time ago, and her failure to call or answer her phone was making Cooley suspicious. "OK, well, yeah, I'm about to get out of here. See you tomorrow."

"Speak of the devil." Tee smiled as Sahara walked in.

"Hey, Tee." Sahara walked past Tee.

"I'll leave you two alone. See you tomorrow." Cooley nodded as Tee left the room.

"Hey you." Sahara's airy voice echoed through the room as she wrapped her arms around Cooley. "You won't believe the day I have had. Did you see me on the show?"

"Yeah, I saw you." Cooley continued to pack her laptop into its bag. "I saw a lot. So, um, did you lose your phone or something?"

Sahara paused. "No, but as soon as we landed, I was rushed into a planning meeting that just ended. I didn't have a moment to call you."

"And you couldn't send a text or an e-mail?" Cooley tried to keep her nonchalant mild voice.

"I'm sorry I didn't think it was that big of a deal. You know how things can be."

"Yeah, I know." Cooley didn't like the feeling she had. "I just expected to hear from you sooner."

"Aww. I'm sorry hun. It won't happen again. That Bobby Dee really is a nut." Sahara sat on the edge of the desk.

"Really?"

"Yeah, he's cool. I think you would like him." Sahara stood back up.

"Oh. You do, huh?"

"Actually I was hoping you would go with me tonight to Geisha House tonight."

Cooley paused. "Why are you going to Geisha House?"

"To celebrate." Sahara walked closer to Cooley. "I'm singing in Fashion Frenzy."

Cooley's mouth dropped open. "Get the fuck out of here!" She wrapped her arms around Sahara, picking her up off the ground. Cooley planted a kiss on Sahara. "Damn, bae, that's great, and to think I was going just to buy clothes."

Sahara hit Cooley on her arm. "So will you go with me to Geisha House tonight?"

"Sure. Wait." Cooley took a step back. "That might not be a good idea. It's too public."

"I know I was thinking we could arrive in different cars, and—"

"Babe, I can't risk it, and neither can you. James was just in here today with that bull."

"So is this how it's gonna be? We aren't going to be able to be anywhere together?" Sahara folded her arms.

"What the hell do you want me to do? This is my job. And your career."

"I know!" Sahara squealed. She took a deep breath. "I just don't like the idea of having to hide the person that I love."

Cooley's eyes widened.

Sahara stood in front of her. She could see the concern in Cooley's blank expression.

"Yes, I said love. I don't expect you to say it back, so chill out."

Sahara walked over to the chair and grabbed her oversized Jessica Simpson handbag. Cooley closed her laptop bag.

"So, you just gon' leave?"

"I have to go home and change. I have somewhere to be."

"Damn. Why do you want me to go so bad? It's more than just celebrating 'cause we can celebrate for real at the crib." Cooley grabbed her laptop case and walked over to Sahara. Sahara's face dropped. She hesitated. "Don't even think about lying."

Sahara let out a loud moan. "I wanted you to come because I really wanted you to meet Bobby Dee."

"Oh, so that nigga is gonna be there."

"Along with my agent and publicist." Sahara sat in the chair. She couldn't look at Cooley's face. "See, after seeing the way Bobby was acting toward me, his people and my people thought it would be a good idea for us to be photographed in public together."

"You have got to be fucking kidding me!"

"Cooley, some pictures came out." Sahara grabbed Cooley's hand before she could walk past her.

Cooley turned around. Sahara's eyes were filling with tears.

"They hit MediaTakeOut today. Some pics of me back in the day with some women." Sahara lowered her head. Cooley leaned against her desk. "At first Tommy wanted me to just ignore it, use the excuse of me being a stripper and it coming with the job. But when he saw the way Bobby was flirting with me and the way the audience responded, well, he figured the best thing is—"

"To make it look like you two are an item." Cooley ran her hand through her head. She knew of other celebrities doing the same thing. "Bobby was cool with that?"

"Yeah, he and his people thought it was a great idea, since, you know, all male R&B singers are hit with the gay rumor at some point in their careers. Not to mention, it would make for a great P.R. story. The hot new R&B singers meet and fall for each other on *106 & Park*."

"So, you wanted me to come for what reason? Seems like the decision has already been made."

Sahara stood up. "I wanted you to at least meet him and be cool with him. I figured it would make things easier."

"So you told him you are gay?" Cooley looked at Sahara, who quickly turned her head. Cooley huffed. "So, this fool has no idea that he's never gonna get it."

"He knows it's for business purposes."

"He's a man, Sahara. You think in the back of his mind he isn't hoping to fuck?"

"That would never happen."

"He doesn't know that." Cooley threw her hand up.

Sahara pulled Cooley's arm. "But I do! Cooley, I'm a fucking lesbian. I don't want that man's dick!"

"Yeah, I've heard that before," Cooley responded under her breath. Misha entered her mind. She could feel her wall building up. Sahara looked disgusted. Cooley shifted her eyes. She couldn't look at Sahara.

Sahara nodded her head. "You know, until you learn that you can trust me and that I'm not that bitch you were with before, we are never going to make it." Sahara picked her purse back up and walked out the room.

A piece of Cooley wanted to follow her, but her pride wouldn't let her.

Denise pressed Farih's lips against hers. Farih sat in her lap with her arms around Denise. Farih's soft lips felt like silk against Denise's. Her hands roamed up and down Farih's backside.

"Get a damn room," Melanie said as she walked into the room. Her cornrows and oversize jogging suit made her look more like a thug than a top fashion designer.

They both laughed.

Farih turned around in Denise's lap. "I'm sorry, Mel. I just can't control myself sometimes." Farih blushed.

Melanie smiled. "It's fine. I love it." Melanie poured a glass of wine. "I knew you two would be perfect for each other, and the publicity. My God, you two are everywhere."

"Yeah, I've been asked to be the model correspondent at the Swagger Style Show during Fashion Frenzy." Farih and Melanie gently tapped their wine glasses against each other.

Melanie glanced at Denise. "I heard you are doing the show as well."

Denise frowned. "Yeah."

Farih put her hand on the side of Denise's face. "Aww . . . my baby is afraid of doing runway."

"You will be fine." Melanie sat back in her chair and crossed her legs.

"Yeah, right. They said I would be walking in tennis shoes. I better, 'cause the last thing they want is for me to bust my ass in front of the world."

They all laughed.

"Denise? Have you heard back about the role yet?" Melanie questioned while taking a sip of her wine.

Denise's face dropped. "Not yet." She looked at Melanie.

"I'm sure you will hear something soon."

"I'm sure she will too. Bobby would be a fool to not use you. She's perfect for the role," Farih chimed in.

"I must say that I am proud of both of you." Melanie pressed her lips together. "And I am happy that I was able to bring you together. You make a lovely couple."

Denise nodded her head. She looked into Melanie's eyes. She looked worried about something. Denise didn't want to press the issue. She just sat and smiled as Melanie and Farih went on about dresses for her to take to Atlanta.

"So tell me, you two are hot in person, are you hot in the bedroom?"

"Mel, I can't believe you just asked that," Farih squealed.

Denise lowered her head. She didn't know what to say. They slept together every night, but never had sex.

"Well, is it?" Melanie laughed. "I bet Denise is an undercover freak."

"I plead the fifth." Farih tilted her head up.

"OK, well, be like that then." Melanie finished the wine with a big gulp.

Farih stood up. "I have to go to the little ladies' room. I'll be right back."

Denise watched as Farih walked away, her ass switching in her short denim skirt. Denise could feel Melanie's eyes on her. She turned her head to find Melanie staring with a mischievous grin on her face.

"What?"

"I must say, Denise, I really like what I am seeing in you." Melanie poured another half glass of wine.

"Melanie, can I ask you a question?" Denise shifted her body around.

Melanie nodded for her to ask.

"Why did you really seek me out? I know you sent Farih to check me out at the go-see. What I don't get is why? It can't be just because I'm gay. There's a million gay models out here."

"I told you I saw something special in you."

Denise's lip curled. She knew she was lying.

Melanie laughed.

"Come on, Mel, please. I really want to know what is so special about me."

Melanie stared at Denise. She uncrossed her legs and stood up. "I can't believe I'm going to do this. Follow me."

The two walked down Melanie's long corridor. Melanie opened the door to her bedroom. Denise walked in behind her.

Melanie's bedroom was nothing like Denise expected. The walls were covered white with a white floral imprint in them. A collection of antique dolls sat in a display case. Her California King bed had an all-white sheet and comforter set on it with tons of white pillows at the head.

"Do you know where I come from, Denise?" Melanie asked. She got on her knees and pulled a box out from under her bed.

"California, right?"

"Not exactly." Melanie opened the box. She pulled out a green photo album. "I'm actually from Memphis."

"Are you serious?" Denise was shocked.

Melanie began to flip through the pages of the book. She stopped at a page. She looked at Denise as she pushed the book across the bed to Denise.

Denise picked up the book. A group of photos of two girls were collaged together. Denise's body froze. She looked at Melanie as a teenager, standing next to her mother, Tammy. Denise looked up at Melanie.

Melanie pressed her lips together and nodded. "She was my bestfriend."

Denise studied the photographs. Her mother looked more like her. Her hair was longer than Denise's. Her body wasn't the frail, crack-filled body she was used to seeing, her mother was thick. Her short shorts showed off her thick thighs and nice frame. Both women looked like they could be models.

"Tammy and I grew up on the same street. I spent so much time at Mema's house and vice versa."

"You knew my grandmother too." Denise looked up.

"Like she was my own." Melanie smiled. "Me and your mother were thick as thieves. You didn't see one without the other."

"How is it that I don't know any of this?" Denise said, staring at the book.

"Well, because it was before your time. When we got into high school we started partying a little too hard." Melanie sat on the edge of her bed, her eyes glistening with water. "We both got out of control. The only difference was that my mother had a sister in California. They shipped me off to go stay with her."

"So, you didn't stay in touch."

"No, I couldn't. When I got to Cali, I was a mess. I didn't want to do anything but drugs. I missed your mother so much; she was all I lived for. I was so miserable that one day I tried to kill myself."

Denise's face dropped.

Tears began to flow down Melanie's face. She couldn't look at Denise.

Denise couldn't believe what she was hearing.

"I went to rehab. That's where I found out the real reason I was so depressed. I was in love. I was deeply in love with your mom." Melanie's eyes met Denise's. "By the time I got out, it was too late. Your mother had run off, broken my heart again and your grandmother's."

Denise felt her knees getting weak. She closed the book and sat on the edge of the bed.

Melanie looked at Denise. "I never got over your mother. When I graduated I came back to Memphis to visit my parents. I came to your grandmother's house, and that's when I saw you. You were just a baby, but you were the spitting image of your mother."

"I tried to find her, but I couldn't. I ended up coming back to California and starting college, but I never stopped caring about Tammy."

A single tear fell from Denise's eye. She wiped her face. Denise looked down at the book; her eyes lost focus, causing two books to appear.

Melanie stood up. "When I saw that Jocku ad, I thought I'd seen a ghost. I knew immediately that you had to be Tammy's daughter. I called your agency and found out your last name. I knew then who you were. I didn't know how you would feel about all of this, so I hid it. But I just wanted to watch after you and help you in the way I wish I could have helped your mom."

Denise's brain was on overload. She could hear the words coming from Melanie, but they sounded so unreal. She closed her eyes, trying to clear some of the thoughts racing through her head

"So my mother is the guilt you felt. So all this you've been doing for me is to try to help you get over your guilty conscience!" Anger set in. Denise felt used.

"No, Denise, it's not like that."

"Why didn't you tell me then?" Denise looked up at Melanie. "Why didn't you just tell me in the beginning that you knew my mother? Why hide this?"

"How could I tell you that it's my fault your mother got on drugs?" Melanie stood up. "Denise, your mom was as good at basketball as you were. She never wanted to party like I did. I would drag her to the parties with me. She tried weed and blow because of me."

Denise felt the room spinning around her. Her eyes shifted back to the book. She noticed Melanie's name on a picture. Melanie Yvette Moore.

"Yvette. Your middle name is Yvette." Denise shook her head in disbelief. Things were making sense; she knew why Melanie looked like she saw a ghost. "My mom named me after you."

Tears rolled down Melanie's face. "It broke my heart when you said that."

Denise's body was shaking. "I knew it. I knew this shit was too good to be true. You didn't do all this to help out a new lesbian. You did it for yourself." Denise knocked the book off of the bed.

Melanie stood in silence.

"Thank you. Now I know the truth. People aren't as good as they appear." Denise stormed out of the room.

Farih stood up when Denise entered the room. Her smile quickly changed when she saw Denise's face. "Bae—"

"Did you know?" Denise stormed up to Farih. "Were you in on this shit too?"

"What are you talking about?" Farih put her hand on Denise's arm, but Denise jerked away.

"Man, fuck this shit! I'm out of here."

Farih's mouth dropped. "Denise!" Denise slammed the door behind her.

Denise looked up and down the empty street. There wasn't a cab in sight.

She took off running down the avenue. She didn't care about anything; she just had to get away from the scene. She ran until she came to a small neighborhood park.

Denise sat on an empty bench. All of the hurt, and pain she had bottled up surfaced. She began to sob.

Denise heard a faint voice in the back of her head. She couldn't make it out. She stared into the darkness of the park. The voice grew.

"*Go back.*"

Denise looked around; there was no one in sight.

The voice grew louder. "*Go back, Neecie.*"

Denise's body froze as her grandmother's voice took over her mind.

"*Go back, Neecie.*"

"I can't" Denise said out loud. "I can't. I just wanna go home."

"*Home is where your heart is,*" Mema's sweet voice echoed. "*Go back.*"

"Denise!" Farih yelled. "Denise!"

Denise looked up to see Farih walking into the park. She stood up. Farih's face was covered in tears. Denise's heart was heavy; Farih had run after her in five-inch stiletto heels. Farih paused when she saw Denise. They walked toward each other.

"I'm sorry, Denise, I didn't know," Farih cried.

Denise walked back to the bench. She sat back down. Farih joined her, sitting next to her. Denise knew Farih was innocent, she wasn't involved.

"This whole time, everything has been a lie." Denise squeezed Farih's hand. It felt good to have her next to her. "I'm sorry. I just need a little time to myself."

"I don't want to leave you here."

"I'll be fine. Just give me a little time."

Farih reluctantly left Denise and headed back to the house.

Denise's mind was racing. She thought about Melanie's face. All the times that she looked at Denise like she had seen a ghost, the whole time was because of her love for her mother.

"*Put yourself in her shoes.*" Mema's voice entered Denise's head again.

Denise thought about Melanie's situation. She thought about Lena, the simple guilt she felt for hurting Lena's feelings. She couldn't fathom the guilt that Melanie had lived with for all of those years.

Denise wondered if her mother knew. She wondered if her mother loved Melanie the way Melanie loved her. Denise knew she had to care about her to give her Melanie's middle name. Her mother obviously didn't hate Melanie, or else she wouldn't have given her that middle name.

"*You can't hate her, Neecie. She cares about you.*" Mema's voice replied. "*Go back.*"

Denise felt calmness come over her body. Melanie had done so much to help her. Now she had the chance to do something for her.

Denise walked into the house. Farih stood up. Denise wrapped her arms around her beautiful girlfriend. She kissed her on her forehead. "Where is Melanie?"

"Bedroom," Farih whispered.

"I'll be back." Denise headed to the bedroom.

Melanie was laying on her bed sobbing. Denise had never seen the strong Melanie Moore look so frail. Melanie turned over and sat up when she saw Denise standing in the doorway.

"It's not your fault. You can't blame yourself for it."

"I should have never let them take me away. I should have kept in touch with her. She would have never got on crack if I was around. We always said we wouldn't try that shit. If I would have just been there . . ."

"It's not your fault." Denise walked closer to Melanie. "You couldn't help the fact that your parents sent you away. I'm sure my mother knew that." The anger Denise felt had faded. She looked at Melanie. She could see the pain in her eyes.

"Don't blame yourself anymore. It's not your fault. My mother never blamed you. She took full responsibility for the things that she did."

"Do you hate me?" Melanie stood up. She sounded like a child afraid of hurting its parents.

"No, I don't hate you." Denise hugged Melanie. "I can't thank you enough for all that you've been doing for me. I really appreciate it, and I know my mother would appreciate it too."

Denise turned to walk out of the room. Melanie called her name, causing her to turn back around.

"When your mother died, was she better?" Melanie's eyes were red and puffy.

Denise smiled. "She was much better, she was clean and living in Mema's house."

Melanie's face lifted. Denise could feel the weight of guilt coming off of her. She had lied to Melanie. Her mother died of AIDS. She knew that the best thing she could give Melanie was peace of mind.

"Thank you for showing me that. I never had any pictures of my mother when she was younger. They were all destroyed over the years."

"You know, you look so much like her, it's hard for me to look at you sometimes." Melanie smiled. "Your mother would have made an amazing model."

They both laughed.

"Go get your girl before she busts in here. I need some time. I'll see you two before you go to Atlanta."

Denise nodded her head and walked out the door. Farih was waiting in the living room, sipping on some wine. She put the glass down and smiled.

"Are you all right?" Farih's eyes slanted with curiosity.

"I am now."

Melanie's words played over and over in Denise's head. Her entire life, she had blamed her mother for doing drugs, not thinking that it could have been something more that pushed her over the edge. She thought about Melanie. Her love for her mother was real. She wished her mother had known.

Denise glanced over to Farih concentrating on the busy street. She wanted to let go, but something was holding her back. She was crazy about Farih, but fear wouldn't let her completely let give her heart to her.

"*She's the one.*" Mema's voice echoed.

Denise looked out at the lights of the city. She realized she didn't want to let it all pass her by.

Denise opened the door to her place. Farih walked past her.

"Well, it's about time I get to see the bat cave." Farih laughed.

Denise watched as she pulled her hair out of the ponytail holder. She walked up to Farih without saying a word. She grabbed her from behind, pulling Farih's ass against her.

"Umm, OK." Farih's face filled with excitement and confusion.

Denise didn't speak. She ran her index finger down the nape of Farih's neck. Farih's body shivered from the cold touch. "Denise. What are you doing?"

"Shhh," Denise whispered as she moved her head in closer. She planted her lips against Farih's lower neck.

Farih's body trembled again. "Wait."

Farih managed to turn around, but still in Denise's arms. Their faces met.

"I thought you wanted to take it slow?"

"Maybe I changed my mind."

"Denise, don't let what Mela—"

Denise kissed Farih's lips.

Farih could feel her body getting weak. She draped her arms around Denise's neck. Her body was aching for Denise, yet she forced herself to pull her lips apart from Denise's.

Denise noticed the concern in her eyes.

"Farih, this has nothing to do with what Melanie said. It has to do with me finally letting go."

Their lips met. Denise held Farih in a loving embrace. They broke apart only long enough for Denise to pull Farih's shirt over her head. Farih didn't say a word; she bit her lip as Denise unbuttoned her pants. Their mouths met again, their tongues dancing the tango.

Denise picked Farih up. Farih wrapped her long chocolate legs around Denise's body. They kissed all the way to her room. Denise slowly laid Farih's body on the bed. Her pink Victoria's Secret bra and panties only made her skin look even more chocolate. Denise loved it.

"Denise, I'm not complaining, but . . . what brought this on?" Farih said as Denise lit three candles on the dresser.

"Let's just say it's time for me to let go." Denise moved toward Farih. She pulled her blue polo over her head with her wife-beater.

Farih bit her lip at the sight of Denise's rock-hard abs and smooth, muscular arms.

Denise put one knee on the bed. She lifted Farih's long leg into the air, kissing her way to her thigh.

Farih's sweet-smelling skin sent Denise's senses into a frenzy. She kissed Farih's flat stomach, right above her belly button. Farih's girlish giggle caused Denise to smile.

Their bodies locked. Denise's tongue curled against the arch in Farih's back. Her chocolate skin excited her in ways she never imagined. Denise wanted to take it slow, savor every moment of their first experience. She held Farih's long limbs in her hands, slowly spreading her legs apart. Heat radiated from Farih; Denise could feel the warmth as her fingers eased closer.

Farih let out a deep breath, her chest rising and falling. She was ready, but Denise wanted to take her time. She studied Farih's body, making mental photographs to keep in her mind.

Denise traced her tongue around the chocolate drops that sat on Farih's breasts. She nibbled on her breasts. The wetness from her mouth mixed with the cool breeze from her breath caused her nipples to stand at attention.

Farih's bottom lip quivered. She bit it. She opened her eyes and met Denise's. Denise leaned down, her lips locking with Farih's. Farih opened her mouth, allowing Denise's tongue to escape into hers.

The softness of their lips pressed against each other caused their fires to grow. Denise's right hand disappeared between Farih's legs, her index finger entered Farih's heat, her wetness covering Denise's finger as she rubbed Farih's clit in a slow circular motion.

Denise and Farih's eyes locked onto each other, their minds connected on a higher level, an orgasmic level. Denise bit her lip as her fingers ran from Farih's clit down to her hollow. They didn't lose eye contact. Denise entered with her index finger. Farih's vagina pulsated; her wetness grew. She ran her perfectly manicured fingertips against Denise's flat stomach. Denise lowered her body. Slowly kissing her way down Farih's chocolate breast to her belly button, Denise's mouth watered for Farih's nectar.

Farih's butt clenched as Denise's breath hit her puffy lips. Her bottom lip fell as Denise's tongue took shelter inside her. She wanted to scream; instead she exhaled a heavy breath laden with the release of her passion. Denise licked Farih from the top to the bottom of her heat. Farih's arms extended, she rubbed Denise's hair, massaging her scalp until the small ponytail holder popped off. Denise's hair fell. Farih's fingers were lost in Denise's mane.

The tingling sensation of Farih's nails against her scalp caused Denise's body to quiver. Denise's strong arms gripped Farih's thick thighs. She pulled herself deeper into Farih. Farih arched her back, grinding her pussy against Denise's mouth. Denise didn't falter; she worked Farih, claiming her lips, clit, and cave as her property.

"Deee," Farih moaned, her accent heavy as Denise sucked and licked her into a climactic frenzy. Farih's body shuddered; the pleasure grim reaper was creeping up on her, slowly causing her toes to extend.

Denise's body trembled. Her pleasure grew as Farih moaned and panted for more.

Farih grabbed on to Denise's shoulders. Lost in another world, her fingertips dug into Denise's skin, leaving tiny imprints. Denise sucked on Farih's throbbing clit, whose pussy curved to Denise's two fingers as they glided in and out.

"Ayeeee, Deeee." Farih's voice and lips quivered. Her legs gripped Denise's body, and her ass shifted.

Denise grabbed her, pulling so close. She wouldn't let her run.

Farih's body jerked like she was going into convulsions. Her hands pushed against Denise's shoulders as her orgasm exploded to the surface.

The explosion of Farih's sweetness on Denise's tongue caused her to cum.

Farih pulled Denise's sports bra. Denise left her warmth. Farih sat up, and their eyes met immediately. Tears were falling from Farih's eyes.

"Are you OK?"

Farih didn't speak. She pulled Denise close. She held both sides of Denise's face as her lips planted softly against Denise's. Farih sucked Denise's lips, tasting herself in the process. Farih lay back down, pulling Denise with her.

They embraced. Their bodies were one as they held each other. It was unlike anything Denise had ever experienced. Denise stroked Farih's hair as she fell asleep. She thought about her grandmother. She was right. There was no better love than black love.

41

The gossip blogs were covered with images of Sahara and Bobby Dee on *106 & Park* and walking into Geisha House. Cooley felt a lump form in her throat. The plan had worked; the urban community was more concerned with the idea of Bobby and Sahara as an item than anything else.

Cooley sat at the kitchen table. She woke up early to prepare a special apology breakfast for Sahara. A lavish edible arrangement covered in strawberries, pineapples and grapes sat in the middle of the table.

Cooley looked up from the laptop when she heard the bedroom door open. She quickly closed the computer and put it on the floor. Sahara walked out rubbing her eyes. Her boy shorts and tight-fitting wifebeater hugged her body. Her eyes widened, the spread causing her to pause in her tracks.

Cooley stood up. "How did you sleep?" Cooley asked as Sahara walked to the table.

Sahara gave Cooley an upset stare. "Fine." Sahara looked down at the table then looked back at Cooley. "What's all this?" She pulled a strawberry off of the centerpiece. Sahara slowly sucked the strawberry, biting the tip off of it.

Cooley smirked. "It takes all that to eat a strawberry?" She knew what Sahara was trying to do with the strawberry, and it was working.

Sahara cracked a smile. "Maybe." She sat down at the table. "You know it's gonna take a whole lot more than a centerpiece."

"I know." Cooley clapped her hands.

On cue Tee walked out of the kitchen, wearing a long white apron and a tall, paper chef's hat. "Welcome to Café Apology. My name is Tee and I am your chef for the day." Tee set a square plate with a large Belgian waffle and some turkey bacon in front of each of them.

Sahara shook her head. "Oh, Tee, I hope she is paying you overtime for that."

"Don't worry. I'm well taken care of." Tee cheesed from ear to ear as she sat Cooley's plate in front of her. "Will there be anything else?"

"No, we are fine." Cooley said as she continued to look at Sahara.

Sahara nodded her head.

Tee took a bow and walked back into the kitchen.

Sahara picked up her fork. She felt Cooley's eyes on her. She looked up and curled her lip.

"What?"

Cooley smiled, and her deep dimples appeared. "You know I think I like you most, just like this."

Sahara blushed. She pushed her hair behind her ear. "Stop it."

"What? I'm serious."

"OK, who are you, and what did you do with Carla?" They both laughed.

"I'm just trying to apologize here."

"All you had to do was say it."

"I thought this was more unique." Cooley winked her right eye. Sahara's cheeks were flushed.

They sat in silence for a moment. Cooley reached for the silver water pitcher and caught an unwelcomed glimpse at her face.

"I think I'm going to go see a surgeon about my scar."

Sahara looked up from her meal. "Carla, why?"

"I just think I need to get it taken care of now. I'm tired of seeing this shit when I catch my reflection. I want to see my old self again."

"Carla, I've told you that it—"

"It's not a big deal to you, I know, but it is to me. I look like a fucking monster."

"Dramatic much?"

Cooley sighed. "You don't understand. You aren't living with a fucking scar across your face."

"All scars you can't see, Cooley. Remember that."

Cooley turned on her stereo to take the edge out of the tense room. Soft music began to play from her iPod. They both began to eat the food Tee created. Beyoncé's rendition of Etta James' "Trust in Me" began to play.

Sahara began to sing along, sounding almost just like the record. She focused on Cooley, and their eyes met.

Cooley admired Sahara as she sang the song to her, each word resonating in Cooley's soul.

Sahara stood up. She held her hand out. Cooley smiled as she stood up, taking Sahara into her arms. They slow-danced as Sahara sung along with Beyonce.

Cooley couldn't take her eyes off of Sahara. Her voice sent chills down Cooley's spine. She hated that the song was so short.

They held on to each other for a few more moments as the next song came on.

Cooley peered into Sahara's eyes. "You know that I care about you right?"

"I know," Sahara whispered.

"It's just I was brought up to believe that you don't let women in. I broke that rule with Misha and it backfired. So as much as I want to take that leap of faith with you, the other half of me is steadily pulling me back."

Cooley expected Sahara's face to be filled with disappointment, but to her surprise she looked happy. "Cooley, when I got into this with you, I knew who I was getting. I accept you the way you are."

"I just want you to understand that I do care about you."

"I already know that. I just want you to trust in me." Sahara sang the words.

They both laughed.

"I promise I'll work on it." Cooley's expression was serious.

Sahara rubbed her hand down Cooley's cheek. They shared a kiss. "Now let's eat before Tee kills us for ruining her food."

They sat back down and continued to eat.

"So, how was Geisha House?" Cooley asked while eating a piece of bacon.

Sahara sipped her orange juice. "It was cool, very chill mode. I really think you will like Bobby when you meet him."

"I still don't wanna meet your boyfriend." Sahara threw her middle finger up at Cooley.

Cooley blew a kiss back at her. "But I will say your plan worked. You hit the blogs already."

Sahara looked up, wide-eyed. "Are you serious?"

"Yup. Speculations are stirring that you are the hot new couple." Cooley stuck her finger in her mouth and pretended to gag. "You better not kiss that nigga."

"Oh, chill out." Sahara stood up. She walked in between Cooley's legs.

Cooley sat back in her chair.

"What's wrong with a harmless little kiss for the cameras?"

"Don't play with me!"

Sahara moved the plate of food out of the way and hopped on top of the table. Her boy shorts raised up,

Sahara spread her legs, placing them on the outside of each of Cooley's legs. "Baby doll missed you last night." Sahara licked her top lip.

Cooley's right eyebrow lifted. "Did she?" Cooley looked at the camel print formed in Sahara's boy shorts. She took her index finger and pushed the small piece of fabric to the side, exposing Sahara's lips. Cooley moved her hand. "Tee is in the other room."

"So." Sahara raised her wife-beater, exposing her washboard stomach. "Where's your sense of adventure?"

Cooley smiled as Sahara planted kisses on her face. Sahara looked deep into Cooley's eyes. Cooley closed her eyes as Sahara leaned and planted a soft kiss on Cooley's scar.

"You are still the most beautiful, and sexy woman I've ever met," Sahara whispered.

Sahara's words heated Cooley's icy heart. Cooley could feel her nature rising. She scooted her chair closer. Her face aligned perfectly with Sahara's pussy, she rubbed her nose against the cotton fabric.

Sahara held on to Cooley's curly hair with both hands. She pushed Cooley's head farther into her warmth.

Cooley fought to resist the temptation. She bit the underwear with her teeth.

"Did you need . . . Oh . . ." Tee froze, quickly turning her head. "I'm sorry."

Cooley and Sahara's heads jerked in Tee's direction.

"I'm so sorry." Tee covered her eyes and walked back into the kitchen, as Cooley and Sahara erupted in laughter.

***

The sound of the doorbell woke Lena up out of her sleep. She pulled herself out of the bed, threw her robe on, and headed to the door. Terrin turned over, still sleeping soundly.

"I'm coming!" Lena yelled as she made it to the door. She pulled the door open, and her mouth dropped.

"It's about time. I was about to use my key." Karen removed her Gucci shades and walked in the house.

"Mother, what are you doing here?"

"Can't a mother come by and check on her struggling daughter?"

Lena placed her hand on her forehead. She glanced at the door to the hallway. She silently prayed Terrin didn't wake up. "You could have called."

Karen turned to her daughter. "Now, what good would that have done? You never answer my calls."

"Mother, it's seven in the morning." Lena yawned as she sat in one of her dining room chairs.

"Well, I have a meeting at the college to discuss renovations to Jamerson Hall. I wanted to come by and get an update on things with you." Karen sat down across from Lena. "You're twenty now and about to be divorced. This is not a favorable situation for you. Think men are going to line up to date a divorced college drop out? You need to have a plan."

"I know, Mother. I am going to register."

"And things with Brandon?"

"We are OK. Actually, very good. We are working on regaining our friendship."

"That's wonderful, honey." Karen shifted her eyes. "So, I saw your little friend on TV. Seems she's dating Farih Okoro."

Lena felt her heart drop. "Yes, I know."

"I heard she's making quite a name as a model herself. I swear I never would have imagined it. She was so butch."

"Mother, is there anything else that you want?"

Karen slated her eyes at Lena. "Well, since I'm bothering you so much, let me go." Karen stood up. "It's a horrible world when your own daughter can't make time for you."

Suddenly they heard a toilet flush. Lena's heart began to race. Karen looked at the hallway. Karen looked at her daughter's frightened face.

"Mot—"

"Shhh." Karen held her hand out at Lena. She proceeded to walk toward the hallway.

Lena jumped up. "Mother, what are you doing? This is my house!" Lena protested to deaf ears.

Karen continued to walk down the hall. She pushed Lena's door open and gasped.

Terrin stood in shock in her boxers and sports bra.

Karen turned to Lena. Lena lowered her head.

Karen walked past Lena without saying anything. Lena followed calling out, but Karen wouldn't respond. Karen picked her purse up. Her hands shaking so hard, she fumbled to get her keys.

"Mother, it's not what you think."

Karen turned around and threw her finger up. "Lena, do not try to justify what I just saw. How could you do this to yourself and to your family?"

Tears filled in Lena's eyes. "I can't help how I feel, Mother. You don't understand."

"I don't understand what, Lena? That you are a *gay* now? You're right. I can't understand that because you aren't!"

"Mother, I don't know what I am." Lena cried.

"And is that the way to find out? Sleeping around with random trash you pick up off the street?"

"She's not trash. She is smart, has a great job, and she lives in this building!" Lena couldn't tell if she was more embarrassed that she was caught or angry at her mother's comments about Terrin.

"Oh, I don't care where she lives." Karen threw her hands up. She took a deep breath. "What happened to my little girl? What happened to my child who would never lie to her mother? Now you lie constantly, hiding things from your father and me. Why are you constantly trying to hurt us?"

"See that right there. That is why I don't tell you anything anymore." Lena paced the floor. "I don't want to hear how I'm disappointing you and Daddy. I don't want you trying to control my every decision."

"Well, if you would make good decisions, I wouldn't have to."

"They aren't your decisions to make!" Lena yelled. She turned back to her mother. "What would you have said if I would have told you that I like women? Really, Mother, what would your reaction have been?"

"I don't know, Lena. You never gave me the option to find out!"

They stood in silence, each staring at the other.

Karen sighed. She picked her purse and keys back up.

"Lena, you think you know know everything, but you don't. I am only trying to protect you like I am supposed to. I am your Mother!"

"Mother, I don't want to hurt you or Daddy. I just needed to figure out what I wanted before I came to you two with anything."

"So have you figured it out? What are you doing with yourself, Lena?"

The question echoed in Lena's mind. "I don't know."

"Well." Karen placed her shades on her face. "Call me when you do." Karen pulled the door open and walked out without closing it.

Lena wanted to close the door, but she couldn't move her feet.

Terrin walked from the back fully dressed. She walked past Lena and closed the door. She turned around. Lena's whole body was shaking. Terrin walked over to Lena and put her arms around the sobbing woman. She silently offered her support.

42

"A'ight, bruh, you there?" Cooley said after pressing flash on her iPhone.

"Yeah." Denise sat on the couch, drinking a bottle of water. Another line began to ring on their conversation.

"Hello?" A high-pitched, happy voice answered.

"Hey, C. Denise is on the phone too," Cooley replied.

"Hey, Dee. What's going on?" Carmen sat down on her couch next to Nic. She put the phone on speaker, so Nic could listen.

"Look, we have something to tell you, but you gotta promise not to get mad at us," Cooley replied, while rocking back and forth in her chair.

"Oh my God, what?" Carmen's face dropped. "You better not be calling to tell me you bitches are missing my birthday."

"C, we're sorry, but we have to work," Cooley tried to sound upset.

"We're really sorry, C. We were going to try to come, but Farih and I both have to be in ATL for Fashion Frenzy. We both have gigs all week, and that weekend is when we are really busy."

"Are you trying to make me shoot myself!" Carmen's happy voice was gone. "Damn, I don't ask for much. All I asked was that my best fucking friends take one weekend out of hanging out with supermodels and rock stars and come see me."

"Carmen."

"This is really fucked up. I had things planned, you know. Ugh. I can't believe y'all are doing this to me."

"Nic, are you there?" Denise's voice echoed through the speaker phone.

Carmen tossed the phone to Nic.

"Yeah, I'm here," Nic said, holding the phone up.

"When Carmen calms down, can you tell her that since we can't be there with her, we thought it would be a great idea if you two came here with us," Cooley smiled.

"Yeah, all expenses paid by us."

Denise and Farih both grinned.

Carmen looked at Nic. Her frown turned into a smile. Nic handed her the phone.

"Are you serious?"

"Yes." Denise said. "Hold on. Farih wants to say something."

Farih leaned toward the phone. "Hi, Carmen."

"Hey, girl!" Carmen squealed, trying to hold back her excitement.

"I'm sorry that we can't make it to Memphis, but I also wanted to throw in All-Access passes to Fashion Frenzy for you two as well."

"Oh my God! Are you serious?" Carmen started bouncing up and down.

Nic just smiled.

"Yes, I've heard so much about you. I can't wait to meet the infamous Carmen." Farih looked at Denise and smiled.

"I can't wait to meet you either. I'm so excited. Thank you, guys. But you are soooo wrong for doing that to me."

Denise and Cooley laughed.

"You didn't really think we would do that to you on your birthday," Denise added.

"Well, I don't know. Y'all all superstars now. You may have forgotten all about little ole Carmen."

"Girl, if you don't shut that shit up," Cooley interjected.

Carmen blew a kiss into the phone.

"Thanks, guys. I can't wait to see you both."

"All right, well, we have to go, but see you next weekend," Denise said.

"OK."

When they hung up, Carmen looked at Nic and squealed. "I have to get my hair and nails done, you do know that, don't you?" She jumped up. "And, baby. What am I gonna wear?"

"Try not to spend all of our money, honey." Nic flashed a smile at Carmen.

"I won't. Oh, baby." Carmen sat back down and snuggled into Nic's arms. She was overjoyed. "We're going to Fashion Frenzy in Atlanta. With our friends. All-Access! Do you know what that means? I wonder who we will see. Oh, man!"

Nic started laughing. "Girl, you're gonna bust!"

"I know, right." Carmen had to laugh at herself. "Know what, Nic?"

Nic looked lovingly at Carmen's beaming face. "What is it ,sweetie?"

"We really have some terrific friends, and I am really proud of them. And of us." She snuggled in a little closer to Nic, who took her cue and wrapped her arms around Carmen. "We have all come through some adversity, but look how far we have come."

"I know. You are right. And we always have to remember just how lucky we are."

"And how blessed."

"That's one of the things I love about you." Nic leaned in and passionately kissed Carmen's full, expectant mouth. She reached down and pulled one of Carmen's thick thighs over her leg and pulled her closer.

Carmen responded and lifted herself up to straddle Nic. She pressed her body close as Nic lowered her face into Carmen's breasts.

"You know you're gonna miss the stores if you stay here, right?"

"They'll be there tomorrow." Carmen lifted Nic's hands to massage her breasts.

Nic gladly obliged and moved her face in to take a nipple through the thin fabric of her silk shirt.

"Right now, I have some celebrating to do with you. And I am pretty sure it's going to take all night."

"I kind of hoped you would say that." Nic lifted the hem of Carmen's shirt and buried her face between the two large melons, taking first one nipple then the other into her mouth.

"Mmmmmm. Start the celebration, 'cause Lord, there sure is gonna be fireworks up in here." Carmen laughed.

The wall was Lena's new favorite thing. She lay on her back on her couch staring at her wall. John Mayer's "Dreaming of a Broken Heart" blared through her sound system.

Lena knew she was a wreck. Terrin had missed three days of work watching over her. She finally convinced Terrin that she would be all right so she wouldn't miss any more work. She was starting to regret that decision.

Lena called her mother over and over, but never got an answer. She left countless messages until the message box was full. She had broken her mother's heart, which hurt more than anything.

Lena stared at the ceiling, thinking. She tried to pinpoint where things went wrong. Denise, Brandon, and now her own mother, she couldn't seem to stop hurting the people she loved.

Lena turned over on her side. *Good Times* was playing on mute on her plasma. She picked the remote up and flipped the channels. Carrie Underwood's "Look at Me" began to play. Denise entered her mind. The lyrics brought tears to her eyes. She thought Denise was the one for her, but Denise had moved on and was happy.

Terrin appeared in her mind. She cared about Terrin more than she realized, but she couldn't shake the feelings she had for Denise.

A loud knock at her door caused her to jump. Lena sighed. She slowly got off the couch and walked to the door. Her strength was gone. She struggled to pull the big door open. She finally mustered up enough strength to open it. Nic's long ponytail hung down her back. She turned around and smiled.

"Hey, Lena, is this a bad time?" Nic looked down the hall.

"Oh no, come on in." Lena stepped to the side, allowing Nic to walk in. She noticed the giddy appearance. Nic was fidgety, anxious about something.

Lena sat in a dining room chair. "So what's up?"

"Well, you know that Carmen was really bummed that Denise and Cooley couldn't make it for her birthday. Well, to make up for it, they are flying us in for that big fashion week in Atlanta.

"Fashion Frenzy, that's awesome. I hope you two have fun." Lena put her arm on the table.

"Well, see, that's the thing. I really was hoping that you and Terrin would make the trip too. I really wanted everyone to be there, because—"

Nic put her hands in her pockets, pulled out a little black box, and sat it on the table. "I'm going to ask Carmen to marry me."

Lena's eyes bulged, she shook her head. "Oh my God. Nic, that's great!" Lena squealed as she hugged Nic's slender frame. "But I don't think that's such a good idea that I come."

More depressing music played from her speakers. Nic looked around the room. She looked at Lena's sullen demeanor. Nic's smile faded slowly. She sat down in the chair next to Lena.

"Lena, what's going on here? Are you all right?"

Tears began to form in Lena's eyes. "Not really."

Nic held Lena's hand. "What's going on? Talk to me."

Lena raised her head. "My mom caught me with Terrin, and she's not talking to me." Lena cried. Nic rubbed her hand. "And as much as I like Terrin, I can't get over my feelings for Denise."

"Oh, come here." Nic extended her arms. Lena embraced Nic. "Lena, it's going to be OK. Your mom will talk to you. Just give her a little time to get over the initial shock of things."

"Everything in my life is so fucked up. As much as I would want to be there for you and Carmen, I don't know if I could face Denise and her girlfriend." Lena sat up. She wiped the tears from her eyes.

"Lena, I know everything seems to be messed up, but trust me, everything happens for a reason. Think about Carmen and me. She left me for Tameka, remember?" Nic rolled her eyes, thinking about Carmen's ex, who she broke up with Nic for their junior year. "But like the saying goes, if something is meant to be, it will be."

"I feel so bad. I have Terrin here, and I can't give her my all because of Denise. It's like I continue to wonder what if? What if I would have just done right by Denise to begin with? Then the way we ended. I have so many thoughts, so many questions."

Nic looked Lena in her eyes. "Well, there is the problem. You have unfinished business with Denise. It's not that you don't want Terrin, and you might not really want Denise. But until you get closure, you won't be able to truly give yourself to anyone else."

"You really think so?"

Nic nodded her head. "I think about Carmen and Tameka. When Carmen finally got the closure that she needed she was a completely different woman."

Lena looked at Nic's sincere face. She thought about the way things ended with Denise. Denise wasn't in her normal state of mind.

"But what if I go and I don't get the answers that I want?"

"It's not about getting the answers that you want. It's about getting the answers that you need. They might not be what you want to hear, but once you know the truth, you will have to take the next steps from there."

Nic stood up. She placed the little black box back in her pocket. Lena stood up as well.

"I really want you to be there, it wouldn't be the same if you didn't come. You are Carmen's best girlfriend, and we owe a lot to you. Bring Terrin if it will make it better."

"It would be nice to try to go see my parents, talk things out with them."

Nic smiled. "See, it seems to me there are a lot of things calling you to Atlanta." Nic winked.

Lena smiled for the first time in a week.

"Nic, I'm really happy that you didn't give up on Carmen. You are really great together. I wouldn't miss it for the world." Lena hugged Nic.

"Thanks, Lena. And, remember, things will work out in the end. I'm sure of it."

Lena closed the door with ease when Nic left. She could feel her depression lifting. She had more important things to do besides moping around. Lena stopped at the mirror on the wall. She looked at her face.

"OK, Lena, this is it." Lena pulled her hair out of the frazzled ponytail. "Lena, you have let yourself go." She checked the split ends on her hair. "You look like crap." She turned to the side. She felt on her stomach. "And you're looking bloated. Well, it is time for"—Lena's eyes widened. She jerked her neck around so fast, she could have gotten whiplash. Lena ran to her purse. She pulled her calendar out and gasped.

"Shit. I'm late."

43

Cooley, Denise and Farih sat in the limo waiting on their time on the red carpet. Cooley did her final primps on her look. She made sure her black button-down was perfectly creased. Denise and Farih laughed in the corner. Farih and Denise kissed. Cooley frowned.

"Damn. I'm in the car," Cooley hissed.

Denise smiled. "I'm sorry, bruh." Denise brushed her straightened hair. Cooley continued to frown.

"See you can't even say that when you looking like that." Cooley waved her hand up and down. Denise was dressed in a pair of black pants and a red halter vest that showed off her flat stomach. Her hair was pressed and wrapped, flowing whenever she moved.

"Come on, man, don't act like that." Denise stuck her bottom lip out. Farih put her hand on Denise's leg.

"Come on, Cooley, you know she looks good."

"Thank you, baby." Denise pecked Farih on her lips.

"Ugh! Gag." Cooley rolled her eyes.

Their limo pulled up to the red carpet. Paparazzi stood on each side of the red carpet, along with a set of bleachers for fans to see their favorite stars arrive. Farih checked her makeup over again. Denise did too.

"Man, I'm one lucky stud to be arriving with such lovely ladies," Cooley joked.

Denise threw up her middle finger.

Farih and Denise's publicists waited by the limo door. The usher opened it and Cooley stepped out of the limo. She gave daps to Big Ron, who had arrived moments before. Denise stepped out of the limo. The cameras flashed double time. Denise lowered her head. She held her hand out.

Farih's long black leg with diamond Louboutin stiletto exited the limo. As soon as Farih stood up, the crowd went wild.

Cooley turned around, thinking it had to be another celebrity. She smiled, gleaming with pride for her friend.

Denise and Farih smiled for the cameras. Denise was surprised by the amount of people yelling her name. Denise squeezed Farih's hand.

Farih turned to her. "Are you all right?"

"It just hit me."

"What?"

"That my life will never be the same."

Farih smiled at Denise. They posed for a few more photos and waved to the fans before they headed further down the red carpet.

The Georgia Aquarium had been transformed into an underwater playground for celebrities, elite models and fashion designers. Jam Zone's Fashion Frenzy kickoff party was the biggest ticket in the city. Aerial acrobats dressed in all types of shades of blue hung from the ceiling, doing various poses. Beautiful spreads of food surrounded by lavish ice sculptures and floral arrangements adorned each table. The various water exhibits gave a variety of unique areas for people to socialize.

The three picked up glasses of champagne as they walked in the door. Farih greeted other famous models and designers. She introduced Denise to everyone.

Cooley watched the relationship between Farih and Denise.

Denise turned around, noticing the look on her friend's face. She excused herself and walked over to Cooley.

"What's up, bro?"

Cooley looked up at Denise. "Have I told you how much I admire you?"

Denise dropped her jaw and covered her mouth. "What brings that on?"

Cooley hit Denise on her arm. "I'm serious. Man, you have gone through some serious shit in your life. Hell, just a few months ago you thought your life was over. Now look at you. You're a model and about to be an actor too."

"I don't know about all that. I haven't heard anything yet." Denise leaned against the blue wall.

"I do. I know you are gonna get it. You deserve it. Hell, you deserve all of this."

"OK. What is bringing on this sentimental shit?" Denise joked.

Cooley sighed. "I don't know. I think it just hit me. Seeing you with Farih, man, that's a real good look. I can tell she really cares for you. I am a bit jealous."

"Ahh, please, you got a girl who cares about you too."

"Yeah, but we can't have what you two have. I can't be all out with her."

"It will happen. Just let her settle in and let that first album come out. When she jump-starts her career and establishes her place in the world, then you can do whatever you want to do."

"Let's hope so."

Denise looked at her friend's worried face. She nudged her with her elbow. Cooley laughed.

"Cooley you know how you were saying you were proud of me and all? I just wanted to say that I'm equally, or even more proud of all the things that you are doing, especially settling down."

The two friends looked at each other. They gave each other daps. Farih walked over to them with a new glass of champagne. Denise put her arm around her.

"Hey, I just heard that your girl is arriving next." Farih handed Cooley a new glass of champagne.

"Well, let's go see this. She's gonna be surprised I'm here so early." Cooley grinned as they headed to the door.

Cooley, Denise and Farih watched the papz go wild when Bobby Dee and Sahara stepped out of the limo together. Bobby Dee was flashy as usual with a black tuxedo with custom Louis Vuitton Air Force Ones. Cooley felt pride as Sahara waved at the crowd. Her pink KLS mini dress looked ravishing on her body. Bobby Dee put his arm around her back as they took pictures for the crowd.

They walked over to the MTV cameras that were set up. Cooley took a deep breath.

Farih put her arm around Cooley.

"He might get to walk in with her, but you get to go home with her." Farih winked.

Cooley kissed her on her cheek. Cooley watched a little longer while Bobby Dee absorbed all of the time in the limelight that he could. He caressed his hand up and down Sahara's back. Sahara stood and smiled, flirting at times when he would hold on to her.

Cooley wanted to scream. "Yeah, I don't want to see anymore of this." Cooley turned and walked back into the party. Denise and Farih followed.

Cooley excused herself from Denise and Farih. She chatted with many of her industry colleagues.

Cooley caught a glimpse of Sahara and Bobby out of the periphery of her eyes. She turned around and walked closer to the action. Bobby Dee had his arm around Sahara while talking to a group of people. Cooley watched as his hand roamed down her back, cupping her butt. Cooley couldn't take it anymore. She made her way through the crowd, ready to rip Bobby's head off.

As she grew closer her eyes focused on Sahara. Sahara's eyes were focused on Bobby Dee. Bobby pulled Sahara close, planting a sensual kiss on her lips. Cooley froze in her spot. The room started to spin.

She started to storm over when someone held her arm.

"Hey, you're Cooley, right?" A beautiful girl flashed a smile at her.

"Yeah. Do I know you?"

"Not really. I was an intern at Jam Zone. My internship ended last week, but they still gave us tickets to the event. My name is Heather."

"Well, it's nice to meet you, Heather." Cooley shook her hand, ready to start back on her mission.

Heather held on to her hand. "I hope this isn't too forward of me. But you have got to be the sexiest woman I've ever seen. I used to feel so . . . wild whenever you would pass by."

Cooley looked Heather up and down. "So why didn't you ever say anything?"

Heather smiled. "It was against the internship rules." Heather walked closer, holding Cooley's hand. Her eyes slanted, giving an alluring vibe. "But I'm not an intern anymore."

Cooley stared at Heather. She could tell she had a nice body from the mini dress that was hugging her frame. Cooley glanced back over at Sahara; she was still next to Bobby Dee, talking to a group of men in suits.

Cooley turned back to Heather. "How about we go check out the sting rays?"

Cooley took Heather by the hand. She flashed her All-Access pass to security. They walked into the exclusive VIP area.

Heather gazed in awe at the beauty of the arctic tunnel. She looked at the fish over her head and the celebrities standing all around her. Cooley didn't notice her excitement. She couldn't take her mind of Sahara.

The large viewing room that usually hosted children and parents was covered in small private booths. The gigantic viewing window combined with blue mood lighting created the perfect romantic hideaway. Cooley and Heather found an empty booth and sat down. Heather scooted her body as close to Cooley as she could. She placed her hand on Cooley's knee and smiled. Cooley paused. She looked into Heather's lust-filled eyes. Sahara entered her mind.

"You know what . . . I don't think I can do this." Cooley removed Heather's hand from her knee.

Heather's smile dampened. "What's wrong? Did I do something?"

"Nah, it's not you."

Heather crossed her legs. She placed her hand on Cooley's thigh, rubbing up and down. "Then what is it?"

Sahara's face entered Cooley's mind. Cooley blinked. Flashes of Bobby Dee grabbing Sahara's ass flashed in her mind. She could see the kiss as though it was happing right in front of her. Cooley blinked again. Heather looked puzzled.

"Fuck it."

Cooley leaned in, planting her lips against Heather's.

***

"OK. I'll see you later then." James smiled until the cute video vixen walked away. His smiled quickly turned into a frown. The video girl was known as an easy fuck and she still wouldn't do him. He restlessly sat in the small, hard booth. He thought about beating his meat right in the VIP booth.

James drank the rest of his bottle of champagne. His manhood finally died down. He stood up, ready to head out to try again. He decided to set his sights on a groupie or a wannabe he could bang with promises of a career.

James stood up and headed out of the VIP room. Something caught his eye. He turned around, his smile immediately returned. He shook his head as he spied on Cooley and some hot chick that wasn't Sahara. Maybe his night would get exciting without sex.

44

Sahara couldn't get away from Bobby Dee quick enough. She finally pulled herself away from his hooks. She was furious. Bobby Dee kissed her in front of everyone, even though he knew it was against the rules. She wanted to be back in the safety of her woman.

"Hey, Denise," Sahara walked up to Farih and Denise. "I've been looking for Cooley and I can't find her."

Denise scanned the crowd. "I haven't seen her in a minute. She was near the door when you walked in. I thought she was waiting for you over there."

Sahara's jaw dropped. "Oh, I hope she didn't see what Bobby did."

"What are you talking about?" Denise questioned.

"Oh, it's nothing. I'm gonna go try to find her." Sahara walked away before Denise could pry.

Sahara was becoming restless. The large aquarium offered too many areas to search, and being stopped by people every few seconds didn't help either. Her text messages to Cooley were going unanswered. She knew something was wrong; she could feel it in her stomach. Her performance time was drawing close and she wanted to find Cooley before she hit the stage.

Sahara noticed the VIP sign hanging under the Ocean Voyage exhibit. She knew that was her last bet. Sahara walked past the DJ booth, smiling and waving at associates.

"Sahara."

Sahara turned when someone caught her arm. She rolled her eyes. "Hey, James."

James stood with his devilish grin. Thoughts of how to get away from him quickly ran through her mind. He took a sip from a glass of champagne. "Looking for someone?"

Sahara put her guard up. "Actually I am, so I have to go." Sahara turned around but James managed to grab her arm.

"Chill out. I know who you are looking for." He gulped down the last of the bubbly. He picked up the champagne bottle. "You are looking for Wade."

"Actually yes, I am. But don't worry I'm not going—"

"It's cool, Sahara." James smiled. "I know how much you care about her. I meant to tell you how sorry I am about tripping over you two."

Sahara's eyes slanted. "Really?"

"Yes, really." James flashed his pearly whites. "I just told Cooley the same thing."

Sahara's eyes widened. "You've seen her?"

"Yeah, I told her about the VIP area. It's real secluded, bunch of naughty shit going on in there. She went to go secure a table, for you."

Sahara's stomach filled with butterflies. The bad feeling disappeared. "Thanks."

"Wait." James handed the bottle of champagne to Sahara. "Take this. I really do wish you all the best. You make a . . . great couple." James flashed his smile again.

Sahara gave a friendly nod and walked away. She didn't know what came over James. She figured the champagne had something to do with it.

James watched as Sahara walked through the crystal beads hanging from the entrance of the VIP area. He knew he couldn't walk in right with her. It would be too obvious. James waited a moment then headed behind her.

"James, this is your lucky night after all."

45

Lena stood on her balcony. The night view of the Memphis Bridge was the only thing keeping her calm. She held the piece of paper her doctor gave her in her hand. She wanted to let go of it, act as if it didn't exist. But the baby inside of her wouldn't disappear that easily.

She heard the door unlock. Brandon walked into the house. Lena took a deep breath. She opened her eyes wide. The cool breeze helped to dry the tears forming in her eyes. Brandon slid the balcony door open.

"What's up, Lena?"

Lena could hear the attitude in his voice. "How are you?" Lena couldn't turn around. She couldn't face him.

Brandon sighed. "I'm fine. You called me to come over. What's up?"

Lena held her hand out.

Brandon looked down at the piece of paper in her hand. He took the paper and read it. Brandon's heart raced.

Tears fell from Lena's eyes.

Brandon looked up at Lena, who still couldn't turn around.

"How is this possible?" Brandon's voice quivered.

"The last time we had sex, it was spontaneous. We didn't use any protection."

Brandon's mind raced. He remembered the angry sex they had. The day they'd separated for good.

He felt his legs going weak. He sat down in the chair.

"I don't know what to say. I don't know what to do. I'm sorry, Brandon. I . . ." Lena began to choke up. She couldn't get the words out.

Brandon turned to his soon-to-be ex-wife. He sighed. He stood up. Brandon moved behind Lena. He placed his big hands on her arms. Lena turned around. Their eyes met.

"Don't cry, Lena. It's going to be OK." Brandon wiped the tears rolling down Lena's face.

"How, Brandon? How is it gonna be OK? We are divorcing. My mother won't even talk to me. And I . . . I'm a mess! I keep messing things up worse and worse. No wonder you hate me. I'd hate me."

"Lena, stop it." Brandon's deep voice rumbled. He held on to her tight. "I don't hate you. Damnit, girl, you know I love you."

"But last time."

"I was pissed off!" Brandon threw his hands in the air. "Lena, do you know how hard it is for me to know I did this to you?" Tears rolled down Brandon's face. "I turned you gay." Brandon walked into the house.

Lena's body froze. She watched Brandon pace back and forth. He stopped, falling down on the couch. Lena ran inside.

"Brandon, this isn't your fault. You didn't turn me."

"If I would have been a better man, you never would have gone to her."

"Brandon." Lena fell to her knees. She put her arms on his knees. "I can't explain how it happened. All I know is that it did. It wasn't your fault or my fault. You . . . you can't help who you . . . fall in love with."

Lena dropped her head. She couldn't bear to look at his hurt-filled face.

Brandon took a deep breath. He looked up and let out a long sigh. He put his hands on Lena's shoulders. Lena's lip trembled as she looked at Brandon's face.

Brandon couldn't take his eyes off of Lena. Thoughts of the happy times ran through his mind. He put his hands under her arms and helped her to the couch. Brandon put his arm around Lena. Lena placed her head on his chest.

"Lena, you know when we first met, you were so real to me. I was so crazy about you, even though I didn't want to show it. I was a freshman in college crazy over a damn sophomore in high school." Brandon cracked a smile.

They could feel the tension clearing.

"I remember. We used to talk about everything. You were my bestfriend." Lena looked up at Brandon's face. She ran her fingers through the beard he was growing.

Brandon took a deep breath, his large chest pushing Lena up and back down.

"What happened?" Brandon whispered.

"I think somewhere down the road we stopped communicating the way we used to, and we grew apart."

"Lena, I look at some of my crew and teammates and the way they are with their exes, it's so brutal. I don't want that to be us. I don't want to bring a baby into something toxic."

Lena sat up and turned toward Brandon. Brandon held her hands.

"I don't want that either. Brandon, you are the only man I've ever loved. You are one of my bestfriends. I think if we can just work on rebuilding our friendship, being honest with each other, we can make things work."

Brandon stared at Lena. "Lena . . . I want you to be happy." He fought to get the words out of his mouth. "Even . . . if it's with a woman?"

Lena gazed into Brandon's eyes.

Brandon let out a loud moan. He covered his eyes and rested his head on the back of the couch.

"Damn, do you really think this is that serious? Lena, for real, can you sit here and tell me that you are gay. Can you say you never want to be with a man again?"

Brandon's questions hit Lena with force. She paused. Lena didn't know the answers. She had been trying to figure it out. Was she completely gay? Did she never want to be with a man again? She still didn't have any answers.

They stared at each other. Lena's hands trembled, her bottom lip quivered.

"I . . . I don't know." Lena held Brandon's hand. "I don't know if this is something that is forever or if it is something that could change. All I know is that I fell in love with someone, and that I really, really like someone else, and they both happen to be women."

"At one time you loved me," Brandon said, placing his other hand on top of hers.

"And I still love you. You are the only man I've ever loved. That doesn't just go away. But I can't deny the other feelings I have. And I think it's something that we are both just going to have to deal with."

They sat in silence. Neither wanted to let go forever, but both knew that the love they felt would never be the same.

Brandon let out another deep moan. His lips curved upward, he smirked."

"This would have been so much easier if you would have given me a good-ass threesome." Brandon started to laugh.

Lena smiled. She hit him with a pillow from the couch.

"Ugh! OK, OK, I'll be all right. My baby mama is a lesbo. But, damn, can you leave these nigga-lookin' girls alone and at least get you a fine-ass bitch? Hell, you too damn fine yourself to be with these little boy-girls." Brandon sighed. He put his arm around Lena."

"Yeah, let me go find an Alicia Keys to date."

"Hell yeah, that will work. Maybe we can do it *She Hate Me* style, and I can date both of you."

"Shut up." Lena hit Brandon on his arm.

They both laughed.

Brandon wrapped his arm around Lena. She rested in his arms again. Lena still felt safe in Brandon's arms, but she knew it wasn't in an intimate way anymore.

"We're gonna be OK."

"Yeah, baby doll, we are."

Lena, and Brandon's eyes met. Brandon leaned in, planting a kiss on Lena's lips. They both knew that the flame that they used to feel for each other was dying out, yet a friendship was rising from the ashes.

46

Sahara's body was on fire. She wanted to feel Cooley next to her. The beautiful atmosphere was making her wet in anticipation. She took a swig out of the bottle of champagne as she walked into the main VIP room. She peeked into each of the booths. Others were involved in their own affairs. She was ready to have one of her own.

Sahara caught a glimpse of the back of Cooley's head. She smiled, walking through the booths to the corner. She smiled, wondering what Cooley was looking at on the wall. Sahara walked closer, and she noticed a small arm wrapped around Cooley's back. She gasped at Cooley kissing someone. Her heart pounded. She rushed over to the table.

"So, is this the new look?" Sahara stood over the table.

Cooley turned to face Sahara. Heather's face filled with fear.

Cooley sat back in the booth. "What's good, Sahara?"

"What's good? You tell me." Sahara turned to Heather. "You got five seconds to get the fuck up out of this booth."

Heather took heed.

Cooley grabbed her hand. "You don't have to go no-where." Cooley looked back at Sahara. "Why don't you go back to ya date? That's where you wanna be right."

"Are you kidding me?" Sahara's high voice caused others to turn around. "You back here, fucking with this bitch because of Bobby?"

Cooley remained calm. "You're causing a scene."

"Does it look like I give a damn about a scene?" Sahara yelled. She pointed at Heather. "You better get the fuck out of here."

Heather was too afraid to move.

"Don't threaten her. She hasn't done anything wrong. Now, like I said, go back to your little date. We're done."

Cooley's words spewed like venom. Sahara's mouth dropped. She couldn't speak.

"We got a hot show coming up for y'all. Sahara is about to hit the stage in a few." The DJ's voice echoed through the building.

Sahara couldn't take her eyes off of Cooley.

Cooley looked at her. She glanced away, unable to look Sahara in the eyes. Sahara shook her head. She took the bottle of champagne and shook it, spewing the contents all over Cooley and Heather.

"Fuck you, Cooley." She threw the bottle down on the table. "I hope it was worth it."

Sahara ran all the way out of the room. Cooley was frozen from shock and the cold champagne. Heather screamed, standing up, shaking her dress. Cooley picked up a napkin and wiped her face. She walked away, leaving the soaked Heather in the corner.

Cooley exited the VIP, her clothes soaked. People looked at her, some curious, others laughing. Cooley saw the entrance to the green room. She wanted to go after Sahara, but something was holding her back.

"Oh my God! Cooley, what happened?" Tee said, rushing up to her boss.

"Nothing! Just get me a cab." Cooley started walking toward the entrance.

Tee followed, obeying her orders without question.

The lights on the stage illuminated. Big Ron walked out on the stage. People turned toward him. Big Ron was handed a microphone. Cooley didn't care to watch; she fought her way through the crowd.

"A'ight, y'all. It's the moment you have been waiting for. The newest star on Jam Zone is about to hit the stage." Big Ron hyped the crowd up.

Cooley couldn't get out of the building fast enough. She made it to the door as soon as Sahara's name was called.

Sahara walked out on stage. She knew the show had to go on, even if she was dying on the inside. She hugged Big Ron as she took the mic, forcing a smile. Her eyes focused on Cooley about to walk out of the door.

"Thank you. Thank you so much." Sahara couldn't take her eyes off of Cooley.

Cooley couldn't fight it. She turned around, immediately making eye contact with Sahara.

Sahara sighed. "I know you are ready to hear my songs, but I wanted to start with a song that I absolutely love and, and a song that I dedicated to someone very special."

Sahara began to sing Etta James's "Trust in Me." The music began to play. Cooley's heart dropped. Sahara sang to Cooley, refusing to take her eyes off of her.

Cooley watched as Sahara poured her feelings into the song.

The crowd was silent, hanging to every word coming from Sahara's mouth.

Cooley wanted to run to the stage, take Sahara in her arm and apologize for everything. She took a deep breath, lowered her head and walked out of the building.

Sahara continued to sing as the tears flowed down her eyes.

47

Cooley didn't want to go home. She walked the downtown streets for hours. She stopped and sat in Olympic Park. The place was swarming with people, but she didn't notice anything. Cooley wanted to cry. She tried to squint her eyes as hard as she could, but nothing would come out. Sahara's song played over and over in her head. She wanted it to all go away.

Cooley finally got into a cab. Even with the traffic, she made it to her downtown loft in less than ten minutes. She looked at the door. She couldn't go in. She had the cab driver keep driving.

By the time she made it back to her place she had run up a hundred-dollar cab fare. She handed the cab driver six twenty-dollar bills. He thanked her for her nice tip. Cooley didn't respond. She walked into her building.

Cooley walked into her dark apartment. She hit the light switch and jumped. Sahara looked up. Her eyes bloodshot, and makeup smeared. Sahara stood up. Cooley couldn't move from her spot.

"I know why you did what you did. Cooley, that was not my idea. He just grabbed me and did it."

They both stood in their spots.

Sahara's eyes twinkled from the water forming. "I cursed him out, told him never to contact me again."

"It doesn't matter now." Cooley walked past her couch.

Sahara turned around. "It does matter. Cooley, I know why you did what you did. I'm not mad. We're OK."

"No, Sahara, we aren't!" Cooley snapped. "I can't do this. I don't want to do this anymore."

"Cooley, please, it wasn't my fault." Sahara ran up to Cooley.

"It's not about that. I just don't want to be in anything. I never did." Cooley's straight expression didn't change.

Sahara took a few steps back. "So, you really want to stand here and just give up on us over something so stupid?"

Cooley couldn't look at Sahara. "It's too complicated. I never wanted a relationship to begin with. So . . ."

Sahara shook her head in disbelief. "No, this isn't you talking. You are angry at me, and I know that. I was wrong for the champagne but—"

"Sahara, I don't want to be with you!"

Cooley and Sahara stared at each. Cooley shifted her eyes away from Sahara's tear-filled face.

Sahara couldn't take it anymore. She picked her purse up and walked toward the door. Cooley wanted to stop her, but she couldn't.

Sahara grabbed the doorknob, she paused. She turned around.

"No!" Sahara dropped her purse and stormed back up to Cooley. She wrapped her arms around Cooley and held on with all her strength.

Cooley's eyes widened.

"I'm not letting you do this, I'm not letting you walk away from us!"

Cooley closed her eyes as Sahara held on to her. Cooley could smell her sweet perfume. She could feel her heart beating. Cooley shook her head. She pulled

Sahara off of her. She turned her back, walking toward the kitchen.

Sahara yelled her name with a high-pitched screech, causing Cooley to stop.

Cooley turned around.

They stood face to face like two cowboys at high noon.

"I know you care about me. I know deep down you don't want to do this." Sahara's voice was calm, but filled with raw emotions. "It's easier for you to run away from it."

"I'm never going to change!" Cooley threw her arms up. "I'm always going to be me. I'm no good for you or anyone else!"

They stood in silence for a moment. Sahara's eyebrows raised. It made sense to her. "I'm not Misha."

"What?"

"I'm not Misha. I'm not going to give up on you because you have a few flaws. I know you are good for me. You are meant for me, and I am meant for you. Cooley, I'm standing here telling you that I accept you for who you are, and I am not going anywhere. Can you honestly stand here and look me in my eyes and tell me that you don't love me . . . that you want me to leave?"

Cooley stared at the woman pouring her heart out to her.

Sahara stood in her spot, vulnerable and open. No tears fell, she couldn't cry anymore. She waited on Cooley to answer.

Cooley's bottom lip trembled. She knew Sahara loved her. She knew it was her moment.

"I don't love you," Cooley responded in a very low tone.

The words hit Sahara like a Louisville slugger. Sahara lowered her head in defeat. She couldn't cry. She was all cried out. She walked slowly toward Cooley. She pulled a keychain out of her pocket, dropping Cooley's house key at her feet. Sahara turned around, grabbed her purse and walked out the door.

Cooley watched Sahara walk out the door. She stared at the closed door, hoping Sahara would walk back in. She knew she was gone for good. Cooley looked down. She saw her single key lying in front of her. She reached down to pick it up. She stood back up, leaving a small puddle of tears on the floor.

48

Lena sighed as the Six Flags roller coasters appeared from the highway. It was the longest six hours of her life. There was no turning back. She was about to face Denise, and her parents. Lena looked at Terrin. She knew it was best to start with the easiest confrontation.

"Terrin, I'm pregnant."

Terrin's smile dropped. She glanced over at Lena. "What?" Terrin looked at Lena dumbfounded, causing the car to swerve, which made her look back at the road.

"I'm pregnant."

Wrinkles appeared in Terrin's forehead. "Brandon's?"

"Yes."

"Does he know?"

"Yes."

"Are you and him still—"

"No." Lena turned toward Terrin. "We haven't been for a very long time. It happened before you and me got serious."

Terrin let out a sigh of relief. "Are you going to keep it?"

Lena paused. "Yes."

Terrin was quiet. She stared at the road. She took a deep breath and exhaled. She glanced over at Lena, placing her hand on her thigh.

"It's OK. I'm shocked, but I'm OK."

Lena was shocked. Terrin continued to drive as though she didn't admit to her that she was carrying a baby by her ex-husband.

Lena gazed at Terrin. "I, I can't believe you are OK with it."

"Lena, you said it happened before me and you. I can't be mad about that. You were married to the man. A child is a blessing from God. I'm not going anywhere just because you're pregnant."

"I can't believe how wonderful you are. I expected you to leave me on the side of the road."

Terrin smiled. "Lena, haven't you realized by now that I'm not going anywhere? I love you."

Lena gasped. Terrin continued to look ahead. Lena felt her body tense up. Her stomach turned. She suddenly felt nauseous.

Terrin noticed Lena's silence. "Lena, I don't expect you to say it back. I just felt it was time to tell you how I really feel about you. I want to be in your life and your baby's life."

"Thank you, Terrin."

Lena dropped Terrin off at their hotel room at the Westin. Terrin wanted to go with her, but there was something she had to do on her own. She drove in silence, no music, only her thoughts. Lena thought of a perfect speech, but it had escaped her memory.

Lena parked in the long driveway to her home. The beautiful mansion looked the same, but it felt completely different from the last time she was there. She had so many wonderful memories. Now she faced creating a horrible one.

She sighed; all their cars were in the driveway. Both of her parents had to be home.

Lena raised her hand to ring the doorbell and stopped. She pulled her key out of her purse. She opened the door and walked in. Lena fell right into her old habits. She placed her keys on the coffee table near the door and dropped her purse in the chair next to it. Lena could hear the television coming from the living room. Her hands were shaking; it was her moment of truth.

"Hello."

Lena's parents turned around. Her father placed his pipe down, her mother's face winced.

Her father smiled. "Lena, baby doll, now this is a surprise." He walked over and embraced his daughter.

His slender body felt better than he ever did. "Hey, Daddy." Lena hugged her father. She wondered if it would be the last hug she received.

Her mother picked up a copy of *Vogue.*

"What on earth are you doing here? Karen, did you know she was coming?"

"No, I didn't," Karen replied, without looking up from her magazine.

Lena thought she was going to have a heart attack. She took a deep breath. "Can I talk to you two about something?"

Her father's happy disposition changed to worry. "Of course." He sat back in his leather chair. "Is everything all right, honey?"

Her mother didn't respond.

"Mother, can you put the magazine down," Lena waited, but her mother didn't move. "Please."

Karen looked up from the magazine. Her mouth curled as she threw the magazine on the couch. "Fine, Lena. Go on with it."

Her father looked at her mother, confused by her attitude.

Lena took a seat in the chair across from her father. They both stared at her.

"Well, first I want to let you know that I love you so very much and I never wanted to do anything to disappoint you." Lena took another deep breath to try to keep from crying.

"Lena, what is going on?" Her father's deep voice rose. "Why are you saying this?"

"Just let her talk," Karen interjected.

"Well." Lena's voice trembled. "I really hope that even if you don't agree with my decisions that you will support me in the end." Lena dropped her head. She couldn't look at them. "I'm pregnant."

Her mother's and father's mouths dropped at the same time.

Karen sat up straight. "Is it Brandon's? Are you getting back together?"

"Yes, it's Brandon's baby."

"So my baby is giving me a grandbaby?" Her father's face filled with joy."

"Are you together again?" Her mother's face stayed straight.

Lena's eyes met her mother's. "No, we are still getting a divorce."

Her mother grabbed her magazine and opened it back.

"Mother, please?"

"Karen."

Her father's stern voice frightened her.

Karen looked at both at them. She slammed the magazine down on the couch.

"Well, what do you want me to say? You want me to get all excited over a baby being brought into a broken home?"

"Mom, Brandon and I have talked about it. Our relationship is good, and we are both excited to have this baby."

"But you aren't staying married."

Her mother's pained expression tore her apart. Lena started to cry.

"Mother, can't you understand that that is not what was best for me or Brandon? I'd rather bring my baby up with him happy than bring a child in a family that isn't."

"Lena, we only want what is best for you." Her father stood up. "If you feel that this is what you want to do, then we support you. As long as Brandon remains a man and takes care of his responsibilities."

"He will."

"Then, we both will be there for you one hundred percent." Her father threw her mother a stern look.

Karen folded her hands. "Is that all you have to tell us, or is there something else you want to tell your father?" Karen gave Lena a glowering look.

Lena looked at her father's face. He knew something else was up. He sat back down, waiting on the rest of the news to hit him.

Lena's parents' eyes were burning a hole in her heart. She opened her mouth, but nothing came out. She blinked. Their eyes were still fixated on her.

Lena's mother shifted her body on the couch. "Well, Lena? Are you still dating that person?"

Lena could feel the walls closing in on her. She felt short of breath. Her palms were sweating. She knew it was now or never.

"Well, Lena?" her mother folded her hands.

Lena took another deep breath. "No, Mother, I'm not. It's over . . . for good."

49

"It's OK, baby. You don't have to come out until you are good and ready." Terrin held Lena's hand as they walked to Cooley's door.

"I just feel so bad. I hate lying to them."

"Lena, you did what was best for you."

They stopped at the door.

Terrin turned to Lena. "Are you sure you want to do this?" She held Lena's hand. Terrin didn't know what to expect. The girl who threatened her future with Lena was on the other side of the door.

"Yeah, let's do it."

They both took deep breaths as Lena knocked on the door.

"Hey!" Carmen hugged Lena. "Welcome to my party."

"Have you already been drinking?" Lena shook her head.

"I sure have. Now time for you two to get drunk right along with me."

Terrin and Lena looked at each other and laughed.

"What's so funny?" Carmen questioned while taking another sip of her blue cocktail.

"I can't drink Carmen." Lena blushed. "I'm pregnant."

Carmen spewed her drink on the floor. Cooley yelled her name, complaining that she better not get her rug dirty. Lena and Terrin walked farther in the house.

Denise and Farih sat next to each other on the couch. Lena and Denise's eyes met. Lena's heart skipped a beat. Denise looked better than she expected. Her hair was down, perfectly flat-ironed. Her basketball shorts were replaced with a pair of jeans and a black button-down shirt. Lena felt her knees wobbling.

Terrin noticed the exchange. She held on to Lena's arm.

"I'm sorry, Cooley. Lena just shocked the shit out of me."

"What's up?" Nic walked up, holding two glasses of the blue concoction.

"I can't drink that because I'm pregnant."

Denise's eyes widened.

Farih smiled, patting Denise on her leg.

Nic hugged Lena. "Congrats, Lena," Nic said.

"We are very happy," Terrin added. She looked at Denise.

"Yes, Lena, congratulations," Denise said very calmly. She stood up, holding Farih's hand.

Lena's heart skipped a beat with each step the gorgeous couple took.

"Lena, this is Farih. Farih, this is Lena, my old roommate, and one of my bestfriends."

Lena saw Denise's mouth moving, but the words sounded like the teacher from the *Peanuts* cartoons.

Farih extended her hand.

Carmen nudged Lena, who snapped back to reality.

Lena extended her arm. "It's so nice to meet you, Farih. I love, your Victoria Secret campaign." Lena's voice slightly trembled.

"Thank you, girl, but you look like you need to be modeling beside me. Denise, you never told me how stunning your friends are." Farih held on to Denise's arm.

Farih's pleasant disposition made Lena wonder if she was aware of her past with Denise.

"This is Terrin, my . . . girlfriend." Lena put her arm around Terrin's back.

Terrin shook hands with Denise and Farih.

"It's nice to meet you, Terrin." Denise forced the words out of her mouth.

"It's nice to finally meet you too."

Terrin and Denise caught eyes again.

"OK, now that all that awkward shit is out of the way, can we start the party?" Cooley's soft voice echoed.

Everyone headed into the house.

"Cooley, is Sahara here? I love her music." Lena's question caused everyone to pause.

Cooley fought to keep a straight face. "Nah, she won't be coming." She took a sip from her Corona.

Carmen quickly changed the subject.

Drinks were pouring, and music was playing. The gang laughed as though nothing was wrong.

Lena felt more at ease than she expected. She caught herself catching glances at Denise and Farih. She had to admit, they made a beautiful couple.

Lena glanced over at Denise again, only to catch Denise's eyes on her. They lingered for a moment. Lena's heart began to pound.

"Um, Cooley, where is your bathroom?" Lena stood up.

"There's one in the back, right past the kitchen."

Lena excused herself and headed to the bathroom. She closed the door quickly. Lena's heart was racing. "Get a grip, Lena," she said out loud.

Lena took a few more moments to compose herself. She knew if she stayed much longer Terrin would be ready to knock the door down. Lena sighed and opened the door. She jumped when Denise was standing there.

"Can we?"

Denise's warm eyes melted Lena's heart.

They both walked back into the bathroom and closed the door.

There was an awkward silence.

Denise leaned against the wall, Lena against the sink. Lena did a double take when she noticed the brown powder on Denise's eyelids.

"Are you wearing makeup?" She smirked.

Denise frowned. "It's the day job."

They looked at each other and laughed.

"So Farih, huh? She's absolutely beautiful." Lena swallowed hard.

"And Terrin seems cool too.

"Yeah, she is."

"Lena, look, I am so sorry about New York." Denise's face filled with regret. "I was so out of it and—"

"Denise, you don't have to. I know what you were going through. I forgive you, I promise."

"Still, there are no words to describe how horrible I feel about that."

"Hey." Lena smiled. "Maybe it was for the best. You have Farih now. You are doing big things. Things way bigger than me."

"Nothing is bigger than Lena Jamerson-Redding."

Their eyes connected, so did their hearts.

Denise couldn't help herself. She took a step forward. Lena followed, taking another step. They stood close, staring into each other's eyes, holding their hands. The connection was electric.

Lena took another step forward until there was no space in between them.

Denise's head moved in. Lena stood on her toes. Their faces met, their lips so close, they could feel each other's breath.

They couldn't resist. They both closed their eyes.

50

The door bell chimed. Cooley stood up, walking slowly to the door.

"See, y'all loud asses about to get me put up out my crib." She laughed as she looked at them while opening the door. Cooley turned around and froze. "Misha."

"Hi, Carla."

Cooley felt like she was seeing a ghost. Misha smiled; her face plumper than normal. Cooley's eyes glanced down. Misha's stomach poked out from her shirt.

Misha rubbed her stomach. "Yeah, I know, I'm huge."

"You look absolutely beautiful." Cooley couldn't take her eyes off of her.

Misha blushed.

Cooley thought about Patrick. She looked up.

"He's not here. I came alone," Misha said, noticing Cooley's defensive stance. "Can I come in or not?"

Cooley moved, allowing Misha to walk in.

Carmen's mouth dropped at Misha's wide, round state. "Oh my God, Misha!" Carmen squealed. "I didn't know you were coming."

"Nic called me. Of course, I was coming. I wasn't going to miss your birthday party."

Misha and Carmen hugged. She handed Carmen a gift bag.

Cooley felt her heart race. Misha was glowing. She knew it was because of her pregnancy, but she didn't care. She wanted to grab her and hold her.

Misha reached into her bag. She handed Carmen a black envelope.

Carmen's eyes widened, and she put the envelope next to her.

Cooley looked puzzled.

Nic stood up. "Well, now that everyone is here. I wanted to say something special about my beautiful girlfriend."

"Oh, hold up, Tee!" Cooley yelled.

Tee walked out with a tray of champagne glasses.

"Oh my God! Tee, don't let Cooley turn you into her personal servant." Carmen hit Cooley on her arm.

"I pay her overtime, damn! Aye, we gotta wait on Denise and Lena."

Terrin looked up. She realized Lena and Denise were gone at the same time. Panic sunk in. She looked at Farih, who was busy typing on her phone.

Carmen noticed the look on Terrin's face. She stood up. "Let me go check on Lena. I'll get Denise out of the bedroom. She said she had to make a call." Carmen briskly walked toward the back.

Terrin knew something was wrong.

51

Lena and Denise's hearts were beating rapidly. Denise caressed the inside of Lena's hand. They both leaned in, their lips so close, they could feel each other's breath.

"Dee, are you off the phone yet?" Carmen yelled.

Denise and Lena paused. Denise sighed. "I can't . . ."

"I know," Lena whispered. "You love her, don't you?"

Denise gazed into Lena's big brown eyes. The eyes that she wanted for so long could finally be hers. She held on to Lena's hands.

"Yes, I do. "

Lena thought she would want to cry, but she didn't. A smile came on her face. She could see the pain in Denise's face. She placed her hand on Denise's cheek.

"I'm happy for you." Lena kissed Denise on her cheek and opened the bathroom door. She wasn't angry. She wasn't hurt. She was happy that Denise was happy.

"Are you two OK?" Carmen questioned.

"We are great." Lena looked at Denise and smiled. "Better than ever."

Cooley couldn't take her eyes off the black envelope sticking out of the side of the couch cushion. She had never wanted to open something so bad in her life.

"Man, y'all some junky-ass people." Cooley stood up. She walked over to the couch and reached for two empty bottles on a small table to the side. She slid the envelope under her shirt without anyone knowing and walked into the kitchen.

Cooley was happy Carmen insisted that Tee take a break. The kitchen was clear. The TV was on the red carpet for the Fashion Jams concert that was happening live on *TV One*. Cooley turned the envelope over. The handwriting was fancy. It had to be an invitation. She unhinged the flaps and opened the envelope.

Cooley read the announcement. Patrick and Misha Donaldson had requested Carmen and Nic's presence at their formal wedding ceremony and reception. Cooley dropped the envelope. Misha was already married to Patrick.

"So what are you wearing?" the *TV One* host asked one of the celebrities walking down the red carpet.

"This is Versace."

The voice sent chills down Cooley's' spine. She turned to see Sahara standing with a smile on her face. She was wearing a strapless Versace dress. Cooley quickly turned the television up to full volume.

"So, Sahara, you have a big number to do tonight." The attractive interviewer held the mic to Sahara's mouth.

"Yes, I'm doing my new single. I'm really excited because it's my first Fashion Jams."

"And arc you here with Bobby Dee?" the interviewer pried.

"No, there is no me and Bobby Dee. We are just friends, nothing more at all."

"Oh, I hear that."

They laughed.

"So is there someone else special in your life?"

Cooley watched as the light that shined when Sahara smiled dimmed a little.

Sahara paused. She looked back at the interviewer. "There was, but . . . unfortunately, not anymore."

Cooley felt her heart breaking as the interviewer finished up her questions before Sahara headed off to the next set of press. A single teardrop rolled down her face.

"Hey, bruh, come in here, Denise said as she noticed Cooley standing in the kitchen.

Cooley wiped the tear and headed into the room.

Lena sat next to Terrin and put her arm between hers.

Terrin rubbed her lips together. She watched as Denise joined Farih, planting a kiss on her lips. Terrin looked at Lena. She didn't seem angry or hurt. She made a sigh of relief, thinking maybe Denise was really taking a call. Terrin caught Denise catching a quick glimpse of Lena. Her stomach turned. She knew something wasn't right.

"Are you OK?" Lena asked when she noticed the dull expression on Terrin's face.

Terrin looked at her beautiful girlfriend. Lena was who she wanted to be with more than any other woman she'd dated before.

"Yeah, I think I just drank a little too fast. Things are wonderful." She planted a sensual kiss on Lena's lips. She hoped Denise took note. She was there to stay.

Cooley stood against the wall. Nic stood up holding her glass of champagne in her hand. Nic turned, cleared her throat.

"OK, well, I wanted to take a moment to say something about this woman right here. When I first moved to Memphis all I could think was that I wanted to go back to LA."

Everyone laughed.

"But then I met Carmen."

The ladies all fawned. Carmen was smiling from ear to ear.

"She didn't make it easy for me. I learned quickly that if you love someone you might have to let them go, and if it's meant to be it will be. I had to let her go, but as you can see . . . she came back."

Carmen blushed from embarrassment.

Nic smiled. "And now, I plan to never let her go again." Nic got down on one knee.

Carmen's face dropped. She covered her mouth.

Lena, Misha and Farih all gasped, covering their mouths.

"Carmen, will you spend the rest of your life with me?"

Cooley watched as Carmen screamed yes. She felt an abundance of emotion come over her as her bestfriend held on to the woman she loved.

Cooley's mind drifted to Sahara. Flashbacks of all the time they had spent together played like old movies in her head. She remembered the first time she laid eyes on Sahara, two years ago on her trip to Atlanta with Denise. She thought about the first time they kissed. Even though they were laying in the bed with Sahara's sleeping ex-girlfriend, it felt as though they were the only two in the room. Cooley could hear Sahara's voice reassuring her that she loved her just the way she was.

Everyone has scars. Sahara's voice repeated in her mind as she remembered their embrace. Sahara's face was so vivid. She could feel her kissing her scar as though it was happening at the moment.

Cooley's eyes began to water as she touched the blemish on her face. Sahara had loved her, flaws and all, and she had let her slip away. Tears began to fall down her face. Carmen looked up and noticed Cooley against the wall.

"Carla!" She walked over and wrapped her arms around Cooley. Everyone was shocked to see Cooley cry.

"I'm sorry." Cooley wiped the tears falling from her face. "Carmen, Nic, I'm really, really happy for y'all but I gotta go." Cooley searched for her keys.

"Bruh, what's wrong?"

"Nothing." Cooley frantically searched for her keys in the pile of stuff on her table. She looked up in the living room. All of the most important people in her life were there, except one. "I gotta go. I gotta go get my girl."

Everyone stood shocked.

Cooley smiled, her dimples set deep. Misha smiled.

Tee stood up, pulling her keys out of her pocket. "I got you, boss. I'll drive you."

"Go, baby. We will be here when you come back with Sahara," Carmen replied. Her day went from amazing to better in a single instant.

""Are you sure you aren't mad?"

"No." Carmen held Cooley's hand. "My moment is nothing without you."

The Fashion Jams concert was in full swing. Cooley flashed her Jam Zone pass to security.

Cooley rushed past all the doors for the celebrity dressing rooms. Celebrities and their entourages filled the rooms. Cooley noticed James standing with a group of groupies. She rushed up to him.

"Wade, what are you doing here?" He tried to keep a smile on his face to hide his anger.

"Where is Sahara's dressing room?"

"Why?

"Just tell me."

"You shouldn't be here, Wade."

Cooley pushed James against the wall. "Look, muth-afucka, where the fuck is my girl's dressing room?"

James could see the anger in Cooley's eyes. He pushed her hands off of him. James stood up straight and fixed his blazer. "OK, her dressing room is right there." He pointed to the door across from them. "But it doesn't matter. She's not in there."

Cooley heard the sound of Sahara's music starting to play.

James smiled. "You know that little stunt is gonna cost you."

Cooley looked at the entrance to the stage. She looked back at James with a grin on her face. "That stunt isn't going to cost me nearly as much as this one."

Cooley ran toward the stage.

James' eyes bulged. "Don't you—security!"

Sahara stood waiting on her cue to come on stage. Cooley grabbed her arm.

Sahara turned around. Shock covered her face. "What the hell are you doing?"

"I . . . I was wrong."

Sahara shook her head. "It's too late for that." She tried to pull away, but Cooley held on to her.

"You said you weren't going to give up."

"That was before you said you didn't love me."

"I'm sorry, Sahara."

"No, Cooley, you made your choice. It's going to take a whole lot more than a damn apology from you. I have to go perform." Sahara jerked her hand away and walked out on stage.

"Right there!"

Cooley looked back to see James pointing at her. Two security guards headed her way.

It's now or never. Cooley took a deep breath and walked out on the stage.

Sahara noticed the crowd looking off. She turned around to see Cooley standing on the stage.

Sahara ran up to her. "Carla, what are you—" Sahara said in a panic.

Cooley rushed up to her. "You said it was going to take more than an apology. How about my job?"

Sahara looked Cooley in her eyes. "You wouldn't?"

"Only if you tell me not to," Cooley said with determination.

The security guards stopped at the edge of the curtain.

Sahara looked at Cooley then looked at the crowd. She held her hand up to stop the security guards. Sahara smiled.

"You have lost your mind, Carla Wade."

"No." Carla grabbed Sahara by her waist. "I've found it." She pressed her lips against Sahara's.

Sahara wrapped her arms around Cooley. They embraced as though there was no one around.

The shocked crowd erupted in screams and applause.

Cooley and Sahara looked out into the audience. Cooley knew her friends were watching. She knew jaws probably hit the floor.

Cooley noticed James standing with security, ready to cart her off the moment they could.

Cooley knew her job was gone, but she didn't care. All she cared about was the woman in her arms. The woman she knew she loved. For once nothing else mattered.

"I gotta do my show."

"I'll be waiting afterward."

Cooley watched as Sahara sashayed back to the middle of the stage. The crowd was going wild, but Cooley couldn't hear them. All she could hear was Sahara's voice.

Sahara's face turned toward Cooley as the band started her intro over again. She smiled, winking her left eye at Cooley. Cooley felt a warm tingle come over her body, a feeling she had never felt before.

Cooley took a deep breath as she headed off the stage. She could almost see the fire blaring out of James's ears. As soon as she was out of the crowd's sight, James instructed two security guards to grab her.

"All this is not necessary."

Cooley didn't fight. She let the guards take her to the wall. They pushed her back to the wall. James didn't care about the rough treatment; if so many people weren't around, he would have instructed more.

"You fucking idiot! You know that's your job, right?" James spewed his words like venom.

Their eyes were locked on each other, neither willing to back down.

The two security guards let go of Cooley. She adjusted her clothes, brushing the wrinkles that the security guards left behind.

"Whatever, man. I don't want to work for a hating-ass nigga like you anyway. What you think? I don't know the real deal?"

"You don't know shit, Wade."

"I know that girl on that stage is mine, and nothing you do or say is going to change that."

James walked a few steps closer to Cooley. "Well, I guess I like my career a little more than you do, Wade. 'Cause I'll take my job over a piece of pussy any day of the week." James smirked. "Pick yo shit up on Monday.

Let's see how long she stays with a broke bitch."

Cooley balled her fist up and swung, making contact with the side of James' jaw. James let out a high-pitched squeal as he hit the ground.

Everyone quickly turned around, thinking a woman had been hit.

The security guards didn't know what to do; they hated James as much as Cooley did. One let out a laugh, causing others to chuckle at James.

Cooley walked off, making her way to Sahara's dressing room, while security helped James back to his feet.

"It's over for you, Wade! You'll never work in this town again!"

James' threats didn't seem to matter to Cooley anymore. Especially after hearing him scream like a girl.

Cooley knew her job was gone. She had given up everything for a woman, something she never thought she would do. It didn't matter anymore. She knew things would work out as long as she had Sahara by her side.

52

"I can't believe you did that." Carmen hugged Cooley as she walked into her apartment. "Girl, what have you done to my friend?" Carmen said as she wrapped her arms around Sahara.

"I haven't done anything." Sahara held on to Cooley's arm. "She did it all to me." She smiled.

Cooley planted a kiss on her lips.

Denise laughed at the new sappy version of her friend. Cooley threw her middle finger up.

"Where is Misha?" Cooley asked.

"She had to get home." Carmen sat back next to Nic. "You know she got married—straight woman curfew."

"Awww, I wanted to meet her so bad." Sahara rolled her eyes.

Cooley nudged her sarcastic girlfriend.

"So for real, Cooley, what are you going to do now?" Farih asked.

"I don't know. I guess, look for another job. Bae, are you going to love me if I'm broke?" Cooley batted her long eyelashes at Sahara.

"Don't worry, honey, you can be my Stedman."

Everyone laughed; they knew Cooley could never be a kept woman.

"You can come to New York, be my manager," Denise added.

"That's a good idea." Sahara smiled. "You can manage me too, baby."

"I don't know."

"For real, bruh, you are a natural. Maybe you should consider it." Denise nodded her head. The thought crossed her mind; management might not be a bad idea.

It was four in the morning, but no one cared. The crew sat around laughing about their past experiences.

Cooley reminisced about the first time she saw Lena, and how she thought she was going to be the one to get her first. She had to catch herself from saying too much when she noticed the uncomfortable look on Terrin's face.

Farih told stories about how photo shoots really went. The women listened as she explained how a sexy, beach photo might look sexy and exotic, but in actuality it was cold and uncomfortable.

Lena noticed how Denise and Farih touched each other frequently. Even if it was in subtle way, they would find a way to touch. She didn't want to touch Terrin like that.

"Man, if y'all could have seen my face when Denise sent me those photos." Cooley shook her head, remembering when Denise had sent photos.

"I remember, she started choking and everything." Sahara laughed. "I didn't know what was wrong with her."

"I'm sorry, bruh. Didn't mean to mess you up like that."

Cooley's lip curled. "Yes, the hell you did. You knew exactly what you were doing."

Everyone laughed as Denise nodded in aggreance.

Lena glanced over at Terrin, while her friends laughed and talked. Terrin sat with a goofy smile on her face. She seemed out of place. Sahara walked in the house and immediately fit in. Lena didn't know why it was different with Terrin. Terrin didn't seem to want to get to know her friends. She wondered if it was all because of Denise.

Lena noticed the smiles on her friends' faces. Carmen and Nic, Cooley and Sahara, and Denise and Farih all had the love glow, a glow she didn't have. Thoughts ran through her mind. She wondered if she would ever have that glow with Terrin.

The group began to disperse when they realized the sun was coming up. Sahara and Carmen talked about her singing at their wedding. Sahara and Farih exchanged numbers. Terrin stood by the door while she said her good-byes to her friends.

Lena walked over to Denise. Denise smiled, walking toward Lena. They embraced instantly. The hug was warm. Lena didn't want to let go.

"So you aren't going to forget me when you blow up as an actress, are you?"

Denise smiled. "Now you know better. I could never forget you. And, hell, you act like we aren't going to be talking."

"Are we?" Lena's face fell.

Denise put her hands on Lena's shoulders. "Of course, we are, Lena. You are still one of my bestfriends, you know."

Lena's face lit up. She hugged Denise again. Denise hugged her back.

Denise felt someone looking at her. She glanced up and saw Terrin's eyes fixated on her embrace with Lena. Denise and Lena let go of each other.

Denise walked over to Terrin, extending her hand. "It was real nice meeting you, Terrin."

Terrin hesitated. "It was nice meeting you too." She forced a smile while shaking Denise's hand.

Denise could feel the tension through the strong handshake. Terrin was letting her know that Lena was hers now. Denise wanted to laugh but just smiled and walked back over to Farih.

Lena walked up to Terrin. "You ready to go?"

Terrin tried to hide her attitude, but she knew it was obvious. She'd had enough of the Denise and Lena reunion and was ready to get the hell out of there. "Yeah, let's go."

Lena frowned. She didn't like Terrin's anti-social attitude all night. She wanted Terrin to be more like Farih and Sahara; she was embarrassed by her attitude.

The car ride was quiet. Lena couldn't stop picturing her friends' faces and the glows they possessed. Lena pulled the vanity mirror down. She looked at herself. She barely recognized the woman she had become. She was twenty, married, about to be divorced, and there was another baby growing inside of her. She tried to remember how all of this happened.

"So my friends want to go out to eat when we get back to Memphis." Terrin put her hand on Lena's thigh. She couldn't wait to get back to Memphis and be around people she wanted to be around.

"Terrin, I can't do this."

"What did you say?" Terrin asked, unable to hear Lena's murmur.

Lena turned her head to Terrin. "I can't do this. I can't."

Terrin's heart skipped a beat. Lena's words almost made her miss their turn. She pulled into the Westin and parked into the first empty spot she could find. Terrin turned the car off. Neither moved.

"What do you mean, Lena?"

"Terrin, I am sorry, but what we have going on is not what I really want or need right now."

Terrin wanted to yell. She took a series of short breaths to calm down. "It's 'cause of her, isn't it?" Terrin wanted to turn around and go let Denise have it.

"No, it has nothing to do with her. But don't think that I didn't notice how you were acting with my friends tonight."

"Whatever. That's bullshit." Terrin opened the car door and got out. She slammed the door behind her.

Lena was shocked. "Terrin." Lena got out of the car, closing the door almost as hard as Terrin did.

"Lena, I've done everything you asked of me. Now you come here and see her, and all of a sudden, you don't want to be with me anymore. How am I supposed to take that?"

"Terrin, please just listen." Lena grabbed Terrin's hand. She could see that Terrin was fighting to hold back tears. "Terrin, I am twenty-one years old, and I can't think of a time that I haven't belonged to someone else. I've been my parents' child, Brandon's girlfriend and wife. I am entering a new time in my life, and I need time to figure out who the hell I am."

"All I want to do is be there."

"Terrin, I don't want anyone there. I have to do this on my own. I'm not ready to belong to anyone else. I don't want to be in a relationship. Hell, I don't know when I will be."

Terrin felt her body trembling. She knew Lena was right, but her heart wouldn't let her accept it. "Lena, I can't just be your friend."

Lena lowered her head. "If that's the way you feel, then I am sorry."

Terrin was irritated. "So you gonna just let me go like that? You fought tooth and nail to keep that bitch in your life, but you are willing to throw me away."

"Why do you keep trying to put Denise in this?" Anger filled Lena's body.

"'Cause even if you don't admit it, I know the fucking truth. You are still in love with her!"

Lena took a step back. She had a familiar feeling; it was déjà vu. She remembered the fight she had with Brandon about Denise. "You know what, this is what I am talking about. All of this, I don't want it. I'm not trying to answer to anyone. I'm only answering to myself." Lena walked away toward the hotel entrance.

Terrin watched the woman she loved walk away. She knew she had no one to blame but herself. She knew Lena was damaged goods, but she didn't care. She knew Lena was worth it, and she wasn't giving up without a fight.

Terrin rushed into the hotel. "Lena, wait!" She caught up with Lena waiting for an elevator. "I'm sorry, OK. I just don't want to lose you."

"I am sorry that I hurt you, Terrin. It's not what I wanted to do. But I have to do what is best for me."

"So this is it?"

"I still want you as a friend. I don't want to lose you in my life."

The elevator door opened. They got off on their floor. They walked in silence to the beautiful hotel suite Terrin had rented in hopes of them having a romantic evening together.

"How about we just go in and sleep on it?" Terrin pleaded. She hoped that a night of mind-blowing sex would bring Lena back to her.

Lena stood with the same blank expression. "I think I'm going to go stay at my parents' house. If it's OK with you, I think I'll stay in Atlanta for a while."

Terrin knew her decision wasn't going to make a bit of difference. Suddenly Lena didn't look as beautiful to her anymore. Instead of the sexy, intelligent woman she fell in love with, Lena just looked like another bitch that was breaking her heart.

Terrin swung the door open, causing it to hit the wall behind her.

Lena jumped; she had never seen Terrin so angry.

Terrin grabbed Lena's Louis Vuitton duffle bag, throwing the few things of Lena's laying on the bed in the bag.

"What are you doing?" Lena walked into the room.

Terrin closed her duffle bag. She peered at Lena with pure anger in her eyes. She walked past Lena and threw her bag out in the hotel hallway. "You want to go, then go. I'm not about to sit here and work my ass off for a woman who obviously can't make her mind up about anything."

"Are you fucking kidding me?" Lena looked at Terrin standing against the door, waiting on her to leave. "You are not really acting like this."

"Please, Lena what do you expect? I should have known better than to get involved with you. But, like a fool, I fell for your ass. Now I see why Denise wasn't willing to continue these games with you."

The words slapped Lena against her face. Terrin was right. She had done the same thing to Denise, and that was why she wasn't with her now. Lena didn't have a leg to stand on. Terrin had good reason to do what she was doing.

Lena lowered her head and walked to the door. She stood in front of Terrin. "I just want you to know that I really do care about you a lot. And I'm sorry for hurting you. You are right, and I know it. I hope one day we can be friends, 'cause I do value your friendship."

Terrin wanted to stay mad, but she couldn't. Lena had her heart. She felt like someone was pulling both of her arms in different directions. One, to close the door forever, the other, wanting to hold Lena in her arms.

"I'm sorry too. Just give me some time. Do you need a ride to your parents'?"

"No, I'll catch a cab."

Lena waited for her cab to arrive. She stood outside. The early morning Atlanta air was cool for a summer day. Her hair began to blow as an unusual breeze swept past her. Standing in the city she had lived in her whole life, she knew a new chapter was about to begin. Not as her parents' daughter, Brandon's wife, or Denise's lover, but simply as Lena.

About the Author

Skyy is a 27-year-old author, screenwriter, and playwright and self-proclaimed weirdo from Memphis, TN. Her first novel, *Choices* was originally released in 2007 and quickly gained popularity both within the gay and lesbian community and within the urban fiction community. In Skyy's spare time she enjoys traveling, watching and spending a crazy amount of money on DVDs, and chatting with fans on online.

Contact Skyy

www.simplyskyy.com

skyy@simplyskyy.com

www.facebook.com/simplyskyy

www.twitter.com/simplyskyy

ORDER FORM
URBAN BOOKS, LLC
78 E. Industry Ct
Deer Park, NY 11729

Name: (please print):_____

Address: _____

City/State: _____

Zip: _____

QTY	TITLES	PRICE

Shipping and handling-add \$3.50 for 1st book, then \$1.75 for each additional book.

Please send a check payable to:

Urban Books, LLC

Please allow 4-6 weeks for delivery

ORDER FORM
URBAN BOOKS, LLC
78 E. Industry Ct
Deer Park, NY 11729

Name: (please print):_____

Address: _____

City/State: _____

Zip: _____

QTY	TITLES	PRICE
	16 On The Block	$14.95
	A Girl From Flint	$14.95
	A Pimp's Life	$14.95
	Baltimore Chronicles	$14.95
	Baltimore Chronicles 2	$14.95
	Betrayal	$14.95
	Black Diamond	$14.95
	Black Diamond 2	$14.95
	Black Friday	$14.95
	Both Sides Of The Fence	$14.95
	Both Sides Of The Fence 2	$14.95
	California Connection	$14.95

Shipping and handling-add $3.50 for 1st book, then $1.75 for each additional book.

Please send a check payable to:

Urban Books, LLC

Please allow 4-6 weeks for delivery

ORDER FORM
URBAN BOOKS, LLC
78 E. Industry Ct
Deer Park, NY 11729

Name: (please print):_____

Address: _____

City/State: _____

Zip: _____

QTY	TITLES	PRICE
	California Connection 2	$14.95
	Cheesecake And Teardrops	$14.95
	Congratulations	$14.95
	Crazy In Love	$14.95
	Cyber Case	$14.95
	Denim Diaries	$14.95
	Diary Of A Mad First Lady	$14.95
	Diary Of A Stalker	$14.95
	Diary Of A Street Diva	$14.95
	Diary Of A Young Girl	$14.95
	Dirty Money	$14.95
	Dirty To The Grave	$14.95

Shipping and handling-add $3.50 for 1ˢᵗ book, then $1.75 for each additional book.

Please send a check payable to:
Urban Books, LLC
Please allow 4-6 weeks for delivery

ORDER FORM
URBAN BOOKS, LLC
78 E. Industry Ct
Deer Park, NY 11729

Name: (please print): _____

Address: _____

City/State: _____

Zip: _____

QTY	TITLES	PRICE
	Loving Dasia	$14.95
	Material Girl	$14.95
	Moth To A Flame	$14.95
	Mr. High Maintenance	$14.95
	My Little Secret	$14.95
	Naughty	$14.95
	Naughty 2	$14.95
	Naughty 3	$14.95
	Queen Bee	$14.95
	Say It Ain't So	$14.95
	Snapped	$14.95
	Snow White	$14.95

Shipping and handling-add $3.50 for 1st book, then $1.75 for each additional book.
Please send a check payable to:
Urban Books, LLC
Please allow 4-6 weeks for delivery